A PLUME B

KEPT IN THE DARK

PENNY HANCOCK grew up in southeast London and then traveled extensively as a language teacher. She now lives in Cambridge with her husband and three children. This is her first novel.

Praise for *Kept in the Dark*

A *Sun* (London) Pick of the Shelves 2012

"It's such a thrill to read a book as deliciously dark and richly evocative as *Kept in the Dark*. From the first page to its shocking finale, it draws you into its world and won't let go. A wonderful debut . . . I took *Kept in the Dark* on my travels, thinking it would last me a couple of weeks. Two days later I'd finished it, having stayed up all night, and was telling everyone I met they had got to read it. Brilliantly written and totally gripping. I loved it."
—S. J. Watson, *New York Times* bestselling
author of *Before I Go to Sleep*

"An impressive debut from a writer we're certain to hear more about . . . There are hints of a young Daphne du Maurier in Hancock's cool, evocative prose as she reveals the terrifying extent of Sonia's obsession. . . . Beautifully worked and with a sharp eye for the menace in the commonplace, it lingers in the memory like a Schubert melody, and casts a distinctive spell."
—*The Daily Mail* (London)

"This creepy, well-written debut is reminiscent of John Fowles's *The Collector* . . . with Sonia, Hancock pulls off the considerable feat of 'writing mad.'"
—*The Guardian* (London)

"A clever, creepy thriller about misplaced affection and abduction . . . in clear, chilling prose."
—*Marie Claire* (London)

"A sparklingly creepy debut thriller with the most brilliant premise. When fifteen-year-old Jez pops round to voice coach Sonia's to borrow some music, she can't help herself—and she doesn't let him leave."
—*Mirror* (4-star review, London)

"A gripping account of a woman on the edge, who commits appalling crimes and offers them up in a tone of quietly rational domesticity."
—Natasha Cooper, author of *No Escape: A Trish Maguire Mystery*

KEPT IN THE DARK

PENNY HANCOCK

A PLUME BOOK

PLUME
Published by Penguin Group
Penguin Group (USA) Inc., 375 Hudson Street, New York, New York 10014, U.S.A. · Penguin
Group (Canada), 90 Eglinton Avenue East, Suite 700, Toronto, Ontario, Canada M4P 2Y3
(a division of Pearson Penguin Canada Inc.) · Penguin Books Ltd., 80 Strand, London
WC2R 0RL, England · Penguin Ireland, 25 St. Stephen's Green, Dublin 2, Ireland (a division
of Penguin Books Ltd.) · Penguin Group (Australia), 250 Camberwell Road, Camberwell,
Victoria 3124, Australia (a division of Pearson Australia Group Pty. Ltd.) · Penguin Books
India Pvt. Ltd., 11 Community Centre, Panchsheel Park, New Delhi – 110 017, India ·
Penguin Books (NZ), 67 Apollo Drive, Rosedale, Auckland 0632, New Zealand (a division
of Pearson New Zealand Ltd.) · Penguin Books (South Africa) (Pty.) Ltd., 24 Sturdee Avenue,
Rosebank, Johannesburg 2196, South Africa

Penguin Books Ltd., Registered Offices: 80 Strand, London WC2R 0RL, England

Published by Plume, a member of Penguin Group (USA) Inc. Originally published in
Great Britain as *Tideline* by Simon & Schuster UK Ltd.

First American Printing, September 2012
10 9 8 7 6 5 4 3 2 1

 REGISTERED TRADEMARK–MARCA REGISTRADA

LIBRARY OF CONGRESS CATALOGING-IN-PUBLICATION DATA

Hancock, Penny.
[Tideline]
Kept in the dark / Penny Hancock.
p.   cm.
Originally published as: Tideline. London : Simon & Schuster, 2011.
ISBN 978-0-452-29833-0 (pbk.)
1. Family secrets—Fiction.   2. Psychological fiction   I. Title.
PS3608.A6984T53 2012
813'.6–dc23
2012012876

Printed in the United States of America

PUBLISHER'S NOTE
This is a work of fiction. Names, characters, places, and incidents either are the product of
the author's imagination or are used fictitiously, and any resemblance to actual persons,
living or dead, businesses, companies, events, or locales is entirely coincidental.

BOOKS ARE AVAILABLE AT QUANTITY DISCOUNTS WHEN USED TO PROMOTE PRODUCTS OR SERVICES. FOR
INFORMATION PLEASE WRITE TO PREMIUM MARKETING DIVISION, PENGUIN GROUP (USA) INC., 375 HUDSON
STREET, NEW YORK, NEW YORK 10014.

For Pauline and Peter

CHAPTER ONE

Friday

Sonia

He comes to me when the chatter of school children along the alley has died away. Later, drinkers will troop the other way towards the pub, the evening riverbus will make its last journey westwards to town, rattling chains and making the pontoon groan. But this is a silent time, almost as if the river and I are waiting.

He comes to the door in the courtyard wall.

'Sorry,' he says, twisting awkwardly about, such a graceful body but he doesn't yet know what to do with it. 'It's just, at the party, your husband mentioned about that album.'

I stare past him. Early February, the light in the sky loosening. I smell brewery yeast drift on the breeze from downriver. Bitter Seville oranges from the marmalade I'm making in the kitchen. Along with the bubble of the preserving pan behind me, I hear Cat Stevens singing 'Wild World' on the radio. Time flips and catches in a tangle in my head.

I look into his face.

'Come in,' I say, 'Of course. Remind me . . .'

'It's by Tim Buckley. You can't get hold of it any more, not even on the internet. He said he had a copy on vinyl. D'you remember? I'll record it and bring it back.'

'No problem.' I speak as if I were his age rather than my own. 'Cool!' Then cringe inside. I can hear Kit. 'Oh God, Mum, don't try and speak as if you were sixteen. It's sad.'

He comes in. He steps through the door in the wall. The wisteria's a black steel scribble like the barbed wire they loop along the top of prison fences. He follows me across the courtyard and over the threshold into the hall. As well as the oranges there's the smell of the wax floor polish that Judy uses. He comes into the kitchen. Goes to the window, looks at the river. Then turns and faces me. I won't deny it, the thought flits across my mind that perhaps he's come because he finds me attractive. Young boys and older women, you do hear of such things. But I pull myself together.

'I was just going to have a drink,' I say, turning down the flame under the marmalade which is bubbling ferociously now and must have reached setting point. 'Have something.'

I never usually drink before six, but I wave bottles recklessly at him, vodka – I know teenagers love vodka – Greg's beer, I even hold up a bottle of red wine we laid down, years ago, waiting for it to mature so we can open it on Kit's twenty-first birthday.

He shrugs. 'OK,' he says. 'If you're opening something.'

'What would you *like* though,' I insist. 'Go on, say.'

'Red wine then.'

The thing with boys of this age is they do speak but you have to ease them into it. I know that from Kit's friends who tramped in and out, day and night, for several years before she left. Those boys were all spots and hair over their eyes and big feet. Silent except for the pleases and thank yous drummed into them by their parents. You had to tease and mention bands to get them to talk. Jez is different. With Jez, I don't have to try. He's easy to be with. For a teenager he's quite unself-conscious. It must be to do, I think, with his living in France. Or maybe it's because we feel we know each other, though we've barely spoken before.

He moves from the window and sits at the kitchen table, one foot crossed over the other long leg, the huge sole of his trainer almost in my face. These children today, these boy-men, did not exist quite like this when I was young. They've evolved since then. With their well-mixed genes, they're more adapted to the modern world. Taller and broader. Softer. Gentler.

'This is a wicked house. Right by the river. I wouldn't sell it.'

He drinks half his wine in one mouthful. 'Though it must be worth quite a bit.'

'Oh, well, I've no idea what this house is worth,' I say. 'It was in the family. My parents stayed here for years, all their married life virtually. I inherited it when my father died.'

'Cool.' His wine's gone in one more gulp. I refill his glass.

'This is the kind of place I want to live,' he says. 'On the Thames, a pub to the right, the market there. You've got everything. Music shops. Venues. Why d'you want to move?'

'I'm not going anywhere,' I assure him.

'But your husband, at the party, he . . .'

'I'll never leave the River House!'

This comes out more curtly than I intend. But I'm hearing things I don't like. Greg thinks we should move, yes, but we haven't agreed to it. 'I never would. I never could,' I say, more softly.

He nods.

'I didn't want to leave this area either. But Mum says London – Greenwich especially – is bad for my asthma. It's one of the reasons we went to Paris.'

His dark fringe has fallen across one eye. He flicks it back, and looks at me from under long, perfectly formed black eyebrows. I notice his sinuous neck with its smooth Adam's apple. There's a triangular dip where his throat descends towards his sternum. His skin has a sheen on it that I'd like to touch. He's of adult proportions yet everything about him is glossy and new.

I want to tell him that I have to stay in the River House to be near Seb. Somewhere in the river's swell, in its daily ebb and flow, he's still there, a flash of multicoloured oil on its surface. A ripple, a bubble, a shooosh, and he's back. I've never told anyone this. It's something few people would understand, and, to use a cliché, so much water's gone under the bridge since then. A whole lifetime. I'm convinced Jez would get it. But I let the moment pass. Something prevents me from telling him. It's something that's so close up, I can't get it into focus. Instead, I say, 'Living in Paris. That must be exciting?'

'It's OK. But I miss my mates and the band. I'm coming back soon anyway. Been looking at colleges. Music courses and stuff.'

'Your aunt said.'

'Helen?'

'Yes.'

A flicker of irritation that he calls her Helen. At the intimacy of it. Which is silly. No one calls their aunts 'Aunty' any more. What did I expect?

'Found anywhere you want to apply to?'

He pulls a face and I can see he doesn't want to have this conversation, the one where the adults ask what you're going to do. He's too alive for this kind of talk. Even though I'm thinking, I could help you. Drama, music, they're my areas.

'Everyone says, "Oooh Paris," but it's rubbish, a city where you have no mates. I prefer London. It's like no one gets it when I say that.'

'I get it,' I say.

I'm aware of the marmalade slowly setting on the stove. I should fetch the funnel and pour it into jars, but I'm unable to move from my chair, from his line of vision.

'You can nip up and get the album if you like,' I say. 'It's in the music room right at the top of the stairs.'

'The room where the keyboard is?'

Of course. He came here once before, I remember now, with Helen and Barney, one or two years ago. It was summer. His voice an octave higher, pink cheeks. A girl glued to him. Alicia. I barely registered him then.

He doesn't move.

'You still doing stuff with those actors and all that?' he asks. 'It's sick.'

'What?'

When he grins, his mouth is wider than I'd realized. I have to clutch the edge of the chair to ensure I maintain my composure.

'Sick. Cool. All those actors you meet. All those TV people. What's your job again?'

I train voices, I tell him. He wants to know what that means, what it involves. I try to explain how the voice can emphasize meaning when words are inadequate. On the other hand it can contradict what's actually said. This is useful for actors of course, but for real life, too.

As I speak he listens in a particular way. I find this more disconcerting than anything. He listens the way Seb used to, eyes half closed. Reluctant to admit his interest. A half smile on his lips.

The bottle of wine is almost empty. The marmalade must have solidified in the pan.

'I guess you know some famous people. Any rock stars? Any guitarists?'

'No rock stars as such. But I know some . . . useful people. People who are always looking for new talent.'

He leans towards me a little, and his eyes widen. Brighten.

I've found what drives him.

'I want to be a professional guitarist one day,' he says. 'It's my passion.'

'Well, when you get the album, you could bring one of Greg's guitars down. There's quite a selection up there.'

'I ought to go,' he says.

Of course he must go. He's a fifteen-year-old boy. On his way to meet his girlfriend, before he gets the train from St Pancras back to Paris tomorrow morning.

'She makes me meet her in the foot tunnel exactly halfway between south and north London.'

'Makes you?'

'We–ell,' he looks at me and all of a sudden he's just an embarrassed teenage boy after all.

'We measured the halfway point,' he says, 'by counting the paving slabs. We were going to count the white bricks but there were too many.'

'How old is she?' I ask.

'Alicia? She's fifteen.'

Fifteen. So. She'll have no idea that nothing will ever be like this again.

'I'll go and get that album,' he says, stumbling a little. The wine has gone straight to his head, he's what Kit would call a lightweight.

'Have one more drink. I'll pour it while you go up. Go on. Go up.'

I listen to his footsteps taking the stairs two at a time and open another bottle. Something cheap this time, but Jez won't notice. I fill his glass, and I add a little whisky. A cloud shifts over the river and a last sliver of sunlight slides across the table. For a second the glasses, the bottles and the fruit bowl are suspended in a rich amber glow.

I remember the marmalade again, but do nothing about it.

The phone rings, and I pick it up without thinking. It's Greg. He launches straight in as if we've already been talking.

'I've spoken to Burnett Shaws.'

'Who?'

'The estate agents. I want them to do an evaluation. It doesn't tie us to anything. But I want to know figures, ballpark, it'll help me choose what to view out here.'

I can't speak. Jez has come back into the kitchen with Greg's acoustic guitar. He bumps into the table as he sits and the guitar reverberates.

'What's that?' Greg asks. 'Have you got someone there?'

'No. Nobody. But I'm not talking about this now. You know where I stand. You can't make arrangements over my head.'

'If we could have a sensible discussion about it I wouldn't have to.'

I bite my lip. It's always Greg's last weapon, accusing me of irrationality.

I want to protest but he's put the phone down.

'Couldn't find the album,' Jez says. 'But I spotted this guitar. Can I give it a go before I leave?' His voice soothes away the tension aroused in me by Greg.

'Of course. Of course you can.' Nothing feels more right at this moment.

The next hour is my favourite this evening. Before the drink renders him incapable of leaving – even should he want to. We sit and talk and he plays. He tells me about Tim Buckley. How for him playing music was 'just like talking'.

'It's like that for me too,' Jez says. 'You teach people to express themselves with their voices. I play the guitar for the same reason.'

He's good. I knew he'd be good. He plays something classical, John Williams maybe, something that ripples and lilts like water. The guitar's an extension of him, the music flows through his body from his soul. His fingers barely seem to move as he plucks the strings. His black hair falls over his face. When the drink begins to take effect and he can't play any more, he rests the guitar on the floor, the fingerboard against his thigh.

He tells me again how he loves my house. The river right outside. The smells! The light. The sounds. Listen! And we sit and identify the sounds I've come to take for granted. The inter-mittent gush of waves against the wall, the clank and thumps from the old coaling pier, the throb of helicopters. Urban music, Jez calls it.

'I want this kind of life,' he says. 'Music, wine, a house on the Thames.'

I, too, am a little drunk by now. I never want this evening to end.

'It's OK you know, Seb. You don't have to go.'

'Jez,' he says.

'What?'

'My name. Jez, not Seb.'

It's late when at last he stands up, and almost topples. Grabs the chair.

'Shall I stay and keep you company?' he slurs, and I almost blush.

'I think,' I say, in my grown-up mother's voice, 'it might be better if you got some sleep.'

He's passed out almost before I can get him onto the old iron bed in the music room. I focus on his socks as I lie him down. There's a hole in the big toe of the right one and I think of a darning thing my mother had that was the shape of a mushroom and how she used to sit and mend our socks in the evenings, and I wonder whether anywhere in the world a darning mushroom still exists. What an odd thought to have as I roll the socks off his feet, then tug his arms out of the sleeves of his hoodie.

I wonder if I should remove the jeans that hang so loose around his narrow pelvis, the muscles sloping in a golden

triangle towards the buttons of his flies. He'd be more comfortable when he woke. But I don't want to humiliate him. So I leave
them. I fill a glass of water in the shower room and place it on
the bedside table so that he'll know, if he wakes before I expect
him to, that I am caring for him.

Before I go out of the room I bend over and pass my nose
from the top of his head with its whiff of shampoo, to his neck,
where I can detect his own male scent, of cedar, salt. He wears a
black horn-shaped thing through one earlobe. His hair lies in
liquid curls against his collarbone. I lift it gently so I may press
my nose into the delicate, pale area beneath his ear. Here, I stop.

On his neck, beneath his hairline is the unmistakable red
mark of a love bite. A hickey, Kit would call it. Bloody specks
spread out from an angry central lesion. Alicia? Sucking his flesh
into her mouth until the capillaries burst and bleed. A red sore
on his flawless skin. And suddenly I'm staring at a livid red gash
left by a rope as it dug its teeth into another buttermilk throat.
For a few minutes I cannot look away.

At last I bend over and kiss the wound gently. 'It's OK,' I whisper. 'I'll keep you safe, I promise.'

Then I pull the duvet over him, tuck it in a little at the edge,
and go quietly out of the room.

CHAPTER TWO

Saturday

Sonia

Living by the Thames you get used to its sounds and secrets. The lifeboats that race up and down, trailing wake behind them. You get used to the number of bodies dredged from its depths. The way it flows one way, no return, though it fills and empties twice daily. To move away from it leaves you severed from the essence of things.

My time with Greg and Kit in the country was a dead time. I longed for the city, for its grime and anonymity. Away from London, I often woke at night, convinced that the river still flowed down below me. I would take a while to orientate myself, even after we'd been there many years. To register that I was a grown woman with a husband and a child, out of town. Then reality snapped into place, and acres of loss opened within me.

When we returned to the River House, five years ago, the furniture was covered in dust sheets. My mother believes in preserving things. She folds clothes into suitcases for the winter, interleaved with layers of tissue paper. It's from my mother that I inherited the tradition of marmalade making, conserving, pickling. I always felt those dust sheets, however, were less a way of protecting her furniture, than a sign of her hidden reluctance to pass the house on to me.

Inheriting the house at my father's behest seemed like a blessing. But no blessing comes without its cost. My mother needs me near her now, to fetch and carry, to listen and endure. But she never really wanted me in her house, as she's at pains to remind me.

It's not quite light when I wake the next morning. There's the *phut phut phut* of a launch on the river. I want to lie here and cherish this feeling. A kind of fullness. A completion. It's like the night after you give birth and stare at the baby you have brought into the world. It's like the moment you know you both feel the same towards each other. Made more precious, now you know how rare these instances are.

I hear footsteps along the alley as the first stallholders hurry towards the market. Soft grey light seeps round the edges of the curtains. I go to the window, pull them back. Outside, the tall buildings on Canary Wharf are pale, the glass walls reflect the pearly sky that gives way to a peach glow where the sun rises beyond Blackwall. It's very cold out there.

The smell from the river is sharp, that rich oily mud stench which means the tide is out. Its swag will be on show. New deliveries will lie exposed on the shore: caskets, tyres, bicycle wheels. I know its regular imports, but there'll be the unexpected, too. However, I have no time for beachcombing this morning. I pull on my kimono and go to look at him.

His face is paler in the early light of the music room and for a split second, I'm gripped by a fear that I may have overdone it. He mentioned asthma. Alcohol, I once read, can bring on an attack. I bend closer, feel with relief his breath upon my cheek.

He doesn't stir, so I pick up one of his hands. Observe the slender fingers, nails long enough to pluck the guitar. One has caught on something and is torn slightly. Pink skin on the pads of his fingers like a child's. No coarse dark hair on the back of his hands, just a few golden filigree threads which catch the light. On his forearm a raised blue vein. I run my finger along it, watching the rise and fall of the blood as I push. Seb's arm had this same vein, most prominent when he was exerting strength, as he grasped a painter that he'd thrown around a mooring ring. As he hauled himself up the pilings. Or as his iron grip closed around my wrists.

I drop Jez's arm and look at his face. He must have inherited his pale-brown skin from his French Algerian father. A square chin, turned up slightly, the stubble so soft, so slight, a faint dusting of black specks beneath his skin. As I drag my lips over it I can barely feel it. I'm back with Seb. My nose, buried into his neck, smells the combination of smoke and male perspiration for the first time. Feels the ridges and valleys of his body through his shirt.

When I've had my fill, I must continue as normal. My mother's expecting her Saturday morning visit and will become difficult if I miss it. If I go now, I can be back here before Jez wakes. He's in a deep sleep and, if I know anything about teenagers, will stay that way for most of the morning. I gaze at him for another minute as he turns, resettles himself. Then, reluctantly, I slip away.

Outside, the early morning sun is bright, though the air's so cold it burns my throat as I breathe. Frost glints on the alley walls and I feel the crunch of ice underfoot. Residue from the tide that must have been so high in the night it came over the footpath.

Only a week ago there was still snow on the ground. I caught a glimpse through the almshouse railings – a cluster of snowdrops that had come through a small circle of grass where the snow had melted. The brilliant white of their bowed heads against the unexpected green took my breath away and I hurried home to find my camera. By the time I came out again the light had gone and the next day the snow had turned to slush. I was afraid the loss of that image would pluck at my brain. It's something I've got to guard against. Regrets burrowing in and feeding off me.

My mother's retirement home is a ten minute bus ride away. She moved here when she could no longer manage the River House, when her mind started to slip, her body to give up on her. I hurry down the softly carpeted corridor trying not to inhale the mix of cooking aromas from the separate flats. Max, who visits his own mother and has become a kind of friend, appears from number 10. He waves a cheery good morning so I wave back. I sometimes wonder if Max thinks I'm single and would like to get to know me better. In some ways it'd be fun to flirt, but I have Greg. My husband. Whatever that word means.

'I brought you your paper, and some gin.' I hand my mother a bag that also contains the incontinence pads I buy for her. It is a matter of delicacy that we never refer to these.

I press my lips briefly against her dandelion-fluff hair. That I should have to bend to kiss my own mother upsets me, this once capable woman who stood half a head taller than I do. She doesn't greet me when I step inside her flat, but turns her back to me and asks if I'll have coffee. Then she starts on about the other residents.

'They've started a film club in the lounge. But the things they choose. Such rubbish.'

'Why don't you make a suggestion yourself?'

'They wouldn't listen. I know, from the TV they prefer. They'd rather watch ballroom dancing than a decent drama.'

'What about Oliver? He seems pleasant.'

'Oh, he's an old bore and so effeminate.'

I think that if she met a new man to share her life with, my mother might become more forgiving. That we might talk more as I imagine other mothers and daughters talk.

I settle into one of her chintz armchairs and let the sunlight from her French windows warm my lap, thaw my frozen lips. Mother works her way towards the sideboard where she's set out cups and saucers and a coffee percolator, one shrunken hand on the sofa back, the other against the wall to steady herself.

'It's early. You can't have had breakfast. I've coffee but nothing else to offer you. Unless you want Grape-Nuts. But I know you sneer at Grape-Nuts.'

'I'm fine, thank you. I'll pick up something on my way home.'

'Of course your father introduced me to Grape-Nuts. He advised leaving them at least half an hour to soak in milk before eating.'

'Yes. I remember.'

'If I'd a proper-sized freezer as I did in the River House I could stock up on pastries. As it is I can offer you a Garibaldi. But that's all.'

It's time to change the subject.

'New drugs mother?'

There's a silver pillbox on the tray where she keeps her medication, one I haven't seen before.

'The doctor's given me those for my sleep,' she says. 'The Co-codamol's OK for the pain, but I have terrible nights.'

'Yes. You said.'

'You've no idea what it's like to wake in the small hours. Not to be able to drift off again.'

I do know, of course. Those eternal nights when nothing will still the soul. They've come back lately, since Kit left and Greg spends so much time away. I lie and fret. I worry for you, Mother, how I will manage your deterioration when there's so little love to sustain us. I worry for Kit, out in the world. And anxiety grips me when I think that you will let Greg win and take the River House from me.

My mother pours coffee, her back to me. I sense her shoulders stiffen. Her white perm bobs softly. I flinch. I know what's coming.

'I don't sleep because I worry for the River House. The windows need replacing. The roof. And then there's your voice consultancy.'

'What do you mean?'

'Greg can't approve of those sessions you arrange in the house?'

'Of course he approves. He helped me set it up! You know that.'

'I don't know what your father would have said. The comings and goings day and night. It isn't the way to run a business, letting people poke about in your home.'

'I've lost some clients in this recession in fact. The business may suffer.'

She's coming back, the bone-china plate held so precariously in one hand that the biscuits are in danger of sliding to the floor. I get up to rescue them but she moves irritably aside. I sit back down.

'Then why are you determined to remain there? When everyone wants to move on? Why do you always make trouble, Sonia? Greg thinks the house is worth ... what was it, something million? No. Impossible! Oh dear me. I do get my noughts mixed up. But it's a gold mine! And yet you insist on staying!'

'You spoke to Greg?' I can hear the flint in my voice.

'He does phone, from time to time. We talk. You know we talk. The River House is a yoke around my neck. It's time you moved on. He understands that. It's only you who digs your heels in, Sonia.'

I'm in danger of losing my temper at this point. I stand up, say I need the loo. In her bathroom I curl my fingers over the porcelain of the basin, count to ten, try to control my fury. She knows how much this subject upsets me. Yet she persists! I think of the things I do for her. The little sacrifices I make, constantly, to keep her happy, yet she cannot let me be where I need to be. Now that Jez lies peaceful in the music room, it hurts me all the more. I've sacrificed being with him for her. What if he leaves before I return? What if I've lost him for the sake of keeping her appeased with gin and newpapers?

Back in her sitting room I apologize, say I can only stay for twenty minutes this morning. Fortunately, my mother appears to have forgotten the subject of the River House. She hands me coffee and spends the rest of my visit recalling the singing teacher who flicked chalk at her across the classroom when she was a girl. She remembers the shade and texture of the teacher's lipstick. Can even recall the hymn they sang that morning.

'Break temptation's fatal power,' she warbles. Her pale-blue eyes water as she drifts back in time. 'Shielding all with guardian care, Safe in every careless hour, Safe from sloth and sensual snare . . .'

It's what's supposed to happen when you're in your twilight years, this slipping from the present into the past, I think as I hurry at last back down the corridor. What's odd is that it's happened to me too recently, since Kit left home.

Memories creep up on me. Push up against me the way a cat rubs itself against your leg, purring, refusing to be ignored. Feelings swamp me out of the blue. There's nostalgia sometimes. More often there's a startling upsurge of guilt, shame, regret. I wish I could talk to my mother about this, but her reactions are always tinged with criticism, with accusation. There are so many places I dare not go with her.

Greg, Kit even, now she's the age I was when I left the house for the first time, argue that the past is gone. You move on. For a long time, I agreed with them. After all, I'd been a student, worked as an actress. I'd married Greg, had a daughter and set up my own business. The past had been erased. Sometimes I reel at the number of years that have flowed away.

But recently I've come to know that time does not pass, it folds. As the river loops back upon itself in Greenwich, so some distant years seem closer than those that have only just passed, and forgotten moments shove their way back in. It is, for example, a shock, a marvellous one, that I awoke this morning with the same sensation I had at thirteen when Seb and I first kissed. A revelation that the desire I had then – to feel his eyelashes against my fingers, my tongue against his lips, is still in me. Time has fallen away, a dust sheet slithering to the floor, to reveal what had always been beneath.

CHAPTER THREE

Saturday

Sonia

On the bus, a memory takes hold of me as I pass the Starbucks that was once our local sweet shop.

A summer's day. The middle of a heat wave. I was thirteen. Where was my mother that day? She must have started her teaching job, because I felt free in a way I never did when she was at home.

I can feel the way the cotton of my sundress teased my thighs as I walked back from the shop along the alley. I sucked an orange ice lolly. My flip-flops caught on the paving stones that were sticky with drink and the dribblings of other people's ice creams. The smell of the river was close and intense. Metallic, mixed with tar and alcohol. Always the residual scent of beer on the breeze round here, from the pubs, from dregs left by those who sat on the wall to drink. The tide was out. At the steep stone mooring steps near our house I went dreamily down, sucking my lolly. The riverweed that often left them slippy had dried out. At the bottom I kicked off my flip-flops and stood at the water's edge. The river lapped at my feet, cooled them. Mud oozed up between my toes. I curled them round little hard objects buried there.

'Sonia! Sonneeeah!'

Startled out of my trance, I looked up. Out in the river, balancing on the edge of some old moored cargo barges, were Seb and his friend Mark, naked but for their underpants gone saggy in the water. Mark shoved Seb hard.

'Hey Sonia, he-elp!' cried Seb. He windmilled his arms, feigned terror, tumbled sideways into the water, and vanished into its depths. Mark collapsed laughing. After a bit, when Seb hadn't reappeared, Mark dived after him. Now both were under the soupy brown water, so thick with gunk it barely reflected the sun. Seconds passed. Minutes. Nothing broke the dense surface. My heart began to thump, my mouth went dry, the lolly stuck to my tongue.

At last, a splash. A head. Mark. He clambered back onto the barge and disappeared into its bows.

Still no Seb.

I stepped into the water. Stared out at the motionless river, a heat haze blurring the wharves down towards Blackwall. Everything fell silent.

A motor launch went past, sending waves hurrying over the surface towards me where they leapt up at my calves, before everything went still again. My heart stopped. I couldn't breathe. The world had ended.

Then, at last, *whoosh!*

Seb appeared a few feet from me, dripping with oil and river muck. He lurched at me, grabbed my arm, and dragged me towards him. I resisted for a bit. Dropped the dregs of my lolly, sank my nails into the flesh of his shoulders. He laughed. I tried to kick him but it was hopeless, he was so much stronger than me. Soon the water was up to my thighs, my dress clung to my skin. He pulled me again and I lost my balance. The cool water was a relief after the heat. I followed him in, splashing furiously, and he taunted me, 'Oooh, scary Sonia.'

Mark joined us. They climbed onto me and pushed my head under. Seb grabbed my legs. I lashed out, reached for their hair, missed, bit Mark's arm hard. He yelled and let go and I gasped lungfuls of muggy air as my face came back into the sunshine.

Wet cloth slapping against me in the cool murky water. Seb's strong hands on my ankles. The sun beating down above us.

'Time for a beer!' Seb cried, letting go of me, and he and Mark began to front crawl, racing towards the barges, rather than the shore. I swam behind them trying not to let the river splash into my mouth. I'd been told there were poisons in the water that could paralyze you. It was thick, it felt sticky on my skin as I swam. I could not see beneath the fetid surface. You could develop photos in it, that's what people said. It was a chemical broth, barely water at all. As I swam I felt things brush against my legs. The ticklish drag of a plastic bag, the nudge of something large and slimy. I tried not to imagine what else might touch me, lick me. Eat me even.

Out in the middle, a riverbus passed, its passengers waving cheerily. On the other side, the wharves of the Isle of Dogs were shrouded in thick grey fumes. At the barges, I tried to haul myself up as the boys had done, but slipped on the algae-covered edge. The wood splintered my hands and my nails broke as I clawed at the sides.

'What a sissy!' Mark yelled. 'Pathetic isn't she, Seb?'

'Leave her alone,' said Seb and my heart swelled. I found a foothold towards the back of the boat where a tyre was attached and managed to clamber in. The boys had fashioned some old fishing net into a bag, tied on a rope, brought cans of lager and packets of crisps out in it. They'd hung the net over the edge of the barge with the lager in to keep it cool in the water. We lay back on the boat's hot wooden floor hidden from view of the outside world and let the sun dry the river-water from our clothes. There was a gentle *knock knock knock* as the barges bumped against each other. Then a police boat passed, trailing a wake that made the barges sway, creak, and bash together alarmingly, so we were tossed about as if in the midst of a storm.

When they settled back down again there was nothing but sun and scalding wood and us. 'Do this,' Seb told me, making an 'O' shape with his lips.

I did as he asked. He took a swig of lager, leant over me, pressed his lips against mine, and let the cold liquid seep slowly into my mouth. It tasted tinny and cool, against the warmth of him. I felt strange, as if my legs were melting in the sun. Then Seb turned to Mark and did the same with him. He asked me to do it back to each of them. He wanted to feel what it would be like, he said. He was always wondering what things would feel like. It was lovely, the cold of the liquid coming in from between warm lips, so we carried on like this for a while longer, drinking from each other's mouths until the lager grew tepid.

'Touch my tongue with yours,' Seb said then, and so I did. Mark watched. Seb wrapped his tongue around mine and kissed me long and hard. He tasted of beer and river.

'Oh yuck, you moron,' Mark said, and Seb peeled his mouth off mine and kissed Mark instead. That shut him up.

'I'm gonna swim under the barges,' said Seb.

'Don't Seb. What's the point?'

'What's the point in anything? Just wanna see if I can.'

'What if you get halfway and run out of breath?'

'Don't be pathetic.'

Mark stood and laughed and said, 'You wally,' as Seb dived into the water and disappeared under the barges.

'What a brain-dead moron,' Mark said as we waited for Seb to reappear on the other side. I wanted him to shut up. I wanted to hold my breath until Seb came back, to check it was possible. To check Seb would live.

It was ages before he reappeared, shaking his head to get the water out of his ears. Then he placed his hands on the edge of the boat and was up and in it before you could blink.

'Go on, your turn,' Seb said, and Mark, who wasn't as brave as Seb, made some excuse about needing to get back. We watched him swim to the shore. Then Seb made me lie on top of him.

'Take off your dress,' he said. I smacked his face.

'Ooof!' he said, moving it aside, laughing. 'Go on,' he said.

'Only if you take your underpants off.'

'It's a deal.'

He slid off his pants and I peeled off my dress. I was still too undeveloped to wear a bra, so I lay with my bare chest pressed against his and we seemed to mould into one another, our bodies slotting perfectly together. We were like pieces of a 3D jigsaw, needing each other's bodies to make a complete, flawless whole. That's the feeling I remember most clearly now as I walk the same route as I walked that day along the alley towards the house. Our bodies, warm from the sun, slightly sticky from the effluent in the river, smelling of mud, locked together.

I loved Seb, that doesn't need saying. I thought he was the most beautiful creature that ever walked upon the earth. That day on the barge, I looked down into his face and wondered how anyone could have been created so perfectly. He had long almond-shaped blue eyes and lips that seemed permanently red and swollen as if he'd been eating strawberry ice lollies. His mouth turned down at the edges as if he thought everyone was too dim for him, as if he was waiting for the world to catch up with him. I could feel his sharp hip bones press into the dips just beneath my own, his skin warm and ridged where he slotted into the gaps between my ribs, my chest, that was only just beginning to soften, yield to his.

'Lie under me,' he said after a while, so we rolled over. I had a vague idea that perhaps I should make him stop. I wriggled beneath him, trying to push him off. But what I remember now is the feel of the warm wood of the barge floor banging against my back as he held me, the sound of his breath in my ear.

I arrive back at the River House, tense with anxiety. What if Jez has already woken? Left before I could say goodbye properly? I should never have left him alone.

I clutch Mother's Flurazepam in my pocket, rub the foil blisters with my thumb. Bound up the stairs to the first floor then on up the steep steps to the landing outside the music room. Light comes in from the narrow windows around the top of the walls. I turn the door handle, and push it open, hardly daring to hope.

He's there. Still drowsy. But his eyes are open.

I go straight to him. Sit on the bed.

'You passed out.'

'What?'

'Last night. Had a few too many glasses of wine.'

I look down at him. A prince emerging from a hundred years' sleep. He tries to lift his head, frowns, then gives up.

'It's OK. You're at the River House. Do you remember now?'

'Oh God!'

'You're not to worry. We all drink too much sometimes, believe me. It happens to the best of us.'

'What's the time? I'm getting the ten thirty to Paris.'

'Oh, it's way past ten thirty! But there are plenty of other trains. We can let people know, all in due course.'

'I feel sick.'

He lifts himself up on one elbow, his eyes screwed up against the light.

'You need to rehydrate. Here.'

I take the glass from the bedside table and hold it to his lips, watching them moisten as he takes a sip. A bead of water clings to one of the specks of boyish stubble on his upper lip. It glistens silver for a second before he licks it off.

'Jesus. What the fuck did we drink last night?'

His voice is still not mature even though it's well past breaking stage. It's got that boyish ring to it. He shuts his eyes and puts his head back down on the pillow.

'You'll feel better later. I'll bring you bagels and coffee in half an hour or so. You can take a shower. In there.' I nod towards the en suite. 'How do you have your coffee?'

He looks up again, his face crumpled, but his skin still so fine, like rippled silk. Full lips. Mick Jagger lips. Singer's lips. One day, I can see, he'll have those lines between nose and lip that rock singers have. Seb would have had them.

'Strong. Not too much milk. Two sugars.'

It's lovely to stand and look but I don't want to alarm him.

'I'll go and make some breakfast.'

'I forgot to text Alicia. Or phone my mum,' he says as I reach the door. I'm glad he says this as it reminds me that his mobile is in the pocket of his leather jacket, which he's left on the back of a kitchen chair.

'All in good time,' I tell him. 'You need to recover first.' I pull the door behind me and stand for a few seconds until I hear him go into the shower room, the water start to swish.

In the kitchen I don't think. I fish the mobile from his pocket and step into the courtyard, go through the door in the wall and across the path to the river. Luckily the tide's coming in and there's no beach left, just liver-coloured water slopping against the wall. I lean on it, gazing out at the barges thrashed together and bumping gently, as a group of tourists goes past behind me. I wait for them to disappear, then let the mobile drop into the depths.

When I go back to Jez's room with the coffee and bagels, he's standing in his jeans but no shirt, rubbing his hair dry with a towel. There's a scent of the lemongrass soap I keep in the shower room. He looks out from under the towel at the breakfast tray. I've got coffee in the Italian espresso thing I use for people who appreciate coffee, toast made with organic bread, bagels, and my marmalade in a dish.

'Sit down. You need to eat,' I tell him. He slumps back on the bed. His shoulders are broad but the bones are still delicate. He's got a lot of filling out to do. Where his stomach is bent, a tiny shallow line runs across it.

He puts two halves of bagel together and takes a huge bite. Leans back against the pillows and slurps at the coffee, then finishes the bagel in another couple of mouthfuls. It's warm in the room with the sun coming in from the high windows in the book-lined walls. Pleasant. Better than pleasant. Luxurious. He's fallen on his feet with me.

'You don't have to go, you know,' I say. 'I'm not doing anything today. You're welcome to stay. You can play the guitar, chill out, and I can book you a ticket on the Eurostar later. But of course it's up to you.'

He looks up at me, weighing his options.

'I do feel a bit rough to travel but aren't I in your way?'

I smile. 'Not at all.'

'Alicia'll be mad at me for standing her up yesterday. And I'd better let Mum know where I am. I said I'd be back today.'

'What a considerate boy you are!' I say.

I am indeed surprised. I used to have to beg Kit at this age to let me know where she was and she never did. If I tried to phone her, her mobile was always switched off or out of battery. When I complained that she could have contacted me she'd say she had no credit.

'I'll go and get my phone,' he says.

It's too late to stop him, and I don't want to frighten him. I have no choice but to watch him leave the music room and head downstairs. I'm taking a massive risk in order to win his trust. There's nothing to prevent him walking right out of my house and away from me forever. I tell myself to treat it as a kind of test so I can be certain where I stand with him. I need to know he wants to be here, as much as I want him to stay.

Those few minutes are torture. I can barely move. I'm aware of every sound downstairs as he searches for his phone. I'll know if he goes for the kitchen door, leaves without saying goodbye. I'll shoot down there, ask him to help me shift some furniture in here before he goes, and being such a conscientious boy he'll be unable to refuse. I cannot lose him.

I lean on the door, immobilized as another memory looms into focus. Another departure. We were in a garage. There was the smell of petrol, oil and adult sweat. Someone tossed a suitcase into the boot. Seb's face is crystal clear, he might as well be with me now. A smirk upon his lips. A look I knew so well, disdain for authority, veiled with smug charm.

'Time to go. Get in the car, Seb.'

He laughed at my rage as he climbed into the passenger seat. Then he looked up at me, his shrug telling me he wouldn't go if he didn't have to.

'Don't then, Seb,' I said. 'Don't go. Don't let them make you.'

The thunk of car doors. I grabbed the handle, but it was already locked and Seb was fastening his seat belt. And when he next looked up I could see he was already changing, already resigned, and even though I couldn't bear to admit it, a little excited about what lay ahead.

'No Seb! Don't give in!'

'My God, calm her down will you. She's going to hurt herself or someone else. Hold onto her. We need to go.'

I knew my kicking and screaming wouldn't work, but I'd run out of other options. An arm gripped mine, hauled me away from the car. Then the engine started and they reversed fast out of the garage. Seb didn't look at me. He stared ahead into his future as if he'd forgotten me the minute the car lurched forward.

It wasn't just his leaving I couldn't bear, it was the terrible sense that if only I'd behaved differently, not displayed my desperation, if only I'd got it right, this would not be happening.

When at last I hear footsteps on the bare floorboards of the staircase, I feel a warm tide of relief and gratitude sweep through me. Jez is coming back of his own accord. I move into the room. Notice the key on the inside of the door. Slip it into my pocket.

I start to tidy a little, check that there's enough soap in the bathroom, a clean towel, loo roll. There are some Bic disposable razors left here years ago by a guest, and I place them on the shelf so he'll know he's welcome to use them. He comes into the room, sits on the bed and I can barely stop myself from putting my arms around him, thanking him for not leaving me.

'It's not there,' he says. 'It's weird, I'm sure I had it yesterday. I hope it hasn't been nicked.'

'Do you want to use mine?'

'I haven't got Alicia's number, it was on my phone,' he says, as I knew he would. 'But I could phone my mum if you don't mind.'

'Who might have Alicia's number?'

'I suppose Barney might.'

'Well, look. I'll give Helen a ring. She can get in touch with everyone. Your mother, too.'

'Cool,' he says. He smiles at me and his teeth flash white and his eyes are the sweet brown of chestnuts.

'Like I said last night, you can try out this equipment if you feel like it. There's a recording thing there, and three guitars to play. Have a go on the twelve-string one.'

'A twelve-string. I've just started playing one!'

'There's an amp you can use with the electric guitar.'

I wave my hand in an arc to indicate the range of wonderful musical equipment at his disposal. Greg spent years stocking the music room, nurturing his failed ambition to become a guitarist whilst climbing higher and higher up the medical profession until he had plenty of money for the latest musical gadget but no time to play. He even soundproofed the room, at my request. Jez, as a young, talented guitarist, could not have asked for a better place to stay.

'And, if you want, I could phone a couple of the contacts I mentioned. See if they can get you some kind of a recording deal.'

'Blimey. Wait till Barney and Theo hear about this!'

I smile. Jez needs me, just as Seb did, though he never admitted it.

'When d'you think they'll be around?'

'Who?'

'These contacts of yours. What are they? Managers?'

'The first one I have in mind is an opera singer. But he knows everyone in showbiz. Including a few band managers. Leave it with me.'

'Sick.' He grins. 'Where's your hubby by the way?'

'Greg? He's away at the moment. Work.'

'He must be a good musician.'

'Ah well. That's another story. He doesn't get to play much these days.'

'So no one uses this stuff? It's just sitting here?'

'There's Kit, too, of course. But she's at uni now.'

'Kit, yeah. She was in Theo's year before we moved to Paris.'

'That's right.'

There's a moment's silence in which he gets up, moves over to the amp, fiddles with one of the knobs. Then he turns.

'So, you're here all by yourself?'

I hesitate before replying.

'Just at the moment. I don't like going away from here. Though Greg often asks me to accompany him.'

'Blimey,' he says. 'I wouldn't want to leave this place either. It's bloody amazing, this room.' He goes over to the windows. 'You can see everything from here. Better than the London Eye! Canary Wharf, Docklands. The O2. It's so cool.'

He says it as if I might never have looked myself. As if I need him to point these things out for me. I find this endearing. I stack the breakfast things on the tray. He's flicking through Greg's vinyl collection, as I stand up to leave.

'Sonia,' he says as I reach the door, and I turn to look at him. 'Thanks,' he says. We smile at each other.

I go out. Stand for a few seconds staring at the door before making up my mind. Then I pull it shut and turn the key in the lock before I start down the stairs.

CHAPTER FOUR

Saturday night

Sonia

One disadvantage of the River House, one that Kit complained bitterly about when we first came back, is that there is no garden. The courtyard between the kitchen door and the wall on the alley side is paved and too small to warrant such a name. I've grown a few things in pots out there, but fight a losing battle against the lack of light. My mother nurtured her climbers, in the beds she made from discarded bricks. Many of those bricks are now broken by frost into jagged pieces. In addition to the wisteria, her Virginia creeper and a *Hydrangea petiolaris* compete with threat of takeover by a persistent dark-leaved ivy. In fact, the whole house suffers for most of the day from a lack of light, with the exception of the music room where the high windows are permanently illuminated by the sky.

We never use the door at the front of the house that faces the street. It is blocked these days anyway by Greg's desk and his old computer. Instead, we come and go through the door in the wall that opens onto the alley on the riverside.

When we moved back to the River House, Kit took the big bedroom at the front, overlooking the street, while Greg and I shared the slightly smaller one at the back that does catch the light from the river in the mornings. This was my room when I was a child. There's another bedroom but we don't use that. One more flight of stairs and you come to the music room. My parents wanted a whole loft conversion but the low pitch of the roof did not allow it. The attic space, whose entrance is in my bedroom, is so low you cannot enter it. So they built the odd square tower with its high windows that give a bird's-eye view of the river, if you stand up on a chair, across to the Isle of Dogs and what is now Canary Wharf. The new room had to be wedged onto one side of the roof, a funny overhang from the outside. Extra windows were put in that let light into the stairwell, which otherwise would be pitch dark. It means I'm able, from the landing, to look in and see Jez without him seeing me.

I watch him. I'm overcome by the way he moves. He noticed the door was locked some time ago. Banged on it. Rattled it. Shouted for me. I was tempted to go to him straight away, to calm him. The last thing I want is to frighten him.

After a while he gives up shouting and walks round the room picking things up, looking for something with which to undo the lock. He finds a hair grip and I watch him inexpertly pushing it into the keyhole. His efforts are heartbreakingly pointless.

When he's given up on this, he goes over to the wall, holds onto the ledge of one of the high windows and pulls himself up with his powerful arms. I love to watch the way his biceps flex as he does this. The way his T-shirt rides up, revealing the golden dips at the base of his spine. He sees that escape through those narrow slits is impossible. They are also locked shut.

He returns to the door, bangs, calls my name. It's painful to resist now, but I'm afraid that if I enter without being fully prepared, he might make a run for it. That I'll lose him.

He sits for a while on the bed, his head in his hands. Then he picks up the guitar – Greg's acoustic, the one he bought while we were on holiday in Spain. The year of the grand silence; the year we almost split up. But I don't want to think about that now. Jez has started to play. This time he plays with a kind of manic ferocity. I can see him strum frantically and slap the body of the guitar. I cannot, of course, hear the music very well because of Greg's soundproofing, but I do not need to hear every note to appreciate the nuances of the slow bits and the fast, the loud and the soft, the percussive and the melodic. I'm not even really listening to that; I'm watching the concentration on his face, the intensity, the feeling. It's as if he inhabits another dimension entirely. He's talented but he's also connected. To something bigger, something other. I'm going to love watching him play the guitar, his head bent over the polished body of the instrument, the feeling passing from his soul to his body and his fingers and coming out in those notes. He holds the guitar the way he will hold women, with such tenderness and rhythm, with an instinctive sense of give and take, of knowing when to hold back and when to give all he's got. The only person I know who ever had this instinct before was Seb.

By the time I go in to him, with a tray of freshly brewed tea, the surface of the river is deep copper, the buildings opposite bathed in sallow light. He looks up as I enter, puts down the guitar.

'I've been banging, trying to call you. Why was the door locked?' He stands up, his eyes fixed on me and takes a step towards the door. I stay where I am, barring his way. Just in case.

'I'm sorry, Jez. How stupid of me. It's force of habit. There's so much expensive equipment in here, Greg insists on me locking up.'

'I was a bit freaked out. I need to go. It must be late?'

'You've plenty of time. Relax. Look I've brought you—'

'Did you ask Helen? To tell Alicia to get in touch?'

'Oh, that. Yes. They could have rung. But for some reason,' I shrug, place the tray down on the bedside table, 'they haven't.'

He stares at me, slightly stupified it seems.

'I've still got a stinking headache,' he says.

'Yes, you will do. I've brought you tea. You must hydrate. And later you must have some supper. I've got some arancini. They're from the Italian place on the market.'

'What?'

'Arancini. Rice balls filled with bolognese or mozzarella, delicious. And there's some white Rioja. You'll love it. '

Mentioning wine is a mistake. He grimaces.

'You might not feel like it now, but you'll need that hair of the dog later.'

'Thanks. For all this. But I really must be off.' He starts to pick up his things, which are strewn about the room: his hoodie, a badge that has come off it, a packet of chewing gum. My heart feels as if it's being squeezed, I can't breathe. I know what he's doing and I can't bear it.

'Don't go.'

'I've got to. They'll be wondering where I've been for the last twenty-four hours.'

'Let them think what they want,' I say. 'Stay.'

'I feel bad. Alicia'll be wondering what's happened. I have to explain why I didn't get the train. My mum will be worried.'

'Jez,' I say before I can stop myself, and I can hear the plea in my voice. 'What about how *I* feel?'

He looks at me, alarm on his face for the first time.

I've broken a basic rule by appearing desperate. I must employ one of my professional techniques. Make my voice serene. Hide the sea of desolation that threatens to engulf me.

'I cancelled an engagement tonight because I believed you wanted to stay. Do, please, have dinner with me. We can have pizza if you prefer, burgers, anything you like. And I'll look out my opera friend's number for you.'

'Thanks, honestly. But I'm going now. I need to get home. You could text me your friend's details. I'll get a new phone.'

I look at him, stare into his eyes, think as loudly as I can: Don't do this. Don't make me force you. But he continues to check his pockets, tie his laces.

'You can't go home with a hangover like that. What will Helen say?'

'I'll have a quick cup of tea. Then I'm off.'

I didn't want it to come to this, but I have no choice. I go to the tea tray, my back to him, and drop one of my mother's pills into his cup.

'Sugar?'

'Two please.'

For good measure I add a second pill with the sugar. I give the tea a good stir before handing it to him.

We sit and sip our tea on the bed next to one another. It should be a lovely moment, like the ones we shared last night but it's spoilt by the way he keeps glancing over towards the door, as if he's nervous, as if he can't wait to finish and get out of here.

It doesn't take long for the drugs to take effect. I'm surprised at their efficiency. I had half thought nothing would happen, that I should have to let him walk away from me. But quite quickly, his eyes grow heavy, he murmurs that he feels too sleepy to finish his tea, puts his mug down and lies back against the pillows. I stare at him. He struggles to open his eyes, his lids flicker. His mouth tries to form a word. He lifts his arm, as if reaching for something he thinks I'm offering him, but then he drops it down as if the effort is too much. His eyes close and his head falls to one side. I'm alarmed by my own audacity. And yet I feel an incredible calm sweep over me that I've got him. He's mine.

I put my cup down and lean over him. The light outside has almost gone. He looks like someone in a black and white movie, the dusk accentuating the shadows on his face. He's even more beautiful than I first thought.

I bend over and kiss him on the lips. Not a deep kiss; my lips rest lightly on his, feeling the tender newness of them. I barely exert any pressure, just let our mouths touch gently without moving or making any sound and I cherish the exquisite softness. I'm back there, with Seb, when the world was laid out in front of us, like a vast, eternal playground.

I pick up one of Jez's feet. It's so big I have to hold it in both my hands. I remove his trainers, his socks. Even here there's nothing unpleasant. Only babies, I'd thought, had this natural perfume. I marvel at the delicacy of the skin. What I'd like to do is take each of his pink, fresh-smelling toes one by one in my mouth. I imagine the way the flesh would feel, the scrape of his nail against the roof of my mouth. But the taste would be something new and tender.

However, there's a sweetness in saving some things for later. To savour the anticipation. Now Jez is here, in the music room, I have all the time in the world again.

CHAPTER FIVE

Saturday night

Helen

Headless and legless pregnant torsos on plinths punctuated the gallery. Helen leant on a pillar, one hand clutching a wine glass. She adjusted her stance, tried to look casual, and took another gulp of wine. Her palms were damp.

In addition to the torsos was a centrepiece, a pool of water with ultrasound scans of foetuses projected above it. There was also a series of vivid orange paintings entitled 'Variations on the Svadhisthana'.

'They are to do with the sacral chakra. The centre of fertility and creativity.' Nadia's voice in Helen's ear made her jump. 'I'm convinced orange agate is what helped me get pregnant. That's why I've used the colour so liberally.' At forty-five Nadia had fallen pregnant for the first time and it was as if no one had ever had a baby before.

'I see,' said Helen. 'But why the casts?'

'Not very original, I know,' said Nadia. 'Everyone has them done these days. But I wanted to capture every stage. I use Modroc. Get it off the internet. It's an extraordinarily versatile medium.'

'They're very realistic,' Helen said. 'You can see every tiny wrinkle and bump in the skin.' She noticed that her damp hand had left a dark print on her skirt where it had rested. She moved to hide it. Glanced over at Pierre, Nadia's partner, who was circulating with a tray of wine.

'Do you know anyone here?' Nadia said. 'Want me to introduce you?'

Helen opened her mouth, closed it, then took an in-breath.

'You didn't invite Ben and Miranda?' The words sounded forced, too loud.

'Oh, no. They're away. Madagascar or somewhere. Winter break.'

Helen digested this information, felt relief that he wasn't here, shock that he was still with his wife. She swallowed.

'What about Greg and Sonia? Thought they might be here,' she said brightly.

'I gave them an invitation,' Nadia said, gazing over Helen's head at some women who had just come in, 'at your Mick's fiftieth. Sonia looked rather amazing I thought. In spite of what Greg's been saying about her.' Nadia placed her hands under her bump and lifted it up and down gently. 'God knows how she does it. Though I've never been happier with my body than I am now.' She closed her eyes and smiled beatifically. 'Overheard one of the youngsters refer to her as a MILF! Mother I'd Like to Fuck,' she added for Helen's benefit, though Helen hardly needed a translation.

'What do you mean, in spite of what Greg's been saying?' Helen asked.

'He was worrying about her to Pierre again. How she's so – unfathomable – I think he called her.'

'Oh?'

'He reckons, since Kit's left home and he's got more work in Geneva, there's no need to stay in her parents' old house. But she refuses to move.'

'She loves the River House,' Helen said. 'Who wouldn't? It's in such a unique location.'

'It wasn't just that. Greg thinks she's depressed. You have to admit, she wasn't exactly the life and soul of the party that night was she?'

'To be honest,' said Helen, 'I haven't heard from her much at all since the kids grew up. She seemed to lose interest in me once Kit went to uni. I assumed I'd gone down in her estimation now both my sons have dropped out. But I miss her company. We'd have been out there having a fag on the pavement once upon a time.'

'Well I'm only saying what Pierre heard from Greg,' Nadia said. 'I mean, where is she tonight?'

'Perhaps it's not my place to say this but I will anyway,' said Helen, accepting another glass of wine from Pierre. 'It's bloody typical of Greg to make out something's wrong with Sonia just because she doesn't agree with him. He's always done that. He's a control freak.'

'And you've never liked Greg,' smiled Nadia.

'Not particularly, since you ask,' said Helen.

Nadia smiled at the group of women who'd entered and Helen felt shame, hot and glaring, that she'd mentioned her dislike of Greg. He was Pierre's friend. She never knew when to keep her mouth shut. So Sonia was a MILF. Ben was in Madagascar with Miranda. Helen felt her nerves slacken, her mood dip. Complimentary gasps and exclamations came from the group of newcomers by the door. Nadia was spirited away by one of the appreciative women and Helen saw that the last of the wine on the tray had gone. Time to go.

She stood for a few moments on thes pavement outside, hugging her blue hooded jacket around her and pulling on the burgundy leather driving gloves she kept in the pockets. Stamped her feet in their suede boots against the pavement that was already beginning to twinkle with frost. She began to walk towards the corner where her car was parked. Across the road, boys piled out of a taxi and into a Victorian warehouse that was now some kind of a club, their breath rising in white puffs as they moved across the road. Helen had been surrounded by teenage boys all week. The needy ones at work, her own two and her nephew Jez at home. Their lanky legs and hunched shoulders seemed to be everywhere all the time. She wished there were more women in her life. People you could actually talk to, share your feelings with. Nadia was too wrapped up in her pregnancy, Sonia clearly preferred her own company these days, and Helen's sister, Maria was far too competitive about the boys. Helen could never confide in her.

Some of the gallery's private viewers were meandering across to the warehouse now too. Middle-aged people trying to be young, Helen thought, before it hit her that they were younger than she was. Middle-aged but younger than her. How could that be all of a sudden? She sighed, took a deep breath. It would have been nice to join them, have another few drinks, stay out, but she was tired and she was driving. And Mick had probably cooked. He would be waiting for her.

In the car, she fastened her seat belt, knowing she was probably over the limit, though she hadn't in all her driving years been breathalyzed yet. *I don't look like the kind of woman who might drink too much,* she thought. Police went for youngsters. Barney and Theo's friends were always being stopped though they never drank and drove.

She was just turning the key in the ignition when she spotted Alicia, Jez's girlfriend, coming along the street from the gallery. She was alone, and looked a little lost. Helen opened the window, leant out.

'D'you need a lift Alicia?'

The girl looked up. 'Oh. Cool.'

Helen opened the passenger door and Alicia jumped in.

'Going home?'

'S'pose so. Thought I might see Jez at Nadia's. I went with some of my art class. We invited him to come along. Do you know where he is? I haven't seen him since Thursday.'

'Thought he might be with you actually,' Helen said. When had she last seen her nephew? It wasn't last night. Maybe it had been Thursday too, when Alicia had come round, and they'd made those badge things on the computer.

She pulled out into the traffic and glanced at the girl. Alicia had been in and out of the house since Jez arrived the previous Saturday but Helen had taken little notice of her. Now she saw that the girl was pretty, fine featured, elfin, pale skin. Just a child really. She was staring straight ahead, with a small frown wrinkling her forehead.

'You OK?' Helen asked, taking Old Street roundabout rather too quickly and braking as she headed off towards the city.

'No. He's not answering his phone or returning my texts.'

'He was supposed to be going back to Paris this weekend.' Helen said. 'I told him to let us know which train he was getting, but I haven't been in much. The boys will know.'

'He wouldn't have gone yesterday. We were supposed to be meeting in the tunnel. He didn't come and I'm worried. It's not like him.'

'Tunnel?'

'The foot tunnel. We always meet there. While he's staying with you in Greenwich. It's like, halfway, and it's kind of . . . our special place.'

God, thought Helen, how could anyone, even a starry-eyed teenager view the foot tunnel as somewhere romantic? The floor damp, as if the river were seeping through. The white tiles and exposed electricity cables. The stink of stale urine. The lifts stopped working at seven so you had to take the hundreds of steps up to the surface hoping no one lurked in the corners and shadows.

'You want to be careful hanging about in the tunnel,' Helen said. 'Where do you want me to drop you? I can take you home if it's not too far out of my way. Or to a tube?'

'Docklands.'

Helen thought of Mick again, at home, griddling something. Tuna steaks with udon noodles were one of his specialities, he often did that on a Saturday night. A bottle of something cold and white and a meal in front of the TV. What more could she want? She shouldn't have bothered with Nadia's preview.

'It's doing my head in.' Alicia sounded on the verge of tears. 'He must be in a mood with me.'

'Jez? I'm sure he's not,' Helen said. 'He's gone home to Paris or he'll be with the band. You know what they're like when they're playing. They forget there are other people out here.'

Alicia shrugged. 'He's the best lead guitarist in all the bands I know. My friends are so, like, jealous I'm with him. But he doesn't know how drop-dead gorgeous he is and he's never just blanked me out before. It's weird.'

A dispatch rider on a motorbike cut across Helen's path as they reached Commercial Street and she had to brake. The lights in front turned to red. She could feel her blood pressure rise. Why did everyone go on about Jez all the time? Maria had phoned every night this week to see how her son had got on with his interviews, to check up on what he'd eaten, to remind Helen how talented he was. Maria treated Jez like a pedigree creature rather than an ordinary teenage boy. Now his girlfriend was professing similar adulation and it was annoying. The effects of the wine were wearing off and she felt a headache approaching. Helen craved another drink. She shouldn't have offered to take Alicia all the way, should just have said, 'Out here if you don't mind, I need to get home.' You offered an inch and . . .

'I'll make him ring you, I promise,' said Helen.

As she turned the car round after dropping Alicia home she wondered whether she felt relieved that Ben hadn't been at the opening after all. She no longer had to go through the kind of tumultuous feelings Alicia described again. No more waiting for an email to arrive in the inbox, the ping of a text coming in. No more agonizing nerves at the thought of seeing someone again. No more crazy romantic rendezvous in impractical locations. The foot tunnel, of all places! She had dealt with that side of things once and for all. Why would she want to open a recently healed wound?

'Think of all the civilized things you and Mick can do now that's all behind you,' Helen told herself as the car descended between towering brown walls into the dark mouth of the Blackwall Tunnel. 'You're going to do more together than you ever used to: the theatre, city breaks, good food. You've both agreed to focus on your relationship. You've done the right thing.'

By the time she was home and turning the key in the lock, she was anticipating the warm smell of a meal ready on the kitchen table. Mick stood in the entrance to the sitting room, a newspaper under one arm, his face grave. There was no welcoming smell from the kitchen. The fire was unlit and the hallway was cold.

'Maria's been on the phone,' he said. 'Jez was supposed to be going back to Paris today. He hasn't arrived.'

CHAPTER SIX

Saturday night

Helen

Helen followed Mick into the sitting room and unscrewed the cap of a bottle of Pinot Grigio he'd put out for her on the table.

'Was Maria sure he was going back today?' said Helen. 'I asked him to tell us which train he was getting, but he didn't. He must still be here.'

'When did you last see him? I don't think I've seen him since Thursday.'

Helen sat down. The room felt bleak. It needed flowers. She leant across to put the lamp on over the fireplace.

'Thursday too, I think. No. I saw him yesterday lunchtime. That's right, he was here when I got in . . . after work. Have you put any supper on?'

'Helen. We need to sort this out. Where is he now?'

'Not with Alicia. I just gave her a lift home from the private view. She says he stood her up in the foot tunnel yesterday. He'll be with the boys.'

'The foot tunnel?'

'Apparently they meet halfway between south and north. It's rather sweet.'

Mick jumped out of his chair and ran his hands through his hair.

'We ought to know where the boy is! What are we telling Maria when she phones back?'

Helen filled her glass.

Mick looked at her pointedly.

'This is urgent,' he said. 'Maria was beside herself.'

'My sister beside herself. That makes a change.' She raised her eyebrows at her husband expecting his collusion in an old joke.

'This is not about Maria. It's about Jez. I'm concerned.'

'Hey! It's not like you to worry. Now you're making me anxious.'

When their boys were younger, Helen was the one to fret about their safety, check the booster seats in the car, make them wear cycle helmets, shin pads, armbands. She was the one to see that their chests rose and fell in the night. Mick had never worried, as far as she could tell. Now he wouldn't sit still, and she wondered if there was something else behind his concern.

'Have you tried his mobile?'

'Of course.'

'And you've seen the boys today?'

'No. They weren't up when I went out and they'd gone when I got back.'

'Then Jez will be with them. Relax Mick, please. Look, have a glass of wine, and I'll make some food. They'll all be in soon, and we can phone Maria.'

Ben and Miranda together in Madagascar. She didn't want to think about it. Couldn't stop thinking about it.

'Where are the boys' mobile numbers?'

'On my phone. In my bag.'

Helen kicked her bag over to Mick. He gave her a look before rummaging through it. He found her mobile and started to press the keys.

'Typical. Both of their bloody phones are switched off,' he said.

It was after midnight when they heard the front door swing open and bang against the hall wall. Mick leapt up as Barney came into the room, hair all over his face as usual, slouching, staggering a little. He brought a blast of frosty night air in with him.

'Shut the door,' Helen said. 'It's freezing. Is Jez with you?'

'Eh?'

'Barney! Tune in!' said Mick. 'Jez hasn't gone back to Paris. And Alicia hasn't heard from him. Have you any idea where he is?'

'Theo might know.'

Theo appeared in the doorway, eyes shining, face pink.

'Theo! Where's Jez?'

'Jez?'

Helen could see Mick's jaw tighten with irritation. She knew what he was thinking: he'd like to take his son by the unwashed hood of his smelly sweatshirt and shake some sense into him. Mick's disappointment in his own sons had become palpable since Jez arrived. Theo flicked the remote for the TV to come on. Mick told him to turn it off. Helen asked Barney to run up and put the heating on to constant. She gave up on the idea of eating, poured herself another glass of wine instead.

'I thought he'd gone home,' Theo said. 'He said he was going home on Saturday.'

'To Paris?'

'Yeah. Where else?'

'He's not there. Was he even at the gig last night?'

Helen watched this new, fraught side of her husband with detachment. His face was scrunched and red. His eyebrows did odd things too, were bushier than before and somehow more mobile. She wondered when she'd last really looked at him.

'We assumed he was with Alicia,' Barney was saying.

'Alicia hasn't seen him,' said Helen. 'He was supposed to meet her in the foot tunnel yesterday afternoon and he didn't turn up.'

Theo and Barney exchanged glances.

'What's that supposed to mean?' said Helen. 'That look.'

'Nothing,' said Theo. 'It's just it's quite funny the way Alicia makes him meet her down there as if it's somewhere romantic. He's a bit scared of saying no to her. Even when he'd rather be with us.'

'He's whipped,' Barney muttered and Theo chuckled.

'Whipped?'

'It means he does what he's told,' said Barney.

'Slave to little Alicia,' added Theo. 'I'll ring him.'

They might be lazy, good-for-nothing layabouts, Helen thought through the consoling mist of the alcohol, but nothing can buoy you up like a son. Two sons.

'I don't suppose there's any chance he's gone to his dad's?' Mick said. 'Might he have gone to Marseilles? Did he say anything to you about it? Rather than stopping in Paris I mean?'

'No. He didn't mention Marseilles,' said Barney.

'It's not connecting,' Theo said. 'Must be switched off.'

'What now?' Mick said. 'What do we do now, for pity's sake?'

The phone call with Maria was long and difficult. Helen tried to sound calm.

'For all we know he's on the train now, on his way back. He probably went into town shopping on his way to St Pancras. There'll be an explanation.'

'So he's got his stuff with him?' Maria asked.

It hadn't occurred to Helen to check whether Jez's stuff was still up in the spare room. She gestured across the sitting room to Barney, who was slumped in front of the TV, to go and check.

'What?' he said, barely taking his eyes off the film he was watching. Helen put her hand over the mouthpiece.

'Is Jez's stuff upstairs? Go and see!' she hissed.

'Should I get on a train now and come over?' Maria's voice had risen to an hysterical pitch.

'Of course you shouldn't,' said Helen. 'What if he turns up there in the morning? Which he will, I'm sure.'

'I can't believe you didn't realize he was leaving today? Didn't you help him pack his stuff?'

'Maria. Jez is nearly sixteen. He doesn't want his aunt fussing over him the whole time. I asked him to say which train he was getting, but I let him sort himself out.'

There was a long silence.

'What?' Helen said. 'What are you thinking?'

'I'm thinking that I wish I'd never let him stay with you. Our whole approach to parenting is different. Yours borders on neglect—'

'Maria! Let's please remain civil if—'

'OK. I shouldn't have said that. I think the current term is *benign* neglect. But Jez is not used to it. He doesn't have all that freedom over here. He's used to a strict timetable, to being driven around. He doesn't know how to use the Metro! So the tube will be a labyrinth to him. Oh my God, what's happened to him, Helen?'

'There'll be a simple explanation. What you need right now is a stiff drink and bed.'

'A stiff drink is your answer to everything.'

There was a charged pause as Helen fought not to take the bait.

Maria continued, 'I'm phoning Nadim. I've no choice. He needs to know his son's disappeared!'

Helen felt herself prickle with indignation.

'Jez has been gone one night. That does not mean he's disappeared. And we are doing all we can over here to find him.' She hung up and turned to the others. Tears had sprung to her eyes, fury at the guilt and inadequacy her sister made her feel, mixed with growing anxiety that Jez might actually have come to some harm.

'She's always been overprotective with Jez. It's probably why this ghastly scenario has happened in the first place,' she said.

'Don't worry, Mum,' said Theo. 'He'll be OK. He's not stupid.'

Barney came back into the room and sat down in front of the TV again.

'Well?' Helen asked.

'What?'

'Jez's stuff. Is it there?'

'Oh right, yes. Still there. He hasn't packed. Clothes all over the floor.'

Helen closed her eyes. Sat down. Put her head in her hands.

'When does one call the police in cases like this?' she asked through her fingers.

CHAPTER SEVEN

Sunday

Sonia

Seb's mouth organ is in a shoebox of special things I keep in the spare room. I feel nervous as I turn the big glass door handle, it's so long since I've been in here. We don't often entertain overnight guests, for one reason or another. It smells musty, of dust and old paper. The grey light comes in through a small window on one side of the house which is overshadowed by the roofs of the almshouses and the tall dark chimneys of the power station beyond. Much of the furniture has remained under dust sheets since we moved back. There seemed little point in uncovering the mahogany chest of drawers that we never use, or the ottoman under the window.

The shoebox is on a shelf in the wardrobe. I bring it out with care, lift Seb's Palestinian scarf, uncover things I haven't looked at in years.

I've come for the mouth organ to soothe Jez. He was agitated and a little befuddled by the after-effects of my mother's drugs when I went to him this morning, and I needed to calm him. He thought he had drunk too much again and felt ashamed. He's far too well brought up to imagine his aunt's friend might have added anything special to his tea, and this makes me feel all the more tender towards him. I reassured him that he'd done nothing wrong, and said I'd get him anything he wanted while he was my guest. He eventually made this humble request for the mouth organ.

As I rummage through the shoebox, I'm distracted by a letter uncovered by the scarf. It's addressed to me, as all Seb's letters were, c/o Mark, Vanburgh Hill. Mark brought the letters and squirrelled them away in a niche in the wall along the alley that we'd agreed was the perfect place for me to retrieve them.

I look at the envelope. There's a nine pence stamp and a post-mark – 1st February. The year is no longer legible. I forget the mouth organ for a moment and let myself part the torn edges and extract the letter. The handwriting belies Seb's stature. Small, neat, tightly formed. The first time I've looked at it since.

Sonia!!!!!!!

I can't stand another month of this hole. No girls here. Not even dippy ones like you to obey my commands! In fact, the whole atmosphere is slowly driving me bonkers and God! I'm only just beginning to realize how bloody far away the river is at the moment.

You have to help me. I've made a plan. The cook leaves her bike outside, unlocked. I'm going to borrow it. It's got to be on 12th Feb. I worked out the tides and everything. I'll leave at lunch-time when they're all too busy stuffing their faces to notice. I'll cycle to the Isle of Dogs. You have to be there. Bring Tamasa! We can have a little raft adventure on our way home. I'll signal in morse code. About 4 o'clock. Don't hang about. The minute you see the lights, you have to come. Row upstream a bit, I'll time it so the tide's on the turn. Coast into the landing stage, and I'll be wait-ing. Once I'm back on our side of the river I'm hiding out for a bit. Make sure you come!

I shut my eyes. Fold my hand slowly over the filmy paper until it crumples in my palm, screw it up into a tight ball.

How long had Seb been gone by then? It can't have been more than one or two months. Yet it felt like a lifetime. If we'd waited another month, the holidays would have been upon us. But time is such a slippery, stretchy thing, even a day back then felt like an eternity. I was more impatient to have him back than he was to get out of the school he hated. I was enslaved to him. I would have done anything for him. It was not as if I had a choice. It's the same now, with Jez. I will do anything for him.

I find the mouth organ in its slim red box. Running my fingers over the holes Seb's breath passed through, I feel a deep satisfaction at the thought of Jez's doing the same.

I take the mouth organ up to Jez on a tray with some warm soup and a roll, and a big jug of iced water. I place it on the floor outside the door while I turn the key. As I step into the music room, something knocks into me from the right, the impact forcing me sideways against the bookshelf, leaving the door swinging open. I grasp the shelves, trying to steady myself, but am unable to get a purchase on the books which slither away. I stagger and fall and find myself on the floor, the door gaping.

'Jez, no, please.'

He's disappeared through the doorway before I can get into a sitting position.

'I've brought the mouth organ for you! Wait for me!'

My voice sounds pathetic even to myself, as I struggle amongst the books that have tumbled all about me, feeling the world draining of colour, dismay filling my head, my heart.

'Please, please, I'll do anything. Don't go.'

Then there's a crash, the sound of glass breaking, and something tumbling down the steep stairs followed by a howl. At last

I manage to right myself, and, pushing the books aside, lurch for the door.

Jez sprawls across the top of the stairs. There's a mess of water and broken glass all over the landing. He twists around and stares up at me as I move towards him. It's the look on his face that upsets me more than anything.

Sheer terror.

He shuffles away from me, clutching his right ankle in one hand. In the other I see he's picked up the soup bowl and is holding it above his head, as if he is taking aim, is about to hurl it at me. I make a grab for his wrist, and he lets the bowl fly but it misses me and shatters on the door jamb.

After a few seconds' silence I go and squat in front of him, gazing at him with all the loving kindness I can express.

'Jez, you've hurt yourself. You must let me help you.'

'I want to go home.' He shrinks back, whimpering.

'You will go home. But you need to let me take a look at your ankle. I've got some gel in the bathroom and a bandage. Let's just get it sorted, and we can take it from there.'

'It's fucking agony.'

I can see he's trying hard to be brave. I tell him he needs to put his foot up on a cushion, that it'd be better for him to go back to the bed.

'Jez. Come on. Let me take a look.'

He tries to get up, winces again.

'Jez,' I say, trying to make eye contact with him. 'There was no need for that. I was bringing you the things you asked for. I only want to keep you safe, to make you happy.'

'I don't like it,' he says. 'I don't like being locked up in there.' His face contorts in pain or maybe, though I hate to think it, in fear.

'Well you're not going anywhere in this state. You'll have to let me sort you out.'

He lets me help him up and limps back to the music room, recognizing after all that he really has no choice.

When he's settled on the bed, I lift the leg of his jeans. His ankle is swelling and turning a nasty colour. There's no break that I can detect, but my guess is he's sprained it badly.

I lock the door and go down for the first-aid box and some ibuprofen for the pain. I'm trembling as I gather the things together. I fill another bowl with soup, make up his lunch again, and take up the new tray, kicking aside fragments of broken jug and bowl on the stairs to clear up later. I'm careful to sidle in the door, all my senses alert. But this time he's acquiescent, in too much pain, or perhaps feeling too ashamed, to try anything silly again. He lets me lift his foot, remove his sock, apply the soothing gel to the swelling. I smooth it on, taking my time, being as gentle as I can. I take the bandage and wind it softly, softly, around his ankle, until it is swaddled in white cloth.

'Is that better?' I ask.

He sighs, lies back, and nods. He drinks a little water with the painkillers. We don't speak.

I'm still shaking as I lock the door and go downstairs. I don't like what happened, it shows me that Jez doesn't trust me yet, after all. In the kitchen, I lean on the windowsill for a while. Stare out at the full river, trying to let its gentle undulations soothe me. But my chest heaves and I feel a sob rise into my throat.

It's some time before my weeping subsides. I wipe my eyes, then wrap myself up in my coat and head out of the door.

There's still a spring tide and though it is ebbing now, the water has come over the footpath in places. Tourists tiptoe along beside the railings of the university, trying not to get their feet wet. It seems astonishing to me that they can chatter and laugh together as if nothing has happened, while I have been through an emotional ordeal that leaves me weak and trembling.

In spite of everything, or perhaps because of it, I want to make sure there is a nourishing meal for Jez this evening.

I get to the market and fill my basket quickly with focaccia, cheeses, and some bits and pieces from the Italian and Greek stalls, then hurry back along the river. The sun is very low in the sky behind me. My shadow stretches east from the alley, where my feet tread the dark path, almost as far as the coaling pier where my head brushes the barbed wire at the top of the wall. I have become a giant.

I decide to walk for a little longer, beyond the River House, as lights flicker on around the O2, letting the smell of the river as the tide retreats rinse my thoughts away, before the gathering darkness drives me back to the door in the wall.

CHAPTER EIGHT

Sunday night

Sonia

By the time I get back, the light outside's completely gone. I take care to look in through the high windows before opening Jez's door. He's sitting on the bed, blowing at the mouth organ, his bad foot propped up on the cushion, so I open the door and slide in, locking it behind me and pushing the key deep into my trouser pocket. I'm prepared for tears or sulks or even anger, so I'm taken aback when he speaks.

'I've been thinking,' he says the minute he sees me. 'About the way you're taking care of me. About locking the door, and that you're Helen's friend and all that. I think it's something you're planning between you for my birthday on Wednesday.'

He looks at me with a triumphant half smile on his lips and I see that he's expecting me not to let on. That he assumes I am under oath to Helen not to tell him. So I just give a little knowing smile back. He shrugs, grins. 'I won't tell,' he says.

I look at him. I don't want to lie to you, I think. But when you came to me at that time on a February afternoon as the light was dying, as if it were meant, you made me feel a strange calm deep down in my soul that has been lost to me for so long I barely remember it existed. I need to keep you here, safe in the music room and I cannot let you go just yet.

I stop. Look up, expecting a response from Jez, and realize that after all I have not voiced any of this, though the thoughts were as lucid as if I'd spoken them.

I put his meal on the table by his bed. It's a lovely supper, though the juice is laced with more of my mother's pills. I don't feel any compunction about this, I know the drugs will help Jez relax, to sleep.

'Let's get you better,' I say quietly. 'Look, I'm lending you my laptop. What film would you like to watch?'

When he's settled, satisfied with the explanation he's come up with, and drowsy with the pills, I go down to lie on my own bed. Overcome with exhaustion, I listen to the sounds outside.

There's the harsh whoop of a police launch bounding east along the river, the drone of a plane coming in to City Airport. The shriek of a car alarm out on the road. How I miss the soft, guttural blasts of the foghorns. You used to hear them on winters' nights out there, long and low, one answering another, call and response, as if those enormous ships were playing together. The house felt safe when I heard that sound. A haven away from the storms and the ravings of the world down below.

The thought of the foghorns conjures a memory. I'm not sure, as this scene comes back to me, whether it happened once, or many times. What I do know is the feeling. The sensation of the silk around my wrists and ankles, accompanied by the bass sound of the foghorns on the river, vibrating through the room, through the springs of the old iron bed.

My mother originally used the music room as a dressing room. It's why it has its own en suite with a shower and a bidet (very chic in the seventies when it was installed). In those days the room was full of coat racks, hat boxes and scarves, and there was a cupboard full of my mother's dresses, coats and fur wraps.

That night, my parents were out. I must have been fourteen. Seb was with me. He and I stood on chairs staring out of the high windows, watching ships, lit up in the dark, move lugubriously upriver towards Tower Bridge. The light was dying, there was a drab mist. Occasionally a foghorn would boom from the river, long, deep and mournful. A fire was alight in the wood burner. At some point I must have annoyed Seb. I don't remember what I said but I do remember the Chinese burn he gave me, taking my forearm between his hands, twisting the skin until I cried out at the sweetness of the pain. He forced my arm around my back, dragged me to him, and stuck his tongue in my mouth. After a while he pushed me down on to the bed kept in there for rare guests. He told me to take off my clothes. I obeyed him. I always obeyed Seb eventually even if I made a show of protesting before doing so. While I peeled off my jeans and struggled with the buttons of my cheesecloth top, he rummaged about in one of the hat boxes and unearthed a pile of silk scarves.

'All of them,' he said. 'Everything off, come on.'

Taking a wrist in turn he tied my hands above my head to the bedstead. Then he fastened scarves around my ankles and pulled them tight around the frame. I struggled and swore at him and he laughed and said I'd asked for it.

'See you tomorrow,' he said, making for the door.

'It's cold. You can't leave me like this.' At this point I didn't believe he really would. I was enjoying the game.

'Sorry,' he said. 'Got to go.'

'What'll I do if they come back? Untie me!'

He shrugged.

'Seb!'

He went to the door. Turned back. Grinned.

'Have a good night!' he said. Then he turned the handle, went out, shut the door behind him. I could hear his feet on the steep wooden stairs that led down to the main floor below. I struggled. Began to panic. Suppose Seb walked out of the house and left me like this all night? What if my parents came in and my mother wanted to shower and change? I tried to hear what he was doing downstairs. There was a sound from the bottom floor – the slam of the door on to the courtyard.

Footsteps on the stairs. I struggled to sit up. Strained to work out whose they were. When the door opened I braced myself, grappling for words of explanation.

'What are you doing naked on the bed like that?' Seb asked.

'You git!' I hissed. 'You bastard. Let me go.'

'What did you say? I didn't hear!'

'Seb, it's not funny any more. I was scared.'

'You want me to let you go?'

'Yes, please, please.'

He leant over me then and I struggled, writhed, reached up and bit him hard on the neck.

'Ouch. Vicious!' he said, laughing, pushing my face back with his hand. Then he pushed his jeans down, unleashed my ankles and lay on top of me.

I turn over. I can't stop thinking of Jez above me, drugged again and asleep on the old iron bed. I can't relax. I remember the silk scarves in my wardrobe.

I get out of bed, pull on my kimono, snatch a bundle of silk and go up to the music room.

I take the opportunity to examine him properly. I pull back the duvet. He's half undressed himself, is wearing a pair of boxers and a T-shirt. He must have fallen asleep as he pulled his hoodie off, he's still got one arm in the sleeve. I watch the way his Adam's apple moves up and down as he breathes, the rise and fall of his ribcage. His navel is not even sunken, but lies in a perfect shallow dip amongst his stomach muscles, three little cushions between two tiny creases. His boxers hang so loose around his narrow pelvis, legs long and smooth and muscular as a horse's. I'd like to freeze him the way Seb is frozen at this very age in my memory.

Instead, I take the first scarf and tie it firmly round his right wrist. Then I wrap it tight around the iron bedpost, the way Seb wrapped mine. I know the exact moves, the exact knots to make him secure. I do the same with his left hand and then his good foot. When he's fully bound, I lie on the bed next to him, stretch my hand across his pelvis, rest it on his hip bone. I feel the warm skin under my palm.

He doesn't stir. I wriggle down the bed, and let myself kiss his stomach. I can't help it. It's perfect: the colour, the contours, the texture. His skin is taut, it springs back into place if you pinch it. I taste salt, and something briney, elemental. Even close up it's flawless. I look carefully at the crystalline surface, examine it to see if I can find a blemish. None. I lap at it, as if it were a bowl of thick hot chocolate, letting myself take advantage of the moment, while he sleeps peacefully, his breath warm and regular above my head.

The silence is broken by the ridiculous high-pitched ring of the phone downstairs. I feel things slide, go a bit out of focus. See myself as if from above, squatting here over this boy's body, my hair trailing over his hip bones. Shocked by this image, I leave Jez alone, still tied to the bed.

The stairway is dark after the subdued light from the moon in his room. I creep down, holding onto the bannister, shivering a little. I stand in the living room and listen. The phone continues to ring. I'm not going to answer it. I'm afraid I'll betray myself, in my heightened state. The machine clicks on to voicemail. After the beep comes the disembodied voice of a grown woman. The girl I brought into the world sounds like someone I barely know.

'Mum, it's me. You didn't answer my text! Are you OK? I'm coming back in a few days. There's a reading week. I spoke to Dad and he said he'd be back on Thursday night too. He wants to talk about moving. Yessss! At last. Oh, and I'm bringing Harry 'cos he's knackered. I promised him a weekend on the riverbank! Give us a ring sometime. Byeeee!'

I stand by the phone for a few minutes after she hangs up, and shiver again.

It's always cold in the living room. I've not been able to settle in it since we came back here. For that reason I let Kit and her friends have the run of it. I encouraged Kit to bring friends to the River House. I wanted her to be like other children in a way I'd never been. My parents didn't let me bring friends home, or to go to their houses. Having Kit made me see how islolated my childhood was. I wanted hers to be different.

So I let Kit have the DVD player in here, a widescreen TV, a laptop and CD player. We dragged beanbags and cushions down from her room and I let her stick her posters on the walls and even stock the old sideboard with cocktail paraphernalia. Kit and her friends bought retro posters and beer mats from the shop up on Creek Road. They had endless parties and get-togethers in here and I was actively kept out. It suited me. Now that Kit's gone, the room is not only too cold, but too still. Greg, when he's here, sits on the sofa in the evenings with the paper, or the TV, before going up to bed, but he agrees it's always chilly even with the fire lit and the heating on.

This house has a life of its own. It breathes and fidgets. And it has its particular sounds. The *whooof* as the heating goes on, the *ping ping ping* of the pipes when you run a bath, the creak of the roof slates on a windy night. But the living room is silent.

I spend most of my time in the kitchen. You could say I live there, but the living room, in spite of its name, is dead space. It's not that it's an ugly room. Far from it. Visitors are always quick to comment on its beauty, with the river view at one end, the fireplace, the polished wood floors and large Persian rugs that have been in here for as long as I can remember. I dislike the sideboard but otherwise the furniture is unobtrusive, tasteful. No, it's not the aesthetics that make me unable to relax in here, it's something else, a shadow in the corner of my eye that slides aside each time I try to focus on it.

I look down at the phone, wondering if I should call Kit back now, or if I can leave it until tomorrow. I decide on the latter. I need to think it through before I can say as I would once have done, yes, it's fine to come, bring Harry, darling. Bring whoever you want.

I push open the door to my room and go to lie down again. For a few minutes I contemplate climbing up to the music room to take the scarves off so Jez need never know, will not take fright. But each time I decide to move, another wave of exhaustion presses down upon me.

The next thing I know, dawn is breaking all over again, a restless grey sky through my windows, and I've left Jez all night with his hands above his head, tied to the bed in the music room, just as Seb trapped me, my love for him intensifying with every attempt I made to wriggle free of his bonds.

CHAPTER NINE

Sunday morning

Helen

Helen peeled her tongue off the roof of her mouth. Screwed her eyes against the light. Something horrible had happened and she felt ragged. She put a foot out to soothe herself by rubbing it against Mick's calf, and encountered only empty space. She sat up. Mick was dressed in his jogging things, doing up the laces of his running shoes.

'What's the matter?' she mumbled.

'It's Jez,' he said. 'I haven't slept a wink.'

'You checked his room?'

'He's not there.'

'Oh, God.'

Mick said last night that they should call the police right away. He spoke to someone, who had asked several questions. In the end he had put the phone down and reported that the police had told him to phone back in the morning if there was still no word from Jez.

'You say he's sixteen, he's been in and out at odd times all week. So it's not completely out of character,' the policeman had told him.

'Well, that's a relief, I suppose,' Helen had said, but Mick had stood up, left the room and gone to bed without speaking to her again.

Now Mick ran downstairs. The windows juddered as the front door banged shut. Helen looked at the alarm clock. 6.45! He never got up this early on a Sunday. It was barely light outside. And bloody cold. She contemplated getting up for water, or juice, was overwhelmed by fatigue and nausea. In the end she took advantage of the space he'd left in the bed, rolled onto her front and stretched across the mattress, her arms flung above her head. Ben's face, suntanned and smiling floated into her mind as she drifted back to sleep.

It was still only 8 a.m. when Mick came back up, sweating a little, red in the face. He went straight into the en suite shower room. Helen could see him from the bed, peering at himself in the mirror, smoothing back his strawberry-blond hair, looking at his face from different angles, then his stomach, holding it in and patting it. Sensing her gaze, he pushed the door shut and she heard the hiss of the shower. Helen wished he would come back to bed, that they could have the kind of warm, fusty, Sunday morning sex that always helped to assuage a hangover.

When Mick emerged from the shower he didn't come to her, but walked over to the window, rubbing his head with the towel. He leant on the radiator, gazing out and tapping his fingers. Helen opened her mouth to ask what was on his mind, but shut it again. She wished they could speak to each other the way they once had done, without thinking, simply voicing any thought that came into their heads. Helen looked at the man she'd lived with for so many years she knew the moles on his back, the fillings in his teeth, and wondered who he really was.

'What time did they say to ring back?'

'Not till ten. At the earliest.'

'I bet he'll be here by lunchtime if he's not back in Paris.'

'The police could take us more seriously.' He spoke through the towel so his voice was muffled. 'How long before they consider someone missing for Christ's sake?'

There was the chink of crockery as Mick unloaded the dishwasher, the thump of cupboard doors opening and closing. Later Helen found the bin full of packets of chocolate biscuits, crisps, even cans of beer.

He came back up at last with a breakfast tray just as the phone began to ring. He shot across the room to pick it up. Helen could tell by his tone that it was Maria.

'No, no. I know. I couldn't sleep either. Of course she apologizes but ... Obviously, of course we *both* feel responsible, but she simply thinks he's old enough ... No, I didn't mean that ... Yes, of course. I'll come. See you later.'

He put down the phone and looked at Helen with such misery and helplessness that she held her arms out to hug him. He stayed where he was.

'He wasn't on the night train,' he said. 'She's booked a flight and is arriving this afternoon.'

'Really?'

'She's told Nadim. He's in the Middle East on some assignment but he's coming straight to London if we haven't heard anything by tomorrow.'

'She still blames me. I could tell by what you were saying.'

'It's not just you, is it? I'm to blame as well. I can't believe this has happened. We should have kept closer tabs on him.'

'No Mick! She's mollycoddled him! Our kids would never get into this type of trouble because they've been given responsibility from an early age. But Jez! He's been pushed and overprotected by Maria all his life. If he has got into some sort of trouble she should have a good look at herself before casting aspersions on us.'

'She asked why we didn't drive him to his last college interview.'

'The one in Greenwich? But Barney went to the same one! We didn't need to taxi him there, did we? They've got legs!'

'You know what I mean,' said Mick. 'We should have kept an eye on him.'

'If anyone gets onto that course it'll be Jez, not Barney. He's the talented guitarist and she knows it.'

'Let's not get sidetracked by your idiotic sibling rivalry,' Mick said. 'This is about the boy.'

At ten o'clock on the dot, Mick picked up the phone in their room and called the police.

'Well?' Helen asked when he'd put it down again.

'They're more interested now he's been gone for another night. Said they'd send someone round to talk to us by the end of the day.'

Helen sighed and pushed back the bedcovers. 'I'd better get up,' she said. 'Maria will have to sleep in Jez's room. If he's back before tonight they'll just have to bloody well share.'

After lunch Mick set off to meet Maria at Stansted. Helen caught sight of herself in the mirror and was shocked. The short hair that she dyed light caramel-brown had gone grey at the roots, her eyes were puffy, red veins had appeared on her cheeks. How had that happened overnight?

There was no way she could let Maria see her like this. She nipped out to buy a hair dye at the Tesco Express and sat on the bed while the colour developed, wrapped in a dressing gown. When she'd dried her hair she dressed in a green wool miniskirt, with a cashmere jumper, purple opaque tights and brown suede boots. She felt better.

She knew it would be another hour at least before Mick and Maria came back. She needed to clear her head. She'd have a walk and a coffee, get some organic bits and pieces to make a nice meal. And she'd buy flowers. It would please the new, health-conscious Mick, and reassure Maria that they looked after themselves and the home they'd invited Jez into.

'You two in this afternoon?' Helen asked Barney, who was making a cup of tea in the kitchen, half asleep. 'In case Jez comes in. I want you to phone me immediately if you hear anything.'

'Don't worry, Mum,' Barney said, putting an arm around her shoulders. Helen wished he hadn't, the gesture brought a tear to her eye. It made her realize how alone and afraid she really felt.

Later, she sat at outside her favourite café in Greenwich Market sipping her cappuccino. It did nothing to shift the hangover and she resolved once again to cut down on the wine. Weak sunlight fell through the corrugated plastic roof, warming her. She wondered whether the plans to renovate the market were being followed up. She wasn't sure she liked the idea of it becoming gentrified. It had become so trendy anyway at the weekends with its craft stalls selling everything from fountains for the garden to velvet corsages, from handmade soap to carved wooden sculptures. But on weekdays when the trivial merchandise fell away as if it had been sieved, only the old Greenwich locals were left chatting and drinking tea and scraping a meagre living from the trades they had always plied. Some of them were here today, too, looking as though they were dressed in clothes they'd dragged from the piles of jumble they sold. Many of them, Helen thought, had probably been here since it started as an antique market, years before, on Sundays in the car park over the road. Their stalls looked more like museum collections, with their shoehorns and military figurines, bowling sets and old leather-booted ice skates, hogs heads and stuffed things in glass boxes. They were part of local history. It would be a shame to lose them.

As she gazed she noticed Sonia wrapped in a scarf over on the far side of the market, near the food stalls. Nadia was right. She did look amazing. Slimmer than ever with that grey cashmere headscarf flung about her hair. More elegant than anyone in the bustling marketplace. She was clearly in a hurry, pointing at food and stuffing it impatiently into a large shopper. Helen remembered that Greg was worried about her state of mind.

She drained her cappuccino and got up. She'd go and say hello. Check that Sonia was alright. She adjusted her own scarf, did up the toggles on her wool jacket, and went inside to pay her bill. The queue was long and slow, the girl at the counter clearly new, fumbling with the cash register. By the time Helen had paid and emerged into the marketplace, Sonia had gone.

Helen thought of pursuing her, but decided against it. Instead, she sat back down. The shops round the edge of the market were doing brisk business as usual. The one selling T-shirts made her think of Jez. He and Alicia downloading that picture of . . . who was it? Some seventies musicians? Jeff someone. And Tim? They were father and son, Jez had explained. Helen hadn't really been listening. The son had drowned in a river one night with all his clothes on. He was only thirty. Only a couple of years older than his father had been when he had died, too young. Tragic.

Jez told Helen they were going to shrink one of the images and make badges, and Alicia said she was getting it put onto T-shirts for both of them. After downloading the image, Jez had found a programme where you could morph a photo of yourself onto the body of an elf doing a jig. He and Alicia had found it hilarious. It had been quite funny, but it was more his infectious laugh that had made Helen join in too. That was on Thursday evening.

But what was it that had been niggling away at her about Jez? That had made her feel so irritable when Alicia had gone on about him, and when everyone had fussed so much last night? Something about the last conversation she'd had with Jez before all this had blown up. She tried to remember it all in detail. It was Friday lunchtime. She had come in, not expecting to find anyone at home. Jez was playing his guitar loudly (but rather brilliantly she must admit) through an amp. She remembered the cross way she stomped up the stairs, opened his door.

'If you're planning on living with us when you come to college, you'll have to be more thoughtful,' she told him. 'We have neighbours to consider, you know.'

Her irritation was unreasonable, she knew. Her boys always played loud music in their rooms, it had never bothered her. But Jez was so bloody good at everything, as Maria was at pains to remind her every night, and Helen had a headache. A stonking hangover, truth be told.

Jez had looked startled by her temper, and had apologized. She'd been taken back by his contrition – Barney and Theo would never have said sorry – they were more likely to tell her to bugger off. She'd left the room without saying any more, and was now ashamed by her lack of graciousness.

Surely Jez hadn't taken her words to heart, gone off feeling he wasn't wanted? Something daft like that? Mick's anxiety combined with her sister's hysteria had forced Helen to remain calm last night. But now she felt a slow terror build within.

Maybe Maria was right. She had been too laid back. Not just laid back though, in some ways, downright negligent. She had not asked where he was going when he went out. Had not worried what time he came in. She'd treated him like one of her boys but he wasn't one of her boys. He was young and innocent and naïve and sweet natured. All these thoughts made her so uncomfortable she had to stand up and move. She hurried back through the park, her head down, dreading what lay ahead.

*   *   *

'You've contacted everyone he knew?' Inspector Kirwin glanced at each of them in turn. She was short and plump and looked too homely to be an inspector, Helen thought. Alongside her sat a boy, a police constable she introduced as Josh, who barely looked Barney's age.

Helen and Mick exchanged glances. They were at the kitchen table sipping tea. Maria, dressed impeccably as usual, nevertheless looked exhausted. It was clear she hadn't slept a wink. She was biting her thumbnail, unable to sit still.

'We could go through Barney and Theo's mobile contacts, and then our phone book,' Mick suggested.

'You haven't done that yet?' Maria stood up, her face drained of colour.

'We only began to think there was something amiss yesterday evening. It was late. We could hardly phone people at that hour.'

Helen looked at Inspector Kirwin across the table for affirmation.

'You've had all morning,' said Maria. 'I don't believe this.'

'There are, believe it or not, other things in our lives apart from Jez!' Helen blurted before she could stop herself.

'Helen!' Mick glowered at her.

'We're just as upset and worried as you are, Maria,' said Helen. 'He's our nephew. But to keep apportioning blame . . .'

'No one's blaming anyone.' Mick glared at Helen and Helen pursed her lips.

'From what you've told me,' said Kirwin, 'there's still a strong possibility he's on his way back home to Paris. You say he was expected some time this weekend but he hadn't said exactly when.'

'He said Saturday,' said Maria. 'But he's left his things here. I know Jez. He'd have been in touch if he changed his plans. He knows I worry if he's late. He always phones or texts.'

'Unlike our two,' Helen couldn't help muttering.

'What was that?'

'I said unlike Barney and Theo.' Helen didn't mean to sound bitter, but she realized the minute she'd spoken that it was how it had come out.

Mick stared at her. 'Drop it,' he said.

Kirwin glanced from one to the other of them.

'Was there a feeling of animosity at all towards your nephew? Did he give rise to any conflict while he was staying with you?' she asked.

Mick shook his head.

'Not at all,' he said.

'He's lovely,' said Helen. 'It's been a joy having him to stay.'

'Which one of you saw him last?'

Mick looked at Helen and shrugged.

'I left for work at, oh, 7.30 on Friday morning. I assumed he was in bed.'

'He was,' said Helen. 'He came into the kitchen for a glass of water just before I left. About quarter to eight. I went off to work as usual. I do a half day on Friday so I came home at lunchtime. He went out again at about three thirty I think.'

'Do you know where he was planning to go?'

Helen decided her irritable words before Jez left were best not mentioned.

'I don't remember. He was in and out such a lot. Off to rehearse in Barney and Theo's band. And he had a couple of interviews last week.'

'Those were over by Friday!' said Maria. 'I can't believe you don't know that.'

'Of course I know,' said Helen. 'But he's nearly sixteen, Maria. He was very responsible about getting himself where he needed to be at the right time. You have to trust kids, you can't breathe down their necks all the time.'

What a suffocating mother Maria was. No wonder he'd gone off on his own for a bit, rather than going home. Helen shifted in her chair and changed the subject.

'I bumped into his girlfriend yesterday. She said he was due to meet her in the foot tunnel on Friday afternoon but he didn't turn up.'

'The foot tunnel?' Maria blanched. 'The Greenwich foot tunnel? You let them meet down there?'

'It's not what it was,' said Mick. 'There are CCTV cameras down there these days.'

'That's true,' said the young constable, speaking for the first time.

'We need to speak to the girlfriend,' said Kirwin. 'Did anyone else see Jez that day? In your family, I mean. Obviously we'll check with your sons too.'

They all shook their heads.

'To clarify, then, you came home on Friday lunchtime and saw him leave the house at about three thirty,' the policewoman said, staring at Helen rather intently.

'Yes, that's right,' Helen said. She felt her face go hot and hoped no one would notice.

'Well thank you,' said Kirwin. 'If you could let us have a look at anything that might help – a laptop or mobile he may have used, before he went missing. We'll need a recent photo of Jez if possible, for our missing persons poster. And if you don't mind, there's a reporter who's interested in your case. I know it can feel intrusive, but it often helps to get publicity out there as soon as possible. Are you happy to talk to someone if they come round later?'

'Of course,' Mick said straight away.

'I have a lovely photo of him,' said Maria, 'on my phone. Could I print it out Mick?'

'Sure,' replied Mick. 'Let's get that done straight away.'

The policewoman smiled.

'You can email it straight to us at the station,' she said. 'I'll give you the address.'

As they all stood up the phone began to ring. Helen picked it up.

'Helen, it's Simon.'

'Simon, just a friend,' Helen told the expectant group, covering the mouthpiece. They trooped out of the room. Helen was relieved to have an excuse to hang back.

'Listen. I've got a spare ticket for Tosca, the dress rehearsal this Friday. You interested?'

'Oh, Simon, how timely. I've had the most horrendous weekend. Thank you. If no one else wants it?'

'I was going to offer it to Sonia but Greg often gets tickets and I thought you'd appreciate it more.'

'I'd love it.'

As she put the phone down, Helen could hear Maria with Mick in the study sorting out Jez's photo. She made for the fridge. She could kill for a large glass of wine.

CHAPTER TEN

Monday

Sonia

I let one end of the silk run through my hand. I'm about to untie it so Jez will never know, but suddenly he opens his eyes. Blinks up at me.

'What are you doing?'

'Nothing. It's fine, Jez. Everything's fine. I have someone coming this morning who's interested in hearing you play. My opera friend. You know, I said he could help you.'

'I don't want help. I'm leaving.'

He struggles, pulling at the bonds, which of course only tightens them. His wrists redden. 'Let me go. I want to go now.'

'Please don't, Jez. Don't say you want to go. It upsets me.'

'But you've tied me up.'

I stand up. 'It was just a little game. Look, I'm popping out to get some things to eat. I can get you croissants, bagels, whatever you prefer. What would you like?'

'I just want you to let me go. This is mad. Mad!'

I sit down on the bed, stroke the hair off his damp forehead.

'You'll be glad of the contact, won't you? Then you'll be free to follow it up in your own time.'

He's quiet for a bit as he searches my face. Then he says, 'If it is a surprise party for my birthday on Wednesday, I think you're going a bit far.'

'What do you mean?'

'Tying me up! Locking me in! You could just tell me I have to stay here now I've guessed. I won't tell Helen I know about it. Honest.'

'OK. But I want to get your ankle better, and I don't want you to do anything rash.'

When *am* I going to let him go? I haven't really thought it through properly. Maybe it will be on his birthday as he imagines. Anyway, soon, before Greg and Kit come home. Before he edges further towards adulthood. Today though, I want to savour every second I have left with him, and I want him relaxed and happy, not anxious like this.

'Tell me what I can bring you, Jez. Remember I'll get you anything you like.'

After a pause he lets his head fall back against the pillows. 'I could do with a smoke. There's some weed in my jacket pocket.'

'I'll bring it.'

'But I need my hands free. I need a piss, Sonia! How am I supposed to go for a piss like this? Or a shit. I've got to go!'

I look at him, spreadeagled on the iron bed. His bad foot wrapped in its bandage, lolling over the edge. He can't go anywhere with his ankle like that.

'I'll take these silly scarves off then, if you promise not to try anything daft like you did yesterday.'

'No. No. I promise.' He says it as if he's weary with playing the game but knows it's in his best interests to continue.

We smile at each other and I untie the knots slowly, watching him all the time. I run my thumb over the red welts the scarves have left on his wrists. 'I haven't hurt you, have I? I didn't mean to hurt you.'

'No,' he says, shaking his hands as I pull the silk away. 'No, it's OK. That's better. Thanks.'

'Good, then I'll be back soon. With weed and croissants. And I'll bring Simon.'

A bustle this morning as I go along the alley to the shops. A brisk spring wind blows ripples across the river so the boats speeding in both directions rock on the choppy water. Students in scarves and hoodies gather in little groups in the university gardens, kids bound along on their way to school. People hurry towards the pier to get the Clipper up to town. Everyone's on their way somewhere. I'm going to buy croissants from Rhodes for me and Jez and Simon who's due later. I may grab some of their fabulous panini, too, for Jez to have for lunch. He'll have an appetite by then. While I'm there I'll treat him to one of their chocolate brownies. It's one of those shops, Kit used to say, where you can't buy just one thing however resolute you are when you go in. She used to make me buy her slices of their Princess Cake, with its marzipan icing, and she'd eat the layers one at a time, licking up the creamy filling between each one as she went.

There's a spring in my step this morning. Michael notices this as I pass. He works in the Anchor and is sweeping the paving stones outside.

'You're looking perky this morning, Sonia,' he says. I wave and hurry on towards the village. I cross the road, about to pass the newsagents, and then stop.

There, staring from the rack where the local papers are stacked, is his beautiful face. What's he doing there, on the front page? Smiling over to his right, caught unawares, his mouth half open, as if he's just spotted someone special. Who? I peer at the caption under the photograph:

Jez Mahfoud, who disappeared on Friday.

I buy the paper and hurry to the steps opposite the Cutty Sark, which has been shrouded in white stuff since the fire destroyed it. The wind keeps lifting the corners of the pages as I start to read and I have to bat them down. The white awnings flap around the Cutty Sark, and the blue hoardings slap and rattle. The wind unsettles me. It takes me longer than it should to grasp the meaning of the words.

Fears are mounting for the safety of a young man who has not been seen since he left his aunt's house in Greenwich to meet his girlfriend on Friday afternoon. Jez Mahfoud was last seen on Friday lunchtime by his aunt, Helen Whitehorn, with whom he was spending a week while on vacation from Paris.

Inspector Hailey Kirwin said it was out of character for him to be missing for so long without contacting a family member or his girlfriend.

This is so premature! For goodness' sake, boys fail to go home after a weekend with mates, after a heavy drinking or smoking session all the time. What's the fuss about? A gust of wind lifts the front page and snatches it from my hand. I lurch to catch it, bumping into a woman who gives me a look as she goes past. Putting my foot on the page to trap it, I almost lose my balance. I sit down again and spread the page against my lap.

The fifteen year old was reported missing 24 hours after he failed to turn up at a gig at which he was supposed to be playing. He had arranged to meet his girlfriend in the Greenwich foot tunnel on Friday evening but did not appear there either. His mother, who lives in Paris, expected him home over the weekend but he did not arrive.

Another small inset picture shows Jez, almost unrecognizable, turning a somersault, mid-air. The caption reads:

Jez Mahfoud, base jumping on the Greenwich Peninsula a week ago. Mobile phone picture.

The article continues:

'An accident involving the river has not been ruled out,' says Inspector Kirwin. 'The Marine Policing Unit (MPU) are conducting a thorough search of the stretch between Greenwich and the Thames Barrier.' Police have also contacted Mahfoud's father, a French Algerian journalist who lives in Marseilles.

The police are urging anyone who might have seen Jez Mahfoud to come forward. He is described as about 5ft 10 inches tall with black hair swept forward over his eyes, and was wearing a leather jacket, jeans and Adidas trainers.

I can't help smiling at the mistake in this last detail. Jez is wearing Nike trainers, the kind that come up the ankles a bit. I look again at the photo and see that he was younger then. A child still. He's filled out now, his hair's longer. Pleasure shudders through me at the thought that he's mine. But as I stand up I find my knees are weak. I stumble. This is silly. The report that he's missing makes it sound as if he's come to some harm. But Jez is safe with me. He's getting everything he wants, and more. Do I need to phone everyone and tell them that Jez came to me and now he's staying for a while? That I'm taking care of him? Why should I? He's comfortable. He is, in fact, in the lap of luxury.

I push the paper into a nearby bin and head for the bakery in a daze. It seems that people in the queue turn and look at me, so I lower my face as I pay for the cakes and sandwiches. My hands seem to be trembling, money drops from my purse onto the floor, coins scattering all over the place so I have to grovel about amongst the shoppers' feet to pick them up. No one helps, and I feel myself grow hot and cross.

*　　*　　*

As I hurry back towards the river, there's a sudden uproar. The judder of a police helicopter, the wail of the pontoon, the clank of the cranes, all rise to a crescendo at once, like a football chant starting up in unison. It's a phenomenon of the river I should be used to, but it's too much right now. It all seems directed at me, a sort of jeering. I stop and lean against the black railings to catch my breath.

At last I reach the alley, and the noise drops. The sun's moved round and the path is in shadow. I shiver, but I'm not sure if it's with the cold. I hurry past the Anchor. Michael's gone inside, leaving his pavement swept clean. He's written on the black-board; they're doing an offer on Shrove Tuesday, seafood platter, followed by pancakes with lemon and sugar. I see early drinkers leaning on the bar and catch the whiff of disinfectant as I pass the doorway. Since the smoking ban, pubs no longer smell of pub, but of cleaning fluids, harsh and accusatory. Oh, for the days when all our sins were veiled in cigarette smoke! I hug the paper bag of patisserie to my aching chest. My footsteps echo off the walls. My breath comes in short, shallow gasps. I have the urge to run. But run where? What for?

Helen! Of course I could phone her, explain. But I haven't spoken to her for ages. She'll want to know why I didn't contact her earlier. She'll find it odd.

Other thoughts elbow their way into my head. It's Monday today. As far as they're concerned, Jez has been missing since Friday. That's three nights. I can't tell them he's been with me all that time. No one'll understand. It won't fit anyone's idea of how the world works. It *doesn't* fit, but that doesn't mean it shouldn't be. And the journalists who already, so soon, have wind of his story will turn it into something smutty. It'll get out there, and they'll defile it.

What the stupid reporter who wrote this doesn't realize is that he's made it impossible for me to let Jez go now. If I do, his face will be plastered across every cheap magazine in the country. He'll be the focus of those gutter-press journalists, of the paparazzi. He'll be offered money for his story. This article has given me no choice but to have him to stay a little longer than I intended, at least until the furore dies down.

I reach the door in the wall. My hands tremble as I put the key in the lock and turn it. Simon's coming. I was going to introduce him to Jez. But what if *he* recognizes Jez's face from the paper, from the billboards all across south-east London? I'll have to keep Simon downstairs for his session. Then, he might ask why we're not using the recording equipment in the music room? We often work up there. And if I insist on remaining in the kitchen, and he decides to use the bathroom in the music room, finds the room locked, peeks through one of the windows, what then?

I'm so twitchy by the time I get into the living room I can barely punch the numbers into the phone.

'Simon, hi, it's Sonia.'

'Babes! How are things?'

'I'm sorry, but I've got to cancel this morning's session. I've woken up with a dreadful sore throat. Aching all over.'

'Oh God, you've got swine flu.'

'Ha!' My voice is dry, dusty. I can't get any saliva into my mouth.

'You do sound rough, darling.'

'Do you want to book in for next week – two weeks' time?'

As I speak, thoughts tumble through my head. How long can I keep Jez before more people start to look for him? And how will I let him go discreetly, without media attention? I think of the locked door, my mother's drugs, the scarves, as if for the first time. I'm *not* hurting him. The pleasure I've got from him so far has been taken quietly without causing him any guilt or pain. So why do I feel a kind of shame? My whole body shudders again. Maybe I really do have the flu.

'Pencil me in for next week, will you, Sonia? Let me know, please, if you're not fully better. I don't want your germs, sweetie. Can't afford to lose my voice while the show's still up.'

When Simon's gone I cancel all today's appointments, saying I've got the flu. I need the house to myself for the next couple of days at least, so that I can concentrate on Jez. I refuse to think as far ahead as Thursday, when Greg and Kit are due back. And I won't contemplate yet how I'm going to let him go, or when. All these things are uncertain, unanswered questions, and I haven't the energy to think about them now.

In the kitchen, I lean on the counter. Put the kettle on. Make toast and breathe its comforting scent. Then I reach for a jar of marmalade, stopping for a moment as a ray of sunlight slants in through the jar, lighting up all the little pieces of orange peel suspended in the amber jelly. For some reason this image calms me, my heart rate slows. We're going to be alright, Jez and me. I'll take it all one step at a time.

My mobile sounds as I'm about to go back up to Jez. I flick it open, concerned it's a client I've missed. It's Kit.

'Mum! You didn't return my call. I was worried.'

'Did you call? When was that?'

'Last night. And I texted. Where've you been? You always go on about me letting you know where *I* am! Then when I do ring, you don't call back.'

'Well I'm here now.' I realize I sound edgy, impatient.

'Where, where are you?'

'At home. In the kitchen.'

'But I called home this morning and you didn't pick up. Are you OK? Dad couldn't get hold of you. He's emailed and everything.'

'Has he?'

'Yes. He's worried about you. He wanted to check you were alright.'

'Is that what he says?'

'Mum! Stop it.' She sounds desperate, on the verge of tears. I take a deep breath.

'OK. I'll ring him. Are you coming on Thursday or not?'

'Aha, so you did get my message.' Relief in her tone. 'Yes, I'm coming on Thursday and I'm bringing Harry. I want you to meet him. He's kind of special.'

I don't answer this. Kit's boyfriends in the past have not been to my taste. Often sporty, usually blond, and always in some fast vehicle or other. I wonder in what way Harry is special, recoiling at the thought of any young man that isn't Jez in the house.

'And Mum,' tentative now, 'I thought we could sleep in the spare bedroom. I know you don't like using it, but it's got that big bed in there and—'

'Please Kit!' I say. 'I need time. I need space. Don't crowd out my brain.' I'm aware I've left Jez longer than I intended to. That time's passing and he must be hungry and thirsty.

There's a long pause. I hear her breathe. Then she sighs and says in a false, calm tone, 'I'm sorry. It can wait, we can play it by ear. But you'll ring Dad?'

'Yes. I'll ring Dad.'

'It'll be nice to be together again. It seems ages since Christmas.'

'Yes darling. Yes,' I say.

I go through to the kitchen, fumble in Jez's leather-jacket pocket and find the tiny pack of weed he mentioned. There are some Rizlas there too.

Through the high windows I see he is sitting on the bed, his bad leg propped up, so I go in to him, brandishing the paraphernalia.

I watch as he rolls the joint in his long fingers, then I strike a match for him and light it and he takes a deep toke.

I explain there's been a slight change of plan. That Simon isn't coming today after all.

'Then when will you introduce me?'

'All in good time. We need to wait a bit. It wouldn't be safe today.'

'Safe?'

'Don't look so alarmed. I don't mean you're in danger, it's just we don't want people talking . . .'

'I get it. You're afraid he'll find out I know about the party.'

The weed relaxes him and he smiles. I feel, at last, that we're getting back to the way things were when he arrived.

Later that afternoon, when the smoke has given him such an appetite he's swallowed a vast meal washed down by a cup of tea with some Flurazepam crushed into it, he falls into a deep, drug-enhanced sleep. I slip into bed next to him and push the hair away from his ear. The love bite is diminishing. I remove the black horn thing from his earlobe, push it deep into my pocket, take the soft flesh of his ear into my mouth.

I can see a sharp crescent moon rise in the pale-orange light of the London sky through one of the high windows. There will be another frost tonight. The water will be icy cold. Just as it was the night of the cygnets.

Seb was determined to prove they were there, though it seemed far too cold for baby swans to survive on a night like this. It was pitch dark. Not even a street light on in the alley. Seb let himself down the wall on the mooring chain to the shore below. I could hear the waves sigh. The tide was coming in. I leant on the low wall opposite the house and gazed down into the dark water. Seb's voice floated up to me.

'They're here, Sonia. The babies are riding the swans, nestled under the wings. It's incredible. Come and see!'

'It's too dark Seb. Come back.'

'Bloody hell this water's cold. My feet are numb.'

'Hurry Seb. The tide's rising. I can hear it on the wall.'

'I'm coming up.'

'Go to the steps!' I shouted.

The indistinct forms of swans bobbed against the dark water. I felt the cold brick of the wall press against my chest. A bell struck twelve in the almshouses, followed shortly afterwards by the bell from St Alfridges over in Greenwich. The two were always slightly out of synch.

'The tide's too far up. I'm climbing back up the chain.'

'That's mad. The wall's too high! You won't make it. Go to the steps!'

I heard the chain creak and clank against the wall as Seb clutched the vast iron links down below. I stretched my arm out into the abyss. Could feel the beat of my heart against the cold of the wall, the frozen ring of steel under my hand. At last I felt hair, Seb's warm head. My hand moved instinctively across it, cupping the perfectly shaped top of his skull. I caught his hand, pulled him back up and over.

'Fuck that,' he said. 'I'd like to follow them but we'll have to wait till it's warmer. We can nick a boat. Or we'll build a raft. Follow the swans upstream to Jacob's Island. Wherever it is they go. Hide out there.'

'It's dangerous, Seb.'

'Or over there, to the Isle of Dogs.'

The dark side of the river was a forbidden zone, where the black windows of grim warehouses stared across the water, and chimneys belched toxic fumes into the contaminated night sky. Dry docks and crumbling landing stages hid who knew what diseases and fetid rubbish. I'd been warned not to wander onto the other side. Not to go into the foot tunnel alone, that the Isle of Dogs was dangerous. Not to ever try and row over there either. When the tide turned, the incoming water met the outgoing: the two tussled and produced currents that were unpredictable and lethal.

Seb said they couldn't stop us. They were always trying to stop me doing this, doing that. They were always telling me I was too young. He told me they treated my spirit the way ancient Chinese people treated a girl's foot. Squashing it into a shape that was too small so it would never grow or develop naturally.

'You and me we know the river, we can deal with it,' he said. 'And as soon as it's warm enough we're building a raft and rowing away and no one will stop us.'

And Seb's plan sat in my heart, as Jez does now, a warm secret, like a cygnet curled into a hidden place under a wing.

CHAPTER ELEVEN

Tuesday

Sonia

I'm on the 386 to my mother's. It's one of those days when the whole of London's being dug up to have drains restored or cables put in or burst pipes replaced. The city's bowels are being dragged into the open, its entrails exposed. There's a whole world down there under the pavements and tarmac, not just the tube system, but warrens carrying electricity and gas and water all over the city, and sewers and tunnels and cellars and basements and drains. Whole chambers and underground rivers. Rats too, and worms and things called cave spiders. Bones and blood and rotting corpses. Most of London's plague victims lie under the turf of Blackheath. The land here is riddled with bones. What we see as we go about our everyday business on the surface is just the fragile tip of a vast graveyard.

This morning there are roadworks everywhere and the traffic crawls along. I think about getting off at the next stop and taking a short cut across the park but just as I get up to do so, the bus jerks into motion. A veil of rain sweeps over the trees in Greenwich park, beyond the white colonnades of the Queen's

House, and I can see Seb and me running up the hill, up through the rain in the empty afternoon, laughing at the shared thrill of being chased. Who were we running from?

We were looking for the small red-brick house that sat mysteriously locked at all times, incarcerated in its own little barrier of iron railings. A cold rain spat into our faces as we ran, releasing a scent of soil and dead leaf. Seb went ahead. He picked up sticks and hurled them back down the hill at our invisible pursuer. It took us some time to find the house, running up and down the park, along the official tarmac paths, and then up and down the unofficial mud paths worn through the grassy areas left to grow wild. We spotted it at last. Way over towards Crooms Hill, snuggled under the boughs of oaks and horse chestnut trees. It was pretty, with an archway over the green door, and a big black knocker, though no one lived there. It had no windows.

Seb leapt over the railings and battered on the door.

'Let us in,' he yelled, shaking the handle.

'Don't be silly. It's always locked,' I said. 'No one lives here.'

The park was deserted, silent but for the patter of rain on leaf. Whoever we'd been running from had disappeared.

'I'm cold. Can we go to the café, get a hot chocolate?' I asked.

'You got money?'

'No.'

'Nor me. I want to know what it's like inside.'

'It's just the entrance to the conduits.'

'What's conduits?' Seb picked up a piece of branch that must have blown off a nearby oak tree and used it as a battering ram against the door.

'Secret tunnels. They all run under the park and the heath,' I said. 'They were put there to carry water pipes and electricity cables to the hospital in the old days.'

'How do you know?'

'We did it at school. They used them as an air-raid shelter in the war, 'cos they go right down underground. It was safe from the bombs down there.'

'I wanna see,' said Seb, taking another charge at the door. It rattled on its hinges this time as he thrust his weight against it. The rain began to come harder, and I shivered and huddled up under the brick arch over the entrance while Seb took out his penknife and began to fiddle with the padlock. Rain fell on the sycamore leaves on the trees overhead, a rich earthy scent rose into the moist air. But I couldn't get warm, my teeth clenched together.

'Let's go Seb, I'm freezing,' I said.

'Shh. You're always wanting to go,' said Seb. 'I'm not going. I wanna get in here.'

He knew I wouldn't argue, however much I craved to be somewhere warm and dry, to feel hot food inside me. He knew I'd do whatever he wanted.

It seemed ages before he forced the door open and it creaked back on its rusty hinges, bringing a waft of stale air as the darkness opened up in front of us. Seb took some tentative steps forward. I followed, clinging onto his anorak. As our eyes adjusted to the gloom, he began to edge down steep, crumbly steps. Through the light from the open doorway at the top, we could just discern a pool filled with water. Seb got out the torch he kept in his pocket with his penknife – always prepared for potential adventures. We made our way round the pool to a low, arched tunnel, bending as we went. There was an eerie silence, interrupted by the occasional magnified plop of water, and a sort of whistling sound that must have been the wind siphoned down from above. But otherwise, the sounds of the outside world above us were muted. They could have been a thousand miles away.

'Sit,' said Seb, and I did, feeling the rough wall against my back. He struck a match and I could see by its light that he had

a pack of cigarettes in his hand. He lit two together and handed
one to me. I drew in the dizzying smoke.

'Where d'you get 'em?'

'Out there. Someone was hanging about behind the trees. He
left his jacket on the ground – they were in the pocket.'

'That's stealing. We could get into trouble.'

'He shouldn't have been sitting there if he didn't want 'em
nicked. He was watching us.'

'What do you mean?'

'Before. In the flower garden. He was hanging about watching.
I saw. Then when we stood up he walked off.'

'Who?'

Seb shrugged. Dragged on his cigarette.

'Let's go. I'm scared,' I said standing up.

'So you should be. I'm going to lock you up in here and leave
you,' Seb said, grabbing me, then pushing me up against the
wall. I could feel his now familiar hardness press against my
thigh.

'Not scared of you! Of the weirdo who's watching us. What if
he's in here?' I whispered.

Seb held my neck in his hand, squeezed so hard I coughed.
But I could tell he was afraid now too.

'What'll you do for me if I let you go?'

'Nothing,' I choked. 'Get off, Seb.'

His hand increased its grip. I could see the blue vein stand up
on his forearm, the muscles tense.

'What'll you do?'

'Anything.' I gasped, giving in to the pressure. 'The thing you
like?'

'Now?'

'Outside. Only if we can go outside.'

'In the park?'

'Yes. Here. But in the air. I don't like it in the dark.'

He let go and we began to make our way quickly through the dark towards the stairwell, where light filtered down from above. I felt my heart pummel against my ribcage as we went.

Outside he told me to lie on the grass.

'It's raining.'

'So?'

As usual, in the end I did as I was told, and I clung to him. But he didn't do what I expected. Instead he clutched me to him and we rolled down the hill. We hurtled over the bumps and tussocks, his weight crushing me, the sky tilting and vanishing and reappearing as we tumbled so the breath was snatched from us as we went. When at last we came to a stop at the bottom of the hill, Seb dragged me up to higher ground. This time there were ledges that he wanted us to roll off, so that we were suspended for seconds in midair. I tried to resist but he lay on top of me, pinned my arms behind my back and we were off.

There were so many occasions when Seb might have hurt me or himself. Yet Seb thought we were invincible and I believed him.

Outside my mother's flat I ring the bell and wait impatiently for her to answer. It's a pity it's this Tuesday and not last or next as every other one my mother goes to meet her local University of the Third Age group to discuss what they are going to talk about next. I don't like to leave Jez alone in the house for too long.

The door opens and my mother regards the bags I'm carrying with suspicion.

'I've brought you some cheese from the market.'

'From the *market*?'

I walk down the hallway, drop her bag of pads off in the bathroom and go through to the kitchen where I place the packages of pecorino and taleggio in the fridge.

'June will only shop at the market. You'd think she was penni-less the way she carries on.'

She stands in the lobby by the door, talking to my back. She's forgotten that she enjoyed these cheeses the last time she had lunch with me, that I told her I'd got them from Alexi at the market.

'Oh, I don't think people shop at the market for economy's sake,' I say. 'It's for the novelty value. You can find things there you don't get anywhere else.'

'If you're trying to tell me you can't buy taleggio at Waitrose you must think I'm daft,' she snaps. 'I'm not completely gaga yet. The computer's playing up but that doesn't mean I'm not perfectly capable of buying my own cheese once I get through to them. The Ocado man knows exactly what I like and the cheese is all pasteurized. You know where you are with Waitrose.'

'Anyway, I've put it in the fridge. I'll do your next order for you now if you like?'

I sit at her computer and try not to let her comments niggle at me while she makes my coffee. Circumstance means I'm left to keep an eye on my mother. There's no choice. There are no other siblings who might have had better luck at pleasing her. At the worst moments, when her searing comments hit a particularly sensitive spot, I remind myself that it is small penance for living in the River House, for being where I need to be.

'I've been going through that case. I decided that now you're selling up, I should coil in my ropes,' my mother says. I bite my lip and follow her gaze. She waves an arthritic finger at an old leather suitcase that's been in this room since she moved in. She left most of her box files of old paperwork and out-of-date albums at the River House when she moved. There is adequate storage space there, including a garage that we never park in, and the attic with the low pitch which is only good for shoving boxes of junk into. But for some reason she insisted on bringing this case, crammed with odds and ends.

'I don't want all and sundry rifling through my personal effects,' she'd told me when I suggested she leave it in the garage.

'No one can get in,' I'd reassured her. 'You know Greg reinforced the doors for security.'

'I need to sort through it. It'll keep me occupied now I haven't got a house of my own to care for.'

Periodically I think of the other cases she's left in the attic and despair at the thought that one day, I'll be the one who has to go through them all. As if reading my mind she says, 'Those boxes in the attic. You can deliver them to me when you clear the house.'

She goads me with this talk of moving but I refuse to be provoked. The suitcase she's pointing to now has got its lid up, wedged against the pouf she uses to rest her feet on in her sitting room.

I join her in the patch of sunlight coming in through the window. The rain's stopped. The gulp of the percolator is soothing. It's still cold out there, but the sun shines directly into her sitting room. She settles herself with her lap tray – an odd thing that has a beanbag sewn onto its underside so it doesn't wobble – and pours coffee. One thing about my mother is she knows how to make decent coffee.

'You can take most of that stuff. I don't want it.'

I glance down at the open case. It's lined in an attractive fabric, with a ruched pocket and diagonal fabric hinges that stop the lid from falling backwards when it's open.

'I'll keep the case, though. It's a *Revelation*. They don't make cases like that any more. They all have wheels these days. As if we can't use our own arms and legs. It's why people are getting shorter and fatter, you know that, don't you? It accounts for this terrible epidemic.'

'Which terrible epidemic is this, Mother?'

'The obesity epidemic. Everyone's fat these days. It's all this wheeling cases around instead of picking them up. It's all these remote controls instead of getting up and turning a knob.'

I smile. Seeing my expression she laughs, and for a brief while we seem in quite high spirits.

I put my coffee on a small side table and bend down to rummage through the case. There's a pile of fabrics, ribbons, sewing things. A darning mushroom! I pick it up in surprise. Where was I recently when a darning mushroom came to mind? With a jolt I remember the hole in Jez's sock and it fills me with such an intense longing to get back to him I can barely face the rest of the morning.

'If you need buttons, take them. I can't sew on buttons any more . . . my fingers.' She nods towards a square biscuit tin tucked into the corner of the case. I prise off the lid and delve my hand into the cool heap of plastic and mother-of-pearl. One particular button, a daisy, catches my eye and I find myself face to face on this early spring morning with Jasmine. I don't want to disturb that memory. It's buried deep within me. I put the lid back on the box.

It's too late. My mother has started.

'Oh, I recognize that button. The one in the shape of a daisy. Open up. Hand it to me! Why do I recognize it? There was a girl. A beautiful girl with a flower name. I always liked flower names but your father insisted on Sonia. Was she a school friend? Oh, who was she? Yes that's it. She sat next to me at Sunday school.'

No she didn't, Mother. You've got your pasts mixed up. You brought Jasmine to the River House. The first time you ever invited another child home. You had some twisted plan. I think you know that, really.

'She left one day, after classes, in such a hurry. Someone had upset her. Who was it?'

It was me, Mother. I upset her. She was going to steal Seb from me. I had never felt such pain. I couldn't contain it. The trouble with jealousy is there's nowhere for it to go. It ricochets back and forth, because if you express it you are reviled, and if you don't, the discomfort is unbearable. It's a curse. Jasmine was a curse on me.

My mother is out of her chair and making for the window. It'll take her some time to fumble with the curtains in order to block the sunlight that's in her eyes. I get up to help but she shrugs me off.

'I can manage, thank you. It's good for my waistline.' She's still in her giggly mood so I humour her and give a little conciliatory chuckle as I sit back down.

She speaks with her back to me, so I cannot make out how genuine her confusion is.

'The buttons, the buttons. In the alley outside the River House. At least three, there were, fallen off the front of that pretty dress she was wearing. It reminds me of that poem.' She throws back her head and chants, '*A sweet disorder in the dress, kindles in clothes a wantonness!* That's Herrick, Sonia.' She edges back to her chair. 'What was her name?'

'Her name was Jasmine, Mother. You wanted me to be friends with her.'

'And you refused. So headstrong you always were. Was it you who made her cry?'

'I don't remember the details. All I know is she's the one with the daisy buttons.'

'The buttons that fell off all along the alley. Who picked them up? How did they end up in my sewing box? Take them Sonia, please do. I don't need these things any more. Make Kit a pretty top with the daisy buttons.'

I stand, gather up the haberdashery, the ribbons and darning mushroom and button box, and stash them in a carrier bag. I'll dispose of them later.

On the bus on the way home I work hard not to let the images of Jasmine and Seb unfurl. To distract myself I pick up a copy of *Heat* magazine that someone has left on the seat. I flick through the pages but feel repulsed by the enhanced, airbrushed celebrity beauty and yearn more than ever to be back with Jez. I toss it aside onto the seat and pass the rest of the journey letting the buttons run through my fingers which I find unexpectedly soothing.

When I get in, there's a voicemail on the phone in the living room from Greg, telling me to ring him urgently. I pick up the phone and dial.

'I've been trying to reach you for several days now. What's going on?'

'Nothing. Nothing's going on.'

'You've not been picking up my messages. Have you been out? Other than to your mother's I mean?'

'Only to the market.'

'You must keep your mobile on, so Kit can get you if she needs you. I've told you time and again.'

'I've had a touch of flu, that's all. Probably slept through your calls. But I'm here as usual.'

He tuts, then speaks to me wearily.

'Well look. I've changed my flight. I'll be back early on Thursday morning.'

What in God's name has possessed him to decide to come home early this particular week? He never usually bothers. If anything, he usually extends his trips, or reports that his flight has been delayed.

'You need to phone the Smythes and tell them we can't make it on Thursday. Kit's home and we'll want to spend the evening together. But that invitation's long-standing so you'll have to make an excuse.'

'What invitation?'

'The Smythes, their silver wedding party. It came just after New Year. It's pinned to the noticeboard over my desk. You'd better do it the minute you put the phone down.'

'Is that all?'

'No. You must check the security people can come this weekend while I'm home. The alarm has to be working when we put the house up for sale. You'll have to find the number on Google. Oh, and Sonia? If the cold weather continues you must keep the heating on, even when you're out. We don't want burst pipes. They could do with lagging but that can wait till I'm back.'

'Greg you know we haven't agreed on the sale. We need to talk before you go racing ahead.'

There's a tense silence on the line.

'Right. I see. So we're still at this point, are we? Well, if you'd just get those things done, we'll discuss it on Thursday.'

When he's gone, another memory sidles up, one that's been curled up in the corners all these years, one I haven't wanted to disturb from its catlike slumber. It's been uncovered by Greg's commandeering voice.

Greg and me, standing outside our new house. Kit was one and a half. We were the perfect little family. I was twenty-five, Greg forty. He had just heard he'd got the professorial chair in Norwich. We'd bought this house in a village in Norfolk and everything was in front of us. I stared at the house, a flint, double-fronted Victorian cottage, at the end of the high street. There was even a rose bush climbing around the door. Beyond it was a new housing estate, still surrounded by orchards of apple trees covered in blossom. I was holding Kit in my arms. It was a blustery day and some of the petals had blown off in the wind. Kit pointed to them with her chubby finger, tiny dimples appearing in the back of her hand. She said 'snow' and we both laughed, finding everything she said amazing, miraculous, believing we'd borne a little genius. Greg held up the key, put his arm around his two girls, me and Kit, and kissed us each on the cheek. And he stepped forward and opened the door to the first home we'd owned. The hallway was light and you could see right down to the back door into the garden. It was very attractive, it was what we liked about it the moment the estate agent let us in. The view from the front door of the green and white and dappled sunlight in the garden. But at this moment, as Greg opened up our new home for us, I had an overwhelming sense that I could not go in. I wanted to turn and run. Walking over that threshold, I felt that a heavily reinforced door was going to slam behind me and that I'd never get out again. I smiled back at Greg anyway, kissed my little Kit on her fine, blow-away hair, and went through.

'Welcome to our family home,' Greg said, walking backwards, his arms wide, letting me and Kit follow. He led us to the sitting room, the last door on the left at the end of the hallway, bright and light and not yet cluttered with all the paraphernalia we would come to gather over the years here. Kit's travel cot was in the corner, with her little blanket and knitted rabbit.

'Put Kit in her cot,' he whispered in my ear, 'and come up to bed with me.'

I put Kit down, willing her not to settle so I wouldn't have to go upstairs with Greg. But she lay and gurgled happily. Within minutes she had her thumb in her mouth and was humming the way she did before falling asleep. I followed Greg up to our new bedroom at the back, overlooking the tarmac road that would soon be the main route through the new housing estate. Greg turned back the covers on our freshly made bed. And I got into bed with him, and as I always did, I closed my eyes and thought of something else, anything other than where I was and who was with me. Greg's hand on me made my skin flinch, his breath in my face made me turn aside. I writhed away from him.

'Oh Sonia,' he gasped as I tried to wriggle free, and he pinned me down and started to breathe more quickly, his rasping breath harsh and too loud in my ears. In the end I let Greg get on with it until it was over. When at last he'd finished he fell asleep and I turned over and cried into our new pillows.

When Helen asked me a while ago, 'But why do you stay with a man you don't enjoy going to bed with?' I stared at her.

'It's not Greg,' I said. 'It's anyone.'

'But . . .'

'Greg is the right husband for me in every other way. He's clever, he earns a good living and, I suppose, he loves me.'

It's only now I have Jez in my house that I remember what really desiring another person once felt like.

The onions soften and turn translucent in the butter as I start to make lunch in the kitchen. So Greg is coming home on Thursday morning! Then I will have to let Jez go on his birthday after all. The thought of him vanishing from me on the very day he turns sixteen, the apex that stands between boy and manhood, fills me with a terrible sense of regret that I am afraid will taunt me for years to come. If I don't snatch the moment while I've got this last chance, it will be lost to me forever.

I go to the window and gaze at the river. As I look, a huge dark seagull lands on an orange buoy. The Clipper passes, churning the water in its wake so the buoy tosses and tips in the river, as if attempting to throw the seagull off. But the big bird clings on to the buoy with impressive determination, rising and falling but not letting go.

It has happened before when I am utterly lost, when I no longer know which way to turn. The river throws up the answer.

CHAPTER TWELVE

Wednesday

Sonia

Unlike Greenwich Market, the one in Deptford sells things people actually need. I walk there along the river, leaning into the perishing wind, screwing my eyes tight against its whip and sting. The skyscrapers on Canary Wharf seem closer than ever. They loom over me, steel grey. The glass is dark this morning, reflecting the stormy sky, the black water.

I'm an anomaly at the market. I am conscious of my lack of expertise compared to the women who prod sweet potatoes and mangoes, who measure out lengths of fabric with their eyes. People sew around here. They buy thread and thimbles and elastic. They sell the results on other stalls, copies of high street fashion at a fraction of high street prices. And they talk. They sit in the cafés and stand in doorways and squat on boxes at market stalls. They pop out from nearby flats to fill blue carrier bags with chilli and mouli and fresh meat.

I move straight to the DIY stall where nuts and screws and bolts are displayed in blue plastic baskets and a Bible lies open upon a pile of batteries. A woman consults the stallholder, 'It's not my thing, you see, DIY. Large or small heads? How should I know?' She is holding a bag of screws in each hand. They laugh together, they seem to have all day.

I pick out a roll of tape.

'Only £2.50 for that,' the vendor tells me, and spotting my obvious ignorance asks what I intend to use it for.

'I'm fixing a burst pipe,' I mutter, and he laughs.

'You'd be better off calling a plumber, though with the cold and the leaks all over London you'll be lucky to find one. You should of lagged 'em,' he says. 'Bit late now. Though they say there's more snow on the way. Here.' He hands me a card. 'My plumber mate. Try him. He can only say no.'

'Thank you,' I say. 'But I'll take the duck tape anyway.'

'It's duct tape,' he says. 'Lot of people make that mistake. Gorilla, Rhino, Gaffer. It's all the same stuff basically. It'll stick anything to anything, darling.'

'I'll take a couple. Be handy to have them in,' I say, as if I'm talking about tins of beans.

In the second-hand yard people scrape a living selling whatever they can. Old car seats. Worn bras. Wooden spoons. Broken keys. At a stall selling used DVDs I find two films for Jez. *The Night of the Hunter* and *Double Indemnity*. I put them in the blue carrier with the duct tape and walk back towards Creek Road.

The shops along the high street are specific: Christine's Pork, the Egg Shop, the Fish Shop, Lobo Halal Meat, the Religious Icons shop. I draw in the smell of fried breakfasts that wafts out of the cafés. There's a constant exchange of goods amongst what seems a merry throng of people. I feel excluded and envious of their sense of community as I pass the pound shops, the hairdressers offering corn rows at special prices for children, the Pie and Mash shop, even the funeral parlour. The whole of London is constantly shifting, being knocked down and rebuilt. The landscape of the river changes daily before my eyes. But Deptford

High Street has managed so far, in its essence, to resist the bang and crash of change.

Back along Creek Road, past the billboards promising a new life experience this side of the river. Luxury apartments and cafés and gardens, they proclaim, will replace the decaying wharves and disused refineries and crumbling abandoned footpaths.

I pop into Casbah records as I come back into Greenwich, and my hand lands immediately on the CD I want: 'The Best of Tim Buckley'.

'Open them.'

As well as his presents I've brought Jez coffee, satsumas I could not resist from a fruit stall, and almond croissants from Rhodes.

This has to be a good day. It has to stay lit up in his memory, radiating golden light. I sit next to him.

'They don't call it sweet sixteen for nothing,' I say. 'Very soon it'll be gone. You as you are now, pffff!'

I'm ashamed to feel tears spring to my eyes. I look him up and down, from the top of his head to his toes. He's got that expectant look on his face, almost as though he was waiting for me to come to him, an innocent, but slightly insolent look.

He pulls the paper off the parcels. '"The Best of Tim Buckley",' he says. 'Hey that's cool. It's the one I wanted. Oh, and some DVDs. Thanks, Sonia.' He looks at me and I can see he's trying to smile but he's in conflict.

'Has Mum called yet? Has Helen?'

When he swallows I can hear the saliva stick, his mouth's dry. He's still worrying about getting home.

'Don't look so forlorn,' I tell him. 'You can listen to the CD, or watch a film. Look, I'll put this on now. I've few things to do, but when I get back, we can go.'

'Go?'

'Yes.'

'So . . . I *am* leaving?'

'You are.'

His eyes widen. Regain their shine. His facial muscles relax and the original beauty that has been somewhat lost under the veil of anxiety and pain from his ankle, returns to his face. It's a little hurtful.

'Greg's coming home soon. You can't stay. I'm sorry. There won't be room. You must collect up your stuff.'

'So,' he says. He can't quite suppress the excitement that flickers in his face. I notice the side of his nose twitch.

'It *is* some sort of surprise you've all been cooking up! You're making out it's because your husband's coming home! You can stop pretending now.' He leans his head back comfortably on the pillows, sighs. 'I *thought* you and Helen and Alicia were planning a surprise party for me! But I'm like, would you go to these extremes? It sounds sad now, I know. I was scared there was something weird going on!'

'Weird?'

'Kind of . . . well you got to admit it looks a bit strange . . . the scarves, the locked door—'

'Jez!'

'Yeah, but then I thought but you've been beast too.'

'Beast?'

'Cool. Good to me, with the guitars, the food and wine and getting me contacts.'

'Of course. I never wanted to frighten you, Jez.'

'I know. I can see that now. It's just – and I'll tell Helen too – it all did seem a bit dodgy.'

That makes me feel dirty. I shake my head.

'Don't ever think things like that about me,' I say. 'Now listen. We just need a little time to prepare things. I'll be back to get you. Enjoy the morning.'

I leave him watching *The Night of the Hunter* and hurry down the alley.

Our garage is in a row of three, just along the alley from the River House, accessible by the side road that goes up to the high street. It backs on to the river, a thirty foot drop below. The one tiny window, no more than a foot square, opens just wide enough to let some air in, but barely any light. It's reinforced in that grid wire that makes me think of primary school classroom doors. The garage smells of damp, dust, mildew. There won't be time to clean it properly and the cobwebs are thick and old and full of dead spiders, hanging suspended in their own webs. As I peer more closely I realize that they're not whole spiders but just the husks, perfectly formed, as if the inner spider had got up and walked away, leaving an inside-out skeleton of itself. I stare for some time at this phenomenon. Perfect replicas of themselves in their own webs.

One of the pieces of furniture I've left in here is a pine bed I never liked. It's been in the garage since we returned from the country and is leaning up against the back wall, its mattress protected from the damp by polythene. Once I've made a space by shifting the office furniture to the side, I pull it down and place it in the middle of the room. I leave the filing cabinet and shelf units, the swivel chair and a pile of old vinyl records, so the room has the semblance of somewhere cosy, habitable. Kit's old cot can stay too, it's in pieces and stacked up in the corner. But there are piles of tools, cans of spray paint, varnish, a ladder and gardening implements including a hoe, all of which I'll have to get rid of or store elsewhere.

I'm standing in the open doorway, surveying all this and trying to decide how best to shift the unwanted stuff when Betty from one of the houses round the corner walks by.

'Having a clear out?' she asks, her breath rising in a cloud of mist in the cold air.

'I need to free up some space,' I say, hoping by my terse tone to put her off any further conversation.

She watches me. I try to look busy.

'You'll be able to put the car in there when you've got rid of all that junk,' she says. 'Your mother always kept hers in there – it's safer than the street.'

I smile. I've always kept the car on the road and I know it's one of Betty's bugbears, though I've never been able to understand why it bothers her so much. After all, it's my problem if it gets stolen. It won't affect her. She trundles towards the corner and I'm relieved to see she's about to disappear. Then she turns and says,

'It's a good job it's secure. There's all sorts of frightful goings-on around here these days. I hardly feel safe in my own home.'

'That's what people have always said about this area,' I say. 'Nothing's really changed Betty. We're lucky to live next to the river. I shall never leave.'

The garage is cold and damp. It's not my choice to move Jez from his lovely music room with its light pouring in where he can sit in comfort playing his guitar. I don't want to entomb him like a corpse. I think of veal then, the way the flesh of young calves is kept pure, remains tender in the dark. A kind of pres-ervation after all. And it'll only be for two days, it can't do my boy any harm. Might even do him good. The important thing is that he'll be safe here. Nothing can happen to him while he's in my care.

I shift some of the old stuff in the garage into the car boot and drive to the tip. Other bits and pieces I carry along to the River House. I put Greg's step ladder, the hoe, and other gardening implements in the corner of the courtyard against the back wall. The jump leads, the jack and tools I put in the cupboard under the stairs. I need to complete the preparation before I take Jez his supper. Then I can relax and spend time with him before we have to make our move.

When I've cleared the garage I return to the house. I rummage through the airing cupboard. A waft of freshly laundered air embraces me, sends me whirring back in time so that I stand for a few seconds, my nose buried in cloth. The cupboard is full of piles of folded linen that have been in the house for as long as I can remember, the texture crisp and smooth, conjuring childhood bedtimes tucked tightly between two crisp sheets. A feeling of deep security you rarely experience again in life.

Then I see him at one end of the iron bed. Late winter, like now. An imperceptible tilt in the earth, the smell of stirrings in the air, the beginnings of new growth, and although it was not daylight, and the room was in shadow, there was a luminous quality to the dark sky even at six o'clock. We were exhilarated from some earlier exertions. Where had we been? Out on the river maybe? My face glowed. My skin tingled. Seb's feet were caked in mud, so we must have been down on the shore. Mudlarking. He went into the shower room and I heard the gush of water as he scrubbed his feet. I was on the bed, knowing what was about to come, filled with anticipation, afraid of the power of it.

The click of the shower-room door, and the pad of bare feet on floorboards. The squish of the mattress as he lay opposite me, his head against the foot board whilst mine was against the pillow in its crisp linen cover.

He pressed his big toe into my mouth. I could taste soap, and the faint residue of the river mud he'd tried to scrub away. It was intriguing, the taste, and the sensation, his toenail scraping the roof of my mouth. I sucked at his big toe and he lay back, his hands behind his head and made happy grunting noises until something interrupted us. What was it? I can't remember now. I only have the vaguest recollection that something sudden, a bang or a crash, intruded on our privacy so that we stopped, startled, abandoned our game. Seb got up and turned on me.

'You're a toe-sucking weirdo,' he said, and I stuck my tongue out at him, not knowing how else to defend myself.

I draw in a deep breath, gather myself. I put two sheets, a single duvet, and two pillows into a bin liner. Jez is going to need more than this to keep warm. I don't have a heater since we had central heating installed in the River House. I'll have to buy an old-fashioned paraffin thing tomorrow, if there's time before Greg arrives. For now, I add an old green and white checked blanket that we used to take camping with us. Packing for Jez's move *is* a bit like preparing for a camping trip. It arouses in me a fizz of anticipation. What I'd really like to do is to plan this *with* him, the way Seb and I planned our adventures. We could compose a list together, enjoy the excitement that precedes a holiday under the stars. We'd unearth big cook's boxes of matches, plastic plates, tinned food. Cans of butane gas for the one-ring gas stove. Little pans that stack one inside the other. But of course this is impossible. Jez would get upset if I told him he was camping in a garage. He'd do something impulsive.

For now I must work alone. I gather tea lights, candles (things my parents must've kept in the kitchen drawer since those regular winter power cuts in the seventies), toilet paper, a bucket with a lid we used for compost at one stage in our lives, before we gave up trying to be green. I secrete a pack of my mother's incontinence pads into a bag; they may be necessary. I unearth the groundsheet that still retains its smell of warm grass, even after being aired and stored for years.

I smile as I think of the tupperware containers of tea bread, the torches, and the windshield we used to stuff into the back of the car when Kit was a little girl. In those days our holidays were taken on the chilly Norfolk coast in campsites full of earnest families. They were always better equipped for the outdoor life than we were. Kit refused to use the communal toilets, because of the daddy-long-legs that coated every surface. Then at night she wouldn't sleep in her own little separate tent. She'd lie tucked between us, wrapped in this very same green and white checked blanket. Who was more relieved that she lay next to us, her or me? At any rate, I ensured she was snuggled up in the middle, a welcome buffer between Greg and me. How old was she in those camping years? Five? Six? We stopped them once Greg was earning serious money, began to go to villas in Italy, Spain or France.

Kit's childhood has become a blur to me. As if it were not me, but some other woman who breastfed her for nearly two years, eased her passage into the outside world. Some other, better woman who smoothed Sudocrem onto her nappy rash, put plasters on her knees, Calpol into her mouth, nit combs through her hair. Who was that woman who attended toddler groups, baked cakes? Later, when we were back at the River House, the person who traipsed with her around the gigantic Top Shop at Oxford Circus? When did I change? Was it a step-by-step process? When she ran to a friend instead of me at playgroup, and I realized I was no longer the centre of her universe? When she went out on her bike alone so I no longer knew where she was every second of the day? The first time I accidentally saw her kiss a boy and knew with a pang she was no longer a child?

Or was it a sweeping catastrophic change? Did it happen suddenly, during the lonely car journey home after leaving her at university? When the terrible realization hit me that everyone we love only comes into our lives to leave us again?

Just before I return to the garage, I take a hot-water bottle and fill it, so that Jez's bed will be warm when he gets in. I drag the bin liner along the alley to the garage. It's almost dark and there's a fine, spitting, icy rain. I could do with a torch after all. It's pitch black inside the garage. I can't leave the door open while I work, in case a passer-by becomes suspicious, takes more interest than they should. But even with the door shut, there's a draft from a crack in the window that keeps blowing out the candles. I manage to get some tea lights lit eventually; they give off a gentle yellow light that's welcoming, even cosy.

Once the bed's made up I begin to feel nervous. How am I going to get Jez into the garage without being seen? Obviously, I'll have to leave it until late, after the pub's shut, after the last drinkers have gone. And I'll need to use the last of my mother's tablets. Enough to keep him compliant, but not too many or he won't be able to walk independently.

There's no guarantee even then that Betty, or some insomniac or late-night reveller, won't see us as we come along the alley. I'll make him wear an anorak with a hood. There's one that Greg bought hanging in the hallway on a hook, probably for one of those long-ago camping holidays. With the hood up no one'll look twice at him. I'll work quickly and keep every sense peeled, alert.

I ram a strip of scarf into the crack under the window to stop the draft, and place a group of tea lights on one of the filing cabinets and light them too. Cars are drawing up outside now, the swift gleam of headlights through the narrow crack between the doors as they sweep round the corner looking for parking spaces. People tramp past on foot to go to the pub, their voices raised, excited. The mattress feels damp, but I cover it in the ground sheet and make up the bed with the clean sheets. I pile the blanket and old eiderdowns on top of the duvet. The smell of earthy walls and chalk is pungent in the darkness. How much more exquisite things will be after he's been deprived of light for a few days. He'll only have to stay here until Greg and Kit have left again. Then how luminous the music room will appear to him.

*   *   *

'What shall I tell people?' Jez asks, looking at me with such trust, such innocence that I feel a tiny glimmer of remorse about what is going to happen.

'What do you mean?'

'Well, I can't say I've been locked in your house, can I? It'll sound odd to people, even if it was because of this surprise thing. I don't want you or Helen to get into trouble for this. And what am I going to tell Alicia?'

'Tell her the truth. That you wanted to stay, to get some music contacts, and I let you.'

'But not getting in touch?'

'Jez! Stop worrying. You needed time to yourself. It's simple.'

He takes an enormous slurp of the tea I've brought him.

'I'm sorry I've been rude at times. It was ungrateful.'

'There's no need to apologize,' I say.

'That first night when we got wasted, I actually hoped you might say you'd rent me a room here. When I come over for college.'

'Really?'

'Well, yeah! Helen'd had a go at me that afternoon so I thought well she doesn't want me living with them. I thought it'd be good to live here, but I didn't think you'd want me. Then, the being trapped freaked me out a bit. I got the wrong end of the stick and I've been ungrateful, so you know, I'm sorry.' He's taken on that self-assured voice again, the one he first used as he sat and drank wine in the kitchen nearly a week ago. It's good to see the more relaxed side of him. Over the last few days he's been too quiet. Too cowed.

'So if I were to say you could stay . . .' It feels as if my heart has had a power surge and I'm zooming forward into another reality entirely.

Jez's mouth widens into a smile and in the corners are two tiny lines, though I can perceive a nerviness, an uncertainty in the way the creases flicker.

'Well, obviously I'd like to get home today. It's my birthday.
And it's already almost over. When are we going?'

'Soon.'

'Not now?'

'There are a few more things to get ready.' I try not to sound
hurt that he's so eager, after all, to leave me. 'Patience, Jez.'

When I return to the high windows I see that the drug's taking
effect. He's on the bed, writhing a little as if trying to fight the
sleep that overwhelms him. I plan to wait until it begins to wear
off, when he'll be able to limp as far as the garage, but won't be
so alert as to work out exactly what's going on. I open the door
quietly and go into the music room. I sit down on the bed beside
him.

'Shall I tell you a story?'

'Is it time to go?'

'A little longer. A story would pass the time.'

'OK then. Alright. '

I lie beside him on the bed, he moves over a little, making
room for me.

'It's called *Mudlarks*,' I tell him. I put my hand up and
stoke his hair. He nestles his head into me. I stroke the
tender skin on his throat. He's giving in at last. It's growing
dark outside as I speak, and still raining hard. It's cold in the
music room. I pull the duvet over us both and speak slowly,
soothingly.

'There was once a fifteen-year-old boy. He lived, as I do, by the
Thames, but he was homeless. So poor he had to scavenge for
rubbish washed up by the tide. Twice a day he went, at low tide,
down to the shore to collect whatever he could find. The bones
of the drowned and decomposed, pieces of wood, scrap metal.
Occasionally he found a coin, or a jewel, but those things were
rare. He had friends who worked with him, but many of these

so-called mudlarkers drowned. Stuck on a mudbank when the tide came in, they'd become marooned and then swept away by the relentless tides.'

I pause for a second. I can see he's almost asleep but I want to finish the tale. It's brought tears to my eyes. I swallow, wipe my eyes on the back of my hand and continue. 'This boy, Edmund, he struck lucky. He found a little medallion with Queen Victoria's face on it and he believed it must be hers, her own medallion. That he should give it back to her.

'He made his way to the palace but the guards refused him. He was a ragamuffin, dressed in muddy clothes and ill-fitting shoes that he'd picked up on the shore. But Edmund was not a boy to give up easily, and he was agile. He shinned up a wall outside the palace and broke in through a window. He found Queen Victoria lying in her bed. It was as if she'd been waiting for him. Edmund handed the medallion to Queen Victoria who was still in mourning for Prince Albert and had barely left her room for months. She asked him to sit on her bed and to tell her all about himself. She was so impressed by his story, and his devotion to her, that for the first time in months, years even, she came out of mourning. She saw beyond the rags and the mud to the soul of the boy. His courage and his selflessness enabled her to see that life was worth living again.'

I stop. Jez has stirred, his eyelids flicker a little, a small smile plays on his lips.

It's about three in the morning.

'Jez. We need to go. You must stand up and come with me. Jez.'

His face lights up, but he's still confused, drowsy. He's floppy, his limbs heavy. I make him put on his leather jacket and then Greg's enormous anorak over the top, to protect it. I hold his elbow as we go downstairs. In the hallway I tell him to put up the hood and to walk alongside me. I open the door and he follows me to the courtyard. I lead Jez out into the night.

'Hmmm. Air!' he says. His words slur a little. 'Oh, thank you. Thank you!'

It's been so long since he's been outside he breathes in deeply, greedily. There's a smell of seaweed, an anomaly of the river I love, the saltiness that washes up from the estuary and reminds you that the river runs into wild open oceans. Oceans that deliver to the river, carrying cargo from other worlds, fish to Billingsgate, silks to the East End, spices, fruits and vegetables, coffee, tobacco, cotton, tea and sugar. This river gives generously and takes greedily. I never underestimate it.

Jez looks at me.

'Cheers,' he mutters. 'Thanks. I'm sorry if I've been unhelpful at times. It was nice of you to have me.'

I lead him across the courtyard towards the door in the wall. I'm on edge. I know that if he decides to make a run for it when we're beyond the walls of the River House, I won't have the strength to stop him. I have to rely on his drugged state and his new-found trust in me. Yet the fact he believes I'm about to drive him home stirs an uncomfortable feeling in me. I don't like deceiving him. I've tried not to tell lies, and most of the time I haven't had to. He's believed what he wants to believe.

I told Kit a lie the summer Greg stopped talking to me. The summer of the grand silence. When freezing me out was Greg's way of punishing me for my frigidity. I hated telling it. But saying Daddy had lost his voice was preferable to admitting that he refused to speak to me, and by extension to Kit too. I did it to protect her.

I let Jez think we're going home, to protect him. I lead him along the alley. Horizontal rain stings our faces. Orange lights reflect upwards from the puddles underfoot. The river sighs impatiently down on the shore. Under the coaling pier it's so dark, Jez reaches for my arm. I take his hand and he doesn't try to remove it. So we continue, his hand sweetly in mine, through the chilly night to the garage doors.

'You keep your car in here?' he says, as I slot the key into the lock.

I don't answer.

CHAPTER THIRTEEN

Wednesday

Helen

Helen didn't know what made her feel worse as she arrived home from work on Wednesday evening. The two backs that were turned to her as she pushed open Mick's office door. Or the police car she noticed drawing up outside the front window a few minutes later.

Maria and Mick were poring over the internet, reading the messages that had been posted on the Facebook page they'd set up. Accolades and messages and memories of Jez from friends and admirers they had not even known existed.

'Hi,' Helen said. They didn't look round. 'Honey, I'm home,' she tried, a phrase she and Mick had used when they were first married in mock seriousness.

Mick turned. 'Helen, please, we're busy.'

He was interrupted by the doorbell. Helen went to answer it. It was about four thirty, the street lights had already come on.

Inspector Hailey Kirwin was accompanied again by the boy who barely looked Barney's age.

'We'd like to ask you a few personnel questions,' he said. 'About the disappearance of Jed. Could we come in?'

'Jez,' muttered Kirwin leaning towards him, 'and you mean personal questions, not personnel.'

'I don't mind,' Helen said. 'What do you want to know? Come in. Sit down, why don't you?'

She led them into the sitting room and switched on a table lamp before sitting down herself. She was buggered if she was going to offer them tea. She'd been about to open some wine.

'If you could just run over everything from the moment Jez arrived to stay with you? We need to get a full profile of his relations with you and your family.'

'OK, I'll try. D'you want my husband and sister as well?'

'Just you at the moment,' said Kirwin.

Helen shrugged. 'Fine. Where shall I begin?'

'From the moment he arrived. He came over for some interviews, is that right?'

'Yes. A week ago last Friday.'

'I understand he was thinking of going to sixth form college over here. So he's still at school?'

'Yes. At a lycee in Paris. He's sixteen today. It's his birthday.' Helen paused as the poignancy of this hit her.

Kirwin nodded . 'Birthdays are always difficult,' she said. 'Take your time.'

Helen smoothed down her skirt and took a deep breath. 'I met him on Friday at St Pancras. I remember worrying as I waited under the international arrivals board, about how short and middle-aged I'd look to him.' She smiled a rueful smile. 'That seems such a trivial concern now. But he's taller than either of my boys, even though he's younger than both of them. I assumed he'd feel a bit awkward, we hadn't seen each other for oh, about six months, so it was a nice surprise when he kissed me, French style, on both cheeks.' She frowned at the police woman. 'Is this the kind of thing you want to know?'

The woman nodded. 'Go on,' she said.

Helen thought for a moment. She remembered how she'd noticed his smell, of some kind of soap and how she'd thought of the sweaty pong of her own sons, which she put down to adolescence.

'I must admit I realized, seeing him, that it's no longer uncool these days for boys to care about their personal hygiene. It made me think my sons could try a bit harder. Oh, but I've always felt inadequate next to my sister. She seems to have done a better job than me as a mother.'

Kirwin leant forward, 'How do you mean, a better job? In what way?'

'Oh, all sorts of ways. Jez only came over for a couple of interviews, but Maria had made him bring his guitar, and had packed several changes of smart clothes. I'd never have been so organized with my boys. Then I was worried I wouldn't be able to think of things to say to him in the car on the way home. You know, teenage boys – mine anyway – can be very monosyllabic. But Jez was – is – charming! Probably because of living with adults. Until recently he was an only child. His father has remarried and he has a little stepsister now but he doesn't see much of them. Anyway, he was far more forthcoming than either of my children would ever be. Of course it makes you wonder if it's your fault. It's the lot of parents to blame themselves I suppose.'

Helen looked at the police boy. But he'd turned to look out of the window, or maybe he was studying his reflection in the dark pane, and was pushing his pen down his sock.

'Josh, I hope you're taking notes,' said Kirwin, and the boy started.

'Sorry,' he said.

'So, you picked Jez up in your car?'

'Yes. I was a bit annoyed that I had to pay the congestion charge. More with my sister than with him. I would have left my kids to get the tube. My sister's more protective of Jez than I ever was of my two, but perhaps it's because he's her only one.'

'Would you say then,' said Kirwin, 'that he isn't streetwise? That he might not have known how to look after himself in London? Just a thought.'

'Possibly,' said Helen. 'He's certainly a little naïve. On the way home he realized he hadn't got any English money! I had to stop at the bank, find somewhere to park, take him to the bureau de change. It wasn't his fault, if anything, it was my sister's. Given that's she's so protective, why hadn't she given him cash when he left? But yes, I'd say he's used to having things done for him. Lacks street cred. Since you ask.'

She paused.

'He might be rather mollycoddled, but he's well liked. Adored even! My boys, the band, his girlfriend obviously, they all idolize him. Though my kids described him as something. What was it? That's right. They said he was "whipped".'

'Oh?'

'It means eager to please,' Josh interjected, tuning in at last.

'Yes,' said Helen. 'Apparently he doesn't like to say no to his girlfriend. To anyone probably. He likes to please. He's polite. That's the phrase they use apparently. Whipped. Funny.'

'We spoke to his girlfriend. They've been together for a while.'

'It's rather sweet. They've kept in touch since he moved to Paris.'

'When was that?'

'Oh. It must be two years now. My sister – his mother – is working over there, in the suburbs. She's in fashion.'

'And he was planning to come over here for sixth form?'

'Yes. He applied to two music courses. One of the colleges is the same one my son has applied to. They were both going for the same course. Down here in Greenwich. They won't both get in. There are hardly any places. Barney might have stood a chance if it wasn't for Jez. But Jez is much more musical. And my sister pushes him. He's dyslexic but it doesn't affect his playing. If anything he seems to be more creative as a result.'

'You say people idolize him. Were you conscious at any time of his receiving unwanted attention from anyone?'

'What do you mean?'

'He didn't mention anyone? He wasn't worried about anything?'

'No. Nothing. You could ask his girlfriend, she'd probably know more.'

'And you didn't at any time fall out with either Jez or his mother during the week he was here?'

Helen shifted in her seat. Was she walking into some kind of trap here? She could murder a glass of wine. She'd had a long day at work and she couldn't help thinking about Maria and Mick at the computer together. Was she mistaken or had their thighs been touching? The more she thought about it, the more sure she felt that they had been leaning up against each other when she'd interrupted them just now. It was mad, but the thought grew in her so she could think of nothing else. Logically she knew the anxious feeling in her belly should spring from the worry over Jez. So why did her mind keep pivoting back to Maria and Mick?

'Helen. I'm sorry, but we do need to clarify this. Was there at any time an argument between you and your sister, or you and her son?'

Helen looked at Kirwin and shook her head.

'Just that moment in the car, when I stopped for his money. I wanted to get back and it meant we were running late. But otherwise no.'

'Were you angry with him? Might he have felt in the way? That he was upsetting you or your family?'

Helen paused. She wondered if she should mention losing her temper with Jez on the Friday he disappeared. How his brilliant playing made her tell him he was thoughtless. But that would mean mentioning yet again how inadequate she felt compared to her sister. Or worse, that she was hungover. She would sound neurotic and irresponsible.

'No,' she said. 'It was a minor irritation. And overall as I say, he is very welcome here, everyone loves having him, I'm sure he knows that.'

'One more thing then. You say you saw Jez after returning from a half day at work on Friday morning?'

Helen blinked. 'Yes.'

'And, you have people who can verify that for you?'

'No one else was at home when he left.'

'No. I mean that you went to work on Friday morning?'

Helen found herself nodding in spite of herself. There was time, surely there was time, to concoct a story. To get someone to cover for her. After all, it wasn't as though she'd been doing anything *that* bad. It wasn't as if she was hiding something criminal.

'You work . . .' Kirwin looked down at her notebook. 'At the teachers' centre in Newnham? You run courses, is that right? On behaviour management for classroom teachers?'

'Yes. I'm an advisory teacher,' Helen said. 'It means I'm peripatetic. But yes, based at the teachers' centre.'

'And you were at the centre last Friday?'

'Yes,' said Helen before she could stop herself.

'Thank you. That'll be all for now.'

'You don't want to talk to Mick? Or Maria?'

'We had a chat with your sister earlier. And with Mick. However, we may need to discuss the family liaison officer. It's been nearly a week now and we like to make sure families of missing children are properly supported. We'll be in touch.'

Helen watched the car disappear down Maze Hill and then went back to Mick's study. The two were no longer there, the computer's screensaver flickered blue and purple. She went to the kitchen.

Was today the same as every other day or was it different? It was as if she'd never seen her own kitchen before. The winter pansies on the windowsill, the box stuffed with pamphlets about films and plays they'd never get round to going to. The shelf of chipped mugs. She needed to replace the vase of chrysanthemums she'd placed on the table. They were wilting already. Everything shimmered in and out of focus. She must be ill. Perhaps she needed some paracetamol. Perhaps she needed a large gin.

Mick came in and rummaged in the freezer.

'So, Maria needed help with the Facebook page?' Helen said. He didn't notice the challenge in her eyes, the accusation.

'What? Oh, no, I wanted to help.'

'I don't get why you're taking it all on your shoulders!' But Helen did know why. It was so he could impress Maria. She was certain now, and couldn't contain herself. 'I never noticed Maria being helpless before. Why d'you have to pay her so much attention?'

'Helen, what is this? I just want to do all I can to find that boy. He's been gone five nights now and you don't seem to give a damn. I suppose you'll be wanting this?' He put a bottle of wine on the counter in a coolwrap.

As she reached for the bottle and a glass, the doorbell rang. Mick went to answer it. Helen looked through the kitchen door to see Alicia approaching her down the hallway. She looked dreadful, thinner than ever, with spots beginning to appear on her forehead.

'Come in, Alicia,' Helen said.

'You haven't heard anything?'

Helen shook her head. 'Sit down, darling. What would you like? You look as if you need a drink.' Helen pointed at the wine, and Alicia shook her head.

'I don't touch alcohol,' she said. 'I wouldn't mind a cup of tea though. I walked here through the tunnel and I'm knackered.'

'I'll make you one.'

'I thought someone ought to just drive about and look out for him,' Alicia said. 'It takes so long on foot. And it's freezing out there. I thought I'd ask you if you'd done that yet?'

Maria, hearing voices, came into the kitchen.

'Alicia wants to go and look for Jez,' Helen told her. 'She wants us to get the car out and just drive around south London until we find him. I think it's a good idea.'

'I've tried everything else,' said Alicia. 'But I'm not giving up.'

Helen was sure she saw Maria's lip curl when Alicia spoke in her rather high-pitched south-east London accent.

'That's the police's job,' said Maria. 'We are more useful here, keeping an eye on the Facebook page. Answering calls.' She looked up at Mick who nodded.

'What can I get you, Maria?' he asked.

She looked at Helen's glass of wine.

'Nothing alcoholic. I need to keep a clear head. Just in case.'

'Go to the sitting room and I'll bring you a cup of tea. I've lit the fire.'

Alicia raised her eyebrows as Mick followed Maria out of the room and Helen pulled a face as she handed Alicia a mug of sweet tea. She found something strangely comforting about the girl's presence.

They sat down at the kitchen table and Helen drank her wine while Alicia talked and ate digestive biscuits. She told Helen how she'd kept in touch with Jez on MSN since he moved to Paris. How well they got on. How easy to talk to he was, for a boy.

'I know she's your sister,' Alicia said, 'and I don't want to be mean, but Jez's mum's weird. And she doesn't like me.'

'Oh, come on,' Helen said. 'How can you tell?'

'She never asks me anything. It's odd because I'm into art and it's what Maria does, sort of. And Jez as well, he's like, my mum's too pushy. She's a snob. She wants him to be the best at everything. It's too much pressure.'

Helen warmed to the girl who clearly adored Jez, but saw through all the superficial stuff to the boy beyond the guitar and the looks.

Maybe, after all, Alicia would become her only ally while all this was going on.

'Look, I'm happy to go for a drive, sometime. But it's dark, we're not going to see much and I'm afraid I've had a drink. Let's give it a bit more time. But I'm glad you've come. Together, Alicia, we're going to find Jez. We don't need Maria or Mick and we don't need the police. We just need to stick together.'

Alicia put her hand up and they high-fived one another.

CHAPTER FOURTEEN

Thursday evening

Sonia

Nothing used to bring me greater joy than my daughter's presence. Her visits since she left home last October were what kept me going. Her overly fastidious habits that I find irritating – wiping surfaces with disinfectant spray, applying anti-bacterial gel to her hands before eating – even these brought a kind of fullness to my heart. That I'd produced this whole, new, grown-up person. But today, the morning of her impending arrival, I'm jittery and on edge.

Since she went back after Christmas, and Greg started to travel more, I've craved solitude. Having the River House to myself at last means I have noticed with amazement things I'd barely registered in the intervening years. The height chart pencilled onto the wall in the narrow alcove between the bathroom and my bedroom. I often run my fingers over a dent in the plaster in the hallway made by a carriage clock thrown in anger. I wangle out long-forgotten pieces of jewellery, old pennies, postcards, and lost photos from between the floorboards.

Friends phone occasionally with invitations, but I make excuses. Many have taken the hint and given up. The truth is I cannot bear to spend too much time away from the house and what it has begun to reveal to me. I feel I'm lifting a layer of padding that muffled everything so that for many years I was unable to properly remember, properly feel. And I suppose what I'm afraid of, now Kit's coming home, and Greg too, is that the padding will go back, and I'll never retrieve what it is I feel I'm so close to uncovering. Since Jez came, I have the sense that the intervening years are about to slip away like unwanted junk between the floorboards and the past and present can converge at last.

Kit arrives as I put the finishing touches to the dining table. We are, of course, eating in the kitchen, though she will go into the sitting room with Greg first for a drink, a gin and tonic probably, and they will talk about anatomy and blood and the latest gene therapy while I prod the lamb to see if it's cooked. I get out the wine glasses, breathe on them, rub them with a freshly laundered tea towel. Kit comes in, her tall thin self, newly woman, no longer the teenager who hung about sullenly for so long. The change in her is difficult to describe. It's to do with a taking charge of herself, a comfort within her own skin I never saw before. She stands in the doorway, dressed as usual in casual sportswear, a red ski jacket, black trousers of some sort. She pulls off her gloves.

'Mum, hi,' she says in her deep, Greg-like voice. 'Lovely smell. What're we having?'

She leans forward, offers me a cool cheek. We never hug these days. Since she left home we've adopted a rather formal approach to greeting one another. I sometimes feel she's nervous of me, and that makes me sad. She's more relaxed with her father.

'Langoustines. Followed by shoulder of lamb. Daddy's choice. But I got you your favourite for pudding. Are you alone? I thought you were bringing your new man?'

'He's coming. He nipped to the offie for some wine for you.'

'That's sweet.'

She looks at me and says with a grin, 'He *is* sweet.' I sense that she's in this relationship quite deep and wonder again what I'll make of him.

She starts to wander about the kitchen, picking things up and putting them down, as she always does when she's been away, seeing whether anything's changed. I feel myself tense, afraid I've left a clue, evidence of my past few days with Jez.

'Go and sit down with Daddy,' I say. 'I have to get on with the dinner.'

'OK. I just want to see if there're any letters for me. You've stopped forwarding stuff.'

'There's been nothing to forward,' I say. 'I'll pour you a drink. Do go and sit.'

'Alright, Mum, just a sec. Please don't try and get rid of me the minute I arrive.'

'Don't be silly. I'm not getting rid of you. Stay here. I'd love you to. Just thought you might be warmer in the sitting room. Dad's lit a fire.'

I begin to quarter a lemon, leaning upon the knife more heavily than is probably necessary.

'Mum, are you OK?'

I turn and look at her. She's standing in the middle of the kitchen, her arms folded, a small frown on her forehead, examining me.

'Of course I'm OK. I'm fine.'

'It's just . . . oh, never mind. Did you decide about the spare room?'

I turn my back on her again, fling the knife onto the side and make a show of rinsing my hands at the sink. I try to steady my voice, to sound sensible. 'If you don't mind making up the bed yourself. There are sheets in the airing cupboard.'

'Cor. I thought I was coming back for a rest!' she quips. 'I have to make my own bed at uni.'

'And I have other things to do as well as prepare beds. It won't do you any harm,' I say, and we exchange an old, affectionate mother–daughter look at last.

Kit straightens, her eyes light up and she takes a step forward, a smile on her lips, as a tall young man appears in the doorway.

He's public-school educated, I can tell by the way he holds out his hand, looks me in the eye. He wears suit trousers, a wool overcoat, glasses with dark frames. He must be a good four years older than Jez. But I can see Harry's the kind of man who's never been young. Jez has none of his sort of veneer. It's what I love about him. About the ephemeral stage he's at. Nebulous, yet to condense into a rigid form from which there's no return.

'Mum, this is Harry. Harry, my mother Sonia.'

'It's nice to meet you, Harry,' I say.

He smiles back at me, shaking my hand for a little longer than I'm comfortable with and examining me through his glasses. I wonder whether they've been talking about me on their way here and if so, what Kit has told him?

I see Kit's face brighten as Greg comes into the kitchen behind me. I move aside and they gaze at one another and laugh. Greg holds her by both shoulders, says, 'Let me look at my daughter,' and Kit beams at him. Then he tugs her, beckoning to Harry, towards the living room.

I'm left to finish the cooking. I've put a CD in the player, a Bach cello suite. I scrub and peel the potatoes, cut them into quarters, salt them and put them in the oven to roast. Greg comes back in, goes over to the wine rack for a bottle of Sancerre to have with the starter, puts it in the fridge.

'Where's the claret? The Château Lafite we put down for Kit's twenty-first?' he asks. 'It should be in the rack.'

Until this moment I haven't given that wine another thought. Once I'd pulled the cork, all I knew was the pleasure of sharing it with Jez. Now I look at Greg and can see a storm about to break.

'Oh that,' I say.

'What, Sonia? What are you saying?'

'Sorry, Greg. It got opened by mistake. It was one evening after a session. We finished a bottle so I said grab another from the rack. I didn't look at the label.'

'We kept it for *years*. Are you out of your mind?'

'Greg, it was just wine.'

'I don't understand this. It was your idea to save it for Kit's twenty-first in June. Not mine. But I thought what better way to mark a significant birthday! And now it's gone.'

He looks at me in a way I don't like, as if he wonders whether I'm suffering an early menopause or dementia, something unmentionable in polite circles. Doctors always have the upper hand. They always act as if they have some secret information about you. They keep you in a constant state of anxiety that they've recognized some dreadful symptom and are waiting for the moment to disclose it to you.

'Greg, I was as upset as you on the night. Then I thought, what am I making a fuss about? It's just a few squashed grapes in a bottle. Worse things happen in the world.'

'Squashed grapes that were picked the year Kit was born, and have been maturing ever since,' he says. 'You can't put a price on that. You can't rewind time.'

'I need to get the mint sauce made.' I sigh and turn from him. 'I'm sorry. What more can I say?'

I crush mint leaves in the pestle and mortar, watching them turn from green to brown as they release their aroma into the air. I add vinegar and sugar and stir the resulting sauce vigorously. But all the time my mind is half elsewhere. Only part of me inhabits this world of roast lamb and Sancerre and sauce, of polished glasses and tablecloths, while the rest of me, the secret self that feels more real, is all wrapped up in Jez. It is Jez whose smell infuses the air around me. Jez's flesh I anoint as I rub the lamb with rosemary and garlic. I remember with a shiver that he is away down the alley, locked in the garage, and wish that he were upstairs, cocooned in the lovely light of the music room.

Greg still hasn't spoken to me when we sit down at the dinner table half an hour later. The Bach has finished and there's an awkward moment when no one seems to know what to say. I've lit candles and put a vase of snowdrops in the middle of the white cloth. The kitchen is warm, and the flames of the candles are reflected in the curtainless windows.

'Harry and I fancy a game of Scrabble after dinner,' Kit says at last, reaching for the wine. 'But I told him how you loathe board games, Mum.'

I smile at her. 'Thanks,' I say.

'Why's that?' Harry asks. 'Is it fear of losing?'

I laugh. 'On the contrary, I don't feel competitive enough,' I say. 'I can't get interested in double and treble letter counts and word scores. But you play, by all means.'

'I always wanted one of those large families who play games after dinner,' Kit says ruefully. 'Mum would never play. And Scrabble between two is no fun. You'll play Scrabble with us, won't you, Dad?'

Greg shrugs. He's always found it hard to refuse Kit anything but right now he says, 'Your mother and I need to talk. Sorry honey.' He stands up, wipes his hands on his napkin and goes to the CD player.

'A little music is called for, I feel,' he says. He puts the Bach back in its case and chooses Mahler's 5th symphony.

'Why this?' I ask Greg.

'What's the matter. I thought you liked it?'

'I do like it, but isn't it a bit . . . grandiose . . . to accompany dinner?'

Greg shrugs and takes it off again. 'OK. We'll stick to chamber music if we must.'

Harry leans across to me.

'Actually,' he says, 'I was wondering if you'd mind me having a mess about in your music room after dinner?'

I feel under siege. It's Jez's room. His sacred space. But I can't possibly refuse. What reason would I give?

'Harry plays keyboard,' says Kit. 'I showed him the stuff up there, you don't mind, do you, Mum? I know you sometimes work in there.'

'Of course I don't mind.'

I wonder whether I've been meticulous enough about clearing Jez's things away. The butt ends he'd left on the saucers, the razors in the bathroom. Did I check the waste-paper basket? I try to swallow my mouthful of food but find I can't.

'What a fantastic spot for an office,' Harry goes on. 'The view! Wow.'

Greg and Kit exchange a glance.

'What?' I ask. 'What's that look for, you two?'

'Nothing,' says Greg. 'Don't imagine things, Sonia.'

'It is. It is a lovely room,' says Kit, taking Harry's hand. 'It's one of the arguments Mum uses for staying here. But one lovely room doesn't mean we should stay here for ever.' She doesn't look at me as she says this because she knows it's going to lead to friction.

Greg says, 'We weren't going to discuss this until later.'

Kit says, 'I know, Dad. Sorry. But did you see the local paper tonight? Harry was shocked. Armed burglaries. Perfectly innocent people being mugged, there was even a shooting, all in a week! If nothing else that's a good reason to move. I just want Mum to think about it.'

'You're preaching to the converted, as you know,' says Greg.

'It's two against one, Mum!' Kit smiles brightly.

'Please,' I say. 'Don't bring this up now.'

Kit turns to Harry. 'Dad's seen a fabulous place in Geneva.'

I look at Kit. What's she playing at?

'I know. You said your folks were thinking of moving out there,' says Harry.

'Imagine the skiing! Mum, I can't believe you won't even give it a thought.'

I purse my lips. It seems all of them, Greg, Kit, even my mother have been talking. Planning. Scheming. Going ahead in spite of my feelings. 'What place have you seen, Greg? This is the first I've heard of it.'

'I did a bit of preliminary research. And honestly Sonia, if you saw some of these places . . . I'm certain you'd come round to it. Your mother thinks it's a good idea. I've got some details in fact, to show you later.'

'You discussed this with my mother, before consulting me?'

There's a pause. Harry wipes his mouth with his napkin and shifts awkwardly in his chair.

Then Greg says, 'Your mother takes an interest. You know she does.'

'Who's going to visit her, do her food order, take her the things she needs when I live in Geneva?'

Kit and Greg look at each other again, as if they have been arranging all this for weeks.

'She's coming with us, of course,' says Kit. 'We wouldn't leave Grandma behind. Dad's seen somewhere with a granny flat and . . .'

I fill up my wine glass and rest my forehead on my hand. There's another tense silence.

Then Kit says, 'Anyway, can I take Harry up to the music room? Can we be excused until pudding?'

Before I speak Greg winks at Harry and says, 'The keyboard is mine in fact. I'm thrilled that a friend of Kit's wants to play it.'

Kit smiles at her father, squeezes his hand.

'Is that OK, Mum?' she asks anxiously.

'Of course,' I say, trying to smile too. 'It wants using. Greg hardly ever plays these days.'

'What was that supposed to mean?' Greg asks, when Kit and Harry have left the room. I blink in surprise.

'It wasn't supposed to mean anything,' I say. 'You don't often play these days. You're not often here.'

'It was a dig,' he says. 'If you've got a problem with my being away more, why don't you say so?'

'I don't have a problem with it.'

'Then why carry on in this passive-aggressive manner?'

'Passive-aggressive?'

'What would you call it?'

'Not passive-aggressive, Greg, that's unfair. I was simply stating a fact. You don't play as often as you used to. You aren't here as much these days.'

He gives me that look again, from beneath a lowered eyebrow, as if he's assessing whether his early diagnosis was correct.

'What is it, Sonia?' he says at last. 'First the wine. Then all these snide remarks about my not playing any more. Was the wine a way of getting at me too?'

'Oh God, the wine again. Please drop it, it was an oversight on my part and I apologize. We'll find another way to celebrate Kit's birthday. I'll buy vintage champagne. It's not as if we're short of money these days.'

'How many times . . . I'm happy to stop the lecturing. I'd do it for you if you wanted me to. You just have to say.'

'Do you think your being at home more would be such a good idea?' I ask. 'The way we seem determined to misunderstand each other these days?'

'No,' he says. 'You're right, perhaps it wouldn't.'

I get up, clear away the plates, scrape leftovers into the bin.

Kit comes in and looks at us sullenly.

'What's up, Beanie?' Greg asks, holding his arms out. She walks into them, lets him hold her.

'You two,' she says. 'I thought you got on better now I've left home.'

'Oh, Kit,' I say. 'We never got on that badly, did we? While you were here?'

'You bickered all the time. I always thought it was my fault. That you'd be OK now I've gone.'

'Honey,' says Greg. 'All parents bicker. It has nothing to do with you. How can you think that? We both love you to bits. Don't we, Sonia?'

'Of course.'

'And we love each other.' He looks at me and smiles, so I smile back.

'But you won't agree about the move?'

She says 'the move' as if it is a definite thing, as if they have already gone ahead with it. I open my mouth but Greg interrupts.

'It doesn't mean we don't love each other, honey.'

'So,' I say. 'Harry. It seems quite . . . serious?'

She shrugs. 'We get on OK. Oh, I told Harry about your acoustic guitar, the one you got in Spain, Dad. But I couldn't find it? Did you get rid of it?'

I can feel Greg's eyes trying to catch mine. I busy myself with pudding.

'Shall we have some Tarte au Citron? It's from Rhodes. Oh, and Kit, I got you some Princess Cake.'

She sidles over to me. I slip my arm around her and something seems, momentarily, to slide away, as if a layer of me is shed. I catch a glimpse of the mother-me I was remembering earlier, who for a while was content.

After Kit's eaten her cake she comes back to me at the sink. I'm scrubbing around the burnt bits of the roasting tin with a Brillo pad. But I'm thinking of Jez again, wondering how he is. Thinking of him makes me anxious. He's out of my reach, and it isn't as it should be. He should be warm in the music room. Things have got out of hand. Something that should be precious and exquisite seems to be slipping out of my control.

'Do you remember that summer?' I say to Kit. She's drying the pans that I've washed, the ones that don't go in the dishwasher. 'The one when everything festered. It was really muggy and damp. All those East Anglian crops just rotted in the soil, and everything stank. There were terrible mosquitoes. The cats got fleas. You caught head lice.'

'Mum! Why're you talking about that? Head lice . . . yuck.'

'Hey! And you're a medical student.'

'Yeah but you can keep the parasites for someone else. Not my thing I'm afraid!'

'Anyway. There was a field of cabbages over the road and the leaves went mouldy. The stench was appalling! I thought there must be a curse on the land. Everything that should've been ripe and fertile turned rancid and sickly. Then we became ill too and spent a week or more in bed fighting off a virus.'

'I don't remember,' Kit says.

'No. I suppose you were only about six.'

'Anyway, why drag up that summer? There were plenty of good ones. When the trees were all covered in May blossom. Remember the cow parsley along the hedgerows? And the cornflowers in the garden in June? God, I miss East Anglia so much sometimes. You could feel the seasons change. You just don't get that in cities.'

Of course, for Kit, the country was her home. Her first forays into the world happened under massive skies and amongst spreading fields of poppies. The first images on her fresh baby retinas were of white cloud shapes against blue, green light filtering through canopies of chestnut leaves. Those first impressions, that are made before we are even conscious that we can see, stay with us, imprinted somewhere on our memories. They form our true image of home.

My first images were the river and its mud, the bones and smooth chalk stones washed up on the beach, clay pipes and discarded car parts and driftwood. Ropes and chains draped in dank weed. Lowering grey skies only just glimpsed above the towering wall of the power station and its dark monolithic chimneys. The steel coaling pier reaching a clanking brown arm out over the water. Kit never experienced East Anglia as I did, as an exile, even at its most radiant.

And why indeed am I talking about that one ugly summer? Why do I want to turn her good memories into something murky, best left forgotten?

'You're quite right,' I say, wiping the surface with the dishcloth and putting on the espresso machine.

'Treasure your good memories. Please darling. Hold them close to your heart. It's very important.'

Later, when Kit and Harry have gone up to bed, Greg comes back into the kitchen and puts some guitar music on the CD player. It's John Williams. My heart lurches. He sits down opposite me at the table on the bench, pours us each a large glass of cognac, leans across and takes my hand in his. He smiles a beseeching smile through pale older-man lips. His stubble is grey. His eyebrows, nostrils, and ears have long hairs growing out of them. Under his skin is a web of tiny red broken veins. He squeezes my hand.

'Sorry about earlier,' he says.

'What? What's there to be sorry about?'

'About accusing you of being passive-aggressive. It wasn't on.'

'It's OK,' I say, sighing. I've withdrawn my hand.

'Come and sit beside me?'

I move around to his side of the table and sit next to him on the bench. He puts his arm around me and I can smell coffee and old wool. It's not unpleasant; it's not that I find it repellent when we sit together. It's familiar. It's accompanied me through the last twenty-five years of my life, it's almost as much a part of me as the smell of the River House, which you don't notice until you've been away from it for a while.

He pulls me towards him and though I resist, he leans over and starts to kiss me on the lips.

I never actively enjoyed kissing Greg, but kissing does not even seem appropriate now we are over forty. Why is this? Do all married couples feel awkward trying to kiss when they get older? I do try. I open my mouth a little bit and he pokes his tongue between my teeth. And it feels like a tongue between my teeth. It doesn't feel like a thing to abandon myself to. It does nothing. I can taste the cognac, and the faint residue of lemon tart. I'm afraid I'm going to gag. I push him away.

'Sonia, I'm not having an affair if that's what you think. That's not why I've taken on all this lecturing. I promise.'

'It's fine,' I say. 'I didn't think you were.'

'I just sometimes feel you don't want me with you.'

'That's nonsense!' I say. 'What on earth makes you think that?'

'Well, look at us. We haven't slept together for three months now. I mean properly sleep together, not just share the same bed.'

'Fuck, you mean.'

'Well if you want to use that word. I'd rather say *make love*.'

'I'm just clarifying what we're talking about here.'

'OK. We're talking about sex, Sonia. Three months. And before that, how long? Six? Eight?'

'Yes, but we're not the kind of couple who spends their every waking moment copulating. We never were. Nothing's changed, Greg. This isn't a marriage of grand passions.'

'Not on your part, no.'

'What?'

'I mean, it's not for want of trying on my part. I want us to . . . have more sex than we do. I still find you desirable, Sonia.'

'What's that supposed to mean? Still? Am I supposed to be past it at forty-four?'

'OK. OK. Sorry. I shouldn't have used the word *still*. I was talking about the fact we've been together for a long time. I know we've had our rough patches, but I thought things were better recently. Since Kit's grown up. I haven't tired of you. Some husbands . . . God, Sonia, some guys I know, they're fed up to the back teeth with the women they married and are having affairs left, right and centre. But that's not for me. You're the one. Always have been. Always will be. It's why I want us to move. Be together more often. In a place that is ours. Not one that really belongs to your parents. Can't you consider it, Sonia? Think of it. Geneva. Clean air. Mountains.'

Why won't he give up?

'Come to bed?'

Later, I'm woken in the night by visions of Jez skeletal, his flesh gone yellow and withered. There's a stench of rotting cabbages, flies and lice crawl over him, eating into his once-flawless flesh. I have to get out of bed, leaving Greg's contented, post-coital snoring mound under the covers. I pull on my kimono and am about to turn and climb up the stairs to the music room when I remember with a jolt that he's not there. I go downstairs instead. I put my long wool coat over my night clothes and pull on my boots. Then I turn the handle of the hall door and slip quietly out into the night.

CHAPTER FIFTEEN

Thursday night

Sonia

He stares wide-eyed at me. He won't speak.

'Is this the only way you can think of, to show me you're upset I've put you in here?' I ask. He won't reply.

'I didn't want to do it, believe me. But I've got people in the house who won't be happy you're staying. I had to hide you for your own good.'

I've lit a candle and am looking at him by its wavering light. I'm dismayed. Something's changed. Jez's face is white and pasty looking, as it was in my dream. His skin is faintly moist. I feel a rush of anger and I am not even sure who it's for. Jez, for losing his vitality? Greg for coming back and forcing me to do this to him? Or for someone – something – else?

I sit on the bed and pour Jez some water and offer it to him but he turns his head aside and refuses to drink it. It's the first time, since Sunday, that he's been so uncooperative.

'Jez, we both dislike this situation, but we have to make do. It won't be for long. I promise. Please eat. Here. I've bought you some cake from Rhodes. There's a choice in fact, Princess Cake or Tarte au Citron.'

He takes a deep breath and spits at me, not once, but again and again. It's so unexpected and so violent I have no time to duck.

Saliva runs down my cheek. I wipe it off with the sleeve of my coat.

'That wasn't necessary,' I say. 'I've come out here in the middle of the night to make sure you're OK, not cold or frightened. That's the only reason I'm here Jez, to look after you. Don't bite the hand that feeds you.'

He doesn't reply.

I sit down on the bed next to him, stroke his damp hair away from his forehead to show that there is no ill feeling after his outburst even though it was hurtful. He flinches from my touch.

'If you're not going to talk to me, if you won't even tell me what's wrong, I don't see how you can expect me to help,' I say. I feel gripped, not by fury this time but by hopelessness, frustration, at the thought that I must keep Jez like this. It's not how I want it to be. I want him back in the music room, to go back to the beginning. Show him I only want to do him good. I never wanted to make this into something unpleasant. Neither do I want him to think bad things about me, to think that I should wish him any harm. That's not how it is. It isn't how I am. Some force is taking what we've got and turning it sour. It's what I predicted in the kitchen when I remembered that East Anglian summer. It's like the way they turned what Seb and I had into something shameful.

'Everything's going to be OK, you know,' I say. 'Everything's going to be lovely. We just need to get through this bit.'

'You were taking me home.'

'Yes,' I say, 'I was. But, you know that isn't possible, the way things are. You said yourself it would be difficult to explain things to everyone. I thought about what you said, and you were right. It would have been impossible.'

'Helen and Alicia have no idea where I am, do they? The surprise party was a lie.'

'I never told a lie, Jez. The party, if you remember, was an idea you came up with by yourself.'

He starts to writhe, tugging at the duct-tape bonds.

'Why am I tied up? And locked in? Where am I?'

'SShh. It's OK. You're still very close to my house. I wouldn't have taken you far from me. I'd never abandon you. You know that.'

I pause, waiting for him to calm down.

'My only regret,' I go on, 'is that circumstances are less than luxurious for you for the next couple of days. I'm being forced to keep you in undesirable conditions. But it's not for long.' I look to see if my words are reaching him at all.

He stops struggling and stares at me with a doubtful expression, wanting to believe, not quite allowing himself to.

'I promise, Jez.'

The cold in the garage makes your bones ache. It's worse than I'd anticipated. Even under his duvet and with the blankets and hot-water bottle, Jez is shivering, and though I am wearing my long, black wool winter coat and a scarf and boots over my night clothes, I too am unable to keep my teeth from chattering together. My lips are so numb it's hard to get words out. I must bring another duvet down as soon as I can. I don't want him to fall ill.

'Think of this as a little adventure, like camping in the woods. I'll bring you anything, you know that. You only have to ask. Look, I've put the acoustic guitar there for you. And there's a torch if you need light to see by.'

'How am I supposed to play when you keep my wrists strapped up with this . . . What is it? Gaffer tape?'

'I didn't want to restrain you, believe me. I was worried if you woke up and panicked you might hurt yourself trying to do something silly.'

Neither of us mention what I've used to stop him soiling himself. I know how humiliating this would be for him.

'I'll cut the bonds off soon if you're good. I'd like to keep them off so you can play guitar, smoke and wash. I wish there was running water in here. I've brought you a flannel so you can wipe your face. And there's water in the plastic container. Jez, I'm making it all as pleasant as I can in the circumstances.'

I say I'll unleash one of his hands now so he can take a drink. I snip the tape off with the kitchen scissors I've brought in my pocket. I put the glass of water to his lips. That's when he starts to get difficult again.

He swipes the glass from me and it smashes against the bedpost. I can see by the state he's got himself into that he's going for me even from this sitting position. He's managed to keep a shard of glass in his fist somehow, and as I back away he lurches off the bed towards me. I swivel away from his hand but he catches me on the wrist with the glass shard and drags it, producing a long line of pinpricks in my skin. Luckily for me, he's still weak from last night's drugs, and with his feet and one hand still strapped to the bedposts he can't move far. I take advantage of this to push him back down. I kneel on him. He cries and tries to lash out again with his one free hand, but I guess it's lost feeling in the cold and he hasn't much strength. I grasp his hand and twist it. He yelps as I rip strips of the duct tape from the roll in my bag and fasten his wrist tightly to the bed frame again.

I stand and look down at him. Seb often frightened me, he often threatened to abandon me. And he could be rough. But he would never have gone for me the way Jez just did. I swallow.

'Jez, believe me, I don't want to have you tied up like this. I'd much rather watch you move, listen to you play. But what you did just then was hurtful.'

I wait a bit and when I see he's not going to reply I speak to the silence.

'Everything I do is for your own good,' I say. I take the scarf from the crack under the window and reluctantly I tie it tightly around his mouth.

'For your own good.'

It's pitch black outside, and such a raw cold my eyes sting. It takes me several minutes to adjust to the darkness. There's not a star in the sky. The tide's up high and the water sloshes against the wall only a couple of feet from the top. There's an insistent *clank clank clank* as if someone's trying to get my attention from up there on the steel structure of the coaling pier. Too regular a rhythm for the wind surely, though I know I'm frightening myself. I strain to see. There's nothing but the thicker black shape of the pier against the black of the night. The *clank* changes rhythm for a moment, as if whoever or whatever is up there has moved. I do know what the sound is, it's there all the time, a large sheet of corrugated iron that has come loose and flaps in the wind, a sound that turns into a *bang* on a particularly stormy night. I walk forward, tentatively. There's the regular slurp of the water against the wall. Then I'm certain. I can hear breathing.

I daren't move. Something's down there below the wall, on the water. I'm drawn to it, to peer over, to check who's there. A gaggle of swans rises up and down on the water's surface, huddled together against the cold, an eerie silver in the darkness. I feel the swift warm shudder of relief. I think of something I heard once, about how Hindus revere swans for the way their feathers don't get wet in the water. The way a saint is in the world without being attached to it. One of the swans lifts its wings and stretches, revealing the muscular white underside, and I remember a production of *Swan Lake*, the sinuous bodies of the ballet dancers as they moved. The image gets confused with the one I still have of Jez, his arms stretched over his head as I left the garage. The regret that he's losing his beauty, as he lies wasting away, assails me again. I move on down the alley towards the entrance in the wall to the River House. The panoply of images, the swans, the ballet dancers, Seb, Jez, all become confused in my mind.

There's a bright amber square of light in one of the windows down the alley, but otherwise everyone's asleep. Not a sign of life. I slip in through the door in the wall, push open the front door, stop to listen before entering the hall. Is that a door closing gently upstairs? I'm on edge. Imagining things. Every sense aches with the strain. My mouth's dry. My fingers tingle.

I stand still for a few more moments barely daring to breathe. Slide through the hall door, leaving my coat and boots in the lobby. Slip into the downstairs loo. Flick the lock across. Wait. Try to breathe silently, but my breath comes in great loud gasps. I run the cold tap and bathe my bleeding wrist in the icy water. The blood refuses to be stemmed, it continues to ooze out of the pinprick cuts that turn the water pink as it swirls down the sink. I listen. Someone's moving about upstairs! I can hear the creak of floorboards, footsteps on the landing. Another door closes. When all's quiet I pull the light cord, slide the lock back. Open the door. A slender figure steps towards me in the darkness.

'Sonia.'

It's Harry.

'I needed the loo. Couldn't remember where the bathroom was up there.'

'Be my guest,' I say, wondering what possesses me to employ a phrase I never use. How absurd it sounds, too, in the dark, in the entrance to the downstairs bathroom. Maybe I imagine it, but I feel as if he stares at my back as I climb the stairs, to return to my bedroom and slide back in-between the sheets next to Greg.

CHAPTER SIXTEEN

Friday

Sonia

The next day, Friday, Greg announces he's got us all tickets for a dress rehearsal of *Tosca* at the Royal Opera House and that he's treating us to a trip upriver on the Clipper, and then champagne and a post-rehearsal supper. Kit's beside herself with girlish excitement. She and Greg go into a huddle over their breakfast coffee to discuss the Soprano while Harry has a shower. All this happens in a blur, beyond me. As if I'm watching them from a parallel universe. I can't leave Jez on his own. Not after the fight last night. I need to make sure he's OK and that we're friends again. The way I left him was so awful, so cruel. I need to make sure he understands that all I feel for him is tenderness.

'Judy's coming,' I complain to Greg. 'I don't like to leave her in the house on her own. She never does a proper job if I'm not here.'

This is nonsense. Never in my life have I bothered to tell Judy what to do. She's been the cleaner of the River House for at least fifteen years and I've always let her get on with it as my mother did before me.

'Oh, darling. How often do we get the chance to take time out, have a little treat, and with Kit home. And Harry.'

I squeeze my eyes tight shut, seeing Jez in the icy air of the garage. Tied up. Gagged. Lonely. In need of clean clothes. Resenting me.

'Leave a note for Judy, and try to relax for once.' Greg comes up behind me, puts his arms around my waist, something I hate, and nestles his nose in my neck.

'We need to go *tout de suite*,' he says. 'Grab your coats and scarves, gang, it's going to be brass monkeys out on the river today.'

'I'll follow you to the pier,' I say. 'You all go on ahead while I write Judy a note.'

'I'll wait for you,' says Harry. 'Go on, Kit. Have a bit of time alone with your father.'

Harry hangs about while I make a great show of writing Judy a note, reminding her we are out of wax for the parquet but that the mirrors could do with a clean, that there's some lime and vinegar spray in the cupboard under the sink. It's such a pantomime. What on earth is Judy going to think? She'll wonder what's come over me, after all these years. If Harry wasn't staring over my shoulder as I wrote, I'd screw the note up and toss it into the waste-paper basket, but I have to keep up the charade now, for his sake. He seems unable to stand a decent distance from me. You get people like this. Unaware of physical boundaries, they glean which way you are about to turn and stand right there, in the square foot of floor space you were intending to occupy. As I go to the sink for a glass of water – for some reason my mouth is still dry – he steps there too and stands with his back to it, arms folded over his Fair Isle jumper. I notice that the dark stubble makes a shadow across his jawline, that the skin beneath it is slightly reddened and he already has the beginnings of jowels. I realize again how transient Jez's youth is, feel it slipping away even as

I watch Harry's mouth, with its thin dry lips, open and close. He's talking about something I'm not in the least bit interested in.

'The rowing club, over there.' He gesticulates through the kitchen window to the other side of the river. 'Are you and Greg members? I wouldn't mind having a go if you're still here in the summer. Though I guess that's unlikely.'

I stare at him.

'We've always kept a dinghy, in a boathouse along the alley. We never had cause to join a club,' I tell him coldly.

'Oh, I know where you're coming from.'

'You do?'

'Oh yes. Societies – mostly a waste of time. Better to go your own way. Though Kit and I enjoy the tennis club at uni.'

I want to add that though there is no question I'll still 'be here in the summer', it doesn't guarantee him an invitation. But he's started to speak again. I can barely make sense of the following words that bubble out of his mouth. Something to do with attachment to houses and the need to move on. I don't want to discuss this with him. I tell him I need to find the rubber gloves for Judy, and rummage under the sink hoping he'll take the hint and go. He stands, his feet planted heavily and wide apart on the kitchen floor, as if he owns the place. How is it that I'm here with this man, when the person I want to be with has to lie, cold and incarcerated, in the garage?

By 10 a.m. we're on the pier. Sheila, who sells tickets, is wrapped up in a thick woollen scarf, her face redder than ever in the raw gusting winds. Neither Greg, nor Kit, are ones for chats with the locals, but I like to exchange words with Sheila, so I tell Harry I'll do the honours with the tickets and at last he leaves my side and goes off to join Greg and Kit in the glass waiting room at the end of the pontoon.

'Next one'll be along in ten minutes,' Sheila says, ripping off the stubs. An orange lifeboat bounds past, heading downriver, and the pier groans and creaks and bounces in its wake.

'They still ain't found that kid,' she says. 'They've been up and down dredging the river for days now.'

'What kid?'

'Ain't you seen the papers?

Sheila's been working on the pier for as long as I can remember. She lives at home in Woolwich with her old dad and so many cats she's lost count. She reads the local paper with avid interest, never missing a trick.

'It's always worse when it's a youngster the river takes. You can't help thinking of the parents. Whatever the papers say, it'll be a suicide. It's that skunk does it. I've seen more than one kid come to grief on the back of it and it's all over the shop now, they sell it outside the primary schools these days. It gives 'em the blues, big black depressions they can't climb out of. He'll have done 'imself in, that's what I think.' She shakes her head and asks how I am.

'I'm very well, thank you, Sheila. Never been better,' I tell her, hugging to myself the knowledge that Jez is neither drowned nor suffering from skunk-induced depression but is alive and well and living with me. That though temporarily he's gagged in the garage, the second my husband and daughter leave tomorrow, I can reinstate him in his beautiful music room.

Sheila and I exchange a few more pleasantries before I join the others in the waiting room. The boat approaches, sending more waves butting against the side of the pier.

The Clipper rolls about on the water this morning. It's a rough day, too cold to go out on deck, my preferred place. As we set off in a great arc out into the middle of the river, the buildings on Canary Wharf seem to undulate, their windows reflecting the leaden sky.

Though the river is more familiar to me than my own skin, it can frighten me. Today is one of those days. The grey swell is hostile, it lifts and drops the boat alarmingly. I can't relax. I don't want to look into the depths as the Clipper builds up speed and we start to bump over the waves.

We leave Greenwich on one side, the tall buildings on the other, and move upriver towards Masthouse Terrace Pier, and then Greenhouse. After twenty minutes we dock at Canary Wharf. It never fails to surprise me that it takes this long on the river to reach, when it appears to be right opposite us at the River House. Yet that the Queen's House, which seems right up there on the other side of Greenwich, can be reached on foot in five minutes.

Greg chats to Harry as we set off again. He's bought him a beer from the bar and they are being all man to man. Kit is texting someone, her head bowed over her mobile in concentration. I'd like to sit next to her, talk about small things, the things I imagine other mothers and daughters pass the time with. But I can't think of a way in. I can hear Greg's voice, droning on. How the river was once busier than the streets, crowded with masts, jammed so boats could barely pass one another. How the tobacco warehouse at Wapping was once the biggest public building in the world. 'Designed, would you believe it, by the same guy who built the prisons of Dartmoor and Maidstone.'

Harry nods thoughtfully, though I wonder how interested he really is in Greg's lecturing.

'See over there. That's where they executed people for crimes upon the "high seas". They used to keep "the saddest book in the world" in the police station. A record of suicides both attempted and successful. Not very cheerful, but the Thames has always had its dark side.' Greg takes another sip of beer.

I huddle into myself. I always feel uneasy passing the recklessly constructed 1980s apartments on the other side, when the

river, it seems to me, has no time for such frippery. The warehouses that Greg speaks of, and the wharves as they were when
I was a child, West India Dock at the Isle of Dogs, had a working relationship with the Thames, receiving the goods brought
in on the barges. There was a kind of mutual respect between the
buildings and the river that fed them. But these apartments and
developments are arrogant of what goes on below them. There's
a disjunction between them and what the river demands. Harry
clearly feels no link with the Thames, either, and Greg's is tenu-
ous, cerebral rather than instinctive. It isn't in his blood as it
is in mine. He'll never fully understand why I cannot live away
from it.

I clutch the sides of my seat and think of the mysteries the
river keeps hidden in its depths, the treasures it churns out at
low tide. *Tamasa.* 'Dark river.' Today the Thames seems darker
than ever.

We arrive at the Pool, the stretch of water between the Tower
and London Bridge and sweep into Bankside Pier, the boat braking violently. The waves churn angrily, tossing the boat about as
great ropes are thrown out again.

As we pass under Blackfriars, Greg tells the long-suffering
Harry that the bridge is named after an order of monks who
used to live here. Then we glide past the South Bank where little
blue lights are strung out along the trees. Kit drags Harry by
the hand away from Greg and they lean on the windows and
exclaim at how pretty it looks. At last we arrive in one piece at
Embankment.

We walk up Villiers Street and across the Strand to the Opera
House. Soon we're ensconced in the plush red and gold heart of
the theatre, as far from the dark reaches of the Thames as it's
possible to be.

Greg's managed to get us seats in the balcony. I survey the
auditorium, take in the faint scent of expensive perfume, clap

with everyone else as the orchestra take their place in the pit. As the curtains sweep back I give in to the music, to the drama, since there is no longer anything I can do until after the final act.

The opera is in fact cathartic. Tosca suffers as I do from a jealous mind, a keen suspicion of anyone who might be about to take her lover's attention from her. Yet she will do anything for him, is willing to kill for him; she is a woman whose courage is to be revered. In spite of all this, the music and the story, part of my mind will not be stilled. I wait for the moment I may leave and go back to Jez. Unleash his bound wrists, let him know that I'm here for him.

But today the fates are against me. For when the interval arrives, and I make my way down the stairs ahead of the others, I run straight into Helen.

CHAPTER SEVENTEEN

Friday

Helen

Helen was relieved to leave work on Friday lunchtime knowing she was going straight to the opera. She wasn't sure if the police were going to check whether she had gone to work the previous Friday. But to cover herself she'd fabricated a story in her head about going to the Turkish baths. She was pretty certain no one could check up on this. The baths were anonymous and the woman who sold the tickets barely looked up from her cubby hole when you paid. Helen would explain, if the police asked why she hadn't told them straight away, that she'd felt ashamed of trying to ward off an incipient cold by going to the baths, when she should have been at work.

Later, Helen would wonder why she'd gone to such elaborate lengths to cover up her true whereabouts, but at that moment the worst thing she could imagine was anyone, including the police, discovering she was in a Smithfield's pub, drinking off a hangover. It made her look like an alcoholic. They'd think she was cracking up and it would give Maria even more ammunition with which to accuse her of being irresponsible.

Helen got the tube down to Covent Garden and headed for the Royal Opera House. She needed an escape after the gruelling week she'd had.

Oddly, Ben had slipped from the forefront of her thoughts to the back of her mind. Mick had stepped forward. All that grooming and hair smoothing. What was that about? She tried to see Mick through Maria's eyes. She had no idea any more whether he was attractive to other women. Perhaps this new feeling, this suspicion and jealousy of her own sister was guilt, she thought. A way of punishing herself for her aberration with Ben. Whatever, it made her realize that she still loved Mick, couldn't bear the thought of losing him.

Helen bought herself a gin and tonic at the bar and knocked it back quickly. When the bell rang for the first act she went to find her seat. A numbness came over her as the alcohol took effect, and she let the music and the performance wash over her.

Helen spotted Sonia before Sonia saw her. She tried to catch her eye, over the heads of the crowds moving away from their seats, but it was impossible. Sonia looked distracted, as she had done that day in the market, and Helen wondered again about the depression Nadia had mentioned. Helen waved to try and catch her attention, but Sonia didn't look up and Helen was ushered down the staircase by people impatient for drinks.

In the bar Helen shoved her way between the bustling audience and saw Sonia at last, coming down another staircase.

'Sonia! What a coincidence,' she said. 'Though then again of course not. You and Greg were bound to be here. Greg would never miss a rehearsal of *Tosca*! Simon gave me a ticket. He was going to offer it to you but guessed Greg would probably have wheedled one off someone.'

Sonia nodded, but her eyes seemed glazed as they met Helen's.

'It's lovely to see you,' Helen said. 'We haven't caught up for ages. Don't suppose you've time to talk? Afterwards, I mean. Are you alright? You look pale.'

'I'm fine,' Sonia said.

Helen was taken aback. She was prepared to sympathize if Sonia felt low, but this response seemed decidedly chilly. She wondered whether Sonia had decided to cut off all contact since their kids had grown up. It was hurtful if that was the case. Surely they could have a civil conversation for old times' sake, if nothing else.

Then Sonia spoke. 'I've had a touch of flu this week. Don't feel one hundred per cent I'm afraid.'

'Oh, yes. Simon told me. Said you'd had to cancel your sessions.' Helen smiled, relieved to have an explanation, warming to Sonia now she understood.

'You've seen Simon?'

'He gave me the ticket. You're not with it, are you, Sonia? You need a drink, honey. Listen, meet me afterwards and I'll buy us champagne. I so need to talk. We're in this hellish situation. To do with my nephew. He's vanished. And ... Oh bugger, I shouldn't start now. I'll get all upset. We are *all* upset, it's unbalanced everything. Please, let's meet afterwards for a drink. If you're up to it? Oh, Greg. Hi.'

'Helen,' said Greg. 'How are you? Sonia, excuse me, just to say, Kit and Harry have gone off to buy a programme. I'm just going to the loo and I'll see you back at the seats.'

'I was asking Sonia if she'd meet me for a drink afterwards,' Helen said. 'If you can spare her? We haven't seen each other on our own for ... God, how long is it, Sonia? Not for months! And I need to talk to her about—'

'Fine by me!' Greg said. 'I'll take Kit and Harry for something to eat. It'll give me a chance to catch up with them both. You and Sonia can gossip the afternoon away.'

*   *   *

When the last act had finished, Helen and Sonia found a table together in the bar. Greg came over, assured them again that they had all the time in the world to catch up. He was going off with Kit and Harry to a restaurant in Covent Garden and he'd come back for Sonia when they were ready to go.

'So,' said Helen leaning towards her friend and pouring them both a large glass of Prosecco. She realized that what she'd been missing, what she really needed was the chance to offload her stress onto an impartial friend.

'I don't suppose you remember my nephew, Jez?'

CHAPTER EIGHTEEN

Friday

Sonia

The Opera House bar is heaving with people all desperate for something to drink.

'My nephew, Jez,' Helen's saying, 'my sister's son, he was staying with us, while he looked at music colleges.'

I look around for a clock. Can't see one. Guess it must be around five. Jez has been alone in the garage, tied up, since last night. Anxiety churns through me. Something will stand in the way of my getting back to him. My desire to hear what Helen has to say is bound to delay me further. Because in spite of myself I'm compelled to hear what's going on in Jez's family, how they feel about his time away. What they think has happened. It may give me vital clues as to when and how I can return him. Helen has started to talk, I'm aware of her mouth moving, but I cannot hear the words. They're drowned by the anxious thoughts tumbling in and piling up in my mind; the Clipper will be cancelled due to stormy weather, there'll be a power cut and the tubes will stop. I won't get back tonight and Jez will be tied to the bed in his duct-tape bonds, unable to eat or drink. He'll die a slow, agonizing death. He'll think this was what I wanted for him when the reality is, I want the opposite.

That's when it happens. I see blue lights, hear sirens and adult voices expressing dismay, and I'm back there.

After the police launches and the ambulances and the blue lights and the noise, I found myself on a hard Formica bench in a chilly corridor. Nothing would warm me. Not the Bovril they gave me in a polystyrene cup, nor the rough grey blanket they put round my shoulders.

The bench was surrounded with people looking down at me, asking me questions.

'I was holding on,' I cried, my teeth gnashing together as I shivered. 'I didn't let go.'

Then a nurse materialized through the sea of faces, her skin pale, golden hair curling from under her little white cap, but it was her eyebrows I noticed, finely plucked and highly arched. They made her look as if she'd had a terrible shock. I remember it vividly, the look of fright upon her face, the way her mouth contorted slightly as she formed the words, 'I'm sorry.'

I waited for an arm around me, reassurance, 'They've made a mistake.'

Instead, the faces altered, crumpled, broke, and one pair of eyes looked at me full of something I'd never seen before but have seen many times since: pure hatred.

I was never sure if the terrible wail as they moved me away down the white corridor came from my own throat or someone else's.

'Sonia,' Helen's saying. 'Are you OK? You aren't ill again, are you? Do you need anything? Some more water?'

The people in the Amphitheatre restaurant are swimming.

The whole room feels suddenly as if it's on the river, swaying up and down like the Clipper. I clutch the arms of my chair.

'It's OK,' I say at last. 'But perhaps I'll have that glass of wine.'

I tell myself I'll give her half an hour. Then I'll make an excuse and go.

'. . . and not just this Jez business,' Helen's saying. 'It's what it's done to the whole family. It started last Saturday. I'd been to a private view in Hoxton. Nadia's. I thought you'd be there! I was longing to talk to you. She'd cast her belly at different stages of the pregnancy. With Modroc.'

'What?'

'Modroc. You know, that bandage stuff they use for broken limbs. You can order it off the internet, replicate your pregnant torso exactly as it is, as it may never be again, I suppose, in Nadia's case. At 45 she's pushing it if she hopes to have another one. Amazing, the detail. It's a trend, Sonia. You and I are out of date! Anyway it was when I came home that we realized Jez hadn't been in since the previous afternoon. He's not been back since.'

In the quiet that seems to descend, I'm worried Helen'll hear the thud of my heart.

'That's terrible,' I manage.

Helen goes on.

'Of course it is. It's ghastly. We've had the police round, they've been dredging the river. I think we're all hanging on to the fact there is no – oh God, I can hardly bear to say it – OK, no body. Until they find one, we keep on hoping he's just gone off for a bit, wants to be by himself. I don't know.'

Helen rubs her face with her hand, smudging her mascara. There are pink circles on her cheeks. She looks terrible.

'And I know this sounds unbelievably self-centred given the circumstances,' she goes on, 'but almost as terrible as Jez going off, is the effect it's had on our relationship. Mick's and mine,

I mean. I had only just been thinking how much better things were, now we'd got through a period of . . . tension. Tiffs and stresses, the constant juggling to pay off the mortgage. All that. Then wham! My nephew disappears and instead of supporting each other, it seems the gulf just got wider. Mick's gone cold on me! I almost feel he blames me, Sonia!'

'You? How can he blame you?'

She pauses and gives me an appealing look. 'From the moment Jez came, Mick's compared our boys to him. Me to Maria. She's always been the perfect one. With the perfect son. Jez is a genius on the guitar. He's going to get into the very music college Barney wants to go to. If he gets a place, poor old Barney won't, and yes at times that's made me – oh, I don't know, resentful.'

'I still don't see why that means Mick blames you,' I say.

'He thinks I was too relaxed with Jez. That I treated him the way I do our boys, giving him too much freedom to come and go. He thinks I should have been more like Maria. Ferried him about in the car. Kept close tabs on him.'

She takes another slug of wine.

'He probably thinks if I was more like Maria, Barney and Theo would have got somewhere by now. But in my opinion Maria pushes Jez too much. I'm not a pushy mother. To be fair, it's probably compensation for Jez's dyslexia. You'd think with all that, and being an only child, her son would be geeky or a bit of a loner. No! My boys and all the band boys love him, and he has been staying in *my* house and Mick seems obsessed with him, it's as if he wants to *be* him. He worries about him in a way he's never worried about our boys. It's all been getting on my nerves to be honest. But now he's gone missing, Mick has gone all self-righteous, claims that we – for which read *I* – should have wrapped him up in cotton wool.'

The Opera House is beginning to fill up again with the evening crowd. It's dark outside. Helen suggests another bottle of wine but I refuse, wanting to keep a clear head.

How long have we been sitting here? Why does no one wear a watch these days? I try not to let Helen see that I'm agitated. Her drinking is a blessing in this respect, her perception of her immediate surroundings dulled.

Jez has everything he needs. He's secure. He's got things to keep him warm. He can't come to any harm. But he must be starving by now. And thirsty. And wet. And freezing. And though I can barely think about it, he'll be soiled. Judy's been in the house alone this morning. Suppose she spotted something I've overlooked? Even Kit, who has bigger and better things to think about, saw that the acoustic guitar was missing. Judy doesn't let things slip by unnoticed. She may be undereducated, but she has an astute brain and uses it to pick up the smallest details of other people's lives.

I shift in my chair. How thorough was I when preparing the garage? How careful to cover my tracks? What might Judy see? That the garage keys are not hanging in their usual place on the hook? That sheets from the airing cupboard are missing? No. Impossible that she should put these facts together and come up with such an outlandish conclusion, even if it is the truth.

As Helen returns with the wine, I excuse myself and rush to the loo. I empty my bowels in the luxurious bathroom of the Royal Opera House then lean on the glass handbasin for a while, attempting to regain my composure. I catch glimpses of women applying lipstick, replacing stray hairs, smoothing down their dresses in the mirrors next to me. Peering at myself cautiously, I'm anxious that the face I spot looking back will have changed, will show all my innermost thoughts and fears. I'm surprised at how normal I look. Still the same grey eyes, the same black hair. Only one or two stray silver ones beginning to show. I take my lipstick out of my bag and reapply, and I'm as good as new. I take a deep breath. I'll invent an emergency text from someone. Anything to get back to Jez.

Helen glances up as I come across the foyer.

'Have you lost weight, love?' she asks, as if this were the first time she's looked at me today. 'My God. You have. You look fab. Nadia said how good you looked. What've you been doing?'

I shrug. I want to be able to say to her it's nerves, it's being permanently on edge. I want to tell her, she was my friend once. I look into her eyes and see that she's already drifted off into her own world, her own story, and I feel that yawning distance that lies between you and someone close when you have a heavy secret you simply cannot share with them.

'I think Mick's going off me,' Helen says. 'He can't bear the sight of me. I'm afraid he and Maria might be getting . . . close.'

'Hey,' I say. 'He feels guilty, that's all, that he didn't take more care of Jez. He wants to assuage his own conscience by blaming you. That's what it sounds like to me.'

'Do you think so?'

'I do. Yes.'

'What about all his hair combing and running and stomach patting?'

I laugh. An odd sound these days, to come from my own mouth.

'Sounds like a classic case of midlife crisis,' I say.

'And Jez. Should I be worrying more about him and less about Mick?'

'No!' I say. 'You're quite right not to be stressing about Jez. Teenage boys. They're free agents.'

'He's very young, Sonia.'

'Whatever. You can't watch over them like children for goodness' sake. Jez has got a mind of his own. Of course you had to let him go. Do his own thing. And Helen, that's what he *will* be doing. His mother, your sister, she sounds so overbearing. Wouldn't you want to get away from a mother like that? No wonder he wants to hide. Who knows, he may have a lover he hasn't told anyone about. He may not *want* to be found. I bet he *wants* to be left alone. Has anyone thought of that? Has Mick? Has Maria? Have the police?'

Helen looks at me. This is the longest speech I've made since we arrived at the bar and I can see it's taken her aback a bit.

'Maybe,' she says. 'But there's something else. The police think that I'm involved in Jez's disappearance. They've questioned me more than once. I admitted to some of the feelings I've just told you about.' She pauses. Her cheeks are redder than ever and her eyes slightly bloodshot from the wine. She sniffs. Looks at me.

'And now they want to question me some more. I was the last person to see him. And the fact is, I *had* thought, before all this, about horrible things happening to Jez. Isn't that awful? I thought, what if he had the kind of accident teenagers often have. Broke his leg while base jumping, or got scarred in a car crash. Nothing life threatening, of course! Just something that would let Barney get that place at music school. Isn't that terrible?'

I stare at her for a moment. It is indeed terrible to think of anyone wishing Jez harm. How could she? I'm tempted to say something to defend him.

'Then I've been so shocked with myself!' she goes on. 'What if my feelings *had* led me to ... to do something terrible to her beautiful son? Of course I never would. But I feel I'm being punished! For having those terrible thoughts! Being suspected of something really heinous ... It makes you think how easy it must be to be an ordinary law-abiding citizen one minute and a criminal the next.'

Helen refills her glass again. I notice the second bottle of wine has almost disappeared, though I have hardly drunk a drop.

'You're not shocked, are you, Sonia?' she goes on. 'I'm only telling you this because I know you're someone who thinks outside the box. You're not judgemental like some people. We've talked about dark thoughts before, remember? It doesn't mean we'd act on them.'

'When have we discussed dark thoughts?'

'You told me about your feelings towards Greg, how sometimes you wished he'd just not come back, remember? How he always tries to control you. Perhaps I shouldn't bring that up now.'

'I'd forgotten we'd had that conversation.'

'Please don't hold all this against me. Oh God, I'm beginning to wish I hadn't said anything. It's the wine. I must stop.'

'It's OK. But look. Where's Maria now, and Nadim? What's everyone doing? When do people give up hope of finding him and go home?'

Helen stares at me for a second before she says, 'I don't think people *ever* give up. We have to take this one day at a time. If we imagined that it was going to go on for much longer I think we would all begin to crack up. But for the moment, Nadim has had to go back to work. Maria wants to be here. I don't blame her, though I wish she would find somewhere else to stay. The only person who I seem to be able to tolerate is Alicia. Jez's girlfriend. She and I both suspect that if Maria was a little less conspicuous, Jez would creep back. But Maria is there, in my house all the time, glaring at me – she forgets we agreed to be civil. Usually it's when I'm having a drink. But God almighty, I need to drink. She and Mick are doing their bit for Jez together. There's the Facebook page, they're giving press reports, everything. Alicia doesn't think he'd like all the limelight. They're right on the case, but in the meantime, they've got it in for me. It might sound callous, taking the only opera ticket for myself after what Maria's going through, but we've all been through it, Sonia. He's my nephew too.'

'Helen,' I say. 'Calm down. You were quite right to take the ticket for yourself. Sometimes, we need to take the only ticket for ourselves. And Alicia is right. Jez will no doubt come home once all this focus is taken off him.'

I tell Helen I have to go. She begs me to agree to meet her, 'Like we used to, when the kids were younger, in the park one day,' she says, and I say OK. OK. Ring me.

Outside, the lights of Covent Garden are garish, the bars are full and the piazza seems to heave as the party-goers gather for a Friday night. I breathe deep lungfuls of city air as I hurry towards Embankment. I'm not waiting any longer for my husband or my daughter or her boyfriend. I have to get the Clipper back to the boy I have kept in the dark.

CHAPTER NINETEEN

Friday night

Helen

'Any news?' Helen asked.

It was the first question any of them asked as they opened the front door. Blank faces in response were all they needed to know there was none.

Helen sat down at the kitchen table. Her heart thumped at the sight of Mick and Maria drinking red wine by candlelight. She poured herself a glass. She could hear Barney open a can of baked beans behind her. He'd clearly only just come in, there was the smell of pub about him, of cold night air. Mick and Maria must have been here alone, together.

'What's with the soft lighting?'

'It helps with my migraines,' said Maria. 'I've had endless problems with them since Jez . . .' Her voice cracked and she didn't continue.

Getting things off her chest with Sonia had helped Helen put things in perspective. She knew what she must do. Rather than letting her imagination run away with her, she must remember the strain they were all under. Particularly Maria. She went over to her sister, put a hand on her shoulder, and squeezed it. Maria shrugged her off.

'How was the opera?' asked Mick.

'It was OK.' Helen sat down and took a large swig of wine.

Her sister was impossible, she wouldn't let Helen get close to her. 'I bumped into Sonia. We had a drink together afterwards. Did you save me any dinner?'

'Sorry, we didn't know if you'd be back,' said Mick.

'You can have mine. I can't eat,' Maria said, pushing a plate of griddled tuna towards Helen.

Helen looked at the food, then at Mick. He didn't catch her gaze and she felt her insides collapse. Udon noodles! Their special meal, and he hadn't done any for her.

Mick turned to Maria. 'Have you met Sonia? The voice coach? Her husband Greg and I used to play together, in that band. He's a neurologist. Though he spends most of his time lecturing these days. You'll probably meet them sometime.'

'Great,' said Maria without interest.

'If they don't move soon. Greg's been talking of moving out to Geneva.'

The air felt dense. It was hard to talk, to force out any conversation that wasn't about Jez. As if they were all on some stage, playing unfamiliar roles.

'Yes. But Sonia doesn't want to go,' said Helen. 'She loves the River House. She got really depressed when they lived in Norfolk.'

'Geneva's hardly Norfolk.'

'She says the Thames is where she needs to be, for her health.'

'Ha! It's generally accepted the Alps are better for the health than London,' said Mick.

'Depends whether we're talking mental or physical,' said Helen. 'Anyway I told her about Jez. Her theory is he might have a lover. Might have chosen to go away without contacting anyone.'

'What would *she* know?' asked Maria. 'Has she ever met him?'

Helen noticed a change in the atmosphere as she brought Jez's name into the conversation. They could breathe at last.

'She's got a daughter Theo's age, so she knows about teenagers. She met him once when you lot were shinning up the walls by the river, do you remember, Barney? We called in there for tea. Oh, and they must have met at Mick's fiftieth recently.'

'They did.' Barney plonked his plate on the table and sat down. 'Now you come to mention it. Her husband, Greg, offered to lend Jez that Tim Buckley album he was always on about. Jez said he was going to pick it up . . . actually, I think it was last Friday afternoon. The day he went missing. You mentioning Sonia reminded me. That's where he said he was going.'

'When did he say this?' Maria asked. All their faces turned to look at Barney.

'I dunno. The night before, maybe. He said that before he left for Paris, he had to pick up the album from the River House. I asked if he knew where it was. He said he'd been there once before. It must've been that time you're talking about, Mum. He was going to go there, then meet Alicia in the tunnel. Before the gig. The one he never came to.'

'Why the bloody hell didn't you mention this before, to the police?' Mick said, reddening.

Maria stood up. 'We must tell them immediately.'

'What sort of brain have you got?' Mick said, standing over his son. 'I know you're a bit doped up sometimes but this could be crucial. What d'you think you're playing at?'

Barney shrugged. 'Nothing. Really, I forgot. Honestly. I hadn't given it a thought until just now when Mum mentioned Sonia.'

'It's ringing,' said Maria, holding the phone to her ear with her shoulder.

'God, I'd like to knock some sense into your skull sometimes,' said Mick, cuffing Barney's head.

Helen stared at Mick. She'd been with this man for over twenty years. Did he usually touch his sons like that? She had a sudden need to examine him, to work out what it was about him that made him the man she thought she knew.

'There's no need for that,' she said at last. 'Barney forgot. It's not the kind of thing you'd remember necessarily. A minor detail like that.'

'It throws a whole new light on Jez's possible movements,' said Mick.

Maria stuck her finger in her ear. 'Shh!' she hissed. 'I can't hear the options.' She took the handset into the hall.

'Dad!' Barney said. 'Bloody hell. He just mentioned it, I didn't think, oh I must make a note of that. I had more important things on my mind.'

'Like where your next smoke was coming from?'

'Oh sod off!'

'Don't speak to me like that!'

'But you're being such a dick over this Jez thing,' Barney said. 'Mum's right. You've changed. You aren't like this with us when we go off for a few nights.'

'No, I'm not having that. We're responsible for that boy. He's gone missing from under our roof and now we're bloody well going to find out what's happened to him.'

Barney stomped out of the room.

'I can't see how Jez saying he might call in at the River House can have anything to do with this,' said Helen.

'If Sonia saw him that afternoon, it means he disappeared *after* that but *before* he was due to meet Alicia. It narrows down the possibilities,' said Mick.

'Yes, but she didn't.'

'How do you know?'

'Because Sonia would've mentioned it when I saw her today.'

Maria came back into the room. 'They said they've made a note of it and will have a meeting in the morning to discuss what to do with the information. Now, I'm exhausted. Does anyone mind if I have a bath?'

'Help yourself,' said Helen without looking at her.

Mick waited until Maria had gone, then lowered his voice. 'I didn't want to tell you in front of Maria. Pauline from your work called this afternoon. I had a little chat with her. She says she's worried about you and all the time you've been taking off. She said you weren't there last Friday morning. The police have been making enquiries.'

Helen felt the blood rush to her face. She stared at Mick rigidly.

'I don't know what's going on with you, Helen,' he said, 'but I think you need to get your record straight.' The look he gave her as he left the room was just like the one he'd given Barney. As if he despaired of them both.

CHAPTER TWENTY

Saturday

Sonia

I'm in the bathroom the next morning, doing my face when the police come. Greg stands at the foot of the stairs and calls up to me. Harry and Kit have their bags packed, they're getting the 10.33 up to Charing Cross.

'Oh God, has something awful happened?' Kit's asking as I come down the stairs. 'Is Grandma OK? I should have gone to see her. We should have gone to see her, Harry.' She plucks at Harry's cuff while he frowns at the police, then glances at his watch.

'It's not your grandmother,' the policewoman says, 'but if you wouldn't mind staying while we ask a few questions.'

Greg takes the two police officers, a young man and the woman, into the living room. There's a fire alight in the grate that he must've lit earlier. Greg and I sit side by side on the sofa, while Kit perches on the armchair under the window and Harry stands behind her, one hand on its back.

The woman introduces herself as Inspector Hailey Kirwin and explains that a boy with whom she believes we have some acquaintance has been reported missing and that he hasn't been seen for over a week.

'I think you know about this,' says the woman turning vivid blue eyes on me. 'You met his aunt at the opera house yesterday.'

'Yes. Helen. It was in the papers too,' I say.

'Jez!' Kit exclaims. 'God! He's gone missing? Why didn't you tell us, Mum?'

'I didn't want to worry you.'

'But he's Barney and Theo's cousin.'

'So you know him?' the woman asks, turning her eyes on Kit.

'I did. He's younger than me. Used to live round here. He moved to Paris but he sometimes stays at Barney and Theo's. I know them better. Our dads used to play guitar together. And our mums were friends. Oh God. That's terrible. What do you think's happened?'

'That's what we're trying to find out. It's out of character for him to go off without telling anyone. And it's been over a week now.'

I have the oddest sensation that a pane of glass has come down, that I'm viewing and hearing everything through the misted panel. I catch some of Inspector Kirwin's words, but they are disconnected . . . no one noticed . . . over twenty-four hours . . . river search . . . never arrived.

'What we need to know,' she continues, and her voice seems thick, muffled, 'is whether he ever turned up here for the album?'

'When was this?' Greg asks.

'A week ago yesterday,' the young male constable says.

'So while I was away,' says Greg, looking at me. 'Did Jez come round while I was away, Sonia?'

My mouth is so dry I can barely get the word 'no' out.

'The album he wanted to borrow, it was apparently . . .' the constable looks at his notebook, 'by someone called Jim Butler.'

'Tim Buckley,' Greg corrects him. 'That's right. I have a copy. It's hard to get hold of. He and I were talking about it at Mick's fiftieth birthday party, under the arches. Do you remember, Sonia?'

'What was that?' I ask.

I feel much too hot. I take off my cashmere scarf, and fling it onto the back of the sofa.

'I told you. He'd been trying to get hold of the album. I said I had a copy that he could borrow. I remember because I was impressed that such a young man could be interested in music like that.'

The fire in the grate crackles and spits as if it is joining in the conversation.

'And I said of course he could borrow it, as long as he returned it in good nick.'

'Oh yes,' I say.

'But he never did come?' says Kirwin, who must wear coloured contacts lenses. No one's eyes are that blue.

'No,' I say again.

'Do you think we could just have a look at the album we're talking about?' she asks.

'Of course,' says Greg. He gets up. 'It'll be up in what we call our music room. I'll go and get it. Or do you want to come up?'

'Perhaps Sonia could take me,' says Kirwin. 'Since she was the one who was here on the day he planned to call in. My colleague would just like to ask you and your . . .'

'This is my daughter Kit and her boyfriend Harry. They've just been here for the weekend. They're students at Newcastle University and actually have a train to catch. They're due back today.'

'We won't keep you long,' says the woman, and smiles. She raises her eyebrows at me. I stand as if in a trance and she follows me up the stairs to the music room.

I know exactly where the Tim Buckley album is because Jez waved it at me the other day when he told me he was leaving, and no longer wanted to borrow it. But I make a bit of a show of not being certain. I rummage through various piles and riffle along the shelf before I find it and hand it to her. Kirwin looks at it, turns it over, puts it down and scribbles something in her notebook. It means nothing to her as an album, but what about as a piece of evidence? Jez's fingerprints must be all over it. I wonder if she's going to take it with her, because if she does, the forensics will have a field day.

Why hadn't I told them he'd come and taken it away?

I could've said, *Yes, he came, I handed it to him, and he left.* You can't think quickly enough in these situations. But then what if she still wanted to search the music room, and had found the album? I'm aware of how precarious my situation is. It's the simplest things that catch you out. Since Greg and Kit came home, I've covered all traces of Jez's visit, and worked so hard to keep him tucked out of sight in the garage, yet I've left his fingerprints all over the music room.

The policewoman turns the album over and over. I wait for the moment where everything crashes in on me. I'm ready to give in, to let everyone else take over. If they arrest me for incarcerating a boy against his will – because without a doubt they'll assume it's against his will – all the tension, anxiety, and emotional turmoil of the last few days will be over. This thought seizes my heart and crushes it. Losing Jez after all we've gone through would be more than I could bear. I need more time. I need to nurture him back to health and regain his trust. I cannot lose him, however hard it has been for us both. I cannot bear for it all to come to nothing.

'Thanks,' she says handing it back to me. 'So he never came?'

She's examining me as she asks this question. Her unnaturally blue eyes flash as she does so. I shake my head.

'And you haven't seen him, out and about along the river, in the pub, anywhere? You know what he looks like, I take it?'

'Oh yes,' my voice seems suddenly loud, high pitched, 'as Kit said, his aunt's a friend of mine. I've met him, though not recently. I don't see Helen as much now our kids are grown up.'

'Apparently he used to do a bit of base jumping on the river walls,' she says. 'You know, jumping off the bridges. Climbing up and down landing stages and things. You don't remember seeing him down there, just over a week ago? No recollections at all that may be of help to us?'

I decide to think about this for a minute. She suspects nothing! I want to talk and laugh and discuss this boy and his extraordinary talents at great length.

'I saw him last . . . Oh, it must be a year ago now, maybe two, with his cousins, shinning up the walls down there, near the pub. I remember his aunt having kittens about it. "Boys!" she kept saying, and I was grateful I didn't have any to deal with. Just the one daughter. I should think myself lucky.'

'So. Nothing recently? You didn't see him about here lately?'

'Lately? I don't think so. Nothing I noticed, no.' I realize I'm gabbling in relief, and try to steady my voice. 'I'm here most of the time. I work from home, so I'm sure I might have noticed.'

She makes a note.

'You say they've searched the river?' I ask, though I already know from what Sheila told me yesterday at the pier, from the paper and from Helen.

'Yes. But they'll keep looking,' she says. 'Thanks for your help. Now let's join the others. We'd like to ask you a few questions about the aunt. Helen Whitehorn. How well you know her and so on.'

My heart starts to thud again. This isn't over. I walk behind her down the stairs. I look at her muscular calves not flattered by the flesh-coloured tights she's probably forced to wear by the police dress code.

'Have you any theories at all?' Greg's asking the young constable. I see he must be barely more than Kit's age. He's still spotty for goodness' sake. Acne, poor lad. Fair sandy hair, and a pink complexion behind the spots.

'In cases like this, if it's not an accident, if there's anything unlawful, it's nearly always the family behind it,' says the boy.

Kirwin nudges him in the ribs and gives him a stern look.

'We have no clear theories at present,' she says. 'Though we're following several leads.'

'Oh well, Helen can't have anything to do with it,' Kit says. 'Or Mick. They're great. Jez always liked staying with them, in fact, he preferred their house to his own home in Paris. Helen and Mick are really laid back. Sound as anything.'

'So you haven't noticed a change in Helen recently?' Kirwin asks.

'Goodness, no,' says Greg, looking at me. 'Nothing, have we, Sonia?'

'Not at all,' I manage. 'She was the same as ever when I saw her yesterday.'

'She hasn't been under any undue stress at work that you know of?'

'We don't see much of her these days,' I say. 'Yesterday was the first time I'd talked to her properly in months. She was obviously distressed about her nephew, but otherwise, no, she was her usual self.'

'You didn't notice her drinking?'

I stare at her. I did notice Helen drank a lot but what is she getting at here? What am I stirring up by mentioning it?

'She enjoys her wine,' I say. 'Always has done.'

'So nothing exceptional. Nothing worrying?'

I shake my head.

'What about the father?' Greg says. 'He's off the scene, isn't he, Sonia?'

I stare at Greg. How much does he think I know about someone else's nephew, for God's sake?

'I've no idea,' I say.

'Yes, Mum, d'you remember Helen telling us? Jez's dad left and went to live in Marseilles. About three years ago.'

'Oh, maybe,' I say.

'We've been on to him,' says the policeman. 'And the boy's mother's staying with her sister. So we've talked to her, too. In this case, at the moment, we're thinking accident, possible drowning, though of course . . .'

'Josh, that's enough,' interrupts Kirwin.

'Have you any clues at all?' asks Kit.

'Not really. But unfortunately, a drowning *is* on our list of possibilities. Not a suicide, from the evidence, more likely a tragic accident. They're more frequent than you'd imagine. Especially when the victim likes climbing up walls and under bridges on the river.'

'That's really awful,' says Kit.

'Thanks for your help,' says the spotty boy officer, standing up.

'Oh please,' says Greg. 'If we can do anything else, anything at all. After all, God, he's almost a friend of ours. It's terrible. Will you let us know if you hear anything?'

'You'll hear all about it, no doubt,' says Kirwin. 'The media love cases like this, I'm afraid. Though the publicity is a mixed blessing. It can help.'

We all stare at each other for a few seconds after they've gone.

'It's so scary,' Kit says. 'I get really freaked out by things like this. Poor Jez! It's horrible!'

'Let's hope for a happy outcome,' says Harry.

'I'm like, you know, pretty resilient to most things I encounter in A and E. But when it's something cruel or violent, especially when it's someone I know, I can't get my head round it,' Kit says. She's on the verge of tears.

'Hey.' Harry puts his arm round her.

'You two need to leave,' says Greg, looking at his watch. 'Try not to let this get you down. I'm sure he'll turn up. Teenage boys, they go off for all kinds of reasons. They'll probably discover he's been doing the hippy trail in Morocco or something, finding himself.'

'Oh God, Dad,' says Kit. 'What century are you living in?'

'Hop in the car,' says Greg. 'I'll drive you to Euston.'

I glance up quickly. 'Haven't you got to get ready to go?'

'Haha! I wondered when you'd ask. I've postponed my next trip. I'm staying at home a bit longer, darling, to be with you.'

He says it with a hopeful little gleam in his eye, as if now we've had sex he's convinced I'll be pleased to have him around.

I feel my jaw tighten. The fury I experienced at having to put Jez in the garage to begin with takes hold of me. It's such an intense burning anger I begin to tremble. It's all wrong! That he had to go in there in the first place. That he had to suffer yesterday's horrible indignities that took us both over an hour to sort out when I got back from the opera. I had to clean him up and change him like a baby, keeping him restrained all the while so he couldn't try anything in his distressed state. Then I had to insist he let me spoon-feed him. It was humiliating for both of us.

I kiss Kit goodbye. As I feel her hair brush my cheek, I have a fleeting yearning for the days when she was little and would hold on to me at night. Sometimes she'd tug me down onto the bed and I'd crawl in next to her and wait for her to fall asleep, her feather-light fingers finding some tense part of my face and stroking the stress away with a child's instinct. Watching her walk across the courtyard now with Greg, and with Harry's arm through hers, it's as though she's got hold of a bit of me, a loose piece, and her walking away unravels me. We never cuddle any more, we barely touch each other. She no longer needs me. Hasn't really needed me for years. She disappears through the door in the wall, and I feel a chasm inside that makes me ache.

Thank goodness, then, that now I have Jez.

CHAPTER TWENTY-ONE

Saturday

Sonia

The minute they've disappeared, I go inside, drop some provisions into a bag and make for the garage. Infuriatingly, Betty is outside her house, on the steps polishing her brass door knocker. I glance up at the CCTV camera. I have a compulsive need to check it each time I come to see Jez, though I know it points away from the garages, at the building site where they're erecting yet more riverside apartments and offices on the land which was once Lovell's Wharf.

'I don't know why they have to keep changing things,' Betty says, following my gaze. 'It was fine as it was. And how they're going to fill all those office spaces when there's a recession I've no idea.'

Betty's a woman I could be friends with, if I had time. I have respect for her and her opinions.

'I know. It's a waste of time and money.' It pains me to see these new builds going up, stripping the riverside walk of its history, tearing its heart out. The constructions could be anywhere, they have no link with the river and its business.

'It creates so much noise,' says Betty. 'It's constant. I some-times think I'll go mad if they don't stop their hammering. And that crane's been there for months now, that blue thing. Hanging over us like a gallows.'

The building site is, in fact, quiet today, but the whine of the drills has been replaced by shrieks of children, the cries of seagulls and a harsh *chip chip chip* of a blackbird in a small tree that overhangs the water. A plaintive warning call. And amongst all this I'm certain I can detect a *thump, thump thump*, coming from the direction of the garages. I'm afraid it's Jez, trying to attract attention. My heart starts to race, the bang of blood in my ears drowning out all other noise. I'll have to use the duct tape to tie and gag him more tightly. I hate using the tape. Finding him there yesterday was hell. It was torture for me as much as for him. But I can't have him making that kind of racket. Anger sweeps over me again. If only Greg had left! And now I must get rid of Betty so that I can go and tend to Jez with-out arousing her suspicions.

'Your doorknob and letterbox look beautiful,' I tell her, hugging my carrier bag of food and drink close to me. 'Shinier than all the others on the terrace.'

'Well I like to take pride in the front of my house, especially now all these tourists have started using our alley as a short cut,' she says. 'They look at everything, you know, they would notice if things weren't spic and span. *You* haven't been to see my snow-drops yet this year. You must come now, before they finish.'

I daren't decline. It's a tradition that I view Betty's garden each season and to refuse now might raise questions. The tiny grassed area lies over the road from Betty's house. On the far side is the long drop down to the river. Only a short distance along from there Jez's window looks out over the same view. We walk slowly amongst the shrubs, and under the little bare trees, her arm in mine.

'The cold has delayed the aconites,' Betty says. 'But the snow-drops are everywhere. They lift my spirits more with each pass-ing year. I do believe they get whiter!'

There's always that clanking from Colliers Wharf, even in a light breeze. And now there's the whoop of a jet launch on the water and the whine of an aeroplane heading for City Airport. It's difficult to pick out separate sounds but there's a thump that is loud and distinct. Just as I decide with another lurch of the heart that it comes from my garage, Betty squeezes my arm and leans close to my ear.

'You're a naughty girl. You weren't clearing the garage to put the car in, after all, were you?'

'And what's it to you?' I ask, unlinking my arm.

She totters a little and looks taken aback. 'You told me you were going to put your car in there. Like your mother did. But it's still on the street!'

'What I do with my car is my business, thank you, Betty.'

'I've told you, it isn't safe. You'd be much better off parking it in your garage. There are vandals, Sonia. I'm only thinking of you.'

'Thank you.' I relax a little. 'But it's actually rather hard to get it into that little space.'

'Well, what else are you going to use it for?' she asks turning away from me.

I see that I've offended her, by overreacting to her comments, and that I had no reason to be alarmed. She's making for the gate, so I call out to thank her for the tour of her beautiful garden and say how I wish there was a garden at the River House, but she disappears into her house without looking at me again. I feel sorry that I've upset her and angry with myself for my abrupt reaction, when all she had in mind was the safety of my old Saab.

My hands are shaking as I fumble with the two padlocks on the garage door and finally manage to unhook them. I turn the

Chubb in the metal inner door, and slip inside, shutting the door behind me and drawing the bolt across.

The garage smells. I feel irritation sear through me again. This place with its bucket and its lack of running water or electricity is demeaning. There were none of these difficulties in the music room.

Jez's face is turned away from me, though I know he's heard me come in. I can see the contour of his cheekbone which has lost its smooth curve. His body under the duvets seems almost flat. His arms and legs are still securely fastened to the bedposts so he must have been making the noise, as I feared, by banging the back of his head against the headboard.

I sit down on the bed.

'Jez, you've been banging your head. I could hear you outside. You must stop it,' I say, as I take off the gag.

'Why should I?' Now his mouth is free I see he's been working himself up into a fury. 'What do you expect? When you've done this to me!'

'I don't want you to hurt yourself,' I say. 'Banging your head is dangerous.'

'But my arms and feet are tied,' he says. 'My head is all I've got.'

'I don't like tying you up either,' I say gently. 'But I need some cooperation from you if we're to get you out of here later. If you arouse suspicion who knows what might happen to us?'

'I'm locked up in this hole! No one's come so far. So what's the point in all this? You could untie me. The window's too small to climb out of.'

'I know. And you wouldn't survive the drop to the river. If the tide was out, you'd break something, your neck or back, and if it were in, the currents would sweep you under in no time.' I don't like scaring him but I don't want him to get ideas.

He stares at me dumbstruck.

'Though Seb would probably have found a way,' I mutter. 'He'd have made a rope ladder, and used something to break the window. Nothing stopped him once he had an idea in his head.'

'Who? Who are you talking about?'

I glance into Jez's face. 'No one,' I say.

'It's freezing in here,' Jez says. 'And it smells and it's disgusting. You've got to let me out.'

'I'm sorry. Really I am. I thought everyone was leaving today. Now I hear Greg wants to stay longer. I'm fed up. It means you have to stay here for at least another night.'

'What?'

'If there's anything you need that would make this better for you, I'll get it.'

'But you won't let me go.'

I look at him sadly, shake my head. 'Not yet.'

He's silent for a while and I'm afraid he's started to cry. But then he speaks. 'If it's sex you want I'll do it. Then you can let me go. Please. I won't tell anyone, I promise. Come on.'

'Don't Jez,' I say.

'Don't what?'

'Don't do this. Don't belittle it.'

'But I don't get it. If it's not sex, why have you done this to me?' He shakes his hands in their duct-tape bangles.

'It's enough having you here, near me,' I say. But I can see he doesn't understand. Or maybe he doesn't want to. Not in the mood he's in. The fact is, I want to explain, I'm overwhelmed by the compulsion to hold onto you. It wells up in me, threatens to overflow. It's exhausting and demanding but I cannot give up.

Then he tries another tactic. He tries to harden his voice, to sound more street than he is.

'I'm not *nice*, you know. I take drugs. I spend too much time alone with my guitar. I can't read or write properly. You don't know me. If you did, you wouldn't be interested in me.'

I laugh. 'You think people only like each other if they're nice? The more I hear about the other side of you, the more I want you here. You could hardly have described Seb as nice. It didn't stop me loving him.'

'Seb again!'

'What?'

'You keep mentioning this Seb person. Who is he?'

'Never mind.' I shiver. I must stop invoking Seb's name, it feels like tempting fate.

Jez continues. 'You just don't get it. My dad gave up on me years ago. I've disappointed my mum by turning out to be dyslexic. The only person who puts up with me is Helen.'

'Helen! Your aunt? What's so great about Helen? You talk as if she's some kind of saint.'

'What?'

He's startled by the vitriol in my words, as am I. Why can't I bear to hear Jez sing Helen's praises, or mention any other woman with affection?

'You seem to put her on a pedestal.'

'Hardly,' he says. 'She's usually too pissed to notice what we're doing, that's all.'

I soften a little. Even if he isn't being entirely honest, he knows what I want to hear. He doesn't want to hurt me. I appreciate that.

'Helen doesn't give a toss what we're up to, me, Barney and Theo.' His tone's changed again, as if for the moment he's forgotten he's tied to the bed, and is simply sulking about his lot in life. 'Whereas my mum's at me all the time. Do this. Practise that. Take another exam. Prove I'm "intelligent" even if I can't string a sentence together.'

He pauses, sighs, looks up at me. 'I could do with a smoke,' he says, quite sweetly now. 'And something to drink.'

'Hmmm. I've got you some drinks here. A choice. But the weed you had has run out. Where am I going to get more from?'

'You could ask Alicia.'

I flinch at the sound of her name.

'I don't know Alicia,' I say.

'Helen knows her! And you know Helen! You can phone her. You know you can.'

'OK Jez, look, I'll get you some dope, but I'm not speaking to Alicia; I think we should keep her out of this.'

He raises his voice.

'Out of what? You still haven't said what's going on! It's weird. It's bloody mad.'

'Out of us. Out of you and me.'

'Look,' he says, as if he's trying his best to be patient with a small child, 'Alicia has dope. If she doesn't have any on her, she knows where to get some from. And I need it.'

'It's not good for you, you know,' I tell him. 'It can mess up your brain.'

'We don't smoke skunk,' he says, and the 'we' riles me. Is he doing this deliberately?

'It's just mild stuff. Grass. I can tell you exactly what to ask for. It would do me so much good. It would make me a nicer boy to be with.' He grins. It's not a real, genuine, happy grin, but it's the first time he's smiled since he came to the garage.

'OK.'

It occurs to me that weed might be of help to me, as it has been already. When Jez smokes he loses the will to resist food, which enables me to administer the sleeping drugs he needs to keep him calm and complicit. And I do have another contact who can probably get me some marijuana.

'I said I'd get you whatever you want. So I will. You need some new clothes too. Tell me what you'd like. You can't stay in Greg's old trousers. And I haven't been able to wash the things I took off you yesterday.'

'Could do with some warmer stuff,' he mutters.

'I need to know your size then,' I say. 'Let me look.'

His eyes go hard, and for quite a few seconds I'm afraid he's going to spit again. I step back in self-defence, but then he capitulates, and gives a little nod.

I step towards him, gently, and he lets me pull out the collar of his T-shirt to look at the label. I ask him to roll over as far as he is able to in the bonds, so I can lift his hair to get a better look. I notice the fine hair that runs down the valley of his neck to the top of his spine. I turn down the top of Greg's trousers, which are far too loose round the waist for him, to look at the label on his boxers. Here, his back narrows, the skin like sand that has never been walked on, a gentle sheen of golden down where it disappears into the waistband of his shorts. Is this all I need? To experience the transient stage his body is at, to have it near me, to sense it with my eyes, my nose. I appreciate this best when he's asleep, when I can indulge myself and float back in time. But even that is not enough. It's something else, something that nags at me so I cannot let him go until I can capture it for once and for all.

'Got it?'

'What?'

'The size.'

'OK. Yes. Sure. So I'll get you jeans, some T-shirts, boxers and a hoodie. Maybe a body warmer and some thick socks.'

'I won't need all that.'

'I think you might.'

'Not if I'm leaving soon, like you said.'

'Better to be on the safe side though,' I say. 'Now is there anything else?'

'There's no music in here,' he says. 'All I can hear is the river.'

'I thought you liked the sound of the river? I remember you saying, you know, that first night we spent together, how it's a kind of urban music. You haven't stopped hearing it, have you?

Because it can happen, when you get used to something. You lose your sensitivity to it.'

He looks at me as if he doesn't understand what the hell I'm on about.

'Listen,' I say, sitting down on the end of the bed. 'When the tide's out, you can hear the water on the shingle. There's a constant background rhythm. But when it's in, the sounds can catch you off-guard. Haven't you heard the pontoon? It sounds like a child crying when it moves. And you get those sudden surges in the waves, when a boat goes by. The ebb and flow, if you tune in, is rhythmic, like life. Reminds us that nothing lasts. Yet everything that goes away comes back in some form or another.'

'All I know is I need music.'

'OK. I'm sorry.' I see he isn't in the mood for one of our deeper conversations. 'I was trying to convince you, but of course. Music is essential to you, Jez. I do understand that. I'll sort it. Don't worry.'

'And I want to speak to them. Mum and Alicia. Because they have no idea where I am. Do they? They'll be worried sick by now. I hate to think of what they must be going through.'

I walk to the tiny window, push it open further. A blast of cold, river-scented air comes in, lifts the cobwebs so they catch the light and gleam.

'Jez, I don't know what to do! You can't speak to them yet. And I can't let you out of here until Greg goes. I can't make him leave, but neither can I bear for him to stay. I feel trapped.'

'You? Trapped?' He laughs, an ironic, bitter laugh. I turn and look at him. The light that comes in through the open window catches him and I see now that he looks nothing like he did that first day. His face is drawn and pale, and there are spots appearing around his mouth. His beauty's fading in this dreadful place.

Is the solution, after all, to let him go? I could simply slash off the tape, walk out, leave the garage door open, let him make his way home. It isn't even far to Helen's house. He could be back there in ten minutes. I imagine the looks on their faces, Maria and Mick and Helen. It would be doing Helen a favour. The dynamics have changed in their household, and I hold the key to restoring them. But would they be restored? This thing I've set in motion by taking Jez into my life has taken on a momentum of its own. There are certain things that can't be altered. I suspect that Mick's loss of respect for Helen is irreversible, that Helen's drinking will continue to escalate. That the simmering passion, if that's what it is, between Mick and Maria will run its course. I can't save them. And where would it leave me? Back to square one, with Greg. Jez would grow into some grotesque adult. His beauty, this perfect state between boy and man would pass, until it vanished altogether. It would be as if the simple twist of fate that brought Jez into my life never happened.

CHAPTER TWENTY-TWO

Saturday

Sonia

I leave the garage. I'm afraid if I stay there I'll cry. With fury, indignation and hurt at Greg, and at the impossibility of the situation for Jez. Instead of going straight home, I go down the steps to the beach. The tide's out. I walk along, wanting to feel the cold air on my face, breathe the river's mingled scents.

The shore is clean these days compared to how it was when Seb and I played here. Yes, there's a car tyre washed up on the shore, a length of pipe, the usual discarded bits of electricals, kitchen appliances. Polystyrene burger containers. Even a pumpkin, hollowed, rolling on the shore, a relic of Hallowe'en, goodness knows how it's survived this long. But they're washed clean from the water and beneath them is sand, stones whitened, pieces of smoothed glass and china. The mud, the oil, the dense chemical stew that Seb and I played in is no more. I sit down on a concrete slab. Behind me the wall is coated up to the tideline in green river weed and above it soar the chimneys of the power station, towering over the great crumbling chalky-white walls. To the right of the power station is the little old hospital, now almshouses, with its black and gold clock on its pretty tower, its delicate crenellated eaves, two incongruous buildings juxtaposed. This is one of my favourite places to sit, the tall protective walls behind me, the river in front.

I have to hug my coat around me, pull up the collar to keep off the vicious wind. I wonder if it might snow. I listen to the water lap the shore. There's the gentle bell-like tinkle of china against stone, or metal on bone, as the waves nudge the debris on the shore.

I stare at the river and suddenly I see us. The day we built the raft. The hot summer of that year had ended. It must have been early autumn. I can remember a mist coming off the river. An acrid reek drifted up from Dartford as if some toxic substance had leaked from a chemical plant. Early morning. Something had happened in the River House. There had been some row, shouting, threats. I'd stormed out of the house in tears. I had the same ache in my chest I have now, as if I were holding in months of misery and hurt. Then I spotted Seb down here on the shore and felt things lift. I joined him at the water's edge. He was staring into the murk.

'What's that?'

Something floated on the tide towards us, wood, part of a fish box by the looks of it.

'Grab it, Sonia.'

I waded obediently through the mud into the water, not heeding the cold – something I challenged myself to do when I was with Seb, so he couldn't accuse me of being feeble. I hauled the fish box towards the shore.

'Ideal raft material!' Seb said. 'Then we can get away and hide from everyone. No one can stop us, Sonia. We'll disappear like the swans. We'll vanish!'

I looked at him and smiled. It was a crazy idea but I loved Seb for it. He always believed we could achieve the impossible.

'Brill. This is perfect as a start. When it's built, we can go across to the Isle of Dogs. Make our escape route from there.'

'Will it be safe?'

'It'll be fine. We need an oar though. And some kind of barrier so we don't tip out. And some buoyancy aids. And a painter. Fetch that car tyre, we can use it to make a kind of seat thing.'

I knew about buoyancy. It's something that's second nature to you when you live by water. I'd learnt about it in the various rowing boats and motor launches I'd travelled in. I collected bits of polystyrene, of which there were plenty in those days, scattered along the tideline, and filled plastic bags with them. Meanwhile Seb collected bits from the shore, oil drums and bits of beer barrel and driftwood and ropes. It took us most of the day to build the raft, wading in and out of the water to test it, starting again, redesigning it until it was ready to take across the river. We spent hours tying ragged bits of discarded fishing net between two long ropes to make a ladder.

'We can use it to scale the wall on the other side,' Seb said. 'We'll have to wait for the tide, though, it'll be useless if it won't reach the top of the wall.'

It was getting dark by the time the water was high enough to launch the raft.

The wind had got up, sending waves hurtling upriver. Yellow lights winked on along the banks, both north and south. In the middle of the river too, they flickered on, on the moored ships, on the smaller river-buses that were making their last journeys of the day along the now bronze waterway.

I wondered what we'd do if a ship came up the river and we were unable to get out of its way but Seb said we'd be alright so I kept my mouth shut. If the worst comes to the worst, I thought, we can just dive off and swim for it. As usual, it was more important to maintain Seb's respect than to ensure my own safety.

I slipped silently back into the River House to fetch waterproof outer garments from the hall. Wet suits weren't used in those days. The house was silent. Whoever had upset me that morning had disappeared. I unhooked oilcloth raincoats for both of us and slithered back down the steps that were being licked by the water at the bottom.

'Now we've got to launch her,' said Seb. 'She needs a name, Sonia. What're we going to call her?'

'Tamasa,' I said.

'Tamasa?'

'It's the old word for Thames,' I said. 'It means "dark river". We did it at school. And the river's almost dark now.'

'OK. We'll smash a bottle against her side. Launch her properly.'

We stood on the steps. Seb tied a piece of rope to the handle of one of the oil drums that made up *Tamasa*'s body, then tied a full bottle of Brown Ale to the other end, and threw it hard against the raft's side. It took several attempts. In the end we had to employ the aid of the stone steps, but at last the bottle shattered and bubbles hissed along the surface of the water, fusing and mingling with the toxic froth that had accumulated at the edge.

We walked down the last two steps into the churning tide, and, resigned to what lay ahead, I ignored the water sloshing over the top of my boots and helped Seb shove the raft out into the waves. We jumped on board and set off across the misty water, lying on our stomachs. Seb got the paddle and rowed like fury but after a few minutes he gave up. The currents were far stronger than his rowing. There was no point in trying to navigate. The river was going to do with us what it liked.

Within seconds we were out near the middle. The shore seemed further away than ever in the gathering dusk. The raft barely floated above the surface of the water.

'Whoaa!' Seb shouted as the tidal currents took us up again and sent us heading upriver.

'Row harder!' he shouted, 'or we'll end up beyond Rotherhithe or Jacob's Island! God! The current's stronger than I thought!'

I think that even Seb was scared at this point. The raft veered around, dipped, bobbed up again, and icy water splashed over the side and into our faces. Soon we swung over to the north of the river, way up. The water had carried us faster and further than we'd imagined it could. Over to our right were the pilings, great wooden posts holding up the street above, linked by chains and with steel ladders reaching to the landing stages. Seb's breathing was coming fast now, and I sensed that he was close to panic.

'Hold on!' he shouted, above the roar of the wind, the slosh of water over the raft, the rumble of traffic and thunder of motor launches that rocked obliviously past us. In the dusk there was no way they'd be able to see us from their brightly lit interiors.

'Stick the oar in and keep it there or— Oh fuck, fuck, fuck!'

I pressed the plank we were using as an oar into the water and the raft swung right.

At last we managed to arrive under a landing stage, though whether this was due to my navigation or the river's will, it was impossible to say. The sounds changed. Gulps and drips echoed in the darkness. Seb's voice bounced back off the walls as he spoke.

'Christ, I thought we were done for. OK. We're safe now, Sonia, chuck the rope. I'll tie us on.'

He lashed the rope round one of the pillars and then stood up, wobbling on the raft and holding his arms out like a tightrope walker, looking as if he'd never had a moment's fear after all.

'What do we do now?' I asked.

'We have several options,' he said. 'One, we wait here till the tide goes out and walk ashore. Two, we climb up a ladder and go home by bus. Three, we turn round and row home again. Four,

I climb up a ladder and leave you on the raft to see how you're going to get out of here.'

'Don't do the last one, Seb, will you? Please? I'm cold and I'm scared under here, it's dangerous.'

'What's dangerous about it?'

'Seb! *Tamasa* is sinking as we speak. No one can see us and the water's rising and we might get trapped.'

I could only make out his silhouette in the dark so I wasn't sure if he shrugged or smiled or just ignored me, but suddenly he'd swung the raft round to one of the pillars that had an iron ladder attached to it, and was shinning up it.

'Seb, come back! Don't leave me here.'

Leaving me was one of Seb's hobbies. What I didn't know then was that I hadn't experienced it properly yet. Not fully. Not for ever.

The raft continued to bob up and down and swing around. It was lashed to one of the pillars so I knew there was no chance of being swept further upriver, or, more frightening still, downriver once the tide turned. But alone in the dark of that overhang, the water heaving up against the pillars, I began to wonder what I'd do if the tide rose so high there was no airspace between me and the roof. And *Tamasa* was dipping below the waterline. Soon she would sink and I'd be left holding on, my arms growing weaker and weaker until I'd have to let go and collapse into the dark depths of the real Tamasa, too frozen and exhausted to swim for it. I ought to follow Seb. But the cold of the river had got into me. My teeth chattered uncontrollably. I made a grab for a ladder, but wobbled as I pulled myself halfway to my feet and almost toppled overboard.

After four or five attempts to haul myself up, unable to get any purchase underfoot from *Tamasa* who kept swinging round and dipping under the water, I gave up. I could barely move my hands any more, let alone find the strength in my arms.

Seb had gone. I sat on what was left of the raft and wrapping my oilcloth closer around me, pulled my knees up to my chin. There was a loud scuffle and a squeal of rats from the wall. I shouted again for Seb. He didn't answer and I imagined him now, ensconced in a pub maybe, ordering a lager – he always got away with ordering alcohol even though he was under age. And I felt the familiar onslaught of rejection and envy and yearning that he always managed to evoke in me.

Soon more pressing concerns pushed their way in. *Tamasa* was definitely sinking. The back end, the end with the big bag of polystyrene bits that were meant to keep her afloat started to disappear beneath the water's surface. I wouldn't have been able to see this in the dark if it wasn't for a beam of light that flashed under the overhang and lit up that end of the raft. My boots were full of water now, I tried to prise them off. Then there was a roar, *Tamasa* rose alarmingly, my vision filled with bright white light and big black arms were all around me.

I awoke later in the police launch whose light had found me. Seb had gone home. I'm not sure whether he ever got over the humiliation of finding the police involved, though if I'd known then what I know now, I would have realized how light his punishment at that point was. A reprimand. A day's grounding. And that was it. Until next time.

My right hand, which has been absently picking up and dropping stones as I sit on the concrete slab, is now loosely holding onto a smooth cylindrical shape. I look down and am startled to see it's a bone. If I'm not mistaken, dredging up the anatomy lessons I once took, it's a human wrist bone. I drop it in alarm and see that all around, in amongst the pieces of chalk and flint and shoe soles, are more and more bones, thicker hollow ones, shorter finger-like ones, many blackened at the ends as if burnt, and one or two chopped off halfway down, raggedly, as if they've been hacked to pieces. The tide has started to come in and there's a wind coming off the water, which swells and sighs. The whole river and the sky is filled with the whoosh and cry of things moving restlessly in discomfort. Moans and rattles, creaks and groans, as if the river itself were demanding attention.

I look up and realize I am not, after all, alone. In the flats that line the river side of the alley there are people on one of the roof terraces, looking down at me. I stand up and brush myself down, filled with a sense of dread, and hurry back to the mooring steps.

CHAPTER TWENTY-THREE

Saturday

Sonia

Back in the River House, I gather the old portable CD player Kit used as a teenager, a pile of CDs, and an ipod. I'm about to return to the garage bearing gifts that I hope will put Jez in a better frame of mind, when Greg arrives back from the station. He comes into the sitting room, his arms open, a daft, boyish grin on his face.

'Well, we have the house to ourselves at last!' he says, drawing right up close to me and placing his hands on my ribcage. I flinch. He presses his nose in the back of my neck and starts to kiss it.

'Put those CDs away. There's no need to start tidying up now,' he says into my hair.

I pull away.

'Don't, Sonia, let's not go upstairs, there's no need. Let's be spontaneous for a change. There's no one here! We can do what the hell we like.' He's breathing quickly and I can tell he's been thinking about this all the way back from Euston, getting himself in a lather. He presses himself up against me and I can feel the hard-on against my thigh as he begins to pluck at my top, burrowing his hand under the neckline and pushing it inside my bra. His hand is hot and slightly sticky.

'Oh God, Sonia, I miss you when I'm away. I think about this all the time, you here, alone in your black skirt and stockings, me coming in and taking you in the living room, right here, while you're trying to get on with the housework.'

I make light of this, pushing him away, trying to laugh.

'In my fantasy you're in here with a duster, polishing the furniture and I come in and take you . . .'

I want to guffaw – *with a duster? I've never held a duster in my life!* – but my sense of humour has left me.

'Greg, I'm sorry, I can't. Not in here. Not in this room.'

'Relax!' he says. 'Relax, enjoy!'

'Look. You enjoy your fantasy, why don't you? And if you must be in here, I'll go, and you can please yourself.' I take his hand from under my skirt, place it on his crotch.

'I've had enough of pleasing myself, Sonia! It's what I have to do when I'm away. I've got you here with me now and I want you.' He puts his doctor's hands on my shoulders and pushes me towards the sofa, then shoves me down onto it and kneels over me.

'Greg, please stop this. I've got jobs to do. I'm not in the mood.'

He frowns at me.

'You're *never* in the mood. Tell me what the hell I have to do to get you in the mood.'

His right hand, where it pushes against my collarbone, hurts me. I move my face to one side so I don't have to smell his breath, don't have to observe the vein that pulsates under the loose skin of his throat. He holds me down with one hand and grasps my skirt with the other. I regret wearing the stockings I put on this morning. Greg was the last thing on my mind when I dressed. I've still got my boots on. These details only make Greg more excited.

'Keep them on,' he breathes into my ear. 'Keep on your stockings and your long black leather boots while I take you on the sofa in the sitting room. Think, just outside the window, people are walking by. Imagine their surprise if they glanced in . . .'

He's red in the face. And strong. He pulls my top up and fastens his mouth to one of my nipples. Nothing happens. I am, as always with Greg, as good as dead. I usually pretend, so frightened am I of disappointing him. Terrified of his anger at my lack of response. And he seems taken in by my acting; I suppose he's happy to suspend his disbelief. Even now, as I turn my face this way and that to avoid his kisses, he imagines I'm simply tormenting him by playing hard to get. He's got his trousers round his knees now, black hairs curling against the goose-pimpled flesh of his thighs. I screw my eyes shut tight and pray that it'll be done with as quickly as possible, so that I may be released from the sense of revulsion I feel. Revulsion is too weak a word. What I feel is not simply a physical recoiling, but a profound loneliness.

At last he gasps, sobs, and collapses on top of me, says one day he'll have a heart attack if he's not careful, I turn him on so much. I push him off me, get up, smooth down my skirt and go to the kitchen. I stand at the sink, turn on the tap, let the silver splash of the water against the stainless steel fill my vision, its gush blot out my thoughts.

'Bring me a coffee, darling!' he calls from the living room, and I fill the kettle, and plug it in, moving as if through some thick, viscous liquid, fetching cups and milk and sugar. A thought I had in the garage earlier, when I told Jez I felt trapped comes back to me. There must be a simple unobtrusive way I could get rid of Greg cleanly and for ever. But I know I can't do it. I haven't got it in me.

I call Greg into the kitchen when the coffee's made. I don't want to sit in the living room with its echoes and ghosts. And now its faint residual odour of sex.

'D'you want a sandwich?' I ask as he comes up behind me again and puts his arms around my waist.

'I could murder a toastie,' he breathes into my ear. 'You've given me an appetite!'

I move away from him and light the grill. Outside there's a lowering brownish light. I wonder again if it's going to snow. I slice bread and grate cheese, trying to look casual as I ask, 'So how long are you planning to stay?'

He glances up, probably wondering whether I'm having a go at him again. I smile sweetly.

'There's a conference in Barcelona next week,' he says. 'I'd need to leave on Monday. But I'm happy to cancel my commitments there. You know that.'

'There's no need. I'm very busy next week with my clients. Even if you were to stay here, we'd hardly see each other.'

'You don't *want* me to go, do you, Sonia?' he asks. His eyes are twinkling. He believes nothing could be further from the truth.

'Of course not!'

'Sonia, I know you've been unwell with this flu, but you're not depressed, are you? You haven't been yourself the last few days. Kit thought you were offhand with Harry. She was upset about it.'

I turn the bread over under the grill, add the cheese and wait for it to bubble.

'Offhand?'

'She thought you didn't make much effort. I told her you were just a bit low, post-viral probably. But is that all?'

'I can't think how much more effort I could've made,' I snap. I think of the meals I cooked, the bedroom I let Harry sleep in. How I let him play in the music room, the trip to the opera . . . Everything I did for the onerous Harry when the one person I wanted to look after was shut up in a draughty hovel, suffering under my own hands.

'Then when the police came yesterday, you looked very pale. Very upset. It *is* upsetting when someone disappears. And frightening, too. To think someone might be out there who . . . Anyway to reiterate, if you're anxious I could – and would – cancel Barcelona.'

'Please don't cancel Barcelona,' I say, and slam the plate of cheese on toast on the table in front of him more vigorously than I mean to.

'Fine,' he says. 'Good. Now. There are a few things I need to sort before I go. You did as I asked, I take it. About the alarm?'

There's a tense pause as he realizes what I'm about to say.

'I haven't had a moment.'

'Sonia! We can't put the house on the market without a functioning burglar alarm! Not with things the way they are around here. OK, I know we've been avoiding the subject of moving but it is something we have to discuss soon.'

'You know how I feel about that. About selling up.'

'And *you* know this bloody-mindedness is irrational.'

'I'm never moving from here.'

He puts his toast down and stares rigidly out of the window as if struggling to stop himself from speaking his mind.

'Anyway,' I say, 'we can ring about the alarm now. In fact, what the police said, you know, about this disappearance. It made me think. You've talked about it loads of times, putting bars up at the sitting-room windows. I'd feel safer here alone if I knew there were bars.'

He stands up. Casts me another of his sceptical glances.

'OK. Leave it to me,' he says. 'I'll sort the alarm and we can discuss the sale again when you're in a better frame of mind. I'll go down to the locksmith's. They may still be open. And then you'll be OK for me to go to Barcelona?'

'Fine,' I say. 'Go tomorrow if you prefer.'

'And Sonia, perhaps you should pop to the GP next week. Have a chat about these mood swings. They can do a very simple test for depression these days, a straightforward questionnaire.'

'I'm not depressed, Greg.'

He looks at me, that look again, as if he knows more than I do.

'That's often part of the whole thing, I'm afraid,' he says.

'What do you mean?'

'Denial,' he says. 'Harry pointed it out. It's a classic symptom of depression that the patient denies there's anything wrong with them.'

'What does Harry know about it. About me?'

'Oh, Harry's not just a pretty face,' says Greg, an expression I find odd coming from my manly husband. 'He specializes in psychiatry. You know that.'

I stare at him. How am I supposed to know that Harry, whom I've only just met, and taken an instant dislike to, specializes in the study of the mind?

'You're not telling me you've been discussing me with Kit's latest fling?'

'Oh, I don't think he's just a fling. I think we'll be seeing a lot more of him,' says Greg. He tucks his shirt in, runs a finger under his collar.

'I'd like to think my daughter has a bit more taste,' I mutter.

'What was that?'

'Nothing.'

'Anyway. These irrational attachments . . .'

'What?'

'The irrational attachment you have to the house, along with a loss of libido and insomnia, are classic symptoms of depression in women of your—'

'I've had enough of this!' I grip the edge of the worktop. Dig my nails into it.

'What Sonia? Enough of what? We only want the best for you. Me, Harry, Kit.'

'You discussed my libido with Harry?'

'No, just the insomnia, mainly.'

'This insomnia. Where did Harry get that idea?'

Greg has gone out of the kitchen door. He pulls a scarf off the hall stand and wraps it around his neck.

'Greg, I want to know. What's he talking about?'

'He says he saw you wondering around at night. That you'd been out for a walk. He met you here, in the hall . . .'

'Oh, for God's sake. What business it is of his if I need a little fresh air at night? But, since you mention it, I have been having trouble sleeping. I could do with something to help.'

'If it means you're less touchy . . .' He whips his prescription pad out of his pocket, scribbles on it and hands it to me. Then he mutters, 'It's no wonder Kit wants to get back to Newcastle. That she doesn't like coming home any more.'

Using Kit is underhand. He knows how to get right under my skin. He turns his back to me as he pulls on his coat, his gloves.

'Kit doesn't like coming home when we argue all the time,' I say to his back. 'Just let me be. Stop haranguing me about moving.'

'She doesn't like it that you seem so on edge. And she hates living here.'

'She's left home, anyway, Greg. And if it's just you and me, well . . .'

'Well what?' He turns and stares at me, his eyebrows raised in query.

'Nothing.'

I don't want to go down the route that will inevitably lead to the talk of separating. In spite of everything, I want us to stay together. For Kit, mainly, but also because on a certain level it works. Greg knows this. I'm a good wife to him. I give him

freedom but make a warm home to come back to. And he's a
provider, and a loving father to Kit. We are an old-fashioned
marriage, coupled together for more pragmatic reasons than
love. It's a conclusion we came to that time after the silent holiday in Spain when we almost split up. I thank him coldly for
dealing with the window bars, and suggest that if he's going to
sort it out, he should get on with it. The shops will be shutting
soon.

'I'm going,' he says. 'Don't worry,' and he bangs the door as
he leaves.

CHAPTER TWENTY-FOUR

Saturday

Sonia

I pick up my prescription at the chemist and go to Bullfrog in Greenwich to choose Jez's clothes. It seems like his kind of place – urban, trendy. Though I know it's hard to get these things right. Kit would often berate me for completely misunderstanding her taste at Jez's age. I bundle the new jeans, T-shirts and hoodie into my shopper.

'For my nephew,' I feel compelled to tell the woman at the cash register. 'I hope they fit.'

'How old is he?'

'Sixteen.'

I wish I hadn't said anything. She wants to check the sizes for me, but I don't really want her opinion. I didn't mean to start a whole conversation. She starts to talk about refunds and credit notes but I tell her brusquely that I'm fine. I feel that she gives me a look as I hurry out of the shop.

Impressively, Greg has already managed to employ the services of the locksmiths, and is supervising them in the living room when I get back. They are drilling at the windows, installing bars and replacing the locks. One of the benefits of a recession, I suppose, is that people are glad of work. If you offer them enough money, as I'm sure Greg did, they'll do anything for you straight away and without hesitation.

'There are two messages for you,' Greg says, coming into the kitchen, *The Times* under his arm.

'You failed to visit your mother this morning and it sounds like you'd better steel yourself for the repercussions. And there's a garbled voicemail from Helen. She sounds pissed.'

I fling my coat over the shopper containing Jez's clothes, ignore the workmen in the living room and go to the answerphone. My mother's voice is curt, full of reproach. She may be forgetful in some areas of her life, but when it comes to my visits she's got a memory as sharp as a child's. My Saturday visit has been programmed in and my failure to turn up will be held against me. I'll have to spend longer with her than I usually do. I'll take her extra gin, flowers, and cheeses. Whatever she might imagine, I don't like adding to her misery when she already spends so much time alone. And I cannot take her disapproval. No matter how hard I find it to gain Mother's affections, I never stop trying.

On the phone I apologize and promise I'll go tomorrow. Then I press the 'next' button and listen to Helen's slurred voice.

'It was lovely to see you yesterday, darling. Can we meet again soon? Any chance of coming to the Pavilion, tomorrow morning about eleven? Let me know, I need to tell you the next instalment of this nightmare. Please come.'

Before long, there are bars at all the windows, better locks on both doors, and a new padlock on the door in the wall.

'No one can get in now, Sonia,' Greg says, happily, when the locksmiths have gone. And presumably no one without a special set of keys can get out either, I think. Greg informs me he's going to the pub this evening to meet a few old mates, the ones he used to play guitar with in the old days. So I'm free to go back to the garage.

Jez looks up as I lock the door behind me. He complains of feeling achy.

'Do you feel like eating?'

'Not much.' His voice is hoarse and weak.

I put my hand on his forehead. I don't think he's running a fever, but he feels a little clammy and says he has a sore throat. I don't much like the sound of this.

'I'm nipping home for a few bits,' I tell him. I rush down the alley to the River House, heat up a tin of tomato soup, pour it into a flask. Then I put a carton of orange juice and some paracetamol in a basket and fill a hot-water bottle.

'Did you get me that dope?' He's shivering.

'Like I told you earlier, I'm on the case,' I say. 'Though smoking isn't a good idea if you're feeling unwell. And on top of . . . Oh, never mind. But, look, let's get you into these new clothes. And here's some fruit juice. It'll do you good.'

I help him change his clothes, then I tuck the hot-water bottle under the covers, place his bowl of soup on the old tea chest by the bed and plump up his pillows.

'Greg's booked a flight for tomorrow afternoon,' I tell him. 'So you'll be out of here tomorrow. That's a promise.'

He glances up at me, searches my face for some time, then drops his cheek back onto the pillow. I can hear the breath whistle as it fights its way in and out of his lungs. I remember him saying his mother had moved partly because of his asthma.

'Jez, come on. You need to keep your strength up. Eat some soup.'

'I'm not feeling great,' he says. 'I may need a doctor, Sonia.'

'You don't need a doctor!' I say, more sharply than I mean to. 'Doctors don't help when you feel like this. I should know. Greg's a doctor. He's useless when anyone's ill.'

I hold out my hand, two white round pills in the palm, and offer him the glass of water.

'How do I know those aren't some other drug?' he asks.

'You can look at them. They've got *paracetamol* etched into them. Why don't you trust me? I don't understand it. What's going on in your mind?'

He doesn't answer this, but lifts his head, lets me place a pill on his tongue. He takes a slug of water.

'I can't get warm,' he says, lying down again. I see that he's trembling despite the new hoodie I've helped him into, the hot-water bottle and the three duvets I've piled over him.

'Tomorrow, I promise we can start again. I'm not going to gag you any more. Show me I can trust you. Then we can take the duct tape off your arms and legs too.'

I stand up. Move towards the door.

'Don't leave me,' he says, suddenly. 'Stay and talk to me.'

I turn and look at him. He's shivering uncontrollably, his teeth chattering. There's a bewildered look in his eyes. Like a child who doesn't want their mother to go. This fills me with unbearable tenderness.

'What do you want me to talk about?'

'Anything. You could talk about Greg. You said he's home. How did you meet? An actress and a doctor?'

'I wouldn't call myself an actress any more.'

'Helen says you are.'

'Does she?'

'Yeah.'

I sit down on his bed. Look to see if he's really that interested. He's got his eyes closed, a shallow childish frown line on his fore-head. So I start to speak. I've never spoken about my marriage in detail to anyone before. I have the sudden urge to tell him everything, while he's acquiescent.

'Greg was the professor of my college. I was never cut out to study medicine but it was what my father decided I had to do and I was so frightened of him, I didn't dare refuse. I'd been to Greg's lecture. Anatomy or something. I only went for something to do. But Jez, you don't want to hear this.'

'No, I do. Honest.'

'Greg was an older man, already turning silver at the temples. I was a little in awe of him. Though I didn't know him then of course.'

I stop. I don't want to give Jez the impression that my relationship with my husband is, or ever was, a happy one.

'Is Greg really clever?'

'Yes, as a matter of fact, he is.'

I want to add that being clever does not make him kind or gentle company, does not make him a man of compassion, though I may have thought the two went hand in hand at one time.

'He doesn't know about me?'

'No.'

'I sometimes look at old people and think I wouldn't mind being like that,' Jez murmurs. 'Not all older people are dull. Like you, Sonia. You're not dull.'

I glance at him wondering what's behind these words. But his face gives nothing away, so I continue.

'Greg told me he would help with the exam marks I was worrying about, to leave it to him, but that I *had* to go for dinner with him. I was so naïve! No student would let a lecturer do that to them now. I was flattered. But not just flattered. Relieved too. It meant I'd get good marks and escape my father's wrath. Of course I thought it just required dinner, being a good companion for one evening. But the reality was, the minute Greg got me alone, he . . . well, you can imagine. I was trapped – if I rejected him I might fail my exams. I'd have to face my father and that was a prospect more terrifying to me than sleeping with Greg against my will. So, before I knew it, we were . . . well, we were going to bed together.' I pause here, wondering whether to explain to Jez how little going to bed with someone can mean. 'Lo and behold, at the end of my first year I got the highest marks of my year group. I didn't really question it. Was just pleased I'd found a way to achieve my father's approval. Though ironically I never actually did receive it.'

It's odd explaining this out loud, as if I'm piecing it all together in my mind for the first time. Finding links I'd not been fully conscious of before.

'After my second year, in spite of my soaring marks, or perhaps because of them, I found the courage to tell Greg I wanted to switch to drama college. I thought he'd object, but he encouraged me.'

'What about your father?'

'What about him?'

'Wasn't he angry that you didn't keep up with the medical training?'

I look at Jez. I don't know why he wants this conversation. But it's just what I've always needed, to explain my marriage. To justify it. I've often imagined I'd tell Seb this story if he ever came back.

'My father was dead by then,' I say quietly. 'I never saw him after those first-year exams.'

'He died young, then?'

'It was suicide.'

'Oh. God. '

'It's OK, Jez. It was long ago.'

'But – why, why did he do that?'

'I couldn't make things better by passing exams.' Stupidly, I feel a tear spring to my eye and wipe it away with the back of my hand.

There's more I could say. A lot more. But there are places I daren't go, either for my own good or Jez's. I'm not strong enough to think about them, let alone say them, and I don't want to put Jez through my own pain. Then he speaks and I'm pleased and relieved that he's decided to open up to me, so I am able to stay silent.

'My mum's divorced from my dad.' His voice is hoarse. 'They fucked up big time. It's pathetic the way they rowed. I only live with my mum because I feel sorry for her. My dad's got someone new. But out of choice, I'd rather live with Dad.'

'Why?'

'My mum never lets up. Sounds a bit like your dad. I have to do this, take that, practise the other. When she found out I was dyslexic she went and bawled out the teachers as if it was their fault. I was so embarrassed. My dad's got this new wife, she's Moroccan, a teacher down in Marseilles, and they've got a little girl, my stepsister. I like staying there. But it's unfair on my mum.'

I gaze at him. When I called him conscientious the other day it was an understatement.

'It's sweet of you to care for your mother so much,' is all I can say.

'I don't get why my dad had to leave her.'

'The thing is, Jez, what you might not realize, is that marriage is often more a question of who you meet at the right time, than of falling for the person of your dreams. It's a question of circumstance. Sometimes those circumstances change and you find you're left living with someone you no longer care for.'

'That's crap,' he says. 'I'd never marry someone just because it was time.'

'Have you ever been in love?'

'Nah! No way.'

'What about this Alicia?'

He shrugs.

I see I've embarrassed him, probed a bit too close. He's sensitive. Still such a young boy.

'I'm not going to mess up like my parents.'

It's tempting to take a wise mature woman role at this point and say we all think that when we're young, but Jez does not want to hear this. He thinks, as all young people do, that he won't make the same mistakes his parents have done.

'You know when you're a child,' I say, 'and you realize the colour blue may be different to what other people see?'

'What, like you think it's blue but maybe someone else sees a colour you never even dreamed of? I've thought that.' He's talking but not looking at me. His eyes are still shut. He's enjoying our closeness, but he's afraid of enjoying it. I understand perfectly.

'Well, it's like that with relationships. What one person perceives may be an entirely different thing to the other person. How can you know that? You both assume you're looking at the same blue and that you'll be working in parallel, with the same aims and shared values. Maybe your mum and dad thought they'd met someone who saw the same blue,' I say.

'They're adults. They should try a bit harder. Other people manage to stay together. Helen and Mick. You and your husband.' He gives me an odd look as he says this.

Dare I admit that my relationship with Greg has been a mistake too? That we only stay together for practical reasons? But Jez seems to want to believe that we are, on some level, happily married, so I say nothing. He looks a little better. There's a faint flush in his cheeks and his breath is flowing more easily. He's so close, I put out my hand, lift a lock of his hair, move my mouth towards his ear. He jerks his head so violently away from me, I feel hurt and ashamed.

I stand up and go to the door.

'Night Jez,' I say.

'Don't go!' he says. 'Please. Don't leave me again. I'm sorry about that.'

'I'm sorry too. But I'm going now. We'll talk some more tomorrow.'

'Let me come outside with you.'

I look at him gently. He must realize how much I'd love him to come with me, sit at the table as he did when he arrived on Friday, while I prepare dinner for us both.

'Have a good night. Try to sleep. I'll be back in the morning.'

'Sonia, no,' he croaks as I reach the door. 'Please don't leave me here alone for another night. I'm cold and it's scary here. And I'm not well. Please.'

But I ignore his pleading, and force myself to walk away from him, out into the night.

CHAPTER TWENTY-FIVE

Sunday

Sonia

At eleven o'clock the next morning I'm settled with a cappuccino at a table on the terrace at the Pavilion Tea Rooms, as they've renamed what was once a simple park café. Tiny shoots are just appearing in some of the flower beds around the terrace, but there's a cold wind. The bare tops of the trees claw at dark scudding clouds.

Helen arrives a few minutes later, like an unseasonal butterfly on this raw day, wrapped in a gorgeous cerise scarf and matching hat, and swathed in a blue-green wool jacket with a hood. Unlike me she is partial to a broad pallet of colour in her wardrobe. It suits her. She kisses me on both cheeks and stares at my coffee.

'You don't fancy a drink?' she says.

'It's a bit early for me, Helen,' I say. 'But you go ahead if it's what you feel like.'

I wonder if a better friend would advise against drinking wine at this time in the morning. Might try to persuade her pal to take it easy. But there are two reasons I don't. The first is that I detest moralizing. After all, who am I to judge another's vulnerability?

Who is anyone? Don't we all have our weak spots? Isn't every one of us subject to a failing of one sort or another? Shouldn't we allow for each others' weaknesses in order to live with and accept our own?

The other reason is that it is to my advantage to have Helen drunk. It means she becomes looser with her tongue. I can store what she tells me without her noticing my curiosity. So when she suggests wine, I offer to go and get her a glass, a bottle even, if she prefers, and she thanks me and says they do half-bottles and she'll compromise and have one of those.

I've only just sat down again, and am pulling my coat around me to keep out the icy wind, when she launches in.

'Well. There've been some new events,' she says. 'Even since I saw you on Friday. I've got myself in a bit of a pickle, and I need your help.'

I stare at her, the coffee cup halfway to my mouth.

'Look, Sonia. I have to tell you this, because I'm not sure what to do about it any more. The day Jez disappeared, Friday, I didn't go to work. But I told everyone including the police that I did.'

I stare at her. My hand starts to tremble. For a horrible few seconds I think she's about to tell me that she was here, in Greenwich and saw Jez come to my door. That she knows he is living with me. That now the police are making enquiries it's time to 'fess up' as Kit's friends would say. The cup rattles against the saucer as I put my coffee down.

'I took the morning off – I only work half days anyway on a Friday. So I didn't think anyone at work would be bothered either way.'

She stares at me, wide-eyed, as if expecting me to guess what she's about to say.

'Now the police think I'm involved in Jez's disappearance. At the moment it's only hunches, instincts, they have no firm evidence. But they're trying to get some.'

'How do you know?'

'The questions! Endless! They've been back to question me, not Mick. Twice. And I told you, they imagine I have a motive, because Barney wanted to get into the same college as Jez. Now they've found out I wasn't at work that morning. But I'd told them I was.'

'Oh God. How ghastly. Then where were you?'

My pulse has slowed now. I watch her carefully as I sip my coffee.

'Not where I said I was. The truth is, and I can only tell you this, it's so humiliating. I was in a bar in Smithfields. Hair of the dog. If Maria finds out, I'll never live it down. Look. I got pissed on Thursday night, sitting up, drinking alone. I know it sounds a bit sad. But sometimes I just need it. When Mick and the boys are all busy doing their thing. I'm lonely, Sonia. I've been lonely for a long time. And facing it is sometimes too much to bear.' Two tears roll in tandem down her cheek. She wipes them away with both index fingers then takes a deep breath and a gulp of wine.

'So. On Thursday, I drank. Far too much. Couldn't face work on Friday. Sat in a pub. Drank again. It's pathetic. And now I've lied to the police to save face!'

'God, Helen, you've got yourself in a right muddle, haven't you?' I'm so relieved that this is all she wants to tell me, I feel like hugging her.

'No. no. The thing is, I think it could be OK. I told them I was at the Turkish baths. All I need is a good friend. Someone unconnected with Jez to say they saw me there. And it's plausible. In fact, perhaps, I thought of you because you're freelance, it's perfectly possible for you to pop to the baths on a Friday morning.'

'Look, Helen. I don't think I should get involved. I'm sorry. Anyway, isn't it a bit late? Surely they'll have checked already if they know you didn't tell the truth the first time?'

Helen fiddles with some change I've left on the table. She takes a sip of her wine.

'What do I do? If you won't help me I'm buggered!'

'You're not, Helen. You tell them that you were in a pub, if that is where you were. Tell them the truth.' I feel impatient now. She's not done anything, for goodness' sake. She's not got everything to lose. Helen looks hurt, as if she might really cry.

'And Mick?' I say at last, more gently. 'How are things with him?'

She sniffs, knocks back the end of another glass.

'It's all more complicated than I'd admitted. Even to myself. The jealousy. I've been doing a lot of thinking. There was someone, oh a year ago now, I was involved with.'

'Right.'

This is unexpected. 'Do you want to tell me who?'

'It's over, Sonia. I finished it. To save our marriages. His and mine.'

'You did the right thing.' I can barely believe these words come from my own lips. Whenever did I know what the 'right thing' was?

'But the guilt has been with me ever since. So how can I confront Mick with this suspicion that he's having a fling with Maria now? He could throw it back in my face! When he found out about me he dealt with it. He didn't like it, but he let it go. Now this thing with Maria is eating away at me. I'm losing all my confidence, all my dignity.'

'Oh, Helen.' I'm acutely aware of the feeling she's describing, the agony I, too, felt with Jasmine all those years ago. That terrible conundrum. If you admit to your hurt you invite contempt, if you don't, you remain in agony. It's a curse. But I say nothing.

'I'd been convincing myself everything was back to normal between me and Mick. But then this comes along and the façade of our so-called happy marriage has been blasted off. There were faults we refused to see. It only took one shift for the whole lot to collapse. Jez goes missing and *everything's* fallen apart.'

We sit silently for a few minutes.

'One good thing is I'm getting to know Alicia, Jez's girlfriend. She's been coming around a lot, of course, poor kid. She's devastated. But she's company. She finds their behaviour nauseating too. She's never got on with Maria. When she's not too distraught about Jez, we manage to laugh about them together. Alicia sticks her fingers down her throat when she sees Mick waiting on my sister hand and foot. In a way, it's a distraction. Stops us worrying about Jez. That's how I'm trying to see it, Sonia, though I'm afraid my feelings could well up at any time and I'll let them see how hurt I am. Not hurt. Angry, upset, guilty, confused. My feelings are all over the place.'

She's beginning to sound a little drunk.

I do want to reassure Helen. I'm fond of her in spite of everything. There's a great pleasure, I seem to remember, in sharing secrets with other women, it can be almost as intoxicating as a love affair in its own right. I've not often had this privilege. My greatest passions have been played out in secret, unable to carry their heads high. But I know from the days when I first met and had doubts about Greg, and from nights spent in bars with confused friends, in love but uncertain, how intimate and exciting such conversations can be.

'I must get back.' She leans across now, squeezes my hand, and I catch a whiff of her vanilla perfume. 'But you promise to keep in touch? Now we've re-established contact? You're the only person I can really talk to about all this. Everyone else is too involved.'

I promise that yes, of course, I'll keep in touch.

When she's gone, I lean back, stare past the trees to the view down the hill and across the river to the towers of Canary Wharf, the HSBC building, the mini Manhattan it's become across there with its skyscrapers and myriads of silver windows glinting now in another sudden shaft of sunlight that's found its way between the clouds. I think of the way it looked in the old days, when Seb and I made the riverside our playground, how the Isle of Dogs was out of bounds. I feel as if I've taken a step too far onto the forbidden side of the river. That everything that happens leads me deeper into the murky streets and hidden bombsites. I wonder how I'm ever going to get back. Or whether I want to.

CHAPTER TWENTY-SIX

Sunday

Sonia

'I'm off, Sonia.' Greg's at the door. His suitcase is packed, he's wearing the tracksuit bottoms, casual jacket and white Adidas trainers he always travels in.

'I've not seen as much of you as I'd have liked. But we've both got work to do. Maybe you can give some thought to the things we've talked about. Don't forget what you promised me.'

'What's that?' I ask.

'To go to the doctor's. Oh, and I've phoned a couple of estate agents. They're coming to take some photos. Just photos, Sonia, so don't get all funny about it.'

'When? When are they coming?'

'Sometime next week. One's on Tuesday I think. They'll be in touch.'

'OK,' I say, smiling outside, seething within. I lean forward and kiss him on the cheek. Greg brushes his dry lips against the sides of mine and pats my shoulder before heading up the alley.

There's a rank stench in the garage this afternoon. It takes a while for my eyes to adjust to the light but when they do I see that Jez is very unwell. He's lying awkwardly on the bed as if he's been writhing about in his sleep and there's a strange brown liquid pooled onto the pillow under his mouth. His glassy eyes are open, but only just. I put my hand on his forehead. He's running a high temperature. Then I see that the sheets are soiled, even though I've used the pads, and there's a pool of vomit on the floor.

'I'll soon get you sorted out,' I tell him. 'I didn't mean to leave you for so long. Let's clean you up and get you back to the music room as soon as possible.'

He looks up at me through glazed eyes. 'The music room?'

'Of course. As soon as the coast is clear. I never meant for you to stay in here.' Look what it's doing to you, I think. You need light and air and music.

'No! It's drowning me, go away. Go away! Go away! There's another one, over there. Oh please!'

At first I think he's talking to me, then I realize he is staring in terror at an imagined monster over my shoulder.

He's delirious. I feel his forehead again, his neck. The skin there, under his hair, burns. I try to recall advice indelibly printed on the minds of young mothers. Remove extra layers of clothing to bring down the fever. Apply cold flannels to the forehead. Give Calpol every four hours. But when is it you seek medical attention? What did I learn the time Kit had suspected meningitis? It comes back vaguely. Rashes that don't fade when pressed beneath a glass. Sickness. Aversion to bright lights.

Jez has already been sick. What will I do if he needs antibiotics? If he does have something awful? I bend over him, pull the covers back, look for suspect rashes. There's a faint red sprinkling of tiny spots on his inner thigh. My heart gives a great thump against my chest. It can't be septicemia. Don't people get rashes after a fever? That'll be the explanation.

I cover him again. Panicking is the worst thing you can do. I must remain calm, sensible. Think it through one step at a time. I try to remember the early days of my medical training, the first-aid courses I did when Kit was a toddler. I must refill his hot-water bottle, bring more water for him to drink and to bathe his face in.

The reek is unbearable. It makes me retch. It's mixed with something down there in the river, a foul stench, not the washed-clean feel of the tidal water. Something must have died down there, and begun to putrify. We do occasionally get corpses washed up on the tide. Seabirds of course. Sacks of kittens. Once I found a donkey, half eaten up by chemicals or some preying fish, its side open, all its bloodied ribs on view. Only when the flesh has completely decayed does the smell disappear, when the bones are washed clean, as if in death there is finally a return after all to purity. Like the shoe soles you find lying around on the beach. It's funny how rarely one comes across whole shoes. The river devours the soft tissue of the uppers but it rejects the soles. They wash up on the tide, hundreds of them, strewn along the shore when the tide's out. Detached footprints of the lost and the drowned.

My plan was to take Jez back to the music room but now he's ill it isn't that simple. Preventing him from making a run for it is not an issue while he remains as weak as he is. But now, even were I to support him, I'm not sure he's capable of walking the short distance along the alley back to the house. He's become an invalid.

The word invalid supplies me with one of my rare but brilliant brainwaves. My mother's wheelchair! I'm supposed to visit her today. I could go right now and kill two birds with one stone. Then I'll push Jez along the alley as if I were simply

taking my mother for one of the pleasant evening walks I did
regularly when I first moved back here. I'll wrap Jez the way I'd
have wrapped her, blankets over the knees, a shawl about the
shoulders, a scarf wrapped about the head and tied under the
chin.

I tell Jez I won't be gone long. He's barely conscious as I tuck
him in, but I check the tape is tight and go back outside.

I have to act swiftly. If this illness is serious, then I cannot afford
to hesitate. I grab the car keys from the River House, and hurry
back along the alley.

I navigate the narrow car-lined roads that wiggle up from the
river to the high street, swearing under my breath at the traffic
that seems deliberately to dawdle in front of me. Every time I
come to a set of lights, they're on red.

At last I cross the high street and take Maze Hill past Helen's
house up to Blackheath Standard.

I find a visitors' parking space in the retirement home car park
and let myself in with the key my mother's given me.

'You missed your Saturday visit,' she starts up before I've
stepped through the door. I hand over the bottle of gin I grabbed
for her from the River House, as a sweetener.

'I'm sorry, Mother. It was busy. Kit was home and Greg—'

'Well you could have phoned at least. You've no idea what it is
to wait all day, seeing no one. I expect you'll have coffee.'

'Please.'

After half an hour sitting and making amends, nodding and
agreeing about how tiresome the other residents must be, I tell
my mother I'm sorting out the garage, that it'd be a help to use
the wheelchair to shift stuff along the alley.

'Can't you use a wheelbarrow?'

'Mother, we don't own one. You must remember. There's no
calling for a wheelbarrow in a house with no garden.'

'Hmmm. I used to nurture those plants at the River House. I made things grow in that courtyard that defied nature's own laws. Everyone told me that wisteria would never flourish on the shady side of the house but I made it flower like there was no tomorrow. And the clematis! *Purple stars, held in the green night of its leaves.*'

'That's nice.'

'It's Oscar Wilde. Though I wouldn't expect you to know. And the peonies. I even grew sunflowers one year against the wall in the shadiest patch of the courtyard and they grew tall for me, all they asked for was a little love and attention.'

I wonder how my mother was able to give her plants so much love and attention when she spared so little for me.

'Still, Mother, there was never a wheelbarrow at the River House.'

'So, what do you want my wheelchair for?'

'I just said! I'm clearing out the garage. I need it so I can shift some of the heavier stuff back to the house.'

'You should do as Greg wants and sell that house. Its hour has gone!'

She waves a hand, holding a glass that's three-quarters drained. It's a little early for gin, but the light's fading outside and she's already put her lamp on, which means it's as good as cocktail hour for my mother. I refill her glass and hand it back to her, dropping the lemon quarter in as she takes it. It fizzes and spits up at her.

'Now what can I do for you?' she asks.

'The wheelchair, Mother. May I borrow it? Just for a day?'

'Take it!' she says. 'Take it away. Looking at it makes me feel old and frail. I'd rather never have to look at that horrible thing. I don't know why you had to make me buy it!'

'If it wasn't for the wheelchair you wouldn't be able to go for your outings to the heath, or the village, or to the park, would you? I'll bring it back as soon as I've finished clearing up.'

As soon as she's settled down in front of the TV, I say I have to leave, and I take the chair down the carpeted corridors to the main entrance.

When you're in a hurry, it's as if the world knows and decides to slow you up. As I reach the foyer, Max comes out of his mother's flat.

'Afternoon, Sonia,' he says, grinning, dimples appearing in his rosy cheeks. Max looks like the kind of man who has been happy all his life, who was probably born smiling and has stayed that way ever since.

'I see Mother's going out? What little mystery trip have you in store for her?'

I explain that I'm storing the wheelchair in my car ready for my mother's next excursion.

'I'll give you a hand with that!' he says. 'Here, let me.'

We push our way out through the double doors. At the car I thank Max profusely. He looks at me for a few seconds longer than I feel comfortable with. Is he about to invite me for a drink?

'It's funny,' he says, 'sometimes I envy my mother her little flat in there, all her washing done, nothing to do all day but play Scrabble and gossip about the other residents.' He stands, hands on hips, as if he has all day.

'I'm sorry, Max, I'm in a bit of a hurry, I'd love to stop and chat . . .'

'Perhaps we could have a cup of tea together sometime . . . meet in the residents' lounge?'

'It'd be a pleasure.'

'I was only joking of course, about the residents' lounge. I meant, perhaps I could take you for dinner?'

I smile. 'If I'm ever at a loose end.'

He looks at me as if trying to find a positive way of interpreting my words, then he nods and folds the wheelchair and puts it into the boot for me.

'There she goes!' he says, a broad grin spreading across his face again. 'All ready for Mum's next day out. Take care now.'

I drive as fast as I can back to the river.

CHAPTER TWENTY-SEVEN

Sunday

Helen

Helen sat down on one of the few empty chairs in the market café with her usual large cappuccino and put her head in her hands. Sonia hadn't wanted to help and who could blame her?

It took sitting alone like this, without a drink, for Helen to let her thoughts and feelings take coherent shape. The Jez situation was far worse than she imagined it could have become. Sonia's theory that he might have a lover was unlikely given his relationship with Alicia. Alicia was convinced Jez would never have gone anywhere without his guitar, and she knew him best. That left them with three possibilities. He had had an accident, perhaps in the river and hadn't yet been found. He had been abducted. Or the most unthinkable possibility of all – he'd been murdered. But there was no body. No clue. Helen banged her cup down in her saucer. She wasn't getting anywhere like this. Any further than the police had already done. Though they at least had a suspect.

Me, she thought.

The police interrogation yesterday had been awful. They'd asked her to confirm again where she'd been on Friday morning and she'd been forced to tell them she was at the Turkish baths. It was obvious that they didn't believe her. May even have checked up on her by now. But rather than pursuing this, they had asked her about the course Jez had applied to. How badly had she wanted Barney to get a place? Did he have any other prospects? Was she angry that Jez had jeopardized her son's chances? She had expressed a feeling of inferiority towards her sister and her nephew – did this ever make her think of doing anything to harm him?

Helen knew they'd let her go. They had no evidence of course, never would. But it was time for her to take stock. Stop letting childish feelings of jealousy towards her sister, insecurity towards Mick enter into her head. Feelings that were putting her in a very unpleasant, even dangerous light.

She never used to suffer from such a profound lack of self-confidence, such violent unpredictable avalanches of self-doubt. This week she'd wondered who Mick was, whether she knew him at all. Now she wondered whether she knew herself. This whole situation was about Jez. Her nephew. She must not let her own stuff cloud the fact he might be in serious danger.

A woman walked past with a new baby in a sling and, seeing its tiny nose pressed against the woman's coat, Helen remembered suddenly and with dreadful clarity the first time she'd ever seen Jez. Maria was ecstatic, the dark-haired baby at her breast making tiny smacking sounds with his lips. Helen had gone to visit her sister the day Jez was born, at home in that lovely flat they'd had at the top of Crooms Hill. The sisters had sat side by side on the bed, propped up on pillows, their knees bent up. They were close at that time, as if once Maria had become pregnant the gulf that had existed between them had closed for a while. There was a fabulous view of the river from that room, a

silver ribbon in the distance, weaving its way through the industrial docks towards the sea.

When Maria had finished breastfeeding she'd slipped the
tiny boy over to Helen. Helen had rested him on the slope of
her thighs, facing her, his tiny limbs folded and pudgy, and he'd
fixed her with those mesmerizing dark eyes, and the overwhelming love she felt was matched only by what she already felt for
her own sons. It had brought tears to her eyes. She had held
lots of newborn babies by then, most of her friends were parents
now, but there was something different about a blood-link, you
couldn't deny it. Jez was her baby nephew, her sister's own son,
and she loved him. She still loved him. Of course she did. It was
impossible to imagine that he had come to any real harm.

She left the café, still thinking, and walked between the
wrought-iron gates of the park. As she passed the sign saying,
'No itinerant ice-cream sales' she could hear Theo read it aloud
to Jez, as if they were right there with her now. 'What's "itinerant"?' Jez had asked.

'Exactly!' Theo had said. 'Why use a word like that?'

They'd run along the path beside her, passing a stone as if
it were a football and cracking jokes about the long words you
could use on signs directed at people who couldn't be expected
to understand them.

'People like me,' said Jez, who was dyslexic.

'Yeah,' Barney said. 'For you, the sign'd say, "No inebriated
musicians!" and you'd just carry on being wasted and strum-
ming your geeetar!'

There was never any animosity between her sons and Jez. They
all seemed to exist in a benign world of male camaraderie that
hadn't changed much since they were little, making fun of each
other. Scrambling up things. Going to see bands.

She had just reached the foot of the hill when her mobile
went. It was Alicia.

'I need to talk to you. I've found a clue.'

'Where are you?'

'Outside the university. On the river path. Can you come here? Then I can show you where I found it.'

Helen hesitated. She wanted to go home, felt in need of a bath and a drink. But this might be an opportunity to do something constructive.

'I'm in the park. I'll come to you. Wait there.'

Helen found Alicia on a bench staring out over the river. The tide was up and the water lapped at the wall only a few feet below. It was beginning to get dark and lights were coming on, yellow ones along the path and spangles of red, white and blue on the river and the opposite bank. Alicia looked up at Helen and held out a tiny, ragged piece of cardboard in the palm of her hand.

'What is it?' asked Helen, sitting down on the bench beside her, noticing how cold the seat was.

'It's a roach,' Alicia said. 'Jez's. I found it on the path along there,' she gestured to her right. 'Just outside the power station.'

Helen glanced in the direction Alicia pointed. The river was black towards the east, bottomless, rather threatening in the gathering dusk. The other way, towards the city, it still reflected the remains of a silvery sunset.

'What makes you think it might be Jez's?'

'It's made of a piece of ticket from a gig we went to. I know it. I recognize it. We rolled spliffs the night before he disappeared. Never smoked them because you came in.'

'Me?'

'Yeah, well, we thought you wouldn't like it.'

'And you found it down there?'

'Yes. He left your house on Friday to come and see me in the foot tunnel. This is the way he'd of come. Down the hill, past the Cutty Sark pub, and then along the path. The entrance to the foot tunnel is just over there. ' She nodded to her left. 'I decided to do a search myself. No one else is looking properly.'

Helen doubted the roach was Jez's. She suspected Alicia needed to believe she was on to something, that the roach gave her hope. She wished she didn't have to play along with what was almost certainly a red herring, but at the same time you can't ignore anything, that's what the police had said.

'So you found it near Sonia's?'

'Sonia?'

'She's my friend. The one Jez was going to borrow music from. Her house is that way, but this side of the power station. He might have been on his way to hers when he dropped it.'

'What should we do?'

'Well let's walk back that way now and you can show me exactly where you found it.'

They stood up and hurried along the river path away from the light. Helen shivered at the sound of the water as it sucked and slurped at the wall. Dark shadows cast by the bars of the iron railings, and their own misshapen forms, loomed in front of them, grew, then vanished each time they passed through the glow of the lamps. They went by the pub, then along the alley. Sonia's house was in darkness and the light outside wasn't working. The path was all in shadow and eerily quiet and remote-seeming, in contrast to the floodlit O2 over on the bend of the river, and the white lights of Canary Wharf on the other side. They continued along the footpath to the power station, enormous and lowering above them. Underneath the coaling pier, Alicia stopped.

'Here,' she said, pointing at the ground by the wall. 'This is where I found it.'

The wind lifted something large in the black structure above them that clanked and banged and Helen felt a strange uneasiness sweep through her.

'Let's go,' she said, and not wanting to alarm Alicia she added, 'at least we know he got this far. As soon as we've found somewhere warm to sit, we'll discuss what we're going to do.'

CHAPTER TWENTY-EIGHT

Sunday

Sonia

It's almost dark when I get back from my mother's. Lights blink on along the river.

I unload the wheelchair and push it to the garage, unlock the inner doors, shove the chair in. Jez is lying on his back still, his arms tied above his head. He is sweaty and pale.

'Jez, we're going back to the music room where I can look after you properly,' I tell him. He gazes at me. There is no reaction. His face is gaunt and his lips look drained and blue. He mutters something incoherent, then closes his eyes.

'You're unwell,' I say. 'We need to get you somewhere comfortable. Just slip into the wheelchair so I can push you home.'

I slice the bonds at his arms and legs with the kitchen scissors I've brought in my pocket, and swing his legs off the bed so he's forced into a sitting position. I support his back from behind. Somehow between us we manage to get him into the chair. I put Greg's anorak back over him, making sure the hood covers his head, then wrap him in blankets. As a precaution against him making a run for it, even though I'm almost certain he's too weak, I strap his hands and feet together again with the tape. I want to gag him, just in case someone stops and tries to talk to him, but I'm afraid that if I muffle his mouth he won't be able to breathe at all. Already he is coughing and wheezing. Instead, I cover his face, pulling the hood down low and wrapping the scarf loosely over his nose. Only his eyes are visible once I've finished. I'm desperate to get him home. To nurse him back to health.

I squat by the garage doors, push them open them a crack to see out, and survey the part of the alley that's within my view.

A gaggle of drinkers comes past, fooling about, pushing one another and laughing loudly. I watch as the girls teeter about on heels and lurch into the boys who sing and jeer and stagger from one side to another. They disappear up the street, their voices gradually fading away. More footsteps, the soft voices of two women talking. I squint through the crack in the door and gasp. One of the women looks like Helen. *Is* Helen. What's she doing down here? She's with someone slim whose face I can't discern as she's on Helen's other side. I pull the door closed, and squat behind it, trying to control my breathing. After several minutes, I open the door a crack again.

The alley's in darkness now, only slices of it lit up by the street lamps. There are more footsteps coming from the direction of the pub. Two police officers, striding along, their fluorescent jackets glowing bright yellow in the dark, chatting together as they go. I withdraw into the garage.

I pull the inner door shut, lock it, lean against it, my heart going so fast I'm afraid it'll burst. I look at Jez. His head is nodding against his chest, he's half asleep. I feel his forehead under the hood. Yes, he still has a temperature. His breath is laboured, wheezy. He needs an inhaler. I have to get him to the warmth and comfort of the River House. I can't leave it much longer.

At last the alley quietens down. There's just the usual clank of the sheet of metal up on the coaling station and the smack of waves against the wall, some delayed wake from a passing boat has set them rolling across the river. I push open the doors, wheel Jez into the alley and back towards the door in the wall.

I spend the whole night in a chair, beside Jez, holding his hand in the music room. He struggles for breath. Some of his coughing fits seem so gruelling it's as if he doesn't have the strength to push the air out of his lungs. Several times I'm afraid I will have to phone an ambulance. His breath is empty, it feels as if it is neither entering not leaving his lungs as it should. I rummage through the pockets in his leather jacket and the hoodie he wore when he arrived and find an inhaler in one of his pockets. I hold it to his mouth and pump it. This eases things a little but he remains virtually unconscious.

At around four o'clock, when he still shows no signs of improvement, I realize I have to formulate a plan if I am to keep Jez safe. In this case, now, safe equals alive. I think it through step by step, trying not to let my feelings of loss or regret take hold. Jez must live.

What I'll do is take him to a hospital before first light. I can get him to my car in my mother's wheelchair and I'll drive to St Thomas', or even as far as Hampstead and the Royal Free. I cannot take him to the local hospital, it will be too risky. I might be recognized and stopped. And I need time to get away before the family turn up. I'll sedate him before we go, no longer a problem now I have Greg's prescription. And I'll wrap him up warm. I'll leave him in the hospital foyer with a note asking that they look after him, and with contact details for Helen.

Then I must disappear out of his life. Not only his life. I shall have to take myself away from Kit too, so that she will not have to endure the indignity of her mother's crime. For I know this is

how what I've done will be interpreted. And I must take myself
away from Greg, who will want to know why and how, and to
harangue and blame me for not going to the doctor about my
'depression'. I will have to take myself away then from the River
House.

My eyes fill with tears as I think of how I must let everything
go. Kit, and the River House, and Jez at his most exquisite. I
squeeze his hand and let my tears fall onto his upturned wrist.

Later, I will realize that fatigue made me see things in a
distorted light. That the idea of taking Jez to hospital was neither
necessary nor rational. But now, as the high windows begin to
lighten almost imperceptibly in the dawn, I am convinced this
is the end.

CHAPTER TWENTY-NINE

Monday

Sonia

When I wake up later that morning, having fallen asleep at last in the chair, the sun fills the music room with a honeyed light. I can hear Jez's breath flowing more freely. He is still in a deep sleep, but there is a little more colour in his cheeks. For the moment anyway he seems stable. I go downstairs.

At ten o'clock Simon arrives for his voice-coaching session. He takes my hand in his and presses a small cling film-wrapped shape into my palm.

'Your mother's dope, darling. Medicinal marijuana, just as you ordered.'

I kiss the air next to his cheek. 'My dear, middle-aged drug dealer.'

'No problem, Sons. You can knock the price off my bill.'

It's Monday. I've had to reinstate my voice-training sessions. I cannot remain out of circulation for too long or people will want to know why.

'We're going to conduct the session downstairs today,' I tell him, 'in the kitchen.'

'I thought you preferred having me in the music room.'

'We're having some work done up there. The floorboards are up and it isn't safe.' It was having the builders on Saturday, putting up the window bars that gave me this idea.

'If you need the loo, use the one down here. I'll make you some coffee. Sit down.'

'Are you completely better now, sweetie? We were all afraid you'd got swine flu! You look a little tired I must say. But you're more glorious than ever. You've lost weight!'

'A little, maybe.'

'Not that you needed to, of course. But flu can streamline our jawlines which is never a bad thing in midlife'.

'Simon!'

'At my age you have to work at your looks. You can no longer take them for granted.' Simon objects to time passing as if it were a personal affront. 'I'm fifty-five, Sonia! It's a travesty! How can I, Simon Swavesy, be fifty-five? Do I look it? Is it written all over my face?'

'You look no different to the last time I saw you.'

'But my jowls! And I'm sure I'm developing a double chin.'

'Well, our voice exercises will help with all that,' I say, pouring his coffee. 'We must get to work.'

The sun comes in through the kitchen window lighting the ledge inside, lending the kitchen a radiance it rarely displays. Little areas are thrown into relief, the mugs hanging along the shelf of the dresser, the oranges in the fruit bowl. I look at the row of marmalade jars glowing amber in the sunlight. I feel slightly removed from everything, perhaps due to having been awake most of the night.

'How's business then?' Simon asks. 'Not too effected by the economic crisis? One good thing, people always need escapism. Oh, I meant to ask, were you well enough to see *Tosca*?'

'I was – just. And I loved it. You were amazing, Simon, as always.'

There's something exquisite about the precariousness of my secret, this double life. I never foresaw that this might be a consequence of Jez's being here. Each time I get away with something I feel myself rise upwards on a high that is incomparable with anything I've experienced since childhood.

There's a new smell in the breeze blowing in from the river. A freshness after the lowering, cloud-trapped chemical smell of winter.

'What a sublime day!' Simon says, leaning on the windowsill and gazing out over the water. The surface looks almost solid in this light, like satin or polished metal. 'Do you think spring's arrived at last?'

The day does indeed feel sublime. There's a kind of lifting in my heart as if it were a baby spider in its silken parachute sailing up into the spring sky over the river.

I have Jez. He is recovering, thanks to me. I feel like I did as a child on the first day of the summer holidays when I awoke and knew the horrors of school lay so far away I did not have to think about them. That the days within sight were long and free.

When Kit was a child of perhaps six or seven, she said she heard a bat squeal. We told her she was mistaken, that the human ear cannot detect such a sound. Now I'm discovering levels of feeling which were too extreme to be accessible to me before. Peaks of emotion that, like a bat's cry, I had not thought a human was capable of detecting.

After Simon leaves at eleven o'clock I go up to see Jez.

'Where am I?'

'You're OK, Jez. You're back in the music room.'

Even he must feel this lifting, this lightening of the atmosphere, the way the sun's rays come through his high windows warming the covers on his bed.

'What day is it? What time?'

'It's Monday. Late morning. Do you want some coffee?"

He's still unwell, not feeling like drinking coffee, he says.

'You know there's fresh soap and clean towels in the shower room if you want them, don't you? There's all the music equipment. Books, the radio. And you've got me, right here, to wait on you hand and foot. I'm happy to do that for you, Jez, you know that.'

'Mmm.' He's still poorly, but his breathing is better. He's barely able to open his eyes and he's shivering again.

'There's a pain, in my back,' he says. 'Between my shoulder blades.'

'Yes, well you must rest. And you need a wash and to clean your teeth.'

I bring him a flannel and a toothbrush and clean him up as best I can. He's so weak I allow him to get up and go to the bathroom to relieve himself and then he stumbles back to bed and lies down with a sigh.

'I'll bring you a hot-water bottle.'

'Yes, yes please. It's so cold. The ice has frozen my fingers. Look! My fingers have gone thin!'

I tuck the bottle under the sheets and wonder as I do so whether, since he is clearly delirious, I might lean across and kiss him without startling him. But his lips look dry after his illness, and he gives off an acrid scent. This worries me, he may lapse again.

Downstairs I go to Greg's computer in the hallway that blocks the front door onto the street. The door we never use. I feed Jez's symptoms into Google. The most likely diagnosis is pneumonia. It means he will be ill for quite a while, his strength diminished. It explains his cough and the pain in his shoulder blades. However, although it sounds serious, it seems that if I take special care of him, as I of course intend to do, there should be no need for medical intervention.

Having made my diagnosis, I spend a little longer on Google, searching various sites, losing myself. I browse Nadia's sculptures, and follow the link to the site where she got the Modroc for the pregnant torsos Helen told me about. On impulse I order some for myself. Then I find the Facebook page Mick and Maria have set up for Jez. His face, plumper, shinier, smiles out at me, with friends, with adults I've never seen, with a guitar and with a bunch of girls. I can't bear to see these images of Jez with other people, in another life, and I click off quickly.

When I next go up to see him, Jez is in a peaceful sleep, lying on his side. The roll of duct tape lies on the landing so I fetch it, rip off a length, and stretch it round and round his wrists until they are held securely together behind his back. I go downstairs and double-check the locks, the bars on the windows. I make sure the front door is bolted. The door on the river side is also Chubb-locked and bolted. I've taken the extra precaution of closing the curtains, something I rarely bother with since we only look out onto the path and the river, and drawing down the blinds in the kitchen. From the outside, the house must look closed up, as if we've gone away. I stash the Rohypnol Greg prescribed for me in the kitchen drawer, handy for dropping into Jez's glass if the need arises.

Jez is awake when I return to him. He complains that he still aches all over.

'What's happened to my hands?' he asks, a look of alarm on his wan face. I wonder whether the illness along with the cocktail of drugs I've had to feed him have played havoc with his memory. Perhaps he doesn't recall anything about being strapped up in the garage. If that's the case it's a good thing. Neither of us wants to remember that.

I sit down on the bed and look at him with all the compassion I feel in my heart.

'Jez, I think I trust you. But this first time you come downstairs, I'm taking a small extra precaution. When you've shown me you aren't going to try anything foolish, you can come down, hands free. I promise.'

'I'm coming down? Where to?'

I smile. 'To the kitchen. Please don't look so frightened. We're going to spend the afternoon together. I'll cook and you can talk to me.'

'I'm still here?'

'In the River House, yes. You're still here. It's alright.'

'But I'm going home, aren't I? You're going to let me go. You said so.'

I stroke the hair off his forehead.

'Of course you're going home,' I say. 'Soon now, I think. Very soon.'

CHAPTER THIRTY

Monday

Sonia

The afternoon is near perfect. Jez sits at the table, his hands behind the kitchen chair, while I cook. I put the green and white blanket around him to keep him warm. Refill his hot-water bottle, which I rest on his lap under the blanket. I put Jeff Buckley on the CD player and we listen to 'Hallelujah'.

I make him a hot toddy: whisky with lemon, honey and hot water. I take the precaution of giving him a plastic tumbler instead of a glass, even though he can't hold it and has to take sips as I put it to his lips. I don't think he'll do anything impulsive now. Something's changed between us. He understands that I am nursing him back to health. That I really do not want any harm to befall him.

I turn pieces of chicken over in flour for a casserole we'll share if he has an appetite later. I slice shallots, fry them in olive oil, add bacon. I glance over at him while I cook. I suppose I was expecting to see him as he was that first day, relaxed, his feet lolling against the table leg as he drank his wine. So it's a shock to see the tears rolling silently down his face and plopping into the plastic beaker. His nose is running too, long glistening threads dripping off his upper lip, and, when he sees me looking at him, his chest starts to heave.

'Oh Jez,' I say, and I move towards him.

I wipe his nose and bathe his face with a clean flannel and give him water to drink.

'Jez, look, you've been very unwell. But you're getting better now. Please don't cry. I'm here to look after you. To make everything right.'

Eventually his sobs subside, he takes a huge breath and gives me a weak, sheepish smile.

'Sorry,' he says. 'It's just, I feel so ill.'

It's getting warm in the kitchen. Now he starts to writhe about a bit, saying he feels hot. He shakes off the rug I've put round him then asks me to take off his hoodie. This isn't easy with his hands tied up as they are. I tell him I'll roll up his sleeves instead. I'm aware of everything about him as I turn back the cuffs. His broad wrists with the prominent wrist bones. A spearhead of light along the valley between the radius and the ulna. There's a veil of sweat on his forehead. Beads of perspiration in the crease of his elbows.

'You can't just take it off? I'm really hot. Burning.'

I'd love to undo his wrists, lift his hoodie off his head. But even though he's so weak and compliant, I daren't risk it.

When I've rolled up his sleeves I continue to stir sauce, grind pepper.

'Are you OK now, Jez?'

'Yes, that's better.'

After a long while he asks, 'What's in all those jars?'

I follow his gaze. 'Marmalade,' I tell him.

'That's what you were making the day I came here.'

'Yes. I make it every February, as my mother did. It's traditional. The smell . . . it's a smell I love, though it makes me feel sad too.'

'Some of my memories feel sad sometimes. Not because they were sad, but because the time's gone. It's not being able to go back.'

I turn and look at him. At last he's talking more like he did that first day. We're getting somewhere again.

'What is your earliest memory?'

He thinks for a while. I examine his face as he does so. It's thinner, no doubt about it. But there's something else, something wary in his expression that was never there before. His eyes dart about. It's as if he daren't miss a thing, as if he has to stay alert every second. I don't like it. I want him to relax.

'Swans on the river. My dad used to bring me in a pushchair, I guess. We used to throw bread to the swans. He told me they belong to the Queen. Do they?'

'Only unmarked mute swans. And only those who live here on the Thames. Or on its tributaries.'

'And the smell of Marmite on the breeze. When I smell Marmite even now, it reminds me of here. The river. Before everything changed.'

'It's not really Marmite. It's yeast from the brewery. But that smell is one of my earliest memories too. Some people object to it. I like it. And the swans are still here of course. They disappear sometimes. But they always come back.'

'Yes. But it's not how it was then. Mum and Dad will never be together again. I'll never be that little kid again. Some things are gone for ever.' Tears well up in his eyes once more.

'That's not true, Jez.' I put down my knife, and lean on the table, looking into his eyes. 'I used to think that, but I don't any more. Things don't go, the past isn't gone, time is not linear as we imagine it to be. It loops and spirals and plays amazing tricks on us. It's something I've come to know recently. I wish I'd always understood.'

I move around the table to his side. I lean over him and I look right into his lovely, pale face, into the eyes that have sunken during his illness but that are beginning to brighten again now, and I whisper, putting all the passion I feel into my words.

'You came to me. You came just when I needed to know that the past was not gone. You showed me that I had a second chance and that I need never go through that kind of loss again.'

He doesn't reply, just stares back at me, and for a while he seems to look deep into my soul. We are as one.

There's a peaceful calm, as the light fades outside and I return to my cooking. Jez and I are quiet in each other's company. We do not need to talk.

Later, I'm not sure how much later, because time has started to play tricks again and the day to have slipped away in seconds, Jez says, 'I feel shit again. I need to lie down.'

'Let's go through there. I'll light the fire and you can lie on the sofa.'

I roll down the sleeves of his hoodie. Wrap the rug round him and lead him to the living room. He lies on the sofa and I begin to build a fire in the grate, with none of the sense of forboding this room usually evokes. As if, now Jez is with me, I believe that all those aspects of the past that haunted me, however indefinable, have been erased. But something, perhaps his feet lolling on the sofa, the awareness I have of his body supine and inert, ignites it all. Not just the feeling, but every little detail, the picture in the corner of my eye that usually slides aside each time I try to focus on it.

It is illuminated as I put a match to the kindling in the grate, and it brightens as the flames take hold.

An early spring day, the light failing outside. I pushed open the door. There was some kind of table in the centre of the room.

Candles throwing enormous shadows up against the walls. Grown-ups in black, their heads bent. I knew what was on the table, they did not need to move apart. I could see between them the shiny wooden box with its polished brass handles. But I could not go closer. And no one asked me to. No one spoke to me. I stood alone in the doorway waiting for something, a movement, a word. The heads stayed turned away from me. The smell was enough. They had not lit the fire. The room was colder than the river itself.

The phone starts to ring. It's on the table next to the sofa where Jez lies half asleep. Or at least I thought he was half asleep. He sits up so abruptly at the sound, I wonder now whether he was only pretending. I'm on the other side of the room. It takes a couple of seconds to come out of my reverie, to register that he is using his chin to knock the handset off its cradle, that he's speaking into the mouthpiece, 'It's me, Jez!' he shouts.

I'm across the room, my finger ramming down the mute button before he's completed the three little words that could take him away from me for ever.

'How could you?'

'What?'

He cowers back away from me on the sofa.

'Jez! I brought you downstairs. Now you do this to me.'

'I don't understand. What did I do?'

'You were going to try and leave me.'

'No! I picked up the phone without thinking.'

I take a long, deep inhalation, walk once around the room, my hand running through my hair. This must not turn nasty. I sigh. Sit down next to him on the sofa. Put my hand gently on his knee. 'OK. I'll overlook it this once. Let's forget it for now. But it's time for you to go back to the music room. You can't stay down here any longer. Come on. Up.'

I'm trembling as he goes ahead of me out of the room. Shocked that he continues to fear me. But whether it's because he is still feeble, or because he is sorry for upsetting me, he goes forlornly, his hands taped securely behind his back, his head bowed and does not confront me as we climb the stairs.

Once he's locked in again I hurry straight to the answer machine to listen to the message. I need to see if there's any indication that they've detected Jez's voice.

It's Helen.

'Sonia, you won't believe this . . .'

I pick up the phone and dial Helen's number. She answers immediately.

'Can I come over?' she asks.

For a few seconds I can't speak. Did she hear Jez's voice? Is this a trick?

'Sonia? Are you there? Can you hear me?'

'Yes, sorry. Hi.'

'I need to talk to you. Could I come to yours?'

'No.' It's too abrupt. I try again more softly. 'No. Sorry, Helen, not a good moment.'

'Please, Sonia. I'm so alone in this . . .'

Her voice sounds sincere. Recognizing a false note is something I've learnt in my line of work and I'm pretty sure there isn't one. Of course she *could* come over. I could tell her the same as I told Simon, that the music-room staircase has to be cordoned off while the floorboards are up. But Helen would never leave. It's different with Simon and my other clients. They pay for their time. Helen could talk for hours. She has no deadline to meet. And the blanket's still in the kitchen. The plastic cup in which I gave him his hot toddy. The casserole I made for us, uneaten in the oven.

'What? Have you got clients, Sonia? When can I see you? I do need to talk.'

'I'm sorry Helen, I . . .'

Then she says something that makes me change my mind.

'Alicia wants to meet you too. Jez's girlfriend. She's got infor-mation about Jez. I think she's on the brink of discovering what's happened to him.'

'What's it got to do with me? Why does she want to meet me?'

'I'm sorry if this is a nuisance for you. But we both think you can help. Please don't get angry.'

'I'm not angry, Helen. I just asked, why me? What's it got to do with me?

'You are, you're irritable. I'm sorry. I know it's a nuisance to you, this business, but she found something of Jez's near your house, and she's sure you might have seen him without realizing it, the day he went missing. She really needs to talk to you, Sonia. And so do I.'

I take a deep breath. Did I sound angry? I am usually so care-ful to control my voice.

'Where would you like to meet?' I say. 'I could give you an hour. But you can't come here. I've people coming.'

'The Anchor? It's not far for you so it won't cut into your evening too much. I could be there in ten minutes. How about you?'

'OK. I suppose sooner is better than later for me,' I say. 'See you there.'

CHAPTER THIRTY-ONE

Monday evening

Sonia

The Anchor, that would once have been stuffy with smoke and cramped with men in grey suits bumping into each others' beer bellies at this time, early on a Monday evening, is instead bare and chilly and smells strongly of antibacterial cleaning fluids. The men, though their faces look roughly the same as they always have, seem to have flatter stomachs. I miss the smoke. The illicit atmosphere it lent to after-work pubs. The fog. The sense that even the most jaded of us could walk out of our responsible jobs into the promise of a freer world. Why the smoking ban? Look where it's left pubs. Scrubbed. Sanitized.

I can't see Helen in the bar and wonder whether she's gone through to the dining area that overlooks the river. What she told me about Alicia has made me feel unreal, out of my body. But sometimes this heightened state induces clarity of thought. I'll use what they say to make practical decisions about whether, when, and how to release Jez.

Helen's not in the dining area either and I begin to feel impatient. I wonder why she isn't at work today. I go back to the bar and order a double whisky. I never normally drink spirits but I feel I'm going to need it.

'You're drinking!'

I turn. 'Helen!'

'This is Alicia.'

Next to Helen is a skinny, dark-haired, nose-ringed girl, with a gap between her front teeth. Although she's young there's a world-weary look about her. She wears, in spite of the weather, a T-shirt with the image from Tim Buckley's album 'Works in Progress' on the front. I recognize it instantly because it's the same as the image on the badge Jez wears on his hoodie. The image on the album he'd come over to borrow from Greg.

'My right-hand girl and source of emotional comfort. Even though she's been going through hell herself, as you can imagine. What a stalwart she has proven to be. While you're at the bar, get me a large Sauvignon, will you darling. I'll buy the next round. What'll you have, Alicia?'

The girl shrugs.

'Go on. No one's going to ID you if you're with us,' says Helen, which I think is doubtful since the girl who I dimly remember is fifteen, looks about twelve.

'I don't drink.' The girl shrugs and pulls a sulky expression.

'Then have something non-alcoholic. J2O? 7 Up? Coke? Got to keep your strength up, hasn't she, Sonia?'

'Sure,' I say.

'I'll get a grapefruit juice with slimline tonic and a packet of Worcester Sauce crisps,' she says sullenly, without looking at me. I'd like to correct her Americanism. She is not going to *get a* grapefruit juice, she would *like* one *if* Sonia wouldn't mind, *please*, and *thank you very much*.

We sit by the window. Outside, the river is choppy. In spite of the lovely start, the weather has changed, clouds have gathered as the light has begun to fade, and the wind's got up. Everything outside, beyond the window, has returned to monochrome, sludgy water, leaden sky, brown buildings on the other side, grey seabirds bobbing on the waves. What used to be the pub's old terrace has long since come adrift in a storm and is now moored out a little way, a strange wooden reminder of the days when the pub's punters used to stand on it and laugh and drink the evening away. The murky water sloshes over its dingy brown sides, and the once finely carved fence posts around its edges are jagged. Eaten away by the tides.

'So I guess things could change in the next twenty-four hours.'

'What?'

'You've not been listening to a word have you, Sonia! What's distracting you? You've been staring out there for ages.'

The platform. That's what's distracting me. The day I saw them come in on the raft. I was here! Here at the Anchor, standing on that very platform, outside, waiting, waiting for Seb. Leaning over and staring upriver and waiting for him to come back to me.

Images march through my mind like those characters in *Fantasia*, grotesque caricatures of the people who had come to the River House that day. My mother was there of course, tall and haughty, her perm distorted into a vast bird's nest on her head, her lips pink, and to one side of her the couple she introduced as Joyce and Roger from the Choir. Joyce was wide and pudgy and Roger was small and wiry and between them was . . .

'Sonia, this is Jasmine. '

Jasmine, unlike her parents, was perfectly proportioned. Jasmine had long hair the colour of butter and almond-shaped eyes the colour of grass. Jasmine was about my age but taller and better developed and in my imagination now her eyes grow wider and her lashes longer and her stare more penetrating, than they could ever really have been. Jasmine wore a cheesecloth dress with tiny spaghetti straps and buttons down the front in the shape of daisies. Her hair coiled around her as if it were the hair of a mermaid in a fairy tale, wrapping itself in long tendrils about her body, and glowing yellow-gold until it almost blinded me. I stood in the living room and stared at the group until my mother told me to stop looking gormless and fetch Jasmine a drink.

When Seb's voice called me from the door in the wall, I went to him with relief. His trousers were wet and muddy, rolled up above the knee, for he'd been messing about on our raft again. Hair standing in wild peaks. Bare feet. Mud drying between his toes. He'd come to find me.

'I need you, Sonia. Technical problem with *Tamasa*.'

'We've got visitors. I can't come out now.'

'I'll come and say hello, then,' he said, and without waiting for me to agree to it, he followed me into the living room. I saw Jasmine lock her green eyes onto him.

And he was hooked. He couldn't look away. His lips turned up a bit at the corners and he never even glanced in my direction after that.

'Jasmine,' said my mother in a voice that seemed to me to be artificially syrupy. 'Meet Sebastian.'

'Hi,' he said.

Jasmine smiled at him. 'Hi,' she said.

My mother sat on the sofa and poured tea for Jasmine's parents Joyce and Roger, and Roger said, 'What have you been up to, Sebastian, to get all muddy like that?'

'Oh, just messing about on the river,' said Seb.

'Could I go down to the river, Mummy?' asked Jasmine.

'As long as you don't try any funny business like taking a boat out,' said her mother.

'Oh don't worry Mrs . . .' Seb began.

'Harrison, Sebastian, Mrs Harrison,' she said and smiled at him in a flirtatious way.

'Don't you worry, Mrs Harrison. It's not a boat, it's a raft.'

'And it's not as safe as a boat even,' I said. 'It's not even properly buoyant.'

Seb gave me a hard look. 'That's what I wanted you for,' he said, 'To help with the buoyancy aids.'

'Sonia will take care of Jasmine,' my mother said. 'Don't you worry, Joyce.'

I glared at her as hard as I could and she didn't notice.

My mother had always said she was too tired to entertain other people's children, or that Daddy wouldn't like the noise. I no longer expected to have friends home, and they'd stopped asking me to their houses. Why had my mother suddenly conjured Jasmine out of the blue?

'Off you go now. But take care, do,' she said.

'And don't stay out after dark, Jasmine,' said Mr Harrison. 'We'll need to go.'

'Oh, but you're staying for supper,' I heard my mother say as I left the room. People never came to supper either. What was going on?

As I reached the hall Seb said, 'Follow me, Jasmine,' and I could sense them walking behind me as I crossed the footpath to the steps and began to go down.

It took me the best part of half an hour to sort out the buoyancy, getting cold and filthy in the water. But it was worth it to maintain Seb's respect, to prove to the buttery Jasmine that girls did not need to look like Sindy dolls to attract and keep boys like Seb. I was sure that there was no way Seb could take Jasmine out on *Tamasa* when I was the one to have made her river-worthy. Still, Seb held the raft and Jasmine stood on the shore, giggling as he fiddled with the crates and oil drums and swore and ordered me about. And then, when we were sure it

would float again, Seb asked me to run up to the River House
and borrow a torch.

I could hear the voices of the grown-ups, in the living room,
and grabbed the torch without telling them. I wanted to get back
to check Seb wasn't going take Jasmine on my raft without me.

But already, only a few minutes later, as I came back out of the
house, I saw Seb had Jasmine by the hand and was leading her
through the water. She shrieked. She was petrified, and enjoying
it.

It was as if I'd never had anything to do with either the making
or the naming of the raft we'd nearly drowned on, in Seb's quest
to explore the other side of the river. It was as if for Seb, I no
longer existed.

'You can't go! They told you not to!' I shouted. I ran down to
the steps and although they were slippery that day – it had been
raining, and the tide had not long begun to go out – I jumped
down them two at a time. The lower steps still glistened with water,
I didn't bother to be careful but slithered to the bottom banging
my thigh hard as I slipped and not caring about the pain or the
livid bruise that would appear soon afterwards. Seb was leading
Jasmine out to *Tamasa*, which he'd tied to one of the pillars of
the coaling pier, and she was climbing aboard. She'd left her lovely
high, rope-soled wedges on the mud, near the wall and had pulled
up her cheesecloth dress to reveal long golden thighs. Seb came to
the shore, took the torch from me, then waded back. He leapt on
to *Tamasa* next to Jasmine and untied the rope that tethered the
raft to the pier. I watched them as the river swept them upstream.

'See you later, Sonia,' Seb yelled. 'Wait for us in the pub.
Mark'll be there. Buy us a drink for when we get back!'

'I won't get served!' I cried, and my pathetic words were simply
tossed up into the air by the wind.

What choice did I have? I wouldn't let them go off for the
night. I swore I'd keep them within my sight, so I went straight

to the pub where I knew I'd have a better view of their voyage. Mark was at the bar. He offered to buy me a drink and I asked for a coke. Mark was never refused at a bar. You never got ID'd anyway in those days. We took our drinks out to the wooden platform. Mark began to fool about, putting his arm around me to reach his crisps when there was no need to, then dropping an ice cube down my top. I think he fancied his chances, having seen me kiss Seb. But I never wanted to kiss anyone else. I'd sworn to myself that I never would, that Seb would be the only one.

That hour stretched on forever. Mark told unfunny jokes and tried to touch me and laughed so that his spit flew into my face but every one of my senses was straining for sight or sound of *Tamasa* returning.

'Where are they?' I asked Mark at last. 'That raft isn't safe. I should know. I helped to build it. The buoyancy is as basic as it gets. The whole thing's dodgy.'

'Maybe they've been mown down by a pleasure cruiser,' said Mark. 'Their dismembered parts are bobbing about amongst the flotsam and jetsam.'

I ignored this and made him buy me another drink.

'Is that them coming now?' Mark asked at last. He leant over the barrier of the platform. Sure enough there was the tiny beam of light from the torch wedged on to *Tamasa*. The raft bobbed towards us. There was only one person on board! I looked again. Yes. Just Seb. My heart rose. He'd got rid of Jasmine, tossed her overboard, left her on the Isle of Dogs. Tied something heavy round her and sunk her. She was lying with her butter-coloured hair wafting upwards like weed, at the bottom of the Thames. Her bloated figure would wash up in a few days down at Dartmouth, at Tilbury, amongst the car plants. Green and rotting.

The raft came closer, carried by the incoming tide. Seb was not rowing the raft at all but lying on his front.

I ran straight down to the shore to help, all Seb's thoughtlessness forgiven in the second it took to spot that he was alone.

Jasmine was neither lying at the bottom of the river, nor stuck on the Isle of Dogs. She was in my place, underneath Seb, and she had her arms wrapped around him. He didn't seem to be objecting. As they bobbed closer and closer and the vision could no longer be disputed, my whole world turned black.

'So,' Helen's saying, 'Alicia, tell Sonia what you found.'

Alicia looks up at me and I notice that, like Jasmine, she has eyes that are an unusual shade of green. She puts her hand slowly into her little shoulder bag and rummages about for a minute, then extracts something tiny and holds it out for me to look at. I stare. For what feels like a long time I have no idea what I'm supposed to be looking at. In her palm is a tiny, curled, and slightly ragged piece of card.

'What's that?'

'Guess!' says Helen, excited.

'I've no idea what you're showing me, I'm afraid,' I say.

'You tell Sonia, Alicia. It's your story.'

Alicia shrugs. Looks at Helen. 'I dunno what I'm meant to say,' she says.

Helen takes over, enjoying another opportunity to spin a yarn.

'She found a butt end on the path near where you live, Sonia, and the roach – this piece of card in her hand – was made of a piece of a ticket from the gig they'd been to the week before. What was the name of the band, Alicia? Anyway, I'm getting distracted, sorry. Look, she's *certain* it was Jez's. They'd rolled that joint the night before he disappeared, and I'd come in so they hadn't smoked it. As if I don't know they all smoke weed. She says Jez must have been smoking it along the footpath that Friday afternoon. She reckons he's somewhere not far off, being held against his will. He must have been abducted that day on the way to the foot tunnel, the day he didn't turn up to meet her. I told her he was coming to see you to borrow some music, so he would have gone along the river path. She wants to know if you saw him?'

The whole world slows down, as if it is grinding to a halt. As I speak, my words sound like an old vinyl 45 on LP speed.

'How d'you know it was his?'

'It's the piece of ticket. We went to that gig together and, like, used the tickets to make roaches,' squeaks Alicia. Her voice wavers as she continues. 'Jez would never have gone off on his own without his guitar. I know him too well. He tells me everything.'

Jez, tell her everything? He didn't tell her he wanted to stay with me, did he? Snooping along the river path, informing the police about Jez's personal traits, *he would have taken his guitar, he wouldn't have gone off without telling me.* She thinks she knows him best, but she doesn't know him like I do.

'The police will take this theory seriously, Sonia. We haven't told them yet because we want to get more evidence. That he may have been abducted on his way to your house. Seems Alicia may have found a vocation – future DI of the South London Metropolitan Police!'

Perhaps it's the whisky at this time of the day, but I suddenly have a ridiculous urge to giggle. An image has come into my mind of a character from an Enid Blyton series, one of the baddies, who referred to the children who set themselves up as detectives, as 'them meddling kids'. I feel like telling Alicia to mind her own business, that she's nothing but a meddling kid.

'She and I both wondered if you'd help us,' Helen goes on. 'You live on the river. We wondered whether you'd seen Jez, without realizing it was him? He must have been near your house that Friday. Try to remember. Did you see a teenage boy? It's pretty urgent, Sonia. The longer a person goes missing the less likely it is they find him alive. Jez could be in real danger.' Helen's bottom lip starts to wobble.

I glance out at the river again. Jasmine and Seb bob towards me, across the water, a ray of sunlight illuminates them as they come to shore, as if it, too, is conspiring to rub their partnership in my face.

'Sonia?'

'Yes,' I say. 'The police have already asked me about that. The album he was supposed to be coming for. I told them he didn't.'

'Didn't what?'

'Didn't come for the music. I didn't see him. They asked me that too. But I told them no. I saw no one.'

I stare at them. They both look fraught. Pale and petrified. And now I've answered their question, despondent.

'I'm sorry,' I say. 'That I can't help.'

I can see Helen's not been sleeping either. She looks dreadful.

'How are things with Mick?' I ask at last.

'Yes, there have been some . . .' she lowers her voice, 'developments. You know, all that stuff I told you about. The stomach patting and all that. The udon noodles.'

At this, Alicia sticks her fingers down her throat the way Helen told me she'd done and makes a puking sound. I look at her coldly and turn back to Helen. Alicia shrugs and stands up.

'I was about to go anyway,' she says. She picks up her shoulder bag and drags it across the floor, turns briefly and raises a hand in farewell to Helen. Then she goes out of the pub, not bothering to thank me for the drink, nor to say goodbye.

I sigh. Turn to Helen. 'The last time I heard from you, it all sounded rather . . .'

'It's all awful,' she says, now Alicia's gone. 'I've had to take time off work it's so bad. The doctor's signed me off for two weeks with stress. The family liaison guy suggested I ask for it.'

'Family liaison guy?'

'Oh. They sent a family liaison person over to stay with us while all this is going on. He watches the dynamics. I told him a bit about it, I don't think he would have realized otherwise. I had to talk to someone. He says it's common for people like Mick to react like this by wanting to become 'rescuers' of the victim's nearest and dearest. He's advised me to let him be. But it's still pretty ghastly, Sonia. Watching Mick in some kind of thrall to my sister.'

'Have you talked to her?'

'I've tried. But she's still got it in for me for not looking after her son properly.'

'It does seem tough on you,' I say. 'But this liaison guy sounds pretty astute. Hang on in there while you can.'

'Sonia, you could really help,' Helen says. 'I know you don't want to cover for me, and I understand that. But you could make a few enquiries. Find out if anyone saw Jez that afternoon? Take regular walks along the tideline, and look for clues. I didn't want to say in front of Alicia, but I'm worried that's it's worse than I thought, that something unthinkably nasty's happened to him.'

'Aren't the police going to do another search themselves?' I ask.

'Oh yes. They talk about it. They want to question everyone all over again. But there are certain areas in which they prefer to remain a bit mysterious it seems,' Helen says, looking at me oddly. 'Sorry, does this trouble you Sonia?'

'Trouble me? Why would it trouble me?'

'You look alarmed. No one likes to be questioned by the police. Believe me, I've been through enough of that myself over the last couple of weeks. There's always that niggling worry in your mind that they won't believe you're innocent. I still have it.'

'Oh, that's not a concern,' I say. 'Mind you, think of all the miscarriages of justice the police have been responsible for over the years.'

'Quite,' says Helen. 'Tell me about it. For a while I thought they'd just arrest me whatever I said. I had visions of being convicted for Jez's murder and spending the rest of my days in prison. But this lot do seem pretty sharp. I have to hand it to them. They've changed my opinion of the police, in fact. Don't know if they get some kind of psychological training these days.'

I stand up.

'And you haven't told them where you were on Friday morning?'

'Sonia. I can't.'

'I'll do what I can,' I say. 'I must go.'

'You won't stay for another?' Helen asks as I move towards the door. I shake my head and leave her making for the bar to order another large glass of wine.

CHAPTER THIRTY-TWO

Monday night

Sonia

At home I clear up the kitchen as quickly as I can and go straight up to see Jez. I feel the heat radiate against my face as I lean over him. He whimpers but doesn't wake. There's a smell coming off him of illness, pungent, yeasty. I go down, get him some paracetamol. Shake him awake, make him swallow two tablets with some water. He slumps back, falls asleep again. There's just room on the mattress for me. I lie with him for an hour, maybe two.

'What are we going to do, Jez?' I whisper.

I'm afraid he's lost more weight. His hip bone under my hand feels sharp. It's lost its soft contours. His face, too, is more defined than before, the shadows under his cheekbones darkly angular in the dim light.

There's the intermittent *shoosh* of waves on the shore each time a launch passes out on the river. The occasional flare of light on the wall. As I shift from my side onto my back, releasing the lock of his hair I've taken into my mouth, I notice that the doorbell on the river side is going. I go rigid, my knee between his legs. It rings again, and doesn't stop. If it continues, Jez will wake up, find me here. He might shout out, which, in the silence of the night, may be audible from below. I haul myself from the warm fug of the duvet, pick up my boots and tiptoe across the room. I lock the door, hurry downstairs and across the hall. Someone taps sharply on the window in the living room. A voice calls, 'Sonia, Sonia, *please* open up! I've nowhere else to go!'

Across the courtyard to the door in the wall. The sulphuric scent of mud off the riverbed is overpowering. The tide must be out. There's a brisk wind that stirs an eddy of rubbish on the path. I shiver.

'Helen! What is it? Keep your voice down, will you!' I hold the door close to me. She's distraught. Her face in the orange glow of the lamplight is crumpled. She must have continued to drink after I left her.

'I walked in on them!'

'What?'

'Let me in, will you?'

Instinct tells me it'll be easier to comply than refuse, given the state she's in. I let her follow me across the courtyard and into the kitchen. I sit her on the bench, and pour her a glass of wine.

'We must keep our voices down, Helen,' I say. 'Neighbours, and so on.'

She doesn't query this, just rests her forehead in one hand, groans and starts to talk, quietly at first.

'I had a good think in the pub after you left. Decided I had to talk to my sister. Mick's never going to discuss it.'

She knocks back half the red wine I've poured her.

'It's about ten thirty by the time I get home. All quiet. I go up to see if Maria's gone to bed. Push open the door – and they're in there together. On the bed. *Her son's missing.* And she's with my husband on Jez's bed. Give me another drink, Sonia. God, I need it.'

'What about the family liaison person?'

'Eh?' she looks up, dragging a fist angrily across her cheek, boxing away tears.

'You said he was helpful. He told you Mick's behaviour was typical under the circumstances. To let it float over you.'

'Ah ha. Yes. Where was he when I needed him? He'd gone to sleep at the Clarendon Hotel. So, and I only said it because I was a bit pissed, you know how you say things you don't mean. I said, "That's it. I'm off." And Mick says, and he's half-dressed, Sonia, sitting there on Jez's bed in the Calvin Klein tartan boxers I bought him last Christmas, his arm round my sister, he says, "Fine by me because I'm sick of your drinking." I mean, I wouldn't *be* drinking if it wasn't for the way he's been lately. But he says, "Half the time you wouldn't notice if the boys went out and never came back. It's no bloody wonder Jez has disappeared from under your nose." How dare he say that? He was raving. It was horrible, Sonia. Complete character assassination.'

'Helen, shhh,' I say. 'You're upset. But you mustn't get hysterical.'

Jez might hear, he might call out. I feel ill, as if I might be sick, and I remember that I hardly slept last night, that my nerves are ragged.

'I feel like it,' she wails. 'I feel like howling! What am I going to do? Where am I going to go? He's being so, so . . .'

'Here.' I pour her some more wine, to quieten her.

'Feeble. How can he be so weak Sonia? He won't stand up for me. I'm his wife, for Christ's sake! He thinks that because the police have been questioning me, I might actually be guilty. That Maria's the only one who deserves any sympathy.' She scrapes her fingers down her blotchy cheeks. 'Or has he always had a thing for her? They say only bad relationships crack under strain. So maybe this was coming anyway and I was too stupid to notice!'

She slumps against the back of the bench. The wine's gone in a couple of large swigs.

'I've got nothing left. My kids are dropouts, my husband's unfaithful, my nephew's gone missing and might be dead. They all think it's my fault!'

'They don't, Helen. They can't. Not Mick. Not your sister.'

'They do. I can see it in their eyes. I can't tell them where I was that morning, Sonia, it's too humiliating. But it has nothing to do with Jez. You believe me, don't you? I know it must seem crazy. Better that they think I've been drinking than that I've something worse to hide. Maybe I'll come clean. What do you think? Have I been too proud?'

She stops and shifts back in her chair, her eyes fixed on something under the table. She stoops down, then points. I follow her gaze. Jez's Tim Buckley badge, the one with the image from his album cover, 'Works in Progress', that matches the T-shirt Alicia was wearing today, lies face up on the floor. It must've fallen off his hoodie when I rolled up his sleeves earlier this afternoon. Helen's mouth drops open. She looks at me. I stare back at her, rigid, unable to speak or move.

'What the . . .' she says, looking at me, then back at the badge. 'The motif, it's the same one Alicia was wearing on her T-shirt. The one she got with Jez from that internet site.'

My mouth's dry, my face set. Jesus, don't let her click.

'I should know, I was there, they did it on my computer. The other day. Where did it come from? We must tell the police. It's Jez's. I'm sure it's Jez's. What on earth is it doing here?'

I swallow. Suck my cheeks, try to get some saliva working in my mouth.

'Kit. Picked it up on the river path.'

I get up and move across to the wine rack with Helen's empty glass. I take down another bottle, lean against the sink for a moment and close my eyes. Count, I tell myself. Breathe. I keep my back to her. My hands have lost all feeling. At last I manage to get a grip on the corkscrew. Why didn't I pick a screw-top bottle? I manage to extract the cork and slosh the wine into her glass. Hope she won't notice the slug of whisky I add. Or the Rohypnol.

I steady myself before turning back to her. I sit down, hand her the wine, and brush a stray hair from my cheek.

'You didn't tell the police?' she says.

'It didn't occur to us to. Why would we?'

'It's got that Tim Buckley thing on it.'

'Tim Buckley?' I say. 'I had no idea.'

She leans forward, is about to pick it up and stops.

'Sonia, we must put it in a plastic bag for the forensics. It's crucial evidence! Don't touch it.'

'As I say, Kit picked it up, said she wondered if Harry wanted it, he didn't – hadn't heard of . . . what's his name?'

'It's all extremely odd,' she says. She looks up at me as I hand her the glass. Is she fitting a jigsaw together in her head, even through the mists of the alcohol?

'It's not odd, Helen,' I say, my voice sharp. 'We had no idea it might be Jez's.'

'But think! A roach on the river path, the one Alicia found. Now this! Where did Kit find it? The police must be told. Hey Sonia, I'm a sleuth! I'm gonna solve this mystery. I'm going to find my nephew. I have a feeling I'm close to solving this. Lemme think. I know. He was going to call in here for some Tim Buckley music, wasn't he? Did he come here? Sonia!'

'*No he didn't,*' I hiss.

'No need to get upset!' She's gazing at me over her glass as she drinks. 'Why didn't you make the connection, Sonia? Kit finds a Tim Buckley badge, Jez was supposed to come here for a Buckley album. You're my friend. If you know anything, *anything* about Jez, I'm here for you. But you have to tell me. Do you? Do you know anything? Did you see him that day? Did Kit?'

'No.'

'We have to phone the police.' Her words have begun to slur. She stands up and wobbles a little. 'Where's my bag? I'll use my mobile.'

'Helen, it's after midnight,' I say as gently as I can manage. 'The police won't thank us for ringing them at this time about a badge! If you're sure it's Jez's we'll tell them tomorrow.'

'If he came along the river path, if he came here, they need to know.'

I notice with relief that her voice is losing strength, she's articulating each word as if it's a huge effort.

'You're distressed,' I say. 'We need to deal with *you*. Does Mick know where you are? Do the boys?' My thoughts soar, buoyed by urgency. 'The boys'll be beside themselves after everything that's happened lately. Did you tell them you were leaving?'

'Fuck. I feel completely plastered. I need to lie down. The phone. Oh my God. When I rang here earlier this afternoon, I imagined I heard Jez's voice. But . . . no, that's mad. Isn't it?'

'Completely.'

She stares at me, her eyes bloodshot, her face reddened by drink. I can see doubt in her eyes. She's begun to click, despite the alcohol and, now, the drug. I stare back at her. Why has she put me in this position? She's already standing up, edging along the bench, aiming for the living room. She won't let the police idea drop.

'Gimme the phone,' she says, flopping onto the sofa. She's struggling to keep her eyes open. 'The police . . .'

'Stop worrying.'

'It's urgent,' she says. 'It can't wait.'

Her eyelids are drooping. In a few moments more she's asleep. I stand and stare down at her. The world is collapsing about me. When she wakes up the first thing she'll demand to do is phone the police about that bloody badge and the voice she thinks she heard on the phone. Helen's forced me into this position and I have no choice. I pick up the feather cushion on the sofa next to me. I place it gently over her face. Then I press. She starts to wriggle. When she phones, they'll want to have another look in the music room and I can't move Jez again. He's too ill.

I push the cushion harder over her nose and mouth. They'll find him upstairs.

My eye catches sight of my mother's pile of haberdashery with the darning mushroom lying on top. I reach for it with one hand whilst the other holds the cushion.

They'll take him away from me.

I force the cushion into Helen's now gaping mouth with the handle of the darning mushroom while my other hand holds the rest of the cushion over her nose.

They'll tear us apart and I'm not ready for it. I couldn't bear it.

Living near the river, you get to know the variety of ways there are to cross. There's no bridge on this stretch so the choices are on the water or under. There are no U-turns. You are committed to your destination. Even the Blackwall Tunnel refuses to let you turn around once you've entered its toxic bowels. Sometimes when driving through, I have the urge to go back, gripped by a fear of passing beneath the mass of dark river. But the traffic before you and behind hustles you onwards. You can't stop. You have to plough on, through the grime until you emerge amongst the towering blocks on the other side. I think of this as I lean upon the pillow and know I can't go back. There are no U-turns. I'm committed to my destination.

CHAPTER THIRTY-THREE

Tuesday morning

Sonia

How do you know when it's over? Helen's hands open and close and claw at my sleeves. Her legs twitch. I'd prefer it if this weren't happening in the living room. But I had no choice. I hold on tighter to the cushion. Twist the darning mushroom harder. The fire I lit in the grate this afternoon has long since petered out. A draft scutters in from the chimney, spreads ashes across the rug, lifts one of the curtains. The clock on the mantelpiece whirrs and strikes half past twelve. Helen begins to convulse. To retch. I don't want to hear. I don't want to look. I turn my head to one side, letting my full weight press against her. At last her feet in their lovely suede boots collapse out to the sides. I lift the cushion. It's soaked in vomit. I feel for a pulse. I mustn't think. The cold of the room. The smell of the fluids. The voices.

I leave her for a minute and go to the window on the river side. I lift the curtain and peer out into the darkness. It's hard to see whether the tide's high. I need the river full for this. Carrying her in my arms down the steps with their glycerine sheen would be hopeless.

I slip into the courtyard and through the door to the alley. It's as I suspected. The water has covered the shore and slaps the wall about eight feet below. I'll have to wait at least two hours, maybe three. Perhaps I should have thought of this before using the cushion. Waited a bit.

The smell of Helen's vomit permeates everything. I feel it's got into my hair, my clothes. I go to the kitchen for a J cloth and the Dettox spray and mop up the mess on her chest, take the cushion to the kitchen to wash. On second thoughts, perhaps I should get rid of it. But where? Calm. Breathe. My mind won't be still. There's too much to think about. Like the things Helen drew my attention to. The things the forensics might pick up. I should be far more attentive to the evidence I'm leaving.

In the end, I stuff the cushion into the washing machine on a hot wash and turn it on. Then I fetch Mother's wheelchair from under the stairs. Helen's such a light weight after Jez. I lift her in my arms and shift her into it. She'll be fine sitting there for a couple of hours.

I pick up the incriminating badge and take it up to the music room. In the faint light that seeps from the stairwell through the high windows, I find the hoodie at the foot of Jez's bed and pin it back on. He's still in a feverish sleep, giving off a faint boyish scent that I draw into my lungs to rinse away that other smell of Helen. I lift a lock of his dark hair and rub my nose across the fine down behind his ear, push my finger gently along the blue vein on his arm, down to the palm of his hand that lies upturned as if he's offering me something precious in it. Kiss the pads of his fingers where they are soft like peach skin. I let my eyes roam over the length of his body. Shiver at the anticipated sweetness, once we can be alone again.

Downstairs I tug some rubber gloves from the clutter in the cupboard under the sink and place them on the table ready for the tide. They lie there, pink bloated fingers monstrous after

Jez's slender, golden ones. The next hour is interminable. I try to clear up the kitchen but it's already almost tidy. I put the empty wine bottles in the recycling bin, and wash Helen's glass in the sink, three times, scrubbing it with the washing-up brush before putting it into the dishwasher. Every so often I pop my head round the living room door to check that she hasn't started to breathe again. I have an urge to wrap a rug around her, though she will no longer be able to feel the cold. I don't like to see her slumped there in her orange miniskirt and opaque cerise tights, her cerise crew-neck jumper and orange scarf in the draft that continues to blow from the fireplace. All so nicely co-ordinated. One leg of her tights has wrinkled up around her knee a bit, probably from her struggle with me on the sofa, and I have the urge to pull it up and smooth it out. I don't like to see her like this at all, but I had no choice. What other option did I have?

I find the blanket, the one I wrapped Jez in this afternoon, the green and white check, and drape it around her. The clock strikes again.

I go back to the kitchen. Sit, my head in my hands. Go back to check on her again. Realize that this time I'm hoping she might be breathing. I put my hand under her mouth, her nose, lift her wrist, try to find a pulse.

Nothing.

The phone rings. It's two in the morning. No one phones at two. I consider picking it up, then refrain. It clicks on to answer machine. I hear Mick's voice.

'Sonia. I'm sorry to disturb you at this time. But Helen's gone off and I wondered whether she might be with you. If you could give me a ring in the morning . . . I'm worried about her.'

Why do people assume everyone's with me? If they suspect she's here, how long will it be before they come snooping around? I must get rid of her.

I go out to the door in the wall and stop. There are voices

coming along the alley. Foreign accents. Polish or Russian. Students coming back from a night out. Laughter, a shriek. One of them is probably leaning over the wall to feign jumping into the river. You get used to the pranks played by students, the same old games as if they were the first ones to ever think of them. He calls to his mates, they are just a few centimetres from me on the other side of the door.

Go, I mumble, *move on*, though I don't think there'll be enough water to deposit Helen into yet.

At last the footsteps retreat down the alley, the voices fade. I turn the key in the lock and step across to the wall. As I suspected, the water rolls indifferently, at least six feet below me. Does it always rise so reluctantly?

A police launch bounds past on the river, its lights blazing and the water goes mad, rolling and slapping and splashing up against the bricks. Swirling around the great chain that's bolted to the wall there. There's the mournful wailing sound from the pontoon just along the shore as it creaks in the wake.

I have about an hour until the water should be high enough. How do you sink a body? I need some weights. The obvious place for these would've been the shore but that's no use now the water has crept in and covered it. I unearth a few broken bricks from the courtyard, ones my mother used to raise the flower bed, and carry them into the living room. I stare at Helen in the wheelchair. There's nowhere to put them! Then I remember she had a jacket on when she arrived. I find it in the kitchen. It's the lovely blue-green wool jacket with a hood she had on at the Pavilion the other day. I unwrap the blanket, pull her arms into the sleeves, and place some broken bricks in the coat's deep pockets. I'm not sure, even now, that she will be heavy enough to sink. As a precaution, I put two more half bricks in an old Sainsbury's carrier bag and tie them to the little chain Boden put in the collars of their garments in case you haven't a hanger and need to hook your coat on a peg. The bricks nestle in the hood. This makes me think of Seb, the way he put cans of lager in fishing nets and tied them onto ropes so he could swim out to the barges, dragging them.

I feel light, out of my body. I must stay calm, I must not become hysterical. That's when mistakes are made. I must think logically.

In the end I sit at the kitchen table and listen to the clock tick. My fingers find Jez's horn earring that I've kept in my trouser pocket. The earring! Everything falls neatly into place. It's meant, as I knew it was when Jez first came to me.

I rummage under Helen's coat, find a pocket in her skirt, place the earring deep inside. I take out her mobile. Thumb in a text. Find Mick's number, press send. Then I get up and go back outside to check the tide. I let her mobile follow Jez's into the water. The river is on my side now.

CHAPTER THIRTY-FOUR

Tuesday

Sonia

I release the lock on the wheelchair. Helen's head flops onto her chest. I pull the checked blanket over it. Shove the wheelchair over the threshold, across the courtyard to the door in the wall. Press my ear against it. It's silent at last. I push the door open. The lights are off in the flats along the alley. We go straight across to the wall, to the exact place I dropped the mobiles into the water.

You've got to be careful, this is becoming a habit! mocks a high-pitched voice in my head.

The tide's up and lolls against the wall about three feet below. The tree branches make a tangled black net above my head, and the wall of the flats to my left is covered in a mat of ivy. I'm cocooned on one side at least. The other side is open but deserted as far along the path as I can see, to the power station, to the coaling pier.

It's harder than I thought it would be to lift Helen out of the wheelchair. Have my arms become weaker since I put her into it? Or has her body, empty of its soul, taken on extra weight? The

bricks! I'll have to remove them. My fingers are numb with cold
or nerves. They won't work. I can't untie the plastic bag. I rub my
hands together, try to kick-start the circulation. A police siren
sounds out on the high street. I fumble with the knot of the bag,
straining my ears. Is that a voice? Footsteps? I stop for a minute,
trying not to breathe so I can hear.

I give up on the bricks and use all my strength to heave Helen
up in my arms and hitch her onto the wall. I lift her legs over it
as if she were a child I was putting onto a swing, and shove hard.
She flops forward, face down onto the surface of the water. The
checked blanket is left in my hands. Helen's arms spread out, as
if she were doing the star pose Kit was made to do in swimming
lessons at primary school. She stays there for a few seconds.
Seconds that turn into minutes.

'Go down!' I mutter. 'Go down!'

Her head dips, her bottom rises up, as if she's peering beneath
the surface of the water. Then the bricks start to do their job,
and bubbles rise from somewhere, from her pockets? Her hood?
Her lungs? Her beautiful blue jacket balloons upwards. Then it
too turns dark as the water soaks into it and soon all I can see
is the orange bottom of her skirt and the underside of one foot,
the crepe sole of her lovely boots the only bit of her clothing,
judging by evidence I've gathered from my beachcombing over
the years, that will survive the river's appetite. I rue the fact that
all her gorgeous clothes are wasted.

Why won't she disappear completely? Surely it's exactly this
that keeps the police launches so busy, the tendency of the
human body to sink to the riverbed without a trace?

I go back to the courtyard and find the hoe with the long
handle I retrieved from the garage the other day. I have to
lean over the wall in order to poke Helen with it, prod her.
Still the crepe sole bounces back. I push the hoe harder, and
she bobs away from the wall. At last a current takes her up.

She swirls about, her boot doing a peculiar solo dance in the moonlight.

At last, after I don't know how long, the sole of her boot bobs away, the tide seems to have turned and is carrying her down towards Blackwall. I wait to ensure she doesn't turn around again. That the river doesn't decide to do something perverse and bring her back to me. I wait five, ten minutes.

The moon's up and casts a silver light over the water. It mingles with the street lights that cast their glow deep into the river along the banks. I'm suffused with a sudden sense of peace.

I don't move. A plane passes overhead. Lights crackle on the other side of the river, the bright beacon at the top of Canada Tower flashes on, off, on, off. A gaggle of swans comes past. They gaze into the depths of the water. Then they huddle near the wall together, as if deciding this, Helen's final resting place, was the very spot they were searching for to roost.

At last I turn. I barely bother to look up or down the alley before I push the wheelchair back through the door in the wall, across the courtyard and into the house. I fold the blanket up, stash it in the cupboard in the hall. Collapse the wheelchair, store it back under the stairs. It's done. I feel oddly deflated, as if I deserved a round of applause that didn't come.

I won't be able to sleep yet. For some reason I have a strong urge to go and have a look at Helen's house, to see if Mick's lights are still on after his phone call, to see whether he is still waiting for Helen to come home or has given up and gone to sleep.

I go out again and hurry down the alley to where I park my car. It's not far to Helen's house. I drive carefully, through the now deserted streets, my eyes prickling with fatigue. I leave the car across the road on the park side. I cross and walk briskly to the front gate. The lights are all off. Mick has given up and gone to bed. I look up at the dark windows. Which is her bedroom? I think it's the one on the right. Mick'll be alone in their double bed thinking Helen will come back at any moment. He's oblivious that the expanse of sheet left by her absence is eternal now and it's this that brings a sob to my throat.

I try to walk away, but my feet won't budge. Oh God, oh God, what have I done? I lean on the gate post, a concrete thing that is cold to the touch, rest my head on it. I bang my forehead against it several times.

At last, I manage to get back to the car, and I drive home fast. I'm shaking as I open the door in the wall. I go straight up to the music room, desperate for him.

Jez sleeps so silently it takes me a while to believe he's alive. He's rolled on to the far side of the iron bed now, so I'm able to get in without disturbing him. I sidle up close and lift his hair gently. I slot my lips into the valley in the back of his neck. Draw in the tangy scent of his hair through my nose. Rest my hand on the sharpening mound of his hip bone. I have him. They cannot take him away from me. I've killed for him. Now I've gone this far, I'm going to do whatever it takes to keep him as he is, with me, forever.

CHAPTER THIRTY-FIVE

Tuesday

Sonia

It must be nearly dawn by the time I slip back to my own room. There sleep overwhelms me. I try to fight it but my body won't respond. In the end I have no choice but to give in.

When I do finally wake, it's to the sound of water. It gushes off the roof and down the pipes outside, gurgles along the gutters in the alley. I drag on my kimono and go to the window. The river's veiled in sweeping curtains of rain. The tide is low. I stare out at the brown water. Seagulls have lined up along one of the barges. They come when there's a storm out at sea, beyond Sheppey and Canvey Island. They think the river here is safe.

Something orange startles me, out on the water near the moored barges. It's Helen's skirt. She has floated to the surface, come back to accuse me: *How could you do this to me? I was your friend.* I close my eyes. Breathe deeply. When I open them I see that the orange is a plastic oil drum like the one Seb and I used to make our raft. I feel hot and cold at the same time. I've caught Jez's bug. Must have a fever. That's why the memory that comes is so shiny and raw. So close up.

*   *   *

The night I went to fetch Seb, I paddled through the rain, in the fading light, my heart full of anticipation and longing. I'd taken *Tamasa*, the raft we'd made together, obeying Seb's intructions. The eclectic range of rubber tyres, plastic oil cans, driftwood and rope. Carrier bags stuffed with polystyrene collected from the shore. Our buoyancy aids. I'd repaired *Tamasa* single-handed, planning the day I'd set out to get him. Now I had his letter and I knew the time had come. I dragged the raft from under the coaling pier. It would have its official relaunch once Seb was back on this side of the river. We'd do it together with a bottle of something. Wine or cider. We were too sophisticated now to use a beer bottle.

I set off as soon as I saw him signalling with his torch from the Isle of Dogs. We would be together, after months of enforced separation. Adrenalin pumped through me as I pushed off into the water. I rowed myself out of the pier's shadows, into the brown swirl. Once on the water I sensed an energy I'd never known before. I could conquer the river itself! The tide was high, I could navigate easily, there was no wind, just a calm that I now realize preceded the storm. I used my paddle to take the raft across to the other side. It glided so much more smoothly than the times we'd gone out together, and I was proud of myself, bursting with it. Too proud to notice the change in the weather, the fact the water continued to rise, covering the green tideline on the river walls, lapping over the edge of the footpaths.

I was beside myself with wanting to see Seb. I yearned to feel his tall, newly filled-out body wedged close to mine between the fish boxes and the buoyancy bags on our way back. The waves lifting us as we lay together. We would barely notice the cold that splashed our faces, soaked our clothes.

The light was waning. Clouds that had been hidden behind buildings gathered overhead, the last rays of a low sun left an ominous sickly hue in the sky and threw everything else into

shadow. Over to my right was the landing stage, the pillars holding it up and the dark crevices between them were almost oblit-
erated by the rising tide. I knew Seb was waiting. He was watching for me, preparing to leap aboard as I expertly brought the
raft to shore. I was eager for his praise, for his tacit admiration
as I arrived to take him home.

Later, they asked why Seb hadn't come the way anyone else
would have done. Got a bus over Tower Bridge, or walked
through the foot tunnel from the Isle of Dogs. If he had to take
the river, why not borrow a boat? Why did he want me to bring
him home on a raft? In those days, there were fewer options for
crossing this loop of the river. No Docklands Light Railway. No
tube to North Greenwich. Seb had no choice. That's what I told
them, though I knew he could have come another way if he'd
wanted to. Hitched a lift through the Blackwall Tunnel, or taken
a train from central London down to Westcombe Park or Maze
Hill. I knew it was in Seb's nature to do things in an original way.
He was always on a quest for new experiences. Knowing Seb, he
might have decided we weren't returning to Greenwich at all.
He might have chosen to sail up to the Tower, or drift down to
Dartford when the tide turned. The difference between the raft
and the ferry is on a raft you can go any way you choose, if you
read the river right.

There was another reason and it was my own. I was desperate
to assure Seb I understood the river like no one else. I could navigate it on a raft in the rain as night fell, no problem. He asked
me to bring *Tamasa* and I would not back down. Even when I saw
the storm clouds gather. My pride was what undid me, undid
Seb. I thought I was equal to the river's own will.

I turn from the window. I feel dizzy, light-headed. Have to hold
on to the walls as I go down to the kitchen. I need some sweet tea.
The phone rings in the living room and doesn't stop. I don't want

any more intruders. I don't want human contact with anyone other than Jez. Neither do I want to step inside the room, but I'm afraid the stench of Helen's vomit may have lingered. I push the door and sniff. There's only the faint whiff of wood smoke. I check under the chairs, the cushions. Steady myself with my hands on the sofa. Where's her body now? It will come back. Like the sea, the river returns its dead. Maybe not today. And, if I've gauged the tide right, not here. Blackwall Reach perhaps, or further down, at Woolwich or Tilbury. My mind swings, a boat on its mooring, back to last night, her legs twitching as I leant upon the cushion, the curdled vomit as I drew it out of her mouth. Her orange miniskirt bobbing in the dark water.

I go outside, compelled to look over the wall, convinced the river will have left something. The rain's stopped and the tide is still quite far out. I scan the shoreline for Helen's cerise scarf, a garnet earring. A boot. There's nothing but stones and clay pipes, a white plastic casket. It's a common sight down here. Caskets dropped into the river after the ashes have been scattered. Ashes of people who've died a natural death and been given a proper send-off. I shudder. Helen wasn't. But she asked for it. She should never have come to me and expected me to help her. I've enough to deal with.

It's muggy. A stench comes off the riverbed. Burnt rubber maybe. A lifeboat bounds past, and waves flop onto the shore. After I don't know how long, I turn. It's done, I can't go back. Thoughts jump about in my head. The cushion. I must dry it. But the smell. If it's still there, someone will find out. In the kitchen I pull it from the washing machine, sniff it, peg it to the airer to dry.

At last I go up to see Jez in the music room. Everything's worth it for this. He's awake. A single ray of sunlight from the high windows lights up the hairs on his arm where it lies brown above his head against the white pillows.

He lets me go to him. I put my arms around him. And as he rests his head against my breast, I imagine that he knows, without me telling him, that Helen is dead.

I've got to visit my mother, and then I want to spend the day with Jez. But as I open the courtyard door an hour later, I see Alicia's sitting on the wall, in the place Helen sat, right before I pushed her. If I shoved Alicia right now, she would topple over the wall and go exactly the way Helen went, only backwards rather than face first. Except that she probably wouldn't die. One thing I've learnt is that not all people die that easily.

Alicia's wearing fingerless gloves, and a scarf. She's smoking. Her eyelids are heavy with black eye-liner. She gets up and treads the end of her cigarette out under her foot.

'Helen's disappeared,' she says.

I stare at her. After a while, I say, 'What do you mean, disappeared?'

'She never went home last night. And there was a weird text from her.'

'In what way, weird?'

'They wouldn't show it to me.' She looks straight at me and I see the fear in her eyes, the tears waiting to fall.

'The police are linking her disappearance to Jez's.'

'Hold on,' I say, impressed at how rational I am able to sound, even now. 'Helen didn't come home last night. That hardly constitutes a disappearance.'

'She always comes home, Mick says. Even when she's drunk. He says she must have freaked out. But I'm frightened there's someone out there who wants to hurt us in some way, first Jez, then Helen. Who's going to be next? I'm scared!' Her voice has risen to a hysterical pitch.

'Hey. Slow down,' I tell her. 'Let's get this straight. What was odd about this text? Where does Mick think Helen's gone? Why does he think she's "freaked out"?'

'He's afraid she's done herself in.' She begins to sob. 'I don't believe she'd do that. But he says she's been fraught since Jez disappeared. And the police have been on at her.'

'What about your mother? Shouldn't you discuss this with her?'

She gulps. 'My mum moved out.'

'Your father?'

'He's at work.' She glances quickly up at me and away again. 'I thought . . . Helen said you were the only person she could talk to. Apart from me. She says you listen properly. You don't gossip or take sides.'

'Did she?'

She takes a deep breath. Wipes her eyes on the back of a hand.

'I just don't think the police are doing a very good job of looking for Jez. I found this butt end . . .'

'I remember.'

'But they haven't been searching for him properly. They haven't looked in places like that.' She points at the power station and moves her arm so it swings over to indicate the coaling station.

'It's the perfect hiding place. If I wanted to hold someone hostage, I'd find a place like that. No one goes there. It's derelict, isn't it?'

Alicia thinks the way Seb used to. Without logic. But with a sense that the impossible could become a reality. Her idea is ridiculous, but that doesn't mean the concept isn't appealing.

'You must know a way in. It's almost next door to you.'

I look up at the dark iron arm that once used to transport coal off the boats. Where it meets the huge white walls of the power station, there's a high fence, topped with barbed wire, crisscrossed with netting. The windows are boarded up.

'It *is* used actually. And it's extremely well patrolled. The police know Jez isn't in there.'

'How do *you* know?'

'CCTV cameras. The place is infested with them.'

She stares at me now in a confrontational way.

Then it comes to me. This is a sham! Alicia isn't stupid. She's that meddling kid I recognized in the pub last night. She's put the roach, Jez's plan to get the music from my house, and Helen's disappearance together in her mind and solved the mystery the police are so slow to unravel! She wants to go into the power station because from the high windows in there you can see straight down into my house. My palms start to sweat.

'OK, OK! If you're so certain he's in there, let's go up there shall we? Let's go and take a look.'

This won't take long and then I'll be shot of her one way or another.

Matt'll bend the rules for me, I know he will. We always have a little chat when I pass. And I know he thinks that since I'm usually alone, I must be available. He's been after me for years, never lets me go by without trying it on. He'll let me take Alicia on a 'guided tour'.

And I'm right.

'What'll you do for me if I risk my job and let 'er in?' Matt asks, his eyes twinkling. 'I don't do favours for nothing you know.'

'How about a pint next time I see you at the Anchor?'

'Cor, is that it? You're a tough cookie, Sonia.'

'Come on, Matt. She's only a kid, doing some project on unusual buildings. Does she look like a terrorist?'

'Never judge by appearances, is what they teach us in security,' he says, but he hasn't so much as glanced at Alicia. His eyes lock into mine. 'I expect a smile from you at least. Go to the main entrance and I'll bring you both a hard hat. But you'd better keep schtum about this. I'll be in deep shit if it gets out.'

I enter the power station followed by the girl whose lip-glossed mouth has sucked at Jez's neck. I'm totally unprepared for the effect the place will have on me.

CHAPTER THIRTY-SIX

Tuesday

Sonia

The towering walls of the power station and its four massive brick chimneys have formed the dilapidated backdrop to my life for as long as I can remember. But I haven't been inside it for years. I follow Matt and Alicia across the reception area and into the dark belly of the power station, gazing up at the lofty ceilings. That a human mind could conceive of, and then construct a covered space of these proportions is bewildering. Tiled in white bricks from floor to ceiling, this vaulted part of the building forms a vast ceramic dome. The Tate Modern seems diminutive in comparison. We go up steep, quaking stairways, along metal platforms that sway as we walk. Past towering black tanks that Matt tells us house gigantic turbines. Cranes dangle claws high above our heads.

'OK. I'd better get back down,' Matt says. 'You can have fifteen minutes and then I'm coming to get you. If anyone questions why you're here, call me and I'll do the talking. OK?'

The power station is like an unexplored chamber of my mind. Lately I've become frightened by the realms I'm discovering within parts of myself I never knew were there. The level of passion aroused by Jez is one of them. At the other end of the spectrum, I've found new peaks of fury. And within the walls of the power station, these extremes of feeling open into even larger, wider chambers. For the first time I let the fact I've killed for Jez carry me up on a high. I stand for a minute in a haze of euphoria. I let my determination to hold on to him fill me with dark and intense loathing for Alicia. I have to hold on to a railing and wait. Let this vertiginous feeling subside.

After our tour, Alicia sits in despair at the top of a flight of stairs. She hugs her knees. Frowns.

'Can't we go out? Onto that bit you can see from the river path?' she asks.

'Why would you want to go out there? You can see it from the path anyway.'

She shrugs.

'It gives a good view.'

It gives a good view alright. Of the river, yes, but also of my house. She knows more than she's letting on. She wants to look into the music room.

Alicia stares down at the concrete floor, a dizzying distance below us. Matt and the other technicians who keep the engines working are nowhere to be seen. A girl could easily die if she fell. I'd raise the alarm and the security guards would come running, and I'd be distraught. She'd fall in front of my eyes, perhaps banging her head on the iron stairway as she somersaulted to the floor, and be virtually dead by the time she hit the ground.

Then another picture appears.

I spotted them from below. A sultry day in September. The tide was up, tossing a scum of rubbish against the walls, lolly sticks, condoms, crisp packets, a baby's dummy. I was on my way home from school. A bag weighted down with books banged painfully against my thigh, its strap cutting into my shoulder. Someone had been taunting me again, calling me a weirdo, a freak. And I didn't want to go home either, because I knew my father was there.

The shadows of the railings lay in stripes across the paved path. I stepped carefully between them because I'd lose Seb for ever if I stood on one. It was only as I came close to the power station and into the bigger, denser shadow of the coaling pier, that I glanced up, and the world shaded over entirely. It happened every time I saw Seb and Jasmine together. An eclipse inside my mind. That day, that moment, I was as lonely as I thought I'd ever be.

I stood still and stared up at them. Seb saw me before she did. Our eyes met. Something in my expression must have convinced him. He walked to where Jasmine dangled her feet over the edge and pushed her from behind. Her dress spread out, a yellow parachute as she went down screaming, and landed with a belly flop in the dank high tide. Seb dived straight down after her as if he was going to rescue her. Instead he left her floundering amongst the scum and swam to where the pale-brown froth lapped at the top of the steps. He hauled himself up.

'Sonia,' he called and I went to him. He reached for my hand and dragged me to him. The water seeped into the bottom of my jeans but I didn't care. Seb bit my neck, and my arms went around him. His mouth moved from my neck to my lips and glued itself so fiercely to mine it hurt. He pushed me so the back of my head was wedged on the stone step above, the water lifting my hair, and then he moved so he was on top of me. I shut my eyes and I didn't care about the cold or the hard steps that dug into my back as he manoeuvred himself so that our bodies were sealed tightly between the stone and the water. At some point we heard Jasmine, her voice whiny with indignation from the path above us.

'How dare you? How *dare* you?'

She could say what she liked. Seb would never leave me now.

We must have stayed there for hours because by dusk the tide had gone out. I lay in the mud, and Seb scooped handfuls of the sticky brown mush and spread them over me. He started at my feet, and the mud was warm like a blanket, only turning cold as the tide moved further out and the night air began to dry it. He spread it up my legs and across my thighs, on over my body and up to my neck. I tried to do the same to him, to give him the same peculiar sensation, of cold slime turning warm as it dried on the skin, but I couldn't get the angle right and eventually I just lay and let him do what he liked. When he was finished he stood up and laughed.

'The Tollund man,' he said.

'What's that?"

'A man they found preserved in peat for thousands of years. He never rotted. He never grew old. That's you.'

I look at Alicia on the iron staircase. She starts to speak.

'The police's theory is that Helen got rid of Jez somehow that morning, then said she'd seen him in the afternoon. It's horrible. It's so scary! Helen would never have hurt Jez! But Maria says the police think she had a motive. To do with their history. Maria and Helen's, I mean. I'm thinking, like, if I find Jez, it'll prove them wrong. I don't know what else to do. Helen would never have harmed Jez. She wouldn't, would she? I know she drinks a lot. And she lied about being at work. But she's a softy. Isn't she?'

I stare at her for a few seconds.

'Go home, Alicia. You're too young to deal with all of this. Leave it to the police.'

She looks at me, her large green eyes glittering, and I'm afraid she's going to cry again.

'Here's Matt. Our time's up.'

Back down on the river path I say, 'Now go, get back to college or whatever it is you do. Try to forget, let the adults sort this out.'

I watch her disappear forlornly down the alley, past my house and on towards the university. And as I watch her, I feel something turn over in my heart that hurts.

I don't like to betray a friend. But Helen's already dead. And they've already almost reached their conclusions. I go straight to my car and drive round to her house. I haven't been inside it for years, not since Kit was fifteen or sixteen. I venture up the front path that retains its familiar vulgar smell of privet, and bang on the door. One of Helen's sons opens it. He slouches against the door frame as if he's not used to holding up his own weight, which is considerable. His straw-coloured hair hangs over a face pockmarked with acne. How is it some boys go straight from child to adult? I can understand Helen's inferiority complex. Her son and Jez, there's no comparison.

'Hi Barney. Or is it Theo?'

'Barney.'

'I came to talk to your father. If he's here.'

'Yeah.' He turns, leaving me in the doorway and yells, 'Dad!'

Mick appears from the kitchen, hair on end, eyes ringed.

'Sonia. Come in.'

'I got your message. Last night. Any news?'

He walks ahead of me into their big, light kitchen that overlooks the garden at the back. There's the lingering scent of Helen's vanilla perfume in the air, a tube of the Mac lipstick she uses on the counter next to the fruit bowl. An enormous vase of gerberas. I'd forgotten Helen's passion for cut flowers.

'Can I get you a coffee? Tea?'

'No, nothing. I just wanted to check how things were. I can't be long. Has Helen been in touch?'

He goes to the counter, picks up his mobile.

'Read this.'

I look at the text I wrote, keeping my head down as I make a show of examining it.

'What do you make of it? I haven't told the boys yet.'

'It sounds a bit . . . final.'

'It reads like a suicide note.'

'I didn't want to say.'

'Tom thinks so.'

'Tom?'

'The family liaison man. He's contacted the station. They're starting a search this afternoon.'

'Oh God, Mick, I'm sorry.'

'I feel guilty.'

'No. You mustn't.'

'You don't know what's been going on, Sonia. You've no idea what a tosser I've been. Unless . . . perhaps Helen's talked to you?'

I purse my lips, look at him and he nods.

'It's been fucking mad since Jez disappeared. I'm bollocksed. Can't think straight. It's no excuse, I know, to act like a complete twat. But it's thrown everything.'

He wears jeans that should have a belt holding them up. His T-shirt's ridden up and a roll of white belly, stippled with smooth red hairs, protrudes beneath it. I see him clench his muscles, pull it in.

'What's happening, with the search for—'

'For Jez? Not much. They've drawn a blank.'

I nod. My mouth's dry. Mick examines my face as if deliberating whether to tell me something. He sits down opposite me at the table.

'Alicia – Jez's girlfriend, found a roach she thinks was Jez's on the river path. But it was too disintegrated to prove one way or another. Anyway they've already done a house-to-house enquiry down there. They came to you, didn't they?'

'They did.'

He gets up, goes to the kettle and fills it at the sink. 'Helen's convinced they suspect her of something. They kept questioning her. Don't know if she said anything to you?'

'She mentioned something about it, last time I saw her.'

'It's true she was the last person to see Jez. And there's something else. It meant nothing. It's typical of Helen to be over-dramatic. You know what she's like. Far too open with her feelings.'

I wait.

'You mustn't let this go any further. The police picked up on the fact she was resentful of Jez for applying to a course Barney was going for. It's hardly a motive, I know, but there is an unsolved mystery. She wasn't at work that morning he disappeared. Yet she didn't tell the police. She now says she was at the baths, but they've been making enquiries and even that doesn't seem to be the case.'

He gets a tin out of the cupboard and stands with a tea bag poised over a mug. I notice he's wearing odd socks. No shoes.

'She had this thing about Jez. An obsession almost. Thought Maria, Jez's mother, had done a superior job to her. It sounds bonkers put like that. But I'm afraid Sonia . . . look, d'you mind me telling you all this?'

'No, go on.'

'Since Jez disappeared, I've been trying to console Maria. I think Helen might have imagined it was more than that. It would of course have fed into all her insecurity. Then last night she walked in on us. We weren't doing anything. But it must've looked as if we were. She went ballistic. All our feelings were flying high. I said things I shouldn't have said and I'm afraid. Truly afraid she took it to heart. I couldn't bear it if I'd wrecked everything. I couldn't bear it if Helen thought I'd given up on her and done something stupid and it was all my fault . . .'

I keep looking at Mick, trying not to move my face.

'They're treating Helen going off as a possible suicide, possible hoax. Let's pray she's hoaxing. And who am I to blame her?'

I need to speak, but I can't. His eyes are full of fear. It's clear that whatever Helen imagined he feels for her sister, deep down it's still Helen Mick cares for.

I begin to panic. What have I done to him? To Helen? To their whole family? I can't do what I came to do. Frame Helen after all this. It's too cruel. My heart's racing. I need to get out of here.

'If there's anything . . . please ring. I'd be only too happy . . .' I stand up and move towards the door. 'Helen's been such a good friend to me lately, it was lovely bumping into her again at the opera and spending an afternoon with her, she looked very well. She's always beautifully dressed. More than anyone I know she can put colours together. Sorry Mick. But I have to go now.'

As I reach the kitchen door, Helen opens it.

CHAPTER THIRTY-SEVEN

Tuesday

Sonia

'Maria, this is Helen's friend, Sonia,' says Mick. This woman is dark, not mousy, and slim, not rounded. The eyes are Jez's. Unmistakably Jez's. The long eyebrows, the dark-brown irises with their half-closed lids. But in every other way she resembles Helen.

Maria nods but doesn't smile. Her face is pale, with lines etched all over it. She's small like Helen, not more than five-four, it's hard to imagine her giving birth to Jez. And of course she's white, with that pasty skin that doesn't tan. He's inherited most of his looks from his father, that's obvious. I feel instant animosity towards Maria, the way she's walked into Helen's life, messed up her marriage. If it wasn't for her, Helen wouldn't have come to my house last night. She wouldn't be lying on the riverbed amongst the car parts and oil drums and shoe soles.

'I've been chatting to Tom,' Maria says, moving towards the kettle. She has none of Helen's flamboyant style. She's classically dressed, in a grey wool skirt and an expensive-looking blouse. Agnes B, I hear Helen say. The pushy mother whose husband is tired of her and whose son would rather not have to live with her. I don't like her and I don't expect her to like me. So I'm taken aback when she offers me coffee.

'No, thanks. I was just leaving,' I say, reaching for the door again.

'We're going through hell here,' she says before I can get out. 'You know about Jez, don't you?'

I nod.

'Of course you do, everyone does. We don't know how much more we can take.'

She abandons the kettle, sits down and looks up at me. Her face is even more crumpled than I first thought.

'Sonia lives in the River House,' Mick says. 'She's the envy of middle-class Greenwich.'

'Oh! That's the house Jez went on about!' she says, brightening a little. 'He visited you there with Helen once. He used to say it's where he wants to live when he grows up.' She gives a tight-lipped smile as if to say, how absurd the young can be.

'It's in the most amazing position,' says Mick. 'Views across to the Isle of Dogs and Canary Wharf.'

'Yes, I remember him saying. And you have some kind of vinyl collection in a music room?'

'Ah, that's all Greg's,' I say.

'Greg! Yes. I met him. At your birthday party, Mick.'

'It was his album, the Tim Buckley, Jez was going to pick up the day he went missing,' says Mick.

'I introduced him to Buckley of course,' says Maria. 'Though he likes to think it was his discovery. The arrogance of youth.'

She looks at me, her thin smile seeking some kind of connection. 'It's funny how teenagers think our music's cool. He even plays my old LPs at home! I never liked my parents' music at that age. I guess we were *the* generation, we had it all. Sex, drugs, and rock and roll. They're envious. So they mimic us. But they don't really understand it the way we do.'

Tim Buckley. What was it Jez said about his music? The day he came to the River House? The day he played guitar to me as the afternoon grew dark, as he drained the red wine I should have saved for Kit. How for him playing music was 'just like talking'.

'It's like that for me too,' Jez had said. 'You teach people to express themselves with their voices. I play the guitar for the same reason.' It was Jez's way of connecting with me, of acknowledging the uncanny way we understood each other. Maria's got him wrong. Mothers never know their own children. Only I know the true Jez.

'Maybe I should bring Maria round one day,' Mick's saying. 'You'd like to see Sonia and Greg's house, wouldn't you, Maria?'

'Of course. That'd be lovely,' she says addressing me as if this were my idea. 'Helen loves it too. She's seen a bit of you lately, hasn't she? You didn't see her last night, did you?'

'I've already asked her,' says Mick.

'I'd say she was bloody thoughtless, going off like this on top of Jez,' says Maria, 'if we weren't all so ragged with worry. You know Sonia, it's a living *hell* not knowing a thing. There's a name for this . . . this grief. "Ambiguous loss". There's no closure. You don't know when it will end. You keep on hoping, every morning you awake thinking perhaps it's over. Perhaps it was a dream. He'll be there, in his bed. Then the slow realization, the fear, the dread in the pit of your stomach, it all begins again.'

I can only nod.

'Helen didn't talk to you about him, did she? Because we're seriously beginning to worry that perhaps . . .'

'No, we're not,' says Mick.

'But that text . . . and where was she last Friday? She won't tell anyone. But that's the day he disappeared!'

This is my chance. I swallow.

'She told me she'd been going through a kind of crisis of confidence lately,' I say. 'Said it's why she's been drinking so much. Not feeling good enough.'

'That's exactly what the police are worried about!' Maria says. 'It is, Mick! She's been behaving very oddly. Thinks people are talking about her, criticizing her at work.'

'And you and I have agreed that one does look for someone to blame in these circumstances,' says Mick. 'We want an answer. People grasp at straws when they don't have anything to go by. That's what the police are doing. And now you.'

'Oh!' Maria cries. I see that she's volatile, her emotions seem to change by the minute. 'Please try and see it from my point of view! How can you imagine I *want* to suspect my own sister? It's more painful for me than anyone. But when you add it all up, Helen's always tried to compete with me. Jez's interview was at the same place as Barney's and she knew Jez would get in. She's so jealous, so competitive. And with the drinking, not always rational. I know how hard it is for you. But you have to face it, Mick.'

'I know, and you know, she's got nothing to do with Jez's disappearance.'

'There's a kind of sibling rivalry that's always gone on between us,' Maria says to me as if I couldn't have worked that out for myself. 'It goes back a long way. You'd have to know the background. It's not unreasonable to wonder whether having Jez to stay brought it all up again. The police may have a point. Ghastly though it is to think about.'

'We've hardly been behaving perfectly ourselves,' says Mick glaring at her.

'No one can be expected to behave perfectly when put under this kind of strain,' Maria persists.

I'm aware of time passing, that I've left Jez alone in the music room for longer than I like to. I need to finish what I came to do after all.

'All I can say, and I don't know if it's relevant, is that she asked me to lie about being at the Turkish baths with her that Friday.'

'She asked you to lie?'

'Yes.'

'So she wasn't at the baths. Did she tell you where she really was?'

I shrug. Helen would not want me to reveal that she was in a pub. So I don't.

'Oh God,' says Mick. 'This gets worse.'

The look he gives me is so forlorn I want to reassure him. But they need an explanation for Jez. And Helen is the perfect suspect. Only I can offer them the closure they so badly crave.

'She was obsessed with the fact Jez's ability on the twelve-string guitar would have given him an unfair edge over Barney for the music school,' I say, warming to my task now. 'Kept mentioning it. As if she couldn't get it off her mind. She said Jez would have ruined Barney's future. As if she was justifying something.'

I feel Maria's eyes on me.

'That's very odd,' she says. 'Helen didn't know about the twelve string. It was our secret trump card. For his interview. I made Jez promise me he'd keep it secret.'

My mind whirrs. I've said too much.

'Barney might have told her,' suggests Mick.

'No way,' says Maria standing up, keeping her eyes on me. 'There's no way he would have let anyone, but especially Barney and Helen, know his plans on that score.'

'Well I'm afraid it's what she said.'

She stares at me. 'Did she tell you he'd actually started to learn it? When did Helen mention this?'

'I'm not sure.'

'No, really. I need to know.'

I stare at her, speechless, willing myself to come up with something, anything. I try my best to conjure a voice to get me out of this. But I seem unable to form a word.

Then Maria speaks again. 'Jez was going to borrow the Tim Buckley album from you that very day, wasn't he? Forgive me for asking, Sonia, but why did you come here today?'

'She's concerned about Helen,' says Mick.

'Look.' I find my voice at last. 'I'm sorry. I'm sure Helen will turn up. I must go. Like I said to Mick, let me know if I can help.'

Back at the River House I go straight up to see Jez. Sit on his bed. Stand up again and pace the room. I pick up the twelve-string guitar.

'You do play it, don't you?'

'I've only just begun to learn.'

'It was a secret? Helen didn't know?'

'Ah. No. Mum didn't want me to tell her. I promised her I wouldn't, Sonia. What's going on? Are you going to let me out? I'm better now. I could go.'

I go to the book-lined wall, stand on the footstool, look out of one of the high windows. Boats leave furrows on the water down below. A pale wooden sailing boat, its mainsail keening against the wind, races across the river and I see Seb, one hand on the tiller, standing at the stern, perfectly balanced in spite of the rocking of the boat, leaning forward to sort the jib sheet. His red T-shirt and amber life jacket blend with the sail that points to a crimson streak in the sky above us, and I am speechless as I watch him. Three shades of red merging and reflecting back up from the water. Seb's capable arms, the river doing its best to defeat him. But it never could, I thought, it never would.

'Sonia?

'You love the view, too, don't you? You wanted to stay when you first saw it. Tell me you did.'

'Don't cry, Sonia. Listen. You can open the door and let me go and I won't tell anyone. I'll say I needed time to myself. Please stop. It's alright.'

I do not want his sympathy. I didn't plan to do this and I'm angry with myself for it.

I'm not weeping for Helen or any noble reason. I'm weeping because I can feel him slipping away from me. The rope sliding between my fingers, my arms growing weak. I'm holding on, but to all the wrong things.

CHAPTER THIRTY-EIGHT

Wednesday

Sonia

The doorbell rings. I consider ignoring it, but the fear of who it might be compels me to check. I peer out of the living-room window. No one. I wash my face, go out across the courtyard, and push the door in the wall open an inch.

'We've been trying to phone but there was no answer. We wondered if your phone was out of order. And we've no mobile contact for you.' It's one of the wardens from my mother's retirement home. She's started to speak before I've had a chance to say I'm busy. She's ticking me off, huffing through her puffed-up face, her fierce little eyes narrowed in accusation.

'Your mother's had a stroke. She's alive, she's alright. You're not to panic. But she's been admitted to the Queen Elizabeth Hospital, Woolwich and we think you should go to her.'

I stare at the warden. A small tight mouth. Only just big enough to squeeze words through. 'Alive ... alright ... not to panic.'

Helen is not alive. Nothing's alright. Of course I'm panicking.

The nausea that has swept over me recedes and is followed by an eerie numbness. For a few seconds I'm afraid I'm going to confess. Say I cannot possibly visit my mother because I've just killed someone.

'I'm sorry to be the bearer of bad tidings.'

'You said she was OK?'

'She's talking. It was a mild one. But all the same . . .'

'Thank you.'

Go, will you. Go! The warden doesn't move. She stands panting, her face highly coloured, as if the strain of walking the few yards down the alley has almost finished her off.

''Scuse me, love.' It's the postman. He hands me a package, smiles, holds out his gizmo with its special pencil. I sign and he goes off whistling. It's an ordinary day out there. The warden hasn't moved.

'Thank you for letting me know. I'll check my phone lines.' I shut the door in her face.

'You should go as soon as you can.' She wheezes through it. 'You'll never forgive yourself if you were to miss her. You don't know with strokes.'

I take the package indoors, place it on the kitchen table and watch from the kitchen window as she hobbles away down the alley.

I'll carry on as I would have done before. I'm going to the hospital to visit my mother. I'll buy flowers on the way. Thank a porter in the lobby as he opens a door for me. I'll exchange pleasantries with the staff at the nurses' station. Smile at the other women on the ward. And they will smile back. I'll even have a conversation with the nice young doctor about my mother's prognosis, and thank her profusely for her time. But I will still have killed Helen.

*   *   *

My mother's ward is lined with white-haired old people. I think I've found her several times, then realize that the face doesn't fit. When my eyes do alight upon her I'm overcome by childish relief. My mummy. She may just be another old person as far as the nurses are concerned. One more husk of a woman whose essence has long since drained away. But for me, she's so much more, as if the layers of her that went before this version are still visible through the translucent outer skin. There she is, dressed in a sixties shift dress wheeling the Silver Cross pram along the river path. Bending over me in my bed late at night smelling of gin and Chanel. Then, her hair in a seventies perm, making marmalade in the kitchen, the mordant aroma of Seville oranges permeating the air. Later, versions of her in a suit, marching off to her job at the private school. When did she stop loving me?

I want her to take me in her arms, rock me, tell me everything's alright. Be a proper mother. Now I've almost lost her for ever, I want more of her than she was ever able to give me.

I lean over her, stricken by a mix of fury and pity. How dare age do this to a person? She opens an eye. Takes a while to focus. Then she speaks through one side of her mouth. Her speech is slurred. For some reason she's obsessed with having some old school reports that are stashed away in the River House somewhere.

'I took the wrong case. The Revelation. When I moved from the River House. I won a . . . oh, you know. In fifth year, I need to read the report. It says such nice things.'

'Mother, I'm not sure I can find that now. You don't need it. You should relax.'

I look helplessly up at the nurse who's filling her water jug.

'It'll give your mum a sense of security if you play along with her. Find the things she wants, help her feel at home,' the nurse advises.

So, off I go again. Sonia the grown-up, caring for her sick mother. Doing as she's told by the warden and the nurse. A good daughter. When I'm done, I remind myself, when I've performed my duties, I can return to Jez.

I take the ladder from the courtyard, carry it up to my bedroom and stand it up against the trap door in the ceiling.

It's impossible to get into the tiny loft space. All I can do is poke my arm through the hole and feel about in the dark with my hand. I grasp at the air. There's the gentle tickle of cobwebs on my wrist. A sprinkling of dust as my knuckle bumps the roof. At last, my fingers curl round a chunky leather handle. I drag the suitcase out, balance it at the top of the ladder and slide it down.

The case gives off a familiar whiff of beeswax as I open it – the smell of the River House as it was in my mother's day. The stuff she's kept! Theatre programmes, recipe books, bank statements, postcards. A birthday card made by Kit when she was little. I stand for a moment and examine this. It's been stored in an envelope addressed to my mother at the River House, along with a plastic necklace of pop-together beads arranged in a repeating pattern: pink, orange, blue, pink, orange, blue. A child's depiction of a girl in a triangular pink dress wearing a similar necklace. It transports me back to Norfolk, to Kit coming out of nursery, holding another creation in her hand. My automatic words of praise. How I'd sit with her when we got home and pencil words on her pictures for her to trace over.

Dear Granny, I miss you. I love you, Kit xx

I tried to win my mother's love through Kit. I don't know whether she was moved by her granddaughter's affections. If she was, she never revealed as much to me. Yet now I find that after all, she kept the cards, the letters. She cherished my daughter's overtures even if she rejected mine. This knowledge produces a tiny flicker of warmth, of hope maybe, far off and deep within me.

As I riffle through, looking for the report my mother requested, I find a bundle of envelopes addressed to me, Sonia, in that small neat handwriting that was so familiar to me. I experience the flutter of excitement I got back in the days when a letter from Seb would appear for me in the niche in the wall along the alley.

My stomach flips, as excitement turns to realization. Someone – my mother? – must have found our hiding place, and stashed some of his letters away before I could read them. I freeze. They've been opened with a paper knife, the slit along the top of the envelopes cleaner than any I'd have made in my impatience to tear them open. The letters are in order, with the latest, dated 5th February on the top of the pile. I pull apart the sides of the envelope, my hands shaking. A frail piece of paper, yellow with age slides out.

I read the words.

I look again at the date, then hurry across the landing to the spare room.

I pull the shoebox off the shelf, the one in which I keep Seb's things. I find the letter I read the day I came to get the mouth organ for Jez. It's postmarked 1st February. I'd always thought it was the last letter Seb had ever written to me. Now I'm learning there was another later one that I never got. I open this first letter and read again.

I'll cycle to the Isle of Dogs. You have to be there. Bring Tamasa!

He said to bring *Tamasa* and so I'd brought *Tamasa*. I always did as Seb told me. I craved his admiration, of course. And I wanted to prove my affinity with the river. But if I'd got this letter, this real last letter, dated 5th February, everything would have been different. I was enslaved to Seb. I would have done anything to maintain his respect. But I never got it and so I had taken the raft.

I read them both, all over again. And when I've finished, it's as if all the jumbled images that have come back to me since Jez arrived, pop together in the right order, like Kit's carefully constructed string of beads.

The evening I went to fetch Seb comes back to me, all of it, even the parts I haven't been able to think about since, roaring in like the tide.

Once I reached the other side the weather had changed. The wind had got up and the clouds had closed in. It was impossible to get near the pilings to moor. The waves were relentless, lifting *Tamasa* and smashing her against the walls. Rain swept across the river into my face and hammered on the landing stage. At last I managed to throw the painter around a post and haul *Tamasa* in. Then to get up on the wooden platform. The heavy clouds meant it had grown dark more rapidly than usual. I'd never known the river so noisy, the crash of waves and the creaking of chains and the squeal of the whole wooden structure I was now standing on. Seb was shouting at me, but I could not hear his words. I remember dimly that he looked angry, not pleased to see me as I'd expected. He shouted again and I caught the words, 'No time to lose.' I held the wet rope while Seb jumped down onto *Tamasa* and stood there for a minute, trying to regain his balance. That was when the biggest wave rolled in, roaring, a sound so deafening we could no longer hear each other's voices. It was quickly followed by another, and others sluiced into these so they collided, lifting *Tamasa* up and flipping her over like a paper boat. I held onto the rope with all my might though it was wet and slimy and chafed against my palms. The raft emerged from the water but Seb was already in the river.

'Seb!' I shouted.

My hair lashed around my face in the wind and stuck to it so I couldn't see. I couldn't take my hands off the rope to sweep it out of my eyes. When I did manage to flick it away Seb had become an indistinct shape in the gloom, the pale oval of his face appearing then disappearing under the water, clinging with one arm to *Tamasa*, to her pathetic buoyancy bag. I pulled at the rope again, trying to haul *Tamasa* back to shore but the waves pulled back against me, so we were caught in a dreadful tug of war that I knew, as my arms weakened, I was going to lose.

'Help!' His words only just reached me through the clamour of water and wind and rain, 'Don't let go, Sonia. Hold on! For God's sake, hold on.'

And, as he retreated from me, towards a tangle of chains and ropes beneath the next row of pilings, I gripped tighter to the rope and I pulled with all my might.

CHAPTER THIRTY-NINE

Wednesday

Sonia

'I've brought your things.'

'Pass that . . .' My mother waggles a limp finger at a hand mirror on her bedside locker.

One thing my mother will never be too old or ill for is her vanity. I'll have to take care of this because there's no one else to do it. Nurses don't have time for hands-on care these days. It'll fall upon me to wash her hair, clip her nails, brush her teeth. A peculiar intimacy when we've barely touched each other in our lives before. She plucks pathetically at a long white hair growing from her chin and frowns. I reach for her tweezers. I wonder whether I should not bother her with the letter after all. Let the past remain buried in the old grey box file, as we have always tacitly agreed to bury everything to do with Seb.

I powder her nose and apply the rouge she has worn for the last twenty-five years. She nods when I hold up the mirror. I pour her a glass of water.

I place the package of school reports on my mother's hospital bed next to the other things I've gathered: her clean underwear, a spare nightie, her favourite night cream. She looks up at me through one fading blue eye. Is it my imagination, or has she deteriorated even since my last visit?

She may not have long. I make a decision.

'Mother. Look at this.'

I let her examine the letter for several minutes.

'See who this is from?'

'Is it . . . don't Sonia,' she says.

'What do you mean, "don't"? It's from Seb, Mum. Your son.'

She says nothing. I continue, 'And who is it addressed to?'

'I can't see. I can't see the name.'

She doesn't want to see the name.

'It's addressed to me. Look. *Sonia.* A letter from your son, to your daughter.'

She stares at me, her good eye widening in shock. As if this is the first time she's realized.

'From my brother to his sister. I never got the letter.'

I stop, examining her to see whether my words make any sense to her at all. She tries to turn her head away from me. 'I'm going to read it to you.'

5th February

Sonia,

   I hadn't realized, there's going to be a spring tide on 12th Feb. The forecast is terrible. It will be far too dangerous to bring Tamasa. Get in touch with Mark and come with him in the dinghy, not the raft. I've spoken to him and he agrees there's no point in taking unnecessary risks. I must be growing up over here!

   Anyway, there'll be plenty more chances to go out on Tamasa once I'm free of this place. The whole summer ahead of us! What a thought. But please bring the boat.

   Seb x

My mother takes the letter in her one good hand, looks at Seb's handwriting. She stares at it silently for several minutes through her one good eye. Eventually she rests her hand on the hospital blanket and lets the thin paper flutter onto the coverlet. Then she lifts an arm, pats her hair into place, puts her hand on her chest.

'We sent Seb away to stop you. A brother and sister doing unthinkable things.' A wave of hot shame rolls over me. 'But then you persisted in writing to each other.'

'Seb hated that school. He wrote and asked me to fetch him. I got the letter telling me to take *Tamasa*. I did as he wanted me to do. I never got *this* letter which would have saved his life, because someone, and I guess it was you or Dad, hid it from me!'

'This is upsetting me. I'm ill, Sonia. You're going to kill me if you keep on.'

There's a long silence. A tear has escaped my mother's eye and is rolling down her cheek. The rouge runs. For a few horrible seconds I imagine she's crying blood.

'I would have taken the dinghy with Mark,' I whisper more emphatically. I feel a sudden euphoric sense that I have been wronged. That I am not solely to blame, as I've always believed, for Seb's terrible death. 'Seb would have lived.'

The repercussions pop into my head, reaching far into the future.

My mother seems to shrink before my eyes, to become flatter under the hospital blankets, as if her body were made of paper. She has never talked to me properly about anything, I realize now. She weaves and dodges and quotes poetry, but she never says what she means.

'You sent him away. Then you stole his letters. When you could have talked to me. To us.'

My mother looks directly at me now, determined to regain some authority, taking on her cold schoolmistress persona.

'How could I talk about that kind of thing. It was shameful, it was animal!'

'We were *children*, Mother.'

'I tried, Sonia. I tried to stop you both. I brought Jasmine home when I realized. Have you forgotten?'

I ignore this. She knows what happened. By the time she brought Jasmine onto the scene it was too late.

She suddenly sits up, screws up her face and takes off.

'We only took the letters. We didn't read them. We didn't want to read them. Of course if we had read this one we would have stopped you from going on the raft. We would have stopped him running away at all!'

She turns her face away from me. I wait.

When she finally looks back at me, she seems startled, as if she hadn't expected me still to be here.

'The letters have been opened. Look. With a knife. Who opened them?'

'When you left for university, your father wanted to clear them out, start again. That's when he read them and realized the terrible mistake he had made. That's why, I believe, he took his own life.'

'And you never told me!'

'What was the point in telling you? It was too late. Seb was dead anyway. We couldn't bring him back. Knowing things could have been different would only have made things worse for you. That's what I decided.'

The sky outside the hospital windows is lowering. Inside the strip lights are too harsh. She looks up at me, a pleading look, the kind of look a small child gives its parent when it knows it's done wrong. Surely she must be about to give me what I've asked her for. An admission. A chance to share the blame before she dies. Then I can forgive her, too.

She says, 'Your father left you the River House. Isn't that enough?'

'*Enough?*'

I look at my mother, hoping for something else, some sign of love or forgiveness or *comfort*. I feel the first stirrings of sympathy for her that she finds this so hard.

I want to say something to her, something that will draw us together at last. I want us to share the grief we've both been carrying around all these years. But I don't have the words either. So I just say, 'Mother, speak to me.'

She just looks back at me through the one eye that will open and the words I long for don't come. I stand up, take a step towards the door.

'Sonia.'

I turn around. She's holding one frail old hand out to me.

I go back to her. Our fingers touch, briefly. I bend down and kiss her hair. And then I leave.

I need to go to Jez now, to unlock the door, because I never wanted to force him to stay. He'll have regained his strength. But he won't want to leave. We will wander down to the river together, walk up to our calves in the water, not bothering to roll up our jeans. He might go a bit further, right in, reach the barges, clamber aboard. Shout at me to join him. Stare back at the River House and tell me again how he wishes he could live there. The river will lift the barge suddenly, so he rocks up and down and he will laugh and pretend to fall.

'We'll build a raft, Sonia,' he will shout. 'And get away from them.'

And we'll paddle on our tummies across the glassy water looking for one of those hidden inlets between dark wharves. We'll spend the evening on a secret beach as the river turns fiery in the sunset. Hunt for clay pipes on the tideline. Dig in the mud for treasure. Follow swans with cygnets tucked under their wings. They won't find us. It'll just be us, the swans and the river, forever.

CHAPTER FORTY

Wednesday

Sonia

On the bus on the way home from the hospital I remember the package that arrived today. I will go straight up to Jez. I can't keep him. The only way I can stop them taking him from me is to do it myself, end it all now. This is what I must do. Keep Jez poised for ever, at the point Seb was when he died. And then they can do what they like to me.

As soon as I get home I open the package and take out the rolls of Modroc bandage. I take a bowl up to the music room. Jez watches me.

I fill the bowl in the shower room with warm water and place it at his feet ready to soak each bandage as I go.

The windows have gone tangerine in the evening light. Like boiled sweets. Occasionally this happens over the river, the sky seems scorched, the burnt tinge caused by the pollutants in the air, blurring the sunset. Then this chemical glow bounces off the water, dyeing the banks and bathing the room with the same dazzling amber light.

'What are you doing?' Jez asks. He's smoking a joint. His tea is laced with drugs because I need his cooperation in what I'm about to do, though he's stopped putting up resistance since he returned to the music room on Monday. I think he even mildly enjoys being in the room, while he's unwell, the not having to take responsibility for anything.

The last time I saw Seb, he was embalmed in his coffin, on the table in the living room, his youth caught for ever. I don't think Seb ever looked in a mirror or had any idea of his own perfection. But even in death he was beautiful. His hands folded on his chest, his mouth turned down a little at the corners just as it was in life, as if he were saying, I knew you'd all let me down. I knew you'd never get it.

I tell Jez I need to make a statue of him. He stares at me for a minute. Takes another drag on the joint.

'You want a sculpture of me?' He sounds a little alarmed. Even through the dope. I want him to be calm now.

'Yes. That's all, Jez. That's all I want. To capture you as you are now.'

Of course, he's seen me transfixed by him. By his arms, by the way his Adam's apple rises and falls in his honey-smooth throat. I've tried to keep my admiration covert. But once or twice in the last couple of days he's blinked, and looked up, or turned his head just as I thought he was absorbed. He's caught my gaze, and though I've moved quickly to hide my rapture, he's seen it. I think part of him has grown to enjoy it. He probably knows the power he holds over me. This new-found vanity is useful for what I want to do. It means he'll comply. Yet it spoils the very essence of him that I want to capture. The lack of awareness of his own beauty and youth. This frustrates me to the point of desperation. In getting what I want, I destroy it.

'It won't hurt,' I tell him. 'This is a gentle process. Women use this stuff to model their pregnant bellies.'

'Why do they do that?'

'They want to remember themselves as they'll never be again.'

He stares at me, wide-eyed. My words have the opposite effect to what I intended. He's frightened again.

'I'd be no good to you dead. You do know that?'

'Jez! Please! Try to trust me. This is the last thing I'm asking of you.'

'The last thing? What do you mean?'

'The last thing before you change.'

I feel a cavernous hollow of sadness gape within me.

He's still so weak. His illness has left him wrung out, drained. He can barely resist as I peel off his jeans and his T-shirt. Everything.

'I'm cold.'

'I've lit the wood burner. And it'll be warm once I begin.'

For a few minutes I can't move, pinioned to the spot by the vision of his body on the white sheets.

Then I smooth on the petroleum jelly, first onto and between his toes. They curl as I do so, a fine bone in his caramel-brown foot twitches. I lift each foot in turn, hold it close as I spread on the jelly and as my warm breath touches his sole, his calf muscles tighten, and a smile flickers across his lips. He's like a litmus paper, his response is instant. I wrap his feet individually in the bandages, working up his legs one at a time. I dip my hands in the warm water so they are moist as I smooth and press on the bandages then wrap them around his feet, round and round so they are caught. The wet plaster has to be eased through the fabric then stroked down so it's like another layer of skin, fine, but opaque, over his own.

I think of those spider skins caught in the webs in the garage. The detail of the spider remains in perfect replica after the spider has walked away, suspended in the moment. I reach the concave area of his pelvis, where his muscles are drawn in, and his whole body shudders as I lay on the bandages. I ignore his response and move on up, smearing the petroleum jelly over his pectoral muscles, feeling the sharp protrusion of his nipples as I go, then up to his neck where I press the plaster into the runnel of his clavicle, lingering a little here. My fingers caress his collarbone, the tender cartilage in his neck, his ears. They stray over his square chin, to his face. Soon he's a white silhouette, only his contours visible. He's caught at the exact age Seb was the last time I saw him.

'It's weird. It's going all heavy,' Jez says. His voice is succumbing to the drugs, his tongue must feel like leather. His eyes widen. He looks as if he's had enough.

'It's the plaster drying out,' I tell him.

'I feel trapped. Not sure I like it. It's hot.'

'It's just the chemical reaction between the wet plaster and the air. It won't be for long.'

'What about my face?' he asks.

'Don't speak. You mustn't move or it won't work.'

'But – you can't cover my face. I won't be able to breathe!'

'There's a straw. Take it in your mouth.'

I place the bandages over his face, pushing with my fingertips into the valley between his chin and lips. Lay pieces of bandage over his nose and cheeks. I stroke them over the sockets of his eyes, and with one finger, ease the plaster along his eyelids. Every rise, every dip. At last he's done. He lies, a white shape in the fading orange light immobilized. I've done it. I've got him.

They come to the River House in the early hours of the next morning. The windows in my room throb with flashes of blue light. I get up and go downstairs in a trance. They've already smashed the door in the wall down, and are battering the hall door with crowbars while others bang on the barred windows and helicopters circle overhead. They start up the stairs, heavy boots, protective vests, tasers in holsters, leather gloves. I watch them go. One of them holds me in an armlock, while others mount the steps to the music room. I hear them bang on the door, rattle it. Boot it open. I smile because I know what they're going to find. The Jez in the music room is static and lifeless, every pore of his skin produced in perfect replica. A spider's husk, suspended in a silken web, so that it will never grow old. The live body gone. Not a trace of the real Jez remains, it's as if he were never here. I go with them quietly, because there is nothing left to be done.

CHAPTER FORTY-ONE

A year later

Sonia

You don't know what season it is in here, or even what the weather's doing. The light outside has been pale all day, but it's waning now. The branches on the stubby tree are bare again. And there's not much else to see. A high fence topped with barbed wire, the concrete wall of a multi-storey car park. No river. They took me away from the river.

He comes to me after the teacups have been carried off on trays. He comes into the room in a scarf and wool jacket and I realize it really is winter out there. He sits on the green plastic armchair and looks at me with the same old gaze, eyes half shut as if he's trying to understand. I don't speak, I just look straight back at him. I remember the brush of his eyelashes against my fingertips. His hot skin under my lips. The warm scent behind his ear. But this is not the boy who lay semi-conscious between the pilings where I let him go free. He's larger, broader. I remember the barely there stubble, see that now it's blacker, coarser. His youth's past, like the Clipper hurtling along the river, out of sight and earshot, rocking everything in its wake as it disappears round the bend towards the Thames Barrier.

He stays a while. Tells me he's compelled to return to the River House. Often sits outside on the wall opposite. He feels it's an extension of him. He doesn't know the people who live there now. Greg and Kit left of course to live in Geneva. I only hear from them from time to time.

I open my mouth to explain that even if I'd kept him there, even if the police had not finally deduced from Maria and Mick and Alicia that Jez must be in the River House, it could not have worked. What I wanted was dissolving in my own hands. But the words won't come.

So he asks what happened the night I let him go. And I try to tell him.

It was almost dark when I got back to the music room. I'd tied the dinghy to the chain beneath the wall by the stone steps. The tide was in. Jez was slumped in the wheelchair, ready to go. He slouched forward as I pushed him out, over the alley, to the top of the steps. I'd balanced the oars across the handles of the wheelchair. I took him along the path, under the dark shadow of the coaling pier, to the top of the steps where my boat was wait- ing. I felt light, fearless. Unlike the night I let Helen's body fall into the hungry river, petrified by my own actions. The tangerine glow had long since dissipated. It was dark. Orange lights from the buildings on the other side pierced the water. The dinghy was tied up at the top of the steps, nodding gently on the spring tide as if it were impatient for us.

He slipped easily into the boat. I left the wheelchair at the top of the steps, it wouldn't be needed again. Someone would take it, nothing gets left on the alley. It'd end up at Deptford market or some lost soul would make use of it as a shopping trolley or a pram.

I climbed into the boat behind him, slotted the oars into the rollicks. Then I took a few minutes to arrange him. I'd released him from the plaster. His skin was still warm from its encasement, slippery from the petroleum jelly. I arranged him symmetrically, his head in the bow, feet almost touching the stern. It was only a small boat.

I used my oar to push off across the dark water. We glided easily upriver as I knew we would now the tide was coming in. It was a balmy night. One of those freak days you get in February when you think spring has arrived. Pubs full, people standing out on the wooden platforms. I could hear laughter, snatches of conversation as we passed. All the pubs familiar to me from the years I'd spent on the river, The Trafalgar, the Prospect of Whitby on the north, the Mayflower on the south. Memories of me and Seb reflected like the lights in the water as we passed each one. I rowed upstream, the water dripping off the oars lit up by the lights glittering on either bank. I was in a state of deep peace. Jez at my feet, supine. I wanted that journey to last for ever. The river was gentle, rolling. Jez and me together on the boat, complete. Drifting back east as the tide turned.

We reached the north side, under the overhang of the road, and I took us into its shadows through the pilings. These days, there would have been ghastly, wilting wreaths lashed to them to mark the spot. But we never marked it once they'd released Seb from the rope that had caught around his neck. The rope that was throttling him, as he shouted to hold on to him. As the raft sank beneath the tide. I tugged in the dark. The wake from a passing river-bus rolled over him, and I pulled tighter to stop him from being dragged away. I had no idea that the rope I pulled was strangling him.

'Pull, Sonia,' he cried. 'Pull. Hold me. Help.' And I did. I pulled to save his life.

*   *   *

I stop. Look up. Jez has gone away silently, without saying goodbye.

It's funny, sometimes I think I can hear the river here, though they tell me that is only in my imagination for there are miles of motorway between this place and there. Then the industrial estates and more suburbs before you get to the park, where you can stand at the top on a fine day, encased in green, and hold the whole of London within your sight. Only then do you catch a glimpse of the river, insinuating between the Queen's House and the ghastly eighties constructions on the other side, towered over by Canary Wharf. It's still a good walk, down between the spreading cedar trees of the park, past the Conduit House and out through the grand wrought-iron gates at the bottom. You have to cut through Greenwich Market, and then pass the Cutty Sark shrouded in white plastic while it's being renovated, and only then do you arrive at the river path, where the railings of the old Naval College cast long black shadows like bars across the flagstones. It's a long, long way away.

It's usually at night or sometime soon after waking in the morning, before they bring the medicine trolley round, that I think I hear foghorns, long and deep and mournful. For a few seconds I can actually feel the chill river mist on my skin, smell the chemicals rising off the water, and catch a glimpse of light, the way it bounced off the surface and everything was bathed in silver when the moon was at its brightest. Then I can sense the tide draw the river back, and all I thought I'd ever lost is there, suspended in the mud as if it had never gone away.

ACKNOWLEDGEMENTS

Kept in the Dark would not have been written without the encouragement and companionship of everyone on the MA course in Creative Writing at Anglia Ruskin University in Cambridge, tutors and fellow students alike. In particular, I would like to thank Martyn Waites, Anna D'Andrea and John Davy for reading early drafts, for their contributions and invaluable support.

I am eternally grateful to my friend Suzanne Dominian, whose inspiring conversation helped spark the idea for *Kept in the Dark* in the first place and who has been there throughout.

My thanks also go to:
Everyone at Gregory and Company, in particular Jane Gregory for taking me on, and Stephanie Glencross for her ideas and editorial advice.

The team at Simon & Schuster UK, especially Francesca Main for all her hard work and insight.

Jethro Pemberton for research on the Buckleys and his musical knowledge. Victoria Rance for help with research and providing a base in Greenwich from which to carry it out.

Pip Tabor and Matthew Hancock for their memories of the Thames in the 1970s and 80s.

Polly, Emma and Jem Hancock-Taylor for accompanying me on river trips, and for fending for themselves when I was too distracted to remember to feed them. Andy Taylor for his unswerving patience and for hanging out the washing.

Thank you to Eliot and Mohammed at the Greenwich Power Station.

I am indebted to Peter Ackroyd's *London: The Biography* for information about the history of the Thames.

The story of the foraging boy in Chapter Twelve is based on the film *The Mudlark* (1950) directed by Jean Negulesco, based on the 1949 novel of the same name by Theodore Bonnet (1908–1983).